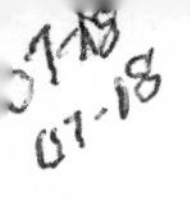

Dinosaur Lake

By Kathryn Meyer Griffith

(The first Dinosaur Lake book…sequels Dinosaur Lake II: Dinosaurs Arising and Dinosaur Lake III: Infestation)

This tale is not based on any scientific facts of any kind, but is a made-up story about a made-up dinosaur.

Dinosaur Lake

by Kathryn Meyer Griffith

Cover art by: Dawné Dominique

This is dedicated to my sweet brother Jim who passed away May 27, 2015.
Hear his music here: ***http://tinyurl.com/pytftzc***

Dinosaur Lake
by Kathryn Meyer Griffith
(a horror/thriller/adventure novel)

Cover art by: Dawné Dominique

Note: This book is not based on scientific dinosaur data... it's a make believe story about make believe dinosaurs. More a thriller than science fiction.

CHAPTER 1

"Ma'am, please watch your step," Henry Shore, Chief Park Ranger for Crater Lake said, cautioning the woman as she inched closer towards the caldera rim overlooking the lake. A leather holster holding the ranger's gun squeaked as he moved.

The ranger was tall and wore a flat-brimmed Smokey the bear hat which often hid his intense blue eyes and shaded a handsome face. It was a movie star's face, his wife, Ann, always said, set off by long dark hair that curled down around his strong neck; hair longer than park regulations allowed, and his one eccentricity. He'd worn it that way since he'd left the New York police force.

His wife maintained he was pining for his hippie youth and perhaps that's why he'd lost so much weight the last few years; he was as slim as the day she'd married him. He looked really good in his dark green and gray uniform.

When he realized the woman hadn't heard him, Henry instinctively reached out and took her pudgy arm, pulling her away from the edge. Visitors (that's what they called the tourists who flowed into the park) rarely listened. They traipsed all over the place never looking where they put their feet, lollygagging along. Always feeding the animals, though they'd been warned not to because it was against park rules. Some of the wildlife could be dangerous, especially the bears. They weren't like the stuffed teddy bears one could buy in the Rim Village toy shop, cute and cuddly–the real ones could bite. At least once a year some naive park visitor was mauled or bitten by an animal because they hadn't heeded the rangers' advice. But park visitors and their money, Henry knew, were what kept the park open and the paychecks coming.

"It's dangerous to get too close," Henry warned the careless woman. "The rim is composed of loose rocks and dirt combined with patches of snow." It was not unusual to have snow on the ground until July. "It's very unstable. Doesn't take much to go sliding over the edge or to start an avalanche."

He didn't tell her about the dog which had escaped from its mistress last week and chased a squirrel right over the edge and all they recovered was the poor dog's dead, broken body. It would only scare her. In most spots, nothing could climb up or down from the rim to the lake. Nothing.

"It's a straight plummet of nearly five hundred feet in some places, and in others as far down as two thousand, to the water. Right here it's about fifteen-hundred."

The woman caught her breath, met Henry's eyes, and nodded gratefully. She clutched her purse closer to her coated side and obediently stepped back. So did some of the others who'd inched too close to the precipice. They were already winded from toiling uphill a quarter of a mile through the close-set trees, slipping on the remaining patches of snow and hunks of lava rock and powdery pumice, weighed down with all the junk park visitors inevitably seemed to drag along: video and regular cameras, cell phones and enough food to last a week.

In the park it was chilly, even though it was mid-June. The summer season lasted barely two months until early September. Then the white stuff would begin to fall and continue falling until early June. There were heavy traces of snow dotting the landscape around them and crusted up along parts of the rim. Last winter the park had had over seventy inches. From December to March, Henry and his wife had holed up in their little stone house after their work days, before the roaring fire, like hibernating bears.

"You say the lake was once a volcano?" the woman covered her earlier indiscretion by asking politely, her eyes studying the blue lake shimmering so far below, a huge sapphire embedded in a setting of multicolored rocks and lush evergreens.

"Yes, ma'am," Henry replied, going into the well-rehearsed spiel he'd learned when he'd first signed on as a lowly park ranger. It was the same speech, the same tour he'd given, in one form or another, at least a thousand times. He could recite it in his sleep, even if he didn't do it daily any longer.

"Ages ago Crater Lake was a volcano called Mount Mazama, part of the Cascade mountain range that stretched from Mount Garibaldie in what is now British Columbia to Lassen Peak in northern California. Geologists estimate it erupted about seven thousand years ago. Fiery magma, ash, cinder, and pumice spewed out in avalanches, some of them coming from underground beneath the base of the mountain. The escaping lava streams left a vast cavity that caused the twelve-thousand foot peak to collapse and form this breathtaking caldera.

"Over the centuries the caldera accumulated water from rain and snow and created the lake you see below. Evaporation and seepage, balanced with precipitation, keep the water level fairly constant; there are no inlets or outlets that we know of. The lava cooled over time and now the water's pretty cold, fifty-five degrees at the surface in high summer; much colder at the lower depths. Right now the surface water is around thirty-eight degrees Fahrenheit."

Henry frowned slightly. But, according to George Redcrow, one of his park rangers and a good friend, the water was steadily warming. George thought it had started with the earthquake they'd had a few years ago.

Henry continued with the rest of his speech.

"The pure water supports little life, except for aquatic moss, which, by the way, is found at extreme depths in this particular lake. Originally the caldera contained no fish due to the lack of adequate food and spawning grounds; but over the years we've stocked it and now there's rainbow and brown trout, and Kokanee salmon in it. No fishing license is required."

Henry didn't notice the women attempting to snag his attention. He was looking in the other direction, still talking.

"Later, additional volcanic activity within the caldera produced the cinder cone, a volcano within a volcano, which you see below to your right." He pointed at a diminutive island that rose out of the water and was covered with evergreens. "The island is known as Wizard Island–which, by the way, is as high as Niagara Falls and covers several acres. The island also holds three or four boat houses where some of the tour boats are kept. There are also two smaller cones in the lake, but both are below water level."

Someone asked, "You don't have any major volcanic activity these days, though, do you?"

Henry recognized the nervousness in the man's voice. Standing there, vulnerable as they were, he could sympathize with the man. Even a tiny earthquake sounded threatening to someone already on steep ground.

"No, sir, that all stopped thousands of years ago," Henry tossed back the standard answer he was supposed to give, though he disliked lying. The key word in the man's question had been *major.* No, no major earthquakes. But he remembered the earthquake they'd had a few years ago. It hadn't done much damage above ground, but no telling, as George had pointed out, what it had done to the magma underneath the caldera and beneath the park's land.

Yet no need to frighten the visitors.

"Over there, you can see Phantom Ship, the only other above-water cone island in the lake." The Chief Ranger directed their attention back to the landscape around them, and the people craned their necks searching for it. "There. That miniature island covered in wildflowers, trees, and topped-off with columns of volcanic rock, which gives it its unique silhouette and thus its name."

"Yes," someone muttered, "it does look like a ship, doesn't it?" A chorus of agreement followed.

"I suggest that, if you have the time, you take one of the day cruises to visit both islands. They're well worth the ticket and the trip. But be prepared for a wait as the boats fill up quickly."

He paused. Beneath his boots he thought he felt a slight tremor. Then nothing. "No private boats are allowed in Crater Lake, only the park run concessionaires' tour boats. I'll warn you all now, in order to preserve the purity of the water, no one is allowed to swim in the lake, either." Yet people regularly snuck into the water, as cold as it was, for a quick swim anyway, just to say they'd done it.

Henry watched what appeared to be two water bugs across the lake leaving Cleetwood Dock. They were really sixty-foot boats heading towards Wizard Island. Probably the last tour of the day and running late.

Below were more people with other tours walking along the crater's rim. Sometimes their voices could be heard drifting on the wind, snatches of conversations or soft laughter that played in whispers around Henry's head.

He acknowledged, with a smile or a tip of his hat, the people in the tour group working their way past them up the two-and-a-half miles from Rim Drive to the fire tower at the summit of Mount Scott. Mount Scott was the highest point in the park at 8,926 feet. It had a wonderful view of the surrounding lands, including the second highest mountain in the park, Cloudcap, and was popular with the visitors.

Henry nodded to the park ranger in charge, Matthew Kiley, returning the other man's grin of amusement, and continued his presentation without a hitch. His men still got a kick out of seeing him with the visitors, especially since his recent promotion to Chief Ranger. They all knew that Henry hated his office and shiny desk. He missed being their friend, their colleague and detested having to boss them.

Henry enjoyed being outside, damn the waiting paperwork, the telephones, the computers, the meetings and the politics of his new position, and grabbed every chance he could to be out in the park. He told everyone that being short-handed as they were, with the budget-cuts and the federal shut-downs, filling in on guiding the tours was the least he could do to help his over-worked men. Truth was, he just plain enjoyed it.

He was disgusted with the way the Federal Government had cut funding to the park and how they'd refused to replace Ranger Griffen, who'd retired last month. His men might have to accept temporary pay cuts, if he wanted to keep everyone on the payroll. Money was tight. If it weren't for the park visitors and their generous donations, the park would have to close.

"To your left," Henry forced himself to smile for the people in spite of his gloomy thoughts, inhaling fresh air into his lungs, "is Cleetwood

Cove. You can't see it clearly because it's five miles away, but it's the only entrance or trail down to the water, weather permitting. Boat tours leave every two hours."

One of the children pestered a grownup to let them go on the boat tour and got a resigned, but weary nod.

"There are only six lakes in the world," Henry resumed in a resonant voice, "deeper than Crater Lake, which, at its greatest depth, has been measured at 1,932 feet. In the western hemisphere, only Great Slave Lake in Canada is deeper, and only by eighty-three feet."

He stared out over the circle of water below, still able to appreciate the beauty of the place after all the years he'd been there. It was a sight he wanted to look upon every day for the rest of his life. Unfortunately, though trained as an E.M.T, a firefighter, commissioned as a gun-carrying law enforcement officer, and a park ranger, he'd eventually be forced to resign someday. Time doesn't stand still for anyone. He and Ann had already decided to relocate after his retirement somewhere in the area, perhaps around Klamath Falls.

Somehow the land, the park, had captured Henry's heart and soul. He'd never felt such a passion for a place before. Ann was always amazed at the love her husband had for their home.

A young woman with fiery red hair peered over the edge, tossing a small rock into the abyss. She was about to toss a shiny piece of quartz, but decided to pocket it instead. Looking up guiltily, the woman pretended to pay more attention to Henry's speech.

"Crater Lake is approximately 25 miles in diameter and the rim that we're standing on is formed of varicolored lava rocks," Henry told the group.

"The water is so incredibly blue," one of them, a short man with a wild-looking beard commented, unintentionally interrupting him. The visitors always noticed the vivid blue color. It was one of the first things they commented on.

"I've never seen such a brilliant blue," said another guy, further back in the crowd, supporting the observation. He was holding the hand of a young girl, about ten years old, with braces that glittered in the sun every time she smiled.

Henry explained. "That's because the water is so crystalline and unpolluted it acts as a prism for the sun's rays, reflecting them to the surface. When it's overcast or cloudy the blue isn't quite as intense."

The water below, a mirror, cast back everything around it in hauntingly muted colors. A hawk swooped down over their heads and with a dip of its wings soared into the billowy clouds above.

It was getting late. Time to wind up the tour and get the people back down to their RVs, or lodge rooms, safe and snug, before the night fell. The park could get very dark after the sun went down.

He sped up the program, shivering with the first arrival of the cold evening air. "The lake was discovered in June 1853, by a party of prospectors led by John W. Hillman as he was searching for the

'Lost Cabin' gold mine. He never found the mine, but while climbing up the slopes of Mount Mazama to get a better view of the area, he and his mule nearly stumbled over the precipice here. Which would have been a really bad step."

A couple of chuckles.

"Though Hillman never found the lost gold mine, discovering the lake was almost as good. I believe this is the most beautiful lake in the world–but, then, I guess I could be biased because I live and work in the park. Well," Henry declared, "it's time to return to the lodge."

Out of nowhere, the red-haired woman blurted out, "Have you ever seen the creature in the lake, Ranger Shore?" She was snacking on a big bag of M&M's and between her words she crunched on the candies.

"What creature?" Henry was smiling.

"Oh, the serpent creature…the one that lives in the lake? My friend, Martha, was here last summer and she told me she saw this…*thing*…swimming in the lake one night. Looked sort of like a huge snake, only with a shorter neck and a fatter body. She swore it was greenish in color, and scaly. A water serpent. Just like that thing in Loch Ness, only smaller. Loch Ness, in Scotland, you know?"

Henry could only nod. He couldn't believe the woman was going on and on about a lake monster. There were no such things. Into his mind stomped the image of Godzilla climbing out of Crater Lake, spiked tail swinging and beady marble eyes scowling as it frantically waved around its tiny, clawed front arms. Henry had to stop himself from laughing.

"My friend said the creature nearly scared her to death. She'd gotten separated from the rest of her tour group exploring Wizard Island, and saw the thing in the water off shore. It circled three times glaring at her. She was terrified it was going to come up on land after her. She wasn't the only one who saw it, either. Herman, her boyfriend, saw it, too."

"Did she get a photograph of it?"

"Well, no. She was so scared she forgot all about her camera, and by the time she remembered the creature was long gone. She said it was really fast."

All eyes were on Henry. He didn't know what to say. Was the woman a crack-pot, or what? She seemed normal enough, no drooling or twitches, but one could never tell.

He sighed, trying not to appear rude. "Ma'am, as far as I know there is no serpent, no huge creature of any variety in Crater Lake. And believe me, if there was one, I'd be the first to know it," he insisted, with a casual shrug. "One of my rangers would have seen and reported it long before this. They patrol the lake every day."

The woman grunted in a dismissive way, didn't say anything else, but her eyes kept squinting out at the water from under her raised palm. The sun was beginning to set in all its splendor. The whole park was bathed in a mist of golden pinks and yellows. Clouds raced across the sky like candy-colored wisps of cotton.

What bizarre things people can come up with,

Henry thought.

With an amused smile, he turned and started to lead the group back down the mountain when the ground began to shake, the trees around them swayed violently and the earth heaved beneath their feet. From far off came the sound of crashing rock and distant screams. Henry barely had time to steady himself against a rock and to see the panic in his tour group's eyes before the quake was over–as suddenly as it had begun.

He quickly checked on his charges. No one seemed hurt. No real injuries though everyone was shaken up and frightened.

Relieved, the ranger hoisted up some of the visitors from the ground where'd they'd fallen or had simply plunked down in surprise. While they brushed off, he apologized for the unusual and unfortunate occurrence. Then, to get their mind off any aftershocks, exclaimed, "I think that's the last of it. It was only a slight earth tremor, folks. No danger at all. So why don't we just keep on moving? Hot chocolate and a nice warm fire's waiting for you down at the lodge. Our treat."

As swiftly as he could, without starting a full-blown stampede, he herded them down the trail towards the lodge. Waiting for the big one to hit. Praying it wouldn't.

He wondered how bad the damage below the rim was this time.

They were a third of the way down when the guy with the beard spied something in the middle of the path. He bent down and snatched up an object in his hands, abruptly careening off through the bushes towards a wall of crumbling rock that hadn't been there on their way up.

"Well, would you look at this," the man shouted over his shoulder. "The earth has split open. There are bones all over the place–animal bones of some kind. They're too big to be human." The man's voice drifted off into silence, as something else caught his attention.

The crowd, lemmings, followed.

Henry nudged through the park visitors and strode up to the bearded man as the guy leaned over something on the broken ground. He wanted the man to rejoin the group and get going again. Besides, he was concerned about Ann, his daughter, Laura, and granddaughter, Phoebe. He hoped Ann had made it home from work before the earthquake had hit. The thought of her caught out alone somewhere on the winding roads with the earth tossing around her and night coming, made him uneasy.

"What are they?" Henry asked.

"Don't have a clue to what they are." The bearded man stood up, dusting the dirt from his hands, the interest fading from his eyes quickly. "But they're damn big, that's for sure. Maybe bear bones?"

"Maybe," Henry speculated, staring at the huge bones strewn about on the ground and embedded in the wall of crumbling earth, trying not to let his shock show. He'd seen plenty of bear bones before and what was in front of him were bigger than any bear bones he'd ever seen. The earthquake must have uncovered them. Must have split the earth open. Whatever they were, they were well-preserved, nearly perfect specimens. For a second, he believed he might be looking at a prehistoric graveyard, full of ancient dinosaur fossils. A remarkable find. Then, reality returned. *Dinosaur fossils?* Impossible!

The man who'd discovered the bones glanced up at the sky. "I guess we should get back, huh? Who cares about a bunch of old bones, anyway?" He strode away from Henry and didn't look back. The others wandered away. They were too shaken up over the earthquake, too eager to get off the rim, to care about dirty bones.

Disbelief muffled Henry's reaction as he glanced at the protruding white bones, but caution silenced his tongue. It was better that he voiced none of his suspicions. He wanted time to come back and have a better look. Until then he'd keep it to himself. Could they really be dinosaur fossils?

Henry had been obsessed with dinosaurs as a kid and had read every book about them he could find. He'd been a shy, fat child with no brothers or sisters and few friends. Most of his time was spent alone, reading books and living either in a far distant future or in a Jurassic dream world.

He'd collected and built model dinosaurs, as well, of every species unearthed. He thought of all the dinosaur movies he'd sat through, all the museums he'd haunted, the countless pictures of fossils he'd studied in books. Though he wasn't an expert on the subject by any means, he knew a great deal more than most amateurs.

For years his ambition had been to become a

paleontologist, go on digs around the world. The dream of a child. That was before he'd grown up and had somehow, one day, found himself a cop. His family hadn't been able to send him to college. They'd needed him to work and help out financially during tough times when his mother had fallen ill. Becoming a cop had been his second choice. But being a cop as long as he'd been had enabled him to achieve Chief Park Ranger in a place as close to heaven as he could have ever found. Not a bad trade, after all.

Now here he was, all these years later, recapturing his first and fondest dream–possibly discovering a dinosaur bone yard. Henry scanned the remnants one last time, trying not to be too obvious or hopeful. They might turn out to be something else entirely.

Henry's tour group had noticed the darkness enveloping them and was getting edgy, shivering in their coats. They wanted to get going. After the earthquake, they were anxious to leave the rim behind and didn't seem interested in the discovery. And he had to get them down to the lodge before nightfall.

Tomorrow he could deal with the bones. He made a mental note to call John Day Fossil Beds National Monument when he returned to the lodge and have them send out a staff paleontologist to check out the site. He'd better do things by the book to protect the find, otherwise he'd have every amateur paleontologist in the country arriving in droves and flooding the park. Henry was elated at the possibilities, but also worried. They'd have gawkers and the curious, as well, no doubt. The bones could turn the park into a circus. He'd seen it before. The park was crowded enough with the usual yearly visitors. He liked things the way they were.

Henry raised his head, his eyes taking in the beauty of the place. A cold northern wind cut across the slope, a mist hung in the air filled with the smell of coming rain. Gray jays cried to each other across the distances, signaling the end of the day. The sun was settling on the horizon in a bed of darkening shades of apricot and pink.

Peering at the watch on his wrist, Henry said, "Well, people, it's getting late." Part of him hated leaving the bones, but the night was taking over and his tour people were spooked and tired. Time to go.

"If we don't arrive back at the lodge in the next hour, they'll send out a search party." Flashing his lazy park ranger smile he gathered them around him for the descent down.

***

Twenty-five minutes later Henry delivered the group to the lodge. Then he checked his office for messages and contacted John Day Fossil Beds National Monument to leave word about the bones for one of their paleontologists. They always had one or two on staff at all times.

He jumped into his cherry-colored jeep and maneuvered the vehicle through the darkening park, making his last rounds of the day. It was another old habit from his time as a lowly park ranger that he couldn't kick now that he was Chief.

There didn't seem to be any lasting harm from

the earthquake. All the buildings and landscape appeared unchanged. Some of the rangers had reported the quake, and reported no measurable damage. As Henry drove past, he could hear the campfire program in progress at the Mazama Campground. Indian Legends of the Park was the story topic for the night and all the park visitors seemed lost in George Redcrow's vivid tales. Ranger Redcrow was a wonderful storyteller, and Henry's best friend, even if the man was a superstitious know-it-all.

Henry pulled into Lost Creek Campground to look over the new arrivals and introduce himself. Didn't take long. He enjoyed meeting the people who sometimes came from around the world to see Crater Lake. Being a ranger had brought him out of the shell he'd forged when he was a New York cop. Early on, he found he liked chatting with the visitors about anything and everything. Not only did he enjoy the social aspect of meeting them, but it helped him keep his finger on the pulse of the park and its needs.

He didn't tarry long with the campers, though, home was calling.

The souvenir shops in Rim Village were closing for the day, and the restaurants were full for suppertime. Henry drove by the dormitories that housed over two hundred park employees, mostly young people working their summer vacations, though the workers' ages had increased with local unemployment the last couple of years. Half the people in the surrounding towns seemed to be working in the park lately. They said there were no jobs left in the outside world.

Everything appeared quiet. Apparently the earthquake hadn't left much of a mark down below in the park. Most visitors he inquired of said they'd hardly felt it.

Satisfied, Henry continued home, a place nestled on the fringe of the woods three miles past Rim Village. It was cozy and simple, fashioned from stone that was plentiful in the area. He pulled alongside the house as true night replaced twilight, releasing much colder temperatures and the nightly forest sounds.

Getting out of the jeep, he stood silently for a few minutes in the gloom under the trees. He treasured this place. Eight years ago he'd been a stressed out cop in New York City, overwhelmed with the gangs, scum-of-the-earth drug dealers and the never-ending rat race of big city life. In the end, the heartlessness of his job had affected Henry's morale.

He'd gotten sick of the hypocrisy of police work long before that August night, chasing those punks through dilapidated welfare apartments, when the kid with the gun, who couldn't have been but ten years old, had stepped out from a shadowy nowhere…and coldly shot him.

Henry had nearly died.

He'd told Ann from the hospital bed that he couldn't live that way anymore.

Months later, after he'd recuperated, he was offered the job at Crater Lake. Then Ann confessed, with a hopeful smile, that she'd always wanted to live in the wild woods of Oregon. And that was that.

Their life was good now.

Through the screen door, Henry saw Ann setting the table for supper. She was a pretty woman, slim, not real tall, with short blond hair and light gray eyes. Henry noticed a touch of gray encroaching into the blond the last year or so. It looked good on her, matching her eyes. She had a soothing way of making everyone believe everything was all right. Nothing riled Ann.

Laura and Phoebe were in the house, too. They were there often since Laura's husband, Chad, had run off a few months ago. Chad was a kid when they married and never could handle the responsibility. Once the baby came, he'd split. Laura hadn't heard a word from him since.

Laura was helping her mother set the table while Phoebe, Henry's granddaughter, sat trapped in her highchair, watching with big innocent brown eyes, a sad baby grin playing over her face. Her blond hair a soft cotton halo.

Ann looked up at Henry and smiled as he walked in the door. "I picked up some fried chicken and all the fixings at KFC on my way home. It'll be ready in a jiff."

"Good, I'm hungry as a bear." Henry kissed his wife and hugged his daughter.

Laura had gained weight since her husband had abandoned her, but Henry could hardly say what he thought, that she looked like the Good Year Blimp. She always ate herself fat when she was depressed. It was a shame, he thought, because his daughter was a lovely woman, otherwise, with long chestnut brown hair and penetrating blue eyes.

Henry placed a kiss on Phoebe's head. "Did you guys feel that earthquake?"

Ann nodded, a biscuit in her hand. "I worked later than usual, so I was at the newspaper when it hit. It shook the town. No real damage, though. Darn." She snapped her fingers in disappointment. "Widespread destruction would have made terrific pictures for this week's edition." With a mischievous grin, she buttered the biscuit and put it to her mouth.

"You ghoul," Henry teased. But he understood her desire to get a good story for the newspaper she worked for. Good stories boosted circulation.

Sweeping off his hat he placed it on top of the refrigerator. His jacket went across the back of the chair that he settled into.

"It rattled some glass in the gift shop," his daughter confided, biting into a piece of chicken. She was already on her second helping of everything. "Didn't break anything, though. Real mild."

"Wasn't as bad as I thought, then," Henry muttered. "It was worse up on the rim. I was worried about all of you."

"That's sweet of you, honey," his wife leaned over to lay a kiss on his cheek, "but we women can take care of ourselves, can't we, Laura?"

"Well, it scared me," Laura huffed between bites.

Phoebe grabbed at her grandpa's arm. "Pa-pa," she beseeched.

Henry released the baby from her highchair prison. As he settled her into his lap, she flung her chubby arms tight around his neck. He was happy that everyone was okay, happy to be home with his family.

Since Chad had taken off, he'd been trying to persuade Laura to live with him and Ann. But Laura, at twenty, was fiercely independent and hard-headed. She'd been that way all her life and wasn't about to change.

Everything they ever wanted Laura to do, finish high school and go to college, meet a decent young man, Laura had done exactly the opposite. She dropped out of school at seventeen, ran away from home at eighteen to marry Chad because she was pregnant. Babies having babies.

In some ways, Henry and Ann blamed themselves for Laura's rebelliousness. They thought they hadn't left New York soon enough and it'd hurt Laura in the early years because she hadn't gotten enough attention and supervision. Henry blamed himself because he hadn't beaten the crap out of Chad the first time he'd laid eyes on him. The litany of guilt concerning his daughter went on and on.

But since Chad had left, Henry and Ann had come to believe they had a second chance with Laura. They accepted what most parents have to accept sooner or later–that it was possible to be the best parent you knew how to be and still have your kids mess up.

Ann had said all along that with time Laura would grow up, do what she had to do and be fine. She'd make it, in the end, because she was a smart, ambitious girl. Like many kids, her youth and her hormones had led her astray. Eventually, she'd wise up, face reality and get back in the game.

Ann was right. Laura was finally growing up. She was changing every day, taking responsibility for her actions and decisions. She wanted to do it on her own while Henry wished she'd let them help more.

Henry's worries evaporated as the three women he loved most in the world vied for his attention.

He ate his chicken, mashed potatoes, and coleslaw with gusto; fed and played with his granddaughter and listened to the women's gossip. The three of them discussed their day. It was a ritual they looked forward to, eating supper together a few times a week and talking. Ann wanted to know about the earthquake, and Henry wanted to know about what was going on in town. Even Laura seemed in better spirits than she'd been in weeks, chatting more than usual about her job and people she'd met that day. She had a sense of humor and would tell funny stories about them which made Henry laugh.

Three hours later, when Laura and Phoebe were gone, Ann and Henry sat on the front porch swing, creaking back and forth, bundled in their coats and snuggling. Porch therapy, they called it.

The woods were pitch black, but a soft glow from the windows behind them spilled into the darkness. Ann pointed to a pair of glowing orbs at the fringe of the forest and a blurry shape hiding in the night's shadows. Then there were two shadowy shapes.

"Look," Ann whispered, squeezing Henry's

hand and pointing with the other. "Deer."

The two humans held their breath and watched the night deer until a forest noise scared the animals off. They were always seeing wild animals from their porch. If they were still, quiet, in the mornings especially, raccoons and squirrels would scramble up, unafraid, and stare at them. Sometimes Ann would feed them. Throw out peanuts or raisins. Sometimes the animals would even run up and eat them.

Ann told him she once saw a black bear in the distance, which was where she wanted it to stay. She was terrified of the larger creatures, especially the ones with teeth and claws. A few times she'd seen bobcats and coyotes, but their appearances were unusual. They tended to avoid people. And no one had seen a grizzly in the park in years. They tended to stay in the back woods.

After the deer were gone, Ann divulged her secret, "Laura told me before she left she enrolled today in GED classes in town. Two nights a week beginning next week. One of her dorm friends is going to watch Phoebe."

"About time," Henry mumbled. "But I'm tickled to hear it."

"She wants to go to night school afterwards. Wants to be a nurse's assistant, maybe even a full-fledged nurse someday."

Henry hugged his wife and placed a kiss on the tip of her cold nose. "That's the best news I've heard all year. I was wondering how long it'd take her to go back to school and get some real direction in her life." Relief was in his voice.

"I agreed that, in a tight pinch, we'd be the back-up to watch the baby," Ann added.

"Sure, no problem." Henry didn't mind watching Phoebe. She was a good child, easy to care for.

Out in the woods something big rustled through the foliage, then it was gone.

Ann put her foot down and stopped the swing. "That was something today, wasn't it, that earthquake? The second one we've had in as many years. Though it wasn't bad in town, it must have done some damage somewhere."

"I thought as much, too."

Henry could just make out his wife's face in the light from the kitchen. A sharp wind ruffled her hair. To him she still looked like the woman he'd fallen in love with all those years ago. She was still beautiful to him, still sexy and vital. His mind wasn't on what she was saying.

"Zeke read the news wires, checked the Internet. They suspect the most damage was done deep underground." Zeke was the managing editor, and Ann's boss, at the Klamath Falls Journal.

"Do they know where the epicenter of the earthquake was?" His attention captured by the serious tone in her voice.

"You're not going to believe this," she hesitated, then went on, "but the information we got at the paper said it was here in the park. The quake was a bad one. Under the lake."

"I was afraid of that." Henry released a sigh. "Up on the rim when it hit, it knocked a bunch of the visitors right on their butts."

Ann didn't laugh.

Henry remembered the wall of bones. He couldn't believe he'd forgotten to tell Ann about it sooner. Too much on his mind with his daughter visiting and the earthquake, probably.

"You'll never guess what the quake uncovered partway up the trail towards the rim."

"What?"

"It ripped open the ground and now there's this wall of...bones. I'm not sure, but I think they could be...prehistoric. Maybe even dinosaurs. Most astonishing thing I've ever seen. They're so damn big."

Now his wife laughed. "Dinosaur bones? Are you sure?"

"No, but they could be. I'm no expert, but as a kid I was really into fossils. Dinosaurs. Live and dead. I know more than the average person about the subject."

"I don't believe it. Dinosaur fossils. What a story. Henry, if it's true, do you know what this could mean to the park? To all of us?"

"Oh, that's the downside, I'm afraid I do. The discovery could screw up the whole park. We'll be overrun by park authorities, reporters–no offense to you, honey–sightseers, scientists and bone nuts from all over the place. All of them wanting to dig up the bones and the rest of the park's land, to boot."

"I sympathize, but, aside from those problems and overpopulating your precious park, it's a fantastic discovery. Look at it that way. You'll have to take me up there so I can get some pictures."

Henry moaned. "And so it begins."

"Have you told anyone else yet?"

"Oh, I've put a request in to John Day's for one of their paleontologists to come out. Take a look. Their paleontologists were gone by the time I called, but the secretary promised she'd give the staff the message. Someone will be sent out as soon as possible."

"Great," Ann said. "I want to get up there and get pictures before they make the entire area off limits. If it's really dinosaur bones, they'll section it off to keep everyone away. You know those paleontologists; they'll want to keep the discovery and all the fame to themselves."

Henry moaned again.

"So," Ann coaxed, leaning in close and snuggling as extra incentive, "will you take me up there tomorrow, first thing?"

"Okay." He gave in. He knew better than to keep Ann from a story. It was like trying to keep a cat away from catnip.

"Promise?"

"I promise." He chuckled, envisioning all those strange bones in the ground. Ancient remnants of the distant past. Dinosaurs. Remarkable.

"Did you know," he spoke, becoming the passionate child again, "that the Apatosaurus, which means *deceptive lizard*, once known as the Brontosaurus, might have measured ninety feet in length, and weighed nearly 38 tons?" Grown up or not, he still loved thinking and talking about dinosaurs.

"Ninety feet. That big, huh?"

"Oh, and they believe the Diplodocus," Henry continued happily, "also a herbivore, a plant-eater, could have been around ninety feet as well, with a whip-like tale forty-five feet long. And Brachiosaurus, from the same time, the Jurassic Period, could have weighed 100 tons." Henry paused, "Come to think about it, I wonder what dinosaurs were common around here sixty-five million years ago?"

"I don't have the slightest idea," Ann responded. "Maybe that paleontologist you've sent for will know."

"He might." Henry yawned. "I can't wait to get another look at those bones in the light."

"I can't wait to see them, either. I hope it's sunny tomorrow. I want good clear pictures. Zeke will positively drool when I take them in. They'll help our circulation for sure." She leaned her head contentedly against Henry's shoulder. "Sweetheart, do you know I love you because you never cease to surprise me?"

He laughed softly. "I hope you always love me and I hope I always surprise you."

"Until we're both old and gray," Ann murmured the promise they gave to each other at every opportunity.

Henry embraced his wife, and whispered, "Isn't it about time we go in?"

"Yeah, it has gotten pretty cold out here, hasn't it?"

Their laughter mingled and, arm in arm, they went in to bed.

CHAPTER 2

The next morning Ann received an early wake-up call from Zeke at the newspaper, something about the final computer layout of that week's edition being wrong, and she had to get into the office right away. She had to help Zeke fix it or the newspaper wouldn't get to the printers on time.

Reluctantly, Ann postponed her trek with Henry to take pictures of the bones. People who work at small town newspapers wear many hats. Ann wasn't only a reporter; she helped sell the advertising, design the ads, help put the paper together every week and send it off to the printers. It was always a delicate balancing act, especially since the Klamath Falls Journal was, as with many small newspapers these days, in financial trouble. Ann did everything she could to help keep it off its death bed. After all, it was her job on the line.

"I'll get that layout fixed and to the printer's quick as a bunny," Ann quipped, crawling out of their warm bed and into her robe, "and return as fast as I can. If you check here later this afternoon, I should be back. Then you can show me that fossil bed, all right?"

"Sure, honey, I'll swing by after lunch, and take

you up there," Henry murmured, sticking his head under the covers, wanting nothing more than to recapture sleep. The alarm clock hadn't even gone off yet. It was barely dawn. Zeke and that crazy newspaper. Didn't the old guy ever go home anymore?

Then the image of those monstrous white bones up on the rim came back to haunt him. He jumped out of bed and fought his wife for the bathroom. In the end, they shared it, and were both dressed and on the move within the hour, going separate ways after a hug and a kiss. No time for breakfast, just a quick cup of coffee.

Henry drove alone to ranger headquarters in a dawn's light which reflected off the frost that covered everything. There were dirty mounds of left-over snow in patches that wouldn't be completely gone until midsummer. It'd taken Henry a long time to get used to the unbelievably long winters in Oregon. Now he didn't mind them.

He figured he'd get another cup of coffee or two while he was checking on his men and his messages. He played with the thought of going up to the lodge later for a real breakfast, but ended up stopping at a place inside the park and bought a large box of donuts for everyone. He did that once and a while as a treat. As he did, his men loved pastries; even though they were bad for the waistlines.

Munching on a glazed donut, he pulled into park headquarters. He strode through the door, opened his office and hung up his coat. Before he could grab a cup of coffee and his third donut, one of his rangers strolled in and took him by the arm.

"Boss, I need to talk to you," his friend, George Redcrow said, shutting the door.

"Well, good morning to you, too, George," Henry announced. His eyes wistfully glanced through the glass window towards the perking coffee pot. "You could have at least let me get my coffee. I was this close." He waved two fingers an inch apart in the air between them.

George grunted, "Time for coffee after I tell you what I've got to tell you."

Redcrow was half Indian, on his father's side, and he looked it. He possessed sharp features in a hawkish face, soul-reading unnerving dark eyes and an earthy wit to match. Nearly as tall as Henry, he was heavier set, his gray-streaked hair longer, wilder, like his eyes and his nature. An excellent park ranger, he had an uncanny wisdom about the land Henry could only attribute to the fact he'd spent most of his life in the woods.

But he was the most superstitious human being Henry had ever known. George actually believed in ghosts, monsters, and U.F.O.s. In every other way, though, he was level-headed, intelligent and intuitive. He was a good man to have on your side or at your back in a tough spot. Henry had seen him take down a rampaging drunk with one swift move; had seen him diffuse tense or dangerous situations many a time with a calming word or two. Henry respected the man.

"Okay, spill your guts, ranger. But make it quick. I've got something very important to attend to and I haven't had enough coffee yet. I'm about to go into serious caffeine withdrawal."

George lowered his voice, "Thought you'd like to know I've been finding a lot of dead animals lately on Wizard Island."

Henry shrugged. "What's so unusual about that, other than the fact the animals swam all the way out to the island and ended up dying there?" Death was a part of nature. Animals grew old and died, or attacked each other and died. Weakened animals froze in the bitter winters and were uncovered, rotting, after the snows melted. Dead. That was nature.

Henry started inching closer to the coffee pot like a man dying of thirst might move towards water. George stuck to him. "The way they died."

"I have to have a cup of coffee, George," Henry said, opening the door. It was early enough, right before the morning shift, that the room was pretty nearly empty anyway. He couldn't understand why George had wanted privacy if he was only talking about dead animals. Henry had assumed it was a personal matter. "What do you mean? How did they die?" He located his cup and reached out for the coffee pot.

"The carcasses, or what was left of them, were mauled and eaten by something that must have the biggest teeth we'll ever see."

"A bear?"

"No, the attacker was much larger than a bear. In fact, one of the carcasses was a bear."

"Oh." Henry's eyebrows lifted and he let his lips smile gently. "Interesting. I guess now you're gonna try to convince me it was one of your aliens…or some monster that's taken up residence in the lake?" George's words had reminded Henry of what the red-headed woman had said the day before.

"Monster in the lake? What are you talking about?"

"Ah, up on the rim yesterday, before the earthquake, some crazy woman told me a friend of hers saw something in the lake last summer. A big water creature of some sort. Have you heard any weird stories like that from any of the other rangers or visitors? Has anyone reported any strange animal sightings in or around the lake?"

"No," George frowned, "but that might explain the tracks."

"What tracks?" Henry raised his cup of coffee to his lips with a contented sigh. The first few cups every morning were sheer ambrosia.

"The tracks around the carcasses, the ones leading back into the water. They were enormous." George looked at him, apprehension in his gaze.

Henry laughed. "Come on, George, lighten up. It was probably some overgrown cougar or an exceptionally big-footed bear that dragged its kills out to the island for feeding privacy. Bears around here do get quite large. You should know that. You've been here pretty much forever."

George's eyes, flint hard, glittered. "Then I should recognize bear or cougar tracks when I see them. And I'm telling you, they weren't either. They weren't like anything I've ever seen. Ever. Not to mention–why would any predator drag its kill all the way out to that forsaken island to eat it?

Swim all that way? Why? Animals don't care where they feed. Maybe we should start looking for something larger something...different. Could be there is something in the lake."

Oh, great, Henry mused, eating another glazed donut and watching his friend, *George has finally gone 'round the bend. Must be all that solitude.*

George lived alone deep in the park in a cabin that was practically inaccessible. He liked it that way. He'd never been married, though he'd had a long string of lady friends. He'd worked odd jobs in the park since he'd been sixteen and had become a park ranger at twenty-one. He knew the park well and was familiar with every animal that crawled or scurried in its woods or swam in its lakes.

"George, you know, you need to get out more. Find a new woman. Not mooch so many suppers at my house," Henry stated flatly.

"Boss, I'm not fooling around."

Wiping sticky crumbs from his fingers on a napkin, Henry gave in. "Show the tracks to me."

"I wish I could, Henry, but the most recent carcass and tracks I found, late yesterday, were in snow and mud, and it rained hard last night. I looked, but the tracks are gone now."

"Well, describe them a little more to me anyway."

"They were gigantic and they were deep, the toes spread wide apart. Looked as if the feet could have been webbed or even clawed."

Henry actually chuckled, but George was serious, so he stopped.

"The animals' remains were left partially in the

water and were gnawed over later by some other animals, coyotes or fish or something. So the other larger teeth marks were hard to make out, unless you knew what you were looking for."

"That's a shame," Henry said. "I would have liked to get a look at them and the tracks." He gave his friend a long, hard look. "Listen, George, tell you what, next time you find those teeth marks on a dead animal or see those tracks, come and get me. No matter what time it is, okay? I'll come. I want to see these monster footprints of yours."

George cracked a smile. "Deal." He stood up straighter, tucking in his shirt, anxious to look as neat and professional in his uniform as possible. "I guess I'd better start my rounds. I've been here three cups of coffee longer than you. You'll fire me if I don't get out there and make the park safe for the visitors."

"Heaven forbid we should endanger the visitors," Henry tossed back. It was a private joke between the two of them. George still thought of Henry as one of those visitors.

"See ya later, then. I have a tour group waiting for me," George finished, slapping him on the back, and strolling out the door into the chilly morning.

***

Water monster sightings and monster tracks. What's next? UFOs? Henry threw an impatient look at his cluttered desk. There were reports to finish, people to call and meetings to arrange; but suddenly the walls were closing in on him. He had to get outside under the beautiful summer sky, breathe in the fresh air and walk among the trees.

And he wanted to get a good look at that fossil bed in the daylight, that's what he wanted.

Getting an insulated go-cup from the office, Henry poured a final cup of coffee. Before leaving, he checked the morning dispatches from the local and park authorities (nothing urgent there), and after answering some procedure questions from a couple of the loitering rangers, he walked out the door and climbed into his jeep. He'd drive as far up the rim as possible and hoof it the rest of the way.

Ah, it was great to be boss. Well, sometimes.

Parking the jeep at the bottom of the trail, Henry hiked up. When he reached the bones, someone was already kneeling before the crumbling lava rock.

Henry walked up and the man turned and flashed a wide, friendly grin, then swiveled around on the balls of his feet and stood up with graceful movements not unlike a panther. The man was young, no more than mid-twenties or so, and was the thinnest person Henry had ever seen for his height. The man was almost as tall as he was.

"Howdy, ranger." Perceptive brown eyes peered at Henry through golden wire-rimmed glasses and took in his uniform. "Sorry…Chief Ranger," he amended. The man's long hair framed a thin, pensive face. As chilly as it was, he wore only a flimsy blue-jean jacket over a sweater, and worn blue jeans. His tennis shoes were dirty from traipsing through the mud.

Henry was usually a good judge of character. It was something he'd perfected as a police officer. He could look at someone, observe their expressions and how well they maintained eye contact, and would know basically what kind of person he was dealing with.

The young man might be dressed shabbily, but something about the way he held himself, the way he moved, the way the brown eyes studied him tipped Henry off. This young man was sure of what he was doing and who he was–and not easily intimidated.

"I see it didn't take long," Henry said, his eyes flicking towards the wall of fossils.

The other man's face registered puzzlement for a fraction of a second and then he said, "No, I got up here as soon as I received your message." He smiled again. "I'm the staff paleontologist you asked John Day's to send out, remember? You are Chief Ranger Henry Shore, aren't you?"

Now Henry smiled. "Yes, I am." He'd been afraid the man was a hiker or a tourist who'd merely happened upon the site. "No offense, but you look awfully young to be a PhD paleontologist."

"No offense taken. I'm older than you think. I graduated college early. Don't worry, I am a full-fledged paleontologist, with a secondary degree in seismology. That's why they sent me. Been on staff at John Day's now, oh, for about two years, but I've been on paleontological digs all over the world with the top people in the field."

"Oh, one of those child prodigies?" He still looked like a kid to Henry.

"No, not exactly." The scientist seemed embarrassed at the remark and Henry changed the subject.

"Well, it didn't take you long to get here, did it?

What did you do, fly?" John Day Fossil Beds National Monument was over three-hundred miles away.

"In fact, yes. As soon as I got your message I had a friend, who has a pilot's license, fly me up as soon as it became light. I couldn't wait to see what you'd discovered. And, from what I can see already, I believe it's an astounding find." The brown eyes were shining with an obsessive glow. The eyes of a true zealot.

"How'd you locate the exact place, though?"

"Simple, Chief Ranger. I asked for you at park headquarters earlier. You weren't in yet, so I moseyed on over to the Crater Lake Lodge to get some coffee and wait for you. I happened to come across this man in the lobby who was going on about these bones he'd seen yesterday up on the volcano's rim after the earthquake. He gave me detailed directions. So, here I am."

He's resourceful, too, Henry thought. "Was he a middle-aged guy with a beard? About this tall?" Henry's hand went shoulder high.

"Yep."

Henry wasn't too happy knowing the guy was blabbing to everyone about the fossils. "I wonder who else knows about it? And what they know."

"I wouldn't worry, Ranger Shore. I don't think the man who sent me up here has a clue to what these bones really are. He was just making conversation and I was lucky enough to overhear. He thought they were bear bones or bones of some other large park animal. And I didn't enlighten him. The fewer people who know about this, for now, the better."

Henry was further impressed. The man knew his business.

"So, Chief Ranger, how did you figure out these were dinosaur bones?" The young man prodded his glasses higher up on his narrow nose. Sunlight glinted off the lenses. He still looked so young Henry had a hard time taking him seriously. It was like talking to a friendly, but precocious kid.

"Dinosaurs have always been one of my great passions." Henry shrugged. "When I was younger, I yearned to be a paleontologist, too. But life sent me on another road."

"So I see."

Henry slid his eyes towards the once-buried treasure. "What's going to happen now?"

The paleontologist coughed, bringing up his hand to muffle it. Dirt clung to his fingers from digging around in the mud. "We notify the proper authorities and, eventually, I'll call in some colleagues of mine to set up a monitored dig. Then we'll begin unearthing and cataloging the specimens; send them back to John Day for further study." He locked gaze with Henry and appeared to make a decision. "But there's no hurry. Not after all the millennia these bones have lain here. I'll report back tomorrow or the next day. Next week, even. I'd like to spend a little time looking over what is here first. In private. Would you mind? I've been waiting for such a discovery my whole career. I've never seen anything like this."

Henry liked the kid more every second. "No. You're right. A week or two one way or another can't matter. I was hoping to do the same thing, look around some before the crowds rush in, the fences go up and the whole place becomes off limits."

The paleontologist nodded in agreement. "Exactly." He knelt down, his back to Henry, making clicking sounds with his tongue as he studied the find. "It's an amazing discovery. Simply amazing. I believe what we have here are genuine dinosaur fossils. But," he scratched his chin, "of what species, I have absolutely no idea. It's an enigma. That's why I want some time with them before I call the troops in. This is much too juicy to share yet."

The man's eyes traveled dreamily over the white fragments protruding from the earth and the clear impressions in the layers of rock. He gently caressed the jagged end of a bone. "Perfectly preserved…must have something to do with the ancient volcanic lava trapped underneath the earth in this area. The earthquake yesterday set them free."

Henry stood behind the scientist. "To think they were once dinosaurs. Real dinosaurs. Any idea how old these particular fossils might be?" He inquired with reverence.

"I've got a rough idea. Ballpark figure. But tests at John Day will have to be performed to gauge their age precisely."

Henry moved closer to the fossil bed, squatting down on his haunches to gain a better look. Tipping his hat back on his head, he reached down, running his hands over the length of a very deep fossil impression. "I'm merely a layman, but I'd guess these bones to be around…sixty-five million years old?"

"Perhaps older." The scientist gazed at Henry, distracted. "You see, I've never seen fossils like these before in any book, in any museum or on any dig. Not anywhere. Not *ever*."

The expert wiped sweat from his forehead and abruptly plunked down on the ground. He seemed overwhelmed.

Henry sat down beside him. Maybe the kid was sun-stroked. "You okay?" he pressed. "The sun and the thin air can be a killer this high up unless you're used to it. It's deceptive because it's so cool."

"Sure, I'm fine. It's the discovery that has me light-headed, that's all. Can you imagine the hoopla, the crowd you're going to have here when we finally release the word about this?"

Henry's eyes rested on the wall, open disdain on his face. "Unfortunately, yes, I can."

His companion searched around with sad eyes. "I'm real sorry, Chief Ranger. It could ruin this place. A damn shame. It's a beautiful park. Hopefully, with restrictions, we'll be able to keep the crowds down and control the damage some."

Henry felt that he'd met a soul mate. It was a relief to know the kid thought as he did.

The young man seemed to recall his manners. "I'm sorry, I haven't even introduced myself properly. The excitement of the moment, you know, and these astonishing fossils, sidetracked me." He stood up, extending his dusty hand for Henry to shake. "I'm Justin Maltin. Dr. Justin Maltin."

Shaking it, Henry responded, "Real nice to meet you, Doc."

"You were here then when the earthquake hit yesterday?" Justin queried.

"Yes. This one knocked half my tour group on their butts."

"This one? You mean there's been other earthquakes recently?"

Henry looked off into the distance. Everything had fallen so silent all of a sudden. Not even bird noises. Strange. His gaze returned to Justin.

"Yes. One last year. Like this one, not much above ground damage."

"Before that?"

"I don't know. I've been here in the park for less than ten years."

"Tell me about both earthquakes." Justin tugged a notebook and a pen from a bulging pack sitting on the ground behind him. He looked up, giving Henry his full attention. "Or anything you can recall. You discovered these fossils–and yes, they're genuine fossils–after the most recent quake?"

"Yes, it uncovered the site."

The scientist nodded. "I'd already been told most of the damage was done below this lake, though."

"Really? How do you know that?"

The young man smiled. "Secondary degree in seismology, remember? And I did the research. Then also, with the lava rivers and tunnels this caldera is supposed to have underneath it, this whole area could become very unstable, if it isn't already. It's something you'll have to keep in mind, not only for your reports, but for the safety of all the people in the park."

"I'd wondered about that myself."

Justin jotted something down in his notebook, the guy was nothing if not thorough, and went back to examining the site. Henry right beside him.

"Never seen any fossils like these, though," Justin repeated, unable to hide his excitement. "As I said, perhaps the bones are an unknown breed of dinosaur altogether. A brand new species. Wouldn't that be fantastic?"

He found the younger man easy to talk to. Soon they were discussing more than fossils.

Justin wanted to know why Henry had become a park ranger and Henry told him the sanitized version he gave most people; that police work in New York had become just too dangerous. It turned out that Justin had been a cop himself, for a short while, after his first two years of college. Unsure of what he'd really wanted and tired of school, Justin dropped out and had attended a local police academy. He'd served on a small town police department for nine months before he decided it wasn't for him.

"For me, it was too boring. Riding around all night in a squad car hoping someone would rob somebody or try to shoot someone, not my thing anyway I discovered…and the dinosaurs were still calling to me." The scientist grinned. "So I went back to school, worked around my classes to pay my way, got my degree in record time and here I am."

They had a lot in common, age difference aside.

"I need to walk down to the lake and take a look around to see if there're more fissures or broken ground, Chief Ranger. How about meeting me later at the lodge for lunch?" Justin asked Henry as they were getting ready to part ways. "We can continue discussing our prehistoric friends here and compare the pros and cons of being a police officer in the United States today."

"Can't make it, I'm sorry to say. I'm supposed to go home and squire my wife back up here so she can take pictures." Henry had previously mentioned that Ann worked at a local newspaper. "And I have work waiting at headquarters."

Justin's carefree expression went serious. "Do you think your wife might hold off a while on publishing those photos where everyone in the world would see them? For a few days?"

"I'll talk to her about it. She'll be disappointed, but I don't see any reason why not. The paper's a weekly and they just put this week's edition to bed. It'd be a week anyway until the pictures come out. That enough time for you?"

"I imagine it'll have to be." Justin crossed his arms, obviously relieved. "Well, then, how about joining me for dinner around six? You and your wife? I'd like to meet her. I can give her some expert input for that article of hers."

"You got a deal, Dr. Maltin. Ann and I haven't eaten at the lodge for…at least a week," he joked. "We need to get out."

"Please, call me Justin."

"Okay, Justin. And you'd better call me Henry, then. Enough of this Chief Ranger stuff."

"You got it, Henry. See you at six."

"See you then."

They shook hands.

Justin collected his duffel bag with an audible groan and, after Henry aimed him in the right direction, started on the path towards the lake. The bag was overstuffed with whatever the boy had in it, probably clothes, snacks and books, and looked larger and heavier than the young man it was being dragged behind. He stumbled around a corner and disappeared, the duffel bag bouncing along in the dust.

Henry returned to headquarters.

That afternoon he attended to business. The Ranger's Station was so busy, he was almost relieved when Ann called from the newspaper and told him she couldn't make it back before dark. Zeke had a couple of timely stories for her to write and they were short-handed again. The assistant editor was out for the day. She couldn't make supper at the lodge by six, either.

"I'll grab something to eat on my way home," she told him. "You have a good time with your new friend and you can show me the bones tomorrow. Zeke promised I could have tomorrow morning off. He really wants those photos."

Henry's day passed slowly, and just before six he made a quick circuit of Rim Village and the campgrounds. One group of campers had parked far away from the others and had left trash out in the open. Bears had come in the night and had made a mess of everything, scaring the campers pretty badly. Henry issued the offenders a fifty dollar ticket for breaking camp rules. He suspected they'd follow instructions better next time.

***

The paleontologist was waiting at a corner table next to the blazing fireplace, hovering over a cup of coffee with a drained look on his face. Something was wrong.

"My wife, Ann, won't be joining us. She's been detained at work," Henry remarked as he sat down.

"Sorry to hear that. I wanted to meet her."

"Oh, you will soon enough, I imagine. She's as excited over the fossils as I am." A subtle hand gesture and Molly, the evening waitress, went off to fetch Henry a cup of coffee. All the waitresses knew him well enough to keep the coffee coming.

"Looks like you've had quite a day, young man."

"You might say that. I've been prowling around since dawn." The kid lifted bloodshot eyes to meet his. "I've been all over the land around the caldera and am so exhausted I can barely stand up. It's a lot of ground to cover. That lake's bigger than it looks."

"Yes, it is. Take it from someone who's been over every inch of it." The coffee came and with it two menus. Henry dropped his eyes to the food list. Steak and mashed potatoes sounded good. Without raising his eyes, he asked, "Find anything interesting?"

A pause. "I did."

Henry glanced up and caught the wary look on the scientist's face.

"I was doing some routine surveying along the

lake and, out of curiosity, believing there's a direct connection between the lava beneath the caldera and the earthquakes, I took some water temperatures." He fell silent.

Henry waited for him to continue as the waitress bustled over with his coffee and her order tablet.

After they'd ordered (Henry the steak and Justin two cheeseburgers with onion rings) Justin said, "I read the data on your lake here. Did you know that the overall temperature of the water has gone up?"

Henry blinked. "You don't say?" So, George had been right about that.

"I took a reading. A couple of them. The temperature of the water is over sixty degrees Fahrenheit. I think it's rising steadily. And–"

"And?"

"I think there's still major volcanic activity going on deep under the caldera, which would explain the temperature rise and other prevalent conditions. The cause could be moving rivers of freed molten lava under pressure. A potentially dangerous situation."

"Then there could be another earthquake?" Henry supplied, unhappily. "Worse than the last two?"

"Eventually. That's highly possible."

"Oh, boy." Henry took a sip of his coffee, his eyes hooded, attempting to absorb the meaning behind it all. He didn't need Justin to explain to him that if what the scientist maintained was true, it could affect the geological make-up of the park. It could even destroy everything.

Their food came, steaming on the plates.

"What else?" Something more was bothering Justin and Henry waited for the young man to tell him.

Justin hunched his shoulders and leaned in closer so no one else could hear. "This has nothing to do with the lake's rising temperature or the volcanic activity, but I also found some...tracks...in the mud down by the water."

"Tracks?" George's worried face floated across Henry's inner eyes.

"Huge animal tracks." Justin rubbed his eyes and shook his head. "The most remarkable thing I've ever seen, except for those bones you discovered yesterday. If I didn't know better I'd swear–" he stopped talking when he caught the look in Henry's eyes.

"Go on, finish what you were going to say. I'm listening." Henry started eating his dinner as if nothing was wrong, but pinpricks of unease had begun to needle him.

He was aware the couple at the next table was having a fight of some kind. Distracting.

Justin's eyebrows lifted and a hesitant grin transformed his face. "If I say anymore you're going to think I'm crazy."

"I can't decide what you are if you don't tell me what you want to tell me first."

"All right." Justin's hands went up in a surrendering gesture. "Based on what expertise I have, I'd swear those tracks were made by some sort of," he whispered the word, "*dinosaur*."

Henry practically choked on his steak. The idea was so ridiculous, he wanted to laugh. And here he'd thought the kid had no sense of humor. Boy was he wrong. "Some joke. You're kidding, of course?"

"No. Dead serious."

"A real one?"

"Yes, a real breathing, walking one," Justin hissed. "A live one."

Now with more than a hint of irritation, Henry mulled over the notion: what if Justin wasn't what he'd presented himself to be, but was some kind of nut case? New York had Jaded Henry in that way. Anyone could say they were this or that but it didn't mean they were. Some people were convincing liars. But the kid's face was sincere; his eyes clear and bright. If he was a liar, he was damn good at it. And why would he be lying anyway?

"It's true. The tracks, whatever they are, seemed authentic. I don't believe it myself. But I saw what I saw." Justin lifted his cup of coffee with a shaky hand. They were nearly clean now, with just a hint of dirt beneath the nails. Exhausted, the guy looked even younger. About fifteen.

"Did you take a picture of them with your cell phone?"

"I would have if I had one. I dropped my last phone a week ago into some crevice I was climbing over. Lost three phones that way in the last year. I need to get to town and buy another."

"You're hard on phones."

"I think I am."

"Doesn't matter. Cell phones don't work well in the park. Bad reception. Don't work well in most places around here. But they still take photos."

"Oh." Justin was watching him.

Henry was a rational man, and he remembered that someone else had claimed to have seen something unusual in the lake. He nearly mentioned it to the scientist, but it was too preposterous to dwell on, much less repeat.

He recalled George mentioning those strange tracks. Merely coincidences?

"The tracks could be a hoax, Justin. Kids are always playing practical jokes around here. Like that Bigfoot scare up in Washington a couple of months ago. They had tracks, photos and everything. In the end, it turned out to be a prank. All of them do. For the attention and the tabloid money."

A negative nod. "No, I don't think this is anything like that. I believe those tracks were made by something alive. Something real. Not any animal I know and not human, either."

"Where'd you find them?"

"Down past Cleetwood Trail, before the steep walls begin again. The prints were going into the water. It's easy to see how they could have gone unnoticed. The location is desolate. Hard to get to. I don't know what made me hike that far off the beaten path." He shook his head again, wonder and fear warring in his eyes. "Any paleontologist in his right mind would give twenty years of his life to see a real live dinosaur walking around–except me. As much as I adore studying the creatures, I believe there was a reason for their demise, their extinction. They'd be far too destructively anachronistic to coexist with humanity. What most people don't realize is some dinosaur species were extremely intelligent. Rapacious in their behavior. I'd hate to come face to face with a live one and I'd hate to try to keep one in captivity. A good dinosaur is a dead dinosaur. They're magnificent monsters, but they don't belong in iron cages like circus freaks or running loose. Too unpredictable. Too volatile. Too *big*."

Henry wasn't sure he agreed with the scientist. It'd be incredible to see a real, living, breathing dinosaur. Just once. A large tranquilizer gun would solve the problem easily.

"Yeah, I remember what happened to King Kong," Henry threw in for comedic relief, but Justin didn't crack a smile.

"Eat your food, Justin," Henry ordered in a calm voice. The kid was a nervous wreck. "Then you can show me those prints. I've got to see them for myself. If we hurry we can make it down there before dark."

"Okay. It'll be good to show them to someone else. Prove they're actually there, that they weren't a figment of my imagination. Maybe then I won't feel like I've lost my sanity."

Justin gulped down his food.

Henry wasn't as hurried. He was convinced their journey down to the lake would turn out to be a wasted trip. Dinosaur tracks. Yeah, sure.

***

The sun was going down by the time they arrived at the water's edge. Trees were bathed in lace cloaks of muted reds and oranges, and the murky shadows dancing around them made it seem even later. They'd taken too long over supper and the trip down from the rim to where the tracks were had turned out to be more difficult than Henry had anticipated. Justin had been correct when he'd said it was off the beaten path.

Trudging through the mud, the scientist led Henry down along the bank, past the boat dock at the mouth of Cleetwood Trail and around the bottom of the caldera. They walked and climbed for what Henry felt was at least an hour. The kid had a great sense of direction. When they came to a spot where the caldera's cliffs were rugged and steep, Justin crouched over and searched the ground in the dimming light, using a flashlight Henry had given him.

"I thought they were here," he muttered, as he moved on.

Henry followed behind in silence. Better find them soon, he thought, light's almost gone.

"Here they are," Justin mouthed just as Henry was getting ready to suggest they give it up and head back. The scientist hunkered down.

Henry came up behind him, bending over to study what Justin was pointing at. They were animal imprints of some kind, true enough. They were approximately eight feet long; narrow at one end and much wider at the other. George had been right about something else–the toes appeared to be webbed claws.

The prints led to the lake and only the impressions made in the soft mud nearest the water were clearly visible.

"See," Justin exclaimed, "I wasn't hallucinating.

Here are the tracks to prove it." He seemed to be talking more to himself than Henry.

Henry didn't know what to say. He was staring at the tracks, but he wasn't believing them. He craned his neck and glanced around. "They seem to have come from below the cliffs somewhere. There are caves along the caldera's base beneath the water line. Some of them are quite large and they vein down into the caverns and tunnel under the lake. I'd speculate that whatever made these prints probably came from those same caves."

The tracks appeared real. They looked like something out of a horror film. So damn big. Henry swallowed hard, his sense of reality blurring. He loved watching old Twilight Zone episodes, but he didn't like living through one.

"They're absolutely not bear or cougar tracks." Henry did some quick calculations in his head: If the size of the body lived up to the feet…then whatever created those tracks was a hell of a lot bigger than any bear.

"Damn," grumbled Henry, "I should have brought a camera along. They're expecting more storms tonight. These might not be here tomorrow." He knew he was behind the times; his cheap cell phone was just a cell phone. It didn't take pictures. Didn't work half the time in the park anyway. He took off his hat and raked his fingers through his hair, a nervous habit. "And there's no way I can run, get the camera and get back here before the light's gone. No way."

Justin was still studying the prints. "Well, at least, you've see them, too. That's a relief to know.

I thought I was losing it."

"You're the expert. Do you think they're authentic?"

"I don't know. They look real. It's just that I've never seen any impressions like these in any of the books or excavation sites. If they are dinosaur tracks, they're tracks of a beast as yet undiscovered in history."

"Or they could be a clever joke," Henry offered, hopefully. "You wouldn't believe how ingenious some hoaxers can be."

"Well, let's hope it doesn't rain tonight. Like you, I wish I could have gotten pictures. I guess I wasn't thinking, either. When I found these prints I thought I had my camera in my duffel bag, but somehow I must have forgotten to put it in this morning before I left. I was in such a hurry. Perhaps it won't rain tonight and these will be here tomorrow." He traced the fading outline of one of the prints. His hair fell forward, covering his face; he slipped the straggly strands behind his ears and rose to his feet.

They stood examining the prints in the flashlight's circle until it was almost totally dark.

"We'd better get back to the lodge," Henry finally said. "The path can be treacherous in the dark."

"Maybe you're right." Justin dropped his muddy hands to his side.

Water lapped softly behind them as they painstakingly made their way to the boat dock using Henry's flashlight.

The cold had crept in with the night and the men

shivered in their coats as they picked their way through the rocks lining the path. Henry chose to take the easiest trail up to the rim and straight down to the lodge.

Henry began to doubt what he'd seen. The impressions could have been a trick of the escaping light; or something the lapping water had created. That was possible, wasn't it?

A full moon, pale and transparent, was riding the horizon above ebony trees. The illumination it gave off was faint. The water of Crater Lake glimmered far below them and they could barely make out the shadows of the trees and the blurry outlines of Wizard Island and Phantom Ship.

Henry glanced behind him when they'd reached the top and before he turned away thought he saw something. "What's that rippling on the surface of the lake there past Wizard Island?" He paused, squinting and staring hard at the water, as Justin waited behind him. Yes, something was swimming down there…a series of bumps in the water.

Then it was gone. The water was placid.

"Did you see that?"

"See what?" Justin asked.

"Never mind." The skin on Henry's arms and neck was tingling. He experienced that strange feeling of unreality again, as if he were dreaming. A cold breeze fluttered across his face.

He was wide awake.

Had that woman the summer before really seen something in the lake? Something that shouldn't have been there? Was that the something he'd just seen?

Nah, he chided himself, chuckling uneasily as he and Justin walked down the trail. The ripple in the water was most likely a big fish. Must have been.

That woman in the group yesterday with her ridiculous accusation had spooked him, that was all. Along with George and Justin and the weird tracks. He was tired; and had obviously seen too many Spook Spectaculars as a kid. Under the cloak of night, anything was imaginable.

But he couldn't explain the great relief he felt when Justin and him strolled through the door of the brightly lit lodge a short while later. The sight and sound of normal, noisy people, the aroma of fresh coffee, and the crackling fire, were comfortingly welcome.

Suddenly he hoped it'd rain again tonight. Hoped it would storm to beat the band so all those tracks would wash away. Then he wouldn't have to deal with any of it.

***

Outside in the night a mournful call echoed across the water of Crater Lake…and slowly pulsed away into the dark. The water rippled and moved and was eventually calmed as the moon rose high and full over the park among the gathering clouds. The waters stilled. The night silent.

CHAPTER 3

It didn't only rain that night, it stormed fiercely, as Henry had wished. In the end, discounting his fancies as childish, he convinced himself he hadn't actually seen anything in the lake. It'd been too far away and too dark.

When he ambled into the kitchen for breakfast, the storm hadn't abated and the rain was beating heavily outside the windows. He didn't waste time gazing out at the solid sheet of falling water, but headed for the sink and made a pot of coffee.

It was his day off, but he'd gotten up early to see Ann off to work. She usually put in half-days on Saturdays and he enjoyed having breakfast with her before she left. Because of the bad weather she'd decided not to go into work that morning, but her boss, Zeke, had called and said he really needed her in the office. Another emergency. What was new? So she'd be going in.

Sitting in his pajamas, reading the paper, he was happy he didn't have to go anywhere and had put the whole weird episode of the night before away as any sane man would have.

He mentioned nothing about the tracks or the sighting to Ann, though he did tell her about his supper meeting with Justin and the lake's continuing rise in temperature.

"Darn," his wife griped over her first cup of coffee, her eyes on the wet windows, "Looks like I won't get those pictures of that dinosaur boneyard this morning, either. I'm beginning to feel as if I'll never get them. I'm cursed. Zeke thinks I'm making it all up."

"Don't fret, hon, you'll get them. The bones aren't going anywhere."

"Yeah, yeah." The disappointment was strong in the way she cocked her head. "With my luck, we'll have another massive earthquake and the ground will swallow the whole area up." She snapped her fingers in the air. "Another missed golden opportunity for fame and fortune."

She was wearing a soft malt-blue sweater, which made her gray eyes seem blue, and her usual blue jeans, which accented her slim figure. Her short hair was feathered around her face, the gray streaks more prominent as they curved along the front. She looked a lot younger than her age, Henry thought. Prettier than she'd ever looked when she'd worked at that big city paper, her life all hurry-hurry. The country air, the slower pace and the woods agreed with her. Her new life agreed with her, as his agreed with him.

"Laura and Phoebe are coming for dinner tonight," Ann informed him cheerily as she was leaving.

"What's new?" he bantered back, with a flicker of a smile, as he looked up from the Everyday section. "Be careful out there, honey. It's been raining hard and visibility is low with the fog. Take the main highways, none of those back road short cuts, ya hear?"

"Yes, honey."

***

Ann opened her umbrella and dashed out to her battered jeep Eagle, splashing through mud puddles all the way. With a sigh of relief she slid into her front seat and closed the door on the cold rain.

If you wanted to live in this part of Oregon, you had to have a rugged four-wheel drive. At least eight months out of the year the roads, especially the back ones, were a nightmare. They were covered with three feet of snow or ice, or were mired in mud, and often impassable. And for another two months, during the tail end of fall and the tail end of winter, it rained so much it was like an Asian monsoon. Summer was brief but sweet. The extreme weather was the only thing that Ann wasn't crazy about.

But her husband loved everything about Oregon. Snow or endless rain didn't disturb him. He was just happy to be living out in the woods. Her mountain man.

When she got to the newspaper, Zeke was busy at his computer. Try as she might, she rarely beat him in.

"Don't tell me you spent the night here?" She clucked as she shook out her umbrella, laid it in the closet, and hung her coat on a hanger.

"Sure, you know me. I live here. I keep a fold-up cot in the closet. Why go home at all?" The older man retorted gruffly, his sharp gaze meeting hers for a moment. Hidden in his eyes was pleasure at her arrival.

"Oh, by the way, Jeff's not coming in today. Had to take one of his kids to the dentist, or something. Says he'll finish his stories at home on his laptop and will email them in first thing tomorrow."

"So it's just you and me today, huh, Zeke?" she said, not surprised. Jeff, a young reporter on his way up, as he liked to put it, wasn't very dependable, kids or no kids. The Klamath Falls Journal for Jeff Spenser was one of those underpaid first steps on his road to the Pulitzer. He'd been with them six months, and Ann didn't expect him to last another six. Few of the young reporters stayed long because the Journal couldn't afford to pay good wages. Maybe that was one of the reasons Zeke valued Ann. She actually cared about the newspaper and didn't want it to go under. Her caring had created a special bond between her and the old editor.

"Not that it matters much lately," Zeke stated. "If the circulation drops any more, we won't need him. We won't need anybody for anything 'cause there won't be a paper."

"Ah, Zeke, this paper's not going to fold, not if you and I can help it. And if you'd listen to me and do a few more circulars for the stores around here to insert in the Journal, we'd made a bundle. And if we also did a shopper–"

"If I told you once," he cut her off gently, "I told you a hundred times, Ann Shore, that if I'd wanted to run a printing company, I would have bought one. This is a newspaper. We print the news, remember?"

"A lot of small newspapers produce circulars and shoppers for extra revenue. It would bring in the money we need to stay afloat." She'd also tried to get him to let her post the newspaper online, but he'd hear nothing about that. No way, he'd said. Newspapers were printed.

"Not us. We're a newspaper, we print the news. Period."

Ann gave up. They'd had the same discussion before, many times, but the elderly newspaper man was stubborn; set in his ways.

Zeke grumbled under his breath and thumped the side of his computer with a loud whack. "Darn thing's acting up again. We never should have thrown away those typewriters."

"Yeah, we should have stayed in the stone age, too." Ann tilted her head. But Zeke was right about their computers. He'd bought them used, to save money, and they were forever acting up or breaking down. Zeke and Ann spent as much time lately babying them as they did writing and producing on them.

Ann knew how shaky things were getting for the Journal. It wasn't only that people these days didn't seem to read as much, which was what Zeke said, and it wasn't that they didn't put out a damn fine product every week, either. According to Zeke, the Journal was the best written little newspaper in the state. No the newspaper's problems were more insidious than low readership. It was the surrounding towns that were the problem. They were dying. People were packing up and moving away to larger cities searching for those ever elusive better living-wage-with-benefits jobs.

Ann believed the scourge of the time wasn't just unemployment, though the government wanted everyone to believe the numbers were down when they weren't because so many people had basically given up ever finding a job and were no longer being counted, but also the prevalence and across the board acceptance of minimum wage no-benefit type jobs. No jobs and lower paying jobs were killing the middle class–if it wasn't already dead. It was destroying America. There were many people desperate enough to take those awful jobs, but no one could live on minimum wage. Newspapers were a luxury, not a necessity.

Ann knew all that. Her daughter worked one of those awful jobs. No medical coverage. No retirement. No time-on-the-job raises. Let a politician try to live on one of those salaries–fat chance–and maybe they'd finally up the minimum wage.

She sighed inwardly. Government and the decline of the middle class were a few of her soapboxes. She'd done a series of articles on the subject last spring and had learned more about the subject than she'd wanted to.

Where she was distressed about the job situation, Zeke was worried about medical insurance and would rattle on to anyone who'd listen that the government ought to give everyone access to affordable universal health coverage and prescription drugs. "I know friends who spend most of their retirement check on doctors and medications and have to eat macaroni and cheese the rest of the month. And there are so many people without coverage who need it desperately. Kids included. It's a shame that in the richest country in the world, so many live in poverty because health care costs so much. Ridiculous." His soapbox topic.

Zeke, preoccupied with his story, had returned to his computer. Since his wife Ethel's death the winter before he'd become more of a workaholic than ever as he fought to hang on to the failing newspaper. He worked harder than most men Ann thought, and he was way past retirement age. "Can't live on social security anyway," he'd complain. "Only a mouse could. A skinny mouse." Another soapbox theme.

The newspaper and his wife had been Zeke's life; now it was only the paper. They'd had two children, Sherry and Tony. Sherry died when a child and Tony lived in Los Angeles with his wife and son, Jimmy, and was a senior reporter on the Los Angeles Tribune. Zeke liked to show Tony's latest articles to Ann for her opinion. Three years ago Tony won a Pulitzer for a story about street gangs. Zeke was proud of his son, though he didn't see much of him, and missed him terribly. But he'd be the last one to whine to Tony about his being too far away. Zeke believed everyone had to live their own lives. Children weren't put on the earth to keep their parents company forever.

How sad it must be, Ann thought, to have a child and grandchild one hardly ever saw. Zeke was a lonely man.

For a while the two worked in comfortable

silence, except for the clicking sounds of Zeke's keyboard. Ann was formatting the weekly ads and bemoaning the fact one of their best client's had canceled his weekly half-page. Things were bad enough without that. Ads were their main revenue.

"Oh, I almost forgot," Zeke announced a bit later as if it'd just popped into his head. "I got a mighty queer call already this morning, Ann."

He ran an age-spotted hand through his white hair, chuckling, and twisted around to look at her through his thick-lensed glasses. "Mighty queer." His eyes, magnified, were a sharp piercing blue. She noticed his slacks were a little threadbare and his button-down tan sweater over a white shirt was frayed at the cuffs.

"Queerer than usual?" Ann asked. The newspaper received odd calls every week; some on the level, some not.

Zeke liked the ones where people spotted criminals they'd seen on America's Most Wanted. He often alerted the police to check them out.

Ann was partial to the ones where little blue aliens visited or had abducted the callers.

Zeke sometimes ran the stranger stories if he could, tongue-in-cheek, as a joke, as if they were real news. Their readers loved them. It was a small town, people knew each other and most had a sense of humor.

At her desk in the back, Ann sipped a cup of coffee, and done with the ads, cleared her work area off a little; the rain a lulling presence beyond the cozy room. She liked things neat and usually ended up straightening up Zeke's and Jeff's messes as well.

She was working on a last minute article about the recent earthquakes for the next edition. All she had left to do was check her facts, a little polish, and it'd be ready to go. Outside, the rain reminded her of the story she truly wanted, but had to wait to get.

In the meantime Zeke continued his story. "Ya, this guy's tale was a doozy. And right in your backyard, Ann. He runs one of those tour boats out from Wizard Island and claims there's a creature, a water leviathan of some kind, in the lake. Can you imagine? We now have our own Loch Ness monster in Crater Lake. Ha! An American Loch Ness monster!"

Ann's hands froze over the keyboard. Her mind went to those bones Henry had spoken of up on the crater's rim. Could there be some connection? Henry believed the bones had once been prehistoric dinosaurs, but they'd lived millions of years ago. Dead now. Just bones now. The weird thing was, this call might be something they'd expect to get later, once the fossil bed was public knowledge, but not now. No one else knew about the bones. Or did they?

Henry had also said the paleontologist from John Day suspected the lava rivers under the lake were flowing again, which was why the lake's temperature was rising. The terrain beneath the volcanic lake was rearranging, shifting and regurgitating ancient rock and dirt. What other repercussions were those changes bringing? What else was the volcano regurgitating?

Certainly not monsters.

Nah. Of course the call was a crank, or an old man's flight of fancy.

"Did the caller sound drunk?" she asked. "Or just mentally unbalanced?"

"No. I've known the guy for years. He keeps his boat in one of those boat houses on Wizard Island and docks it for the tourists at Cleetwood Cove. He always was a little eccentric, and as independent as all get-out. But as far as I know, he's neither a boozer nor a nut. You know the type?"

Oh, Ann knew the type. They spent their lives doing what they pleased and worked when they wanted. Self-employed and obstinate, they were drifters and dreamers. Oregon was full of them. The park was full of them.

She got up, moseyed over and stood looking down over her boss's shoulder as he worked. "Well, what else did he say?"

"Not much. He sounded embarrassed to be calling. I had to pull most of the story out of him, like a bad tooth, after the initial confession. He sounded scared and claimed the creature butted his boat, as it was getting dark, the evening before. Rammed it hard enough to rattle him and the vessel. And you know how big those tour boats are."

"Yeah." They were big; held up to sixty people. "Was anyone with him?" Collaboration was the first thing a good reporter checked on.

"Nope. Claims he was alone. He'd emptied his last tour group of the day at Cleetwood Dock and was heading back to Wizard Island to put the boat away. He swore he wouldn't have said anything, but he thinks the creature is a menace and not only to him, but for everyone on the lake."

"We going to do a story on it?" Ann's thin face was battling a grin. She was too pragmatic a person to believe in boogey men and lake monsters.

"Well, it might be what we need. A good oh-my-god-there's-a-creature-in-the-lake story might stir up some commotion around here, might help bring up the paper's numbers."

"Oh, give me a break." Ann laughed. "It might also help bring all the crazies from miles away to camp out in the park day and night waiting for the thing to reappear, too. Like Loch Ness. Only here it'll be worse because Americans don't respect privacy as much as the Scots."

A slight scowl touched her face. Like her husband, she adored the park the way it was, uncluttered and unpeopled most of the time anyway, thank you. Henry would hate to see his peaceful retreat invaded by hordes of wild-eyed monster hunters. He was fretting enough over the fossil find. Now, monster sightings? He'd have a conniption fit.

"I thought I'd send you out to talk to the guy," Zeke finished.

"Thanks a lot."

"Well, you live in the park. Wouldn't be too far out of your way."

"You don't think it'll create a panic among the park's inhabitants? Reporting about some combative creature lurking in the lake?"

"No, not if we don't play it too seriously. It might turn into an interesting piece if we do it right. Whimsical like."

"It might." Her voice held no sarcasm. It would make a good story. People ate that kind of stuff up. "Okay. I'll go talk to the guy. What's his name?"

"Sam Cutler. He captains a tour boat called the Sea Bird. In the mornings you can find him docked at Cleetwood Cove waiting for his passengers. The boat has a flying bird painted on the side. Can't miss it."

"I know the one. I've seen it on the lake before."

"Good. Try to talk to him sometime in the next couple days and we'll see if we can plug it in the next edition. We're going to be lean on material anyway. We'll need the filler." Then Zeke tacked on: "Hey, you're a fairly good artist, too, as I recollect. So why don't you try to make a drawing from his description of the thing?"

Ann snickered under her breath, shaking her head. Her drawings were a town joke. She could draw, but no one could say she was the next Rembrandt, not by a long shot. But Zeke thought her sketches had character. Kinda like those things Grandma Moses used to do. Yeah. Kinda cute and primitive. They made Zeke chuckle. But most of the townies made fun of them.

"The things I do for you and this rag," Ann groaned with a small smile, pretending he was forcing her to do something she didn't want to do. When in truth, she got a kick out of seeing her doddles in the paper. When she'd worked in New York, her editor would have died before allowing her drawings to accompany her stories. New York was too cosmopolitan for that. Klamath Falls wasn't.

"Okay. I'll try to recreate the mysterious creature of the lake. No promises, though. I'll get photos of Wizard Island and Captain Cutler on his boat, too. Does he know a reporter's coming out?"

"That's the problem." Zeke threw his hands up. "As soon as I mentioned I'd send someone out to take pictures and get more details, he hung up on me. I'm afraid he's sorry he called. He might be a tough sell."

"So he might not talk to me?"

"Oh, but I have considerable faith in your powers of persuasion, Ann. You'll get the story, no sweat. You're a hell of a reporter."

"Flattery, flattery," she said, "will get you everything."

Digging into one of his pockets, Zeke retrieved a tattered brown wallet, slid out a twenty that looked as old as he was and handed it to her with a flourish.

"Offer him this. It'll help. If I know Sam, it'll loosen his tongue quick enough. Money is his life."

Ann took the twenty and tucked it into her purse. Things must be truly bad if Zeke was willing to pay for a story. He never did. But she didn't say a word, merely went back to work.

Soon she'd forgotten about Captain Cutler and the creature in the lake. She had stories to write and ads to sell and was too busy to spend time thinking about mythical monsters.

***

Henry stared out the window, lost in thought. Dressed in a heavy burgundy sweater and faded jeans, a cup of cold coffee poised, forgotten, in his hands, he waited. The rain had abated to a light drizzle, and he was restless.

He longed to see if those strange tracks Justin discovered were still there. Yeah, sure, his good sense told him. They're long gone, washed away from a night of storms.

The imprints had been scored deep, though; perhaps he could get something on film.

Henry put his cup down on the table and got his coat.

He was pulling out of the driveway as the paleontologist came slogging across the muddy yard towards the front door. Henry would have missed seeing him, except for the kid's brightly colored coat fluttering in the wind. He'd gotten smart and was wearing heavier clothes.

Henry zipped back into the driveway and turned the engine off.

Justin sauntered up, a stack of books cradled in his arms, and stood waiting while Henry rolled down the jeep's window. The scientist's expression held restrained excitement.

"What's up?" The wet air hit Henry in the face.

"They said at park headquarters it was your day off, and directed me here. I thought I'd come by and save you a trip down to the lake, Chief Ranger."

"I told you to call me Henry."

"Okay, Henry. The tracks aren't there any longer. Well, they probably aren't. It rained so much the level of the lake rose and covered them. I have no idea now where they are or if they're visible because they're most likely under water."

"Crater Lake has no inlets or outlets. The only

way the level in the lake changes is when it rains, or the water evaporates, so I'm not surprised the tracks are covered."

"We'd have to go under in wet suits with air tanks," Justin grumbled. "I detest the water. And I'm no skin-diver, that's for sure."

"I'm trained as a diver," Henry confessed, "but I don't think I'd have any luck finding those tracks underwater. The lake's water is cloudy. So, thanks, you saved me a trip, I suppose. A wet and muddy one at that."

"That's where you were headed, huh?"

"Yes, that's where I was headed."

"I come bearing information, however, that might shed light on what those prints could have been." The scientist lifted his arms up so Henry could see the stack of books. "Last night after our adventure I called a colleague of mine at John Day's and had him Federal Express some of my research books overnight. There's something quite interesting in a few of them I wanted you to see."

"Good, come on in and you can show me," Henry said, climbing out of the jeep and heading for the front door. "I'll make a fresh pot of coffee, since I have nothing else much to do now." But he was glad to see Justin and his smile showed it. Now he could talk about the fossils.

Henry unlocked the door, Justin trailing behind like a big puppy. Henry had the feeling he'd been adopted or something. Didn't the kid have a family?

"I brought lunch if you haven't had it yet," Justin spoke cheerfully.

"No, I haven't. That was mighty kind of you."

The scientist hesitated as if he wasn't used to being thanked or wasn't used to doing acts of kindness, his long hair uncombed and wild around his head.

"You like cheeseburgers and fries?"

"Doesn't everyone?"

"Some don't. Though I don't know any." Justin produced a sheepish grin. Again, Henry thought how young the paleontologist seemed. Or maybe Henry was just getting old.

"The food's from your lodge's kitchen. One of their picnic lunches."

"I know. I can tell by the box. The visitors buy them up like crazy so they can eat out in the woods with the trees and the wild animals. They like that."

Inside the house, Henry led his guest into the kitchen. Flicking on the overhead light, he motioned Justin to the table. He started a pot of coffee, pulled out two mugs, sugar and cream, and carried them to the table as the java perked.

Justin placed the stack of books and the box lunches on the table and slouched into a chair. "Last night after you left I remembered what had been bugging me about those tracks." He had his lunch open and was devouring it as if he hadn't eaten in days, talking between bites.

"What?"

"I've seen the tracks or something similar to them before in a book." His glasses slid down his nose and he used a greasy finger to shove them upward in an unconscious gesture. He put the cheeseburger down and picked up a book with a strip of torn paper marking a place, and opened it.

"I've studied so many dinosaurs and their habits. My favorites have always been the prehistoric sea and water creatures. I'm fascinated by the myth of Scotland's Loch Ness monster. I've read everything published about Nessie and the sightings. I've even spent time on the Loch searching for it. Unfortunately, I never got a glimpse. But it's made me an expert on the water breeds."

That's it. He thinks he's got a Loch Ness monster here, Henry ruminated. *Good thing I didn't tell him what I thought I saw in the water last night. He'd be camped out on the lake waiting for it right now.*

"Here." Justin held the book out to him.

Henry looked at the open pages. There were artist's drawings of dinosaurs from different angles and close-ups of their limbs and feet. He was surprised to feel the same thrill of pleasure he'd experienced as a kid when he'd look at a drawing of a dinosaur. One footprint caught his eye immediately. It did look somewhat like the tracks they'd seen last night. Somewhat. Not exactly.

As if reading Henry's mind, Justin revealed, "I got a better look at them yesterday than you. That's it, kind of, except the ones I found were a little different and much bigger. They had an extra webbed claw. From the depth of the imprints I'd guess that the beast that made them was quite large and heavy."

Nothosaur, the copy blurb under the footprint illustrations and beside the first picture described, *was a marine reptile that flourished in the Triassic times. It could grow to over twenty feet in length and had a back fin and webbed feet. Water dweller. Triassic period.*

On the facing page, Justin had marked another illustration. *Allosaurus. Probably had a large skull and might have been equipped with dozens of large, sharp teeth. It averaged 28 feet in length, though fragmentary remains suggest it could have reached over 39 feet. Relative to the large and powerful hind limbs, its three-fingered forelimbs were small, and the body was balanced by a long, heavy tail. It is classified as an allosaurid, a type of carnosaurian theropod dinosaur. Land dweller. Jurassic period.*

Henry examined both of the creature's drawings. The Allosaurus had a long snake-like neck and huge gaping jaws full of razor-sharp teeth. Big head for such a slender neck. Fat slick reptilian body with stubby short legs also ended in webbed, almost clawed, feet.

"My fellow paleontologists now believe that Nothosaurs were warm-blooded mammals, and not actually dinosaurs. A powerful swimmer who preferred cooler water, it was probably a ferocious predator that often went after other marine animals, especially short and long-necked Plesiosaurs, if it was hungry enough. It was one formidable, mean creature."

"Triassic was even earlier than the Jurassic period, right?"

"It was." Justin inclined his head. "But, none of that matters. I don't believe the tracks we discovered actually belonged to either of those species in this book. Not totally anyway. They're something like them, but not. Whatever made those prints is a mutant, big time, a more highly developed strain of their ancestors, something *like* a Nothosaur/Allosaurus combination, because it likes the water and the land, but not really either. A cross breed. Or something else entirely–previously undiscovered and unknown–that lives in water but can also move around on the land. Maybe bigger than a Giganotosaurus, believed to be the biggest dinosaur that ever walked the earth. This could be a new kind of dinosaur. A *mind-blowing* discovery."

"You don't say?"

"All theory, of course. Every paleontologist will admit, as much as we know about dinosaurs, there's still so much we don't know."

Out of the mouth of an expert, Henry thought, closing the book. "Well, its original ancestor, if it was its ancestor, sure was ugly. I give it that much." As ugly as the creature that had made those tracks? A shiver tingled Henry's skin. He was being silly. Those dinosaur prints hadn't been real. There weren't any live mutant dinosaurs or undiscovered new breed dinosaurs in the lake or *anywhere* in the real world. Nonsense. It was some kind of joke. That's what it'd been. A big fat joke. There were a bunch of kids laughing their asses off somewhere over it. They'd undoubtedly watched poor Justin going nuts by the water yesterday and had had a good old time.

"Ah, there you'd be wrong. I think it was a beautiful beast." Justin's eyes gleamed with his obsession.

Henry glanced at the boy and laughed. "You

would believe that, wouldn't you? But I bet you wouldn't feel that way if you came face to face with a live one out in the woods? And it happened to be hungry?"

"Probably not." Justin's face broke into a grin. "Unless I had a giant tranquilizer gun with me or I was invisible."

This time both of them laughed.

"So you think some distant descendant of a cross between a Nothosaur and an Allosaurus, or a totally new breed of dinosaur, made those tracks, huh?" Henry asked, as he put sugar in his coffee and gulped it down.

Justin must have caught the disbelief in his voice because he closed his empty box lunch, wiped his fingers on a paper towel, and sighed aloud. His glasses came off, and his fingers rubbed at the bridge of his nose around his eyes.

"You're right, Chief Ranger, this is crazy. As authentic as those prints looked to me yesterday, the idea there's a genuine dinosaur swimming around in Crater Lake is too bizarre to continue going on about. It's insane, isn't it?" He laughed again, but it was flat and tinged with disappointment.

"Yes, it's insane." Henry poured fresh cups of coffee and carried them to the table. Empathy in his eyes. Yet what a discovery of a lifetime a real breathing dinosaur would be for a paleontologist. Poor Justin.

"I guess in some ways we never grow up," Henry said. "Even at my age. For a couple of startling moments yesterday when I first spied those tracks, I *wanted* to believe a real dinosaur could be walking the earth again. Preposterous as the idea is, I wanted it to be true."

"Me, too. It'd be fantastic to discover one. Or a new breed. I'd go in the history books for sure." Justin's gaze was dreamy.

"Well, anyway, it's been an adventure. You've been good company. Interesting to talk with. And we can't forget those fossils, now can we? They're real."

"Yes, they are that."

Finishing his lunch, Henry opened another book and browsed through it. More information paraded before his eyes.

"Dinosaurs," he read snatches aloud and tapped the book with his finger, "were dubbed *the terrible lizards*. Hmm. No doubt. Some of them, they say, were gargantuan in size, and probably as unfriendly as hell. Look at this monster. Palaeoscinus. Do you really think it looked like that? Weighed three tons? How do you guys know that?"

The question spurred Justin into a lecture about the battery of scientific tests they performed on the ancient fossils, and all the other research techniques paleontologists used.

Henry realized the scientist was brilliant on his subject. He really knew what he was talking about. An interesting human being. Impressive. He was beginning to respect the man as much as he liked him.

As they lingered in the kitchen, drank coffee and talked, Henry learned more about the scientist himself. He was thirty-three, not much younger as Henry had thought. Out of college for years, he'd worked other places and had traveled to digs on different continents; as he'd said, he'd been working at John Day's for two years. He wasn't married, or engaged, or involved with anyone at the moment. Had lofty goals to be a director at John Day's and to eventually lead the most prestigious paleontological expeditions around the world. He knew what he wanted. But underneath, Henry sensed a basic loneliness, underlying everything the young man said or did. It was an invisible shadow, but there.

Henry began to look at Justin differently. He was an intelligent man who lacked the knack of making close friends. He'd known men like that, mostly cops.

God, he contemplated more than once, if only his daughter had fallen in love with an ambitious man like Justin instead of that jerk Chad.

They were still gabbing when Ann got home from work. Henry introduced Justin and was pleased when his wife seemed to take an instant shine to the scientist. Before Henry knew it, she'd invited him to supper. Then he recalled that Laura and Phoebe were coming, too.

What a conniving woman he'd married.

***

"So I'm going down there tomorrow sometime and talk to the old man about what he was supposed to have seen." Ann had been retelling the story about Sam Cutler and the mysterious water creature he'd claimed had rammed his boat.

Like Zeke, Henry knew Sam Cutler, too. He'd gone out on Sam's boat with tour groups, many times. Sam was a good guy, but spun a lot of tall stories and exaggerated things somewhat. His boat's compartments were stuffed full of tattered science fiction paperbacks. The old codger had a heck of an imagination.

"Do you believe he saw a monster in the water?" Henry asked softly.

"How do I know, honey? I haven't talked to him yet."

He glanced at Justin, whose interest was captured. He had this feverish glaze in his eyes.

To Henry, as well, the tale seemed to have an uncanny coincidence. Why now, of all times, were people reporting these sightings in the lake? Unless.... No, it *had* to be someone's idea of a practical joke. How many could be in on it? One person could have created the tracks, another mutilated the animal carcasses and another was swimming around in the lake in a monster suit? The thing that baffled him was why would anyone want to go through that much trouble? For attention? Publicity? He couldn't guess.

But he sure as hell didn't believe it was a real monster.

"By the way," Ann turned to catch Justin's eye, "have you already told the place you work for about the bones up near the rim?"

Justin pulled his eyes away from Laura long enough to answer, "Ah, not yet. In a few days, perhaps. There's no hurry. Truth is, I want to keep the discovery to myself for a while, before the crowd arrives. Once I let my colleagues know, there'll be a whole flock of scientists here."

Ann hadn't noticed her husband had fallen silent since she'd mentioned Sam Cutler's story. She was too busy observing Justin's reaction to Laura, and vice-versa.

All evening the young man had been watching her daughter closely, smiling at her and engaging her in conversation. The repartee between the two appeared natural and unforced from the first minute they'd laid eyes on each other. Usually Laura was withdrawn and uncommunicative, but not with Justin. After an hour or so the two were talking up a storm and Laura seemed happier than she'd been in months. She was excited about going back to school, confided the situation to Justin, and he openly encouraged her.

Ann told Henry when they took the empty plates into the kitchen she was positive something was happening between them. Sparks were crackling. They looked right together, even if Justin was older. Henry knew Ann was crossing her fingers under the table, and then she offered the young man another piece of homemade cherry pie.

She was in seventh heaven and was having a hard time hiding it.

Little Phoebe had also taken a fancy to Justin. She was in his lap in no time, cooing and grabbing at his glasses or his long hair; gurgling and grinning impishly up at him as he patiently dealt with her. He seemed unsure with the child, as if he hadn't had much experience with kids, but he went out of his way with her.

"Okay, but what exactly did your boss say Sam told him about the thing in the lake?" Henry asked abruptly, sitting forward.

Justin threw him a funny look.

"Honey, I told you everything I know," Ann spoke. "The man claims some kind of big greenish monster was in the water and it rammed his boat. A serpent-creature is what Sam called it and swears it was after his boat. Doesn't know why it finally left him alone. It sounds to me like nothing more than a big fish tale," she laughed, "but our readers eat up stories like that, you know. So I'll talk to the guy. Sometimes I wonder if I'm working for a small town newspaper or the National Inquirer."

She caught the surreptitious glance between Henry and Justin. "Are you two keeping something from me?"

"No," both of them said too quickly.

"All right, you two. What's going on? I know something is. Tell me now or, I promise I won't give either of you any more pie."

Henry tried not to smile as he confessed about the tracks Justin had found down by the lake the day before.

Ann's reaction wasn't what he'd expected. "My god, maybe there is something peculiar going on in that lake. What a story that'd be!"

"Oh, no," Henry groaned, feigning fear. "You're right. Maybe there is a monster prowling in the water."

He and Justin chuckled as if it were a big joke.

Ann was watching them. Henry knew he wasn't fooling her. Her reporter's sixth sense was humming at full power.

"Well," she simply said, "now it's even more

important I get those photos of that wall of bones. I could tie that in with the mysterious happenings at the lake."

Henry and the paleontologist exchanged another startled look.

She turned to her husband. "Since I have to go to the lake anyway tomorrow, why don't you finally show me where those bones are, at the same time? After I take the pictures, I'll speak to the captain."

"Sure," Henry recovered enough to reply with a faint smile. "Bright and early. You got a deal. No rain in the forecast." He couldn't get what Ann had said about tying in the two stories out of his head. He believed in freedom of the press, but he wasn't sure he liked the idea. It could create problems.

Justin stood up from the table. "I should get going. Let you guys get some sleep."

It had gotten late. Phoebe was asleep, curled up in her mother's lap. Henry was yawning behind his hand. Laura had to get up early the next morning for work.

Ann was obviously tickled when their daughter suggested, "Justin, it's spooky out there, and you haven't seen dark until you've been in the park at night. It'd be easy for you to get lost on your way back to the lodge. But I'm driving by there on my way to the dorm so I'd be glad to drop you off."

Justin didn't hesitate. "That'd be kind of you, Laura. I really wasn't too hot about trekking through the woods in the dark anyway."

"You ready to go then?" As if she couldn't see him standing there, books in his arms, coat already on.

"I'm ready."

Justin smiled at Ann. "Thank you both for a great meal, a nice evening. The food and the cherry pie was delicious, Mrs. Shore."

"You're welcome. But call me Ann. Mrs. Shore makes me feel old."

"If you insist."

"I do and I hope we'll see you again soon. You're welcome here anytime."

"Thank you. I might take you up on that. The way it looks I'll be around for a while." He signaled goodbye to Henry with a salute of his hand.

After Laura hugged him and her mother goodbye, she carried the baby through the door into the night. Justin trailing behind her.

After the sound of the car's engine moved off into the night, Ann glanced at him. That match maker glint he knew so well in her eyes. "Got a feeling about that young man."

"You do, do you?" Henry teased back.

"Yes, I do." Contentment shone on her face and they embraced, knowing each other's thoughts.

Henry helped clear the table, rinsed the dirty plates and put them in the dishwasher. They straightened up the kitchen. But his mind was somewhere else. Ann's remark about connecting Cutler's sighting with the bones haunted him. What would she say if she knew about that other woman's sighting last summer, about his last night?

There were just too many coincidences, his mind told him. The earthquakes…the bones…George's dead animals…those tracks. And now Sam Cutler and his water monster. Too darn many coincidences.

"You ready for bed, honey, or do you want to watch television for a while?" Ann asked as they headed for their room.

"Bed sounds better. We have to get up early, anyway. Remember?"

"And I bet after you show me those bones you'll want to dig around in the dirt with Justin?"

"Possibly." He was getting undressed for bed. "I'd like to be a small part of this thing. The dig. It's a dream come true."

"I know." Ann laid a kiss on his lips and he gently returned it. They made love as they had so many times before, soft and sweet. Comfortable with each other. Sure of their love.

They were long asleep when the strange night noises began down on the lake. Like some ancient beckoning cry on the wind, something called out across the tranquil water and through the silent trees. Lonely sounding.

And somehow unearthly.

CHAPTER 4

Ann enjoyed walking along the rim, peeking out across the circular expanse of Crater Lake's shimmering blue water, knowing she was treading upon what was once the inner wall of a volcano. She treasured the primeval ambience of the place, untouched by civilization, and the air full of the woodsy pine scent.

Henry always joked she must be part mountain goat because the heights never bothered her, or the steep climb. Over the years she'd explored all along the rim's edge and the grounds around it. Each time she found something new, something unique, and was amazed at how much she'd come to love her new home.

She didn't miss New York at all. Well, maybe sometimes a little. She missed the hustle and bustle, the vast variety of people and food–what she wouldn't give for a big fat New York bagel with cream cheese or one of those hand-tossed pizzas they used to get at the corner bistro.

It was noon and the sun was high above as she picked her way down towards the water. Lunch was a good time to catch the tour boats docked in Cleetwood Cove. Most of them puttered in for the meal, and tours resumed at around two o'clock.

Dressed in sneakers, a sweater, jeans and a purple jacket; she'd tied a white kerchief around her head to tame her flyaway hair. She traveled light in the rough terrain, with a fanny pack at her waist, a notebook and sketchpad along with her pencils, snuggled in a cloth shoulder bag as she descended toward Cleetwood Trail, the only entrance to the water.

She'd left Henry and Justin at "the dig", as they'd started calling it. Probably glad to be rid of her and her endless questions about the fossils and dinosaurs. She'd taken a bunch of pictures, seeing right away how an article on the paleontological discovery might become a front page story, with updated installments ongoing afterwards. What a circulation builder.

Justin was certainly knowledgeable on his subject. He knew the long dead dinosaur's ancestors migration and feeding habits, plus their social and sexual structure. Throughout the interview, Henry had chimed in with interesting tidbits Ann had never suspected he knew.

All in all, she had more than enough to write a fascinating story. Justin and Henry had promised her an exclusive. They wouldn't talk to anyone else until her story had run.

With squinted eyes, she scrutinized the docked boats. The Seabird wasn't among them. It was early yet, so it didn't worry her. The Seabird would show up.

Ann plunked her butt down on the wooden dock, her feet swinging out over the water, and pulled out her notebook and sketchbook. She began to jot down ideas and angles for her story, along with questions she'd thought of on the way down to the dock. The sun's rays were soft on her face, the water glistened below her. It was easy to lounge there and daydream. She switched to her sketchbook and her fingers drew a whimsical drawing of a monster with spots, a big grin, and extra-long lashes over huge expressive eyes.

Ann wished Henry was with her instead of up on the hill digging around in the dirt. She hoped he was having fun.

When he'd been shot eight years ago, she hadn't left his side at the hospital for days until he came out of intensive care and had actually spoken to her. *Love you, Ann*, was the first words he'd uttered. *I'm sorry I hurt you and Laura. If I live through this, it's going to change. I promise.* The memory still made her weep. She'd thought she'd lost him that day. The job, finally, and as she'd always feared, had been the death of him. She'd hated him being a cop; always putting her and his family second behind the job. She'd been sick of it. And the night of the shooting she'd been ready to leave him, even though it would have broken her heart. But since the shooting and moving up here, she'd been the most important thing in his life, along with Laura and now Phoebe, and he'd never let her forget it for a moment. It was good they'd left New York. She was happier than she'd been in many years. She had her husband, her friend and her lover back.

She watched the boats fill with visitors and head toward Wizard Island, the Phantom Ship, or to chug around the lake itself, tourists peering up at the steep multi-colored lava walls. She and Henry took at least one or two boat tours a summer. The ride was so peaceful, drifting on the water alongside the cliffs, listening to the call of the wild birds swooping above. Exploring the islands was fun, too. The land was mostly untouched by humans and a person could imagine they'd traveled back in time when the mists billowed in from the water and the silence beckoned.

Ann dawdled on the dock, thinking over what might have happened the night before between her daughter and Justin. Gosh, to have a son-in-law that actually read books, talked in complete sentences and had a real job.

Hey, Ann, she gently scolded herself, *what are you thinking?* Justin and Laura have just met, for heaven's sake. *Ah, well, she could dream, couldn't she?*

Ann didn't carry the same guilt concerning her daughter as Henry did. She fretted at times over where they'd gone wrong with Laura and what to do about the girl when she up and married Chad at such a young age. She'd known the marriage wouldn't last; that sooner or later Laura would end up on their doorstep and they'd have another chance to help set her straight. And she'd been right.

Ann sighed, her eyelashes descending softly, eyes closing. Only so much you could do to help your children, the rest was up to them. Laura had to learn to find her own way in the world.

She opened her eyes and let in the bright sunlight. Laura sped out of her mind, replaced by what she should fix for supper that night.

Ann didn't suspect something was wrong until the fleet of boats began returning from their first two-hour tour of the afternoon. Still no Seabird. Stretching like a lazy cat, she got up off the dock and headed for Willie Sander's boat, the Mermaid, which had just drifted in.

Henry had mentioned that Willie and Sam Cutler were poker pals. They played in the weekly poker game every Friday night at the lodge; everyone knew them. Willie had all the luck and Sam usually lost.

Waiting until after the passengers left, she climbed aboard. A man was busy preparing for the next group of landlubbers. He was in the foredeck cleaning up the litter from the last trip when she strode up to him.

"Willie Sander?" She'd seen him around the lake, like most of the other captains, but hadn't done more than said hi to him before that.

The man, short and muscular wearing blue work pants and a black T-shirt, swung around and winked at her. His arms were loaded with empty Pepsi bottles and crumpled waxed paper. A red ball cap perched on his head of frizzy gray hair, and thin tight lips locked around a dangling cigarette. "Aye, that's me. What can I do for ya, Mrs. Chief Park Ranger?" He dumped the trash into a plastic bag, circled it with a tie, and edging past her, jumping neatly to the dock. Tossing the bag into a trash barrel, he was back again in a matter of moments.

When he was close enough so she didn't have to yell, she explained, "I'm looking for the Seabird and Sam Cutler. Would you know where I might find him?"

Willie Sander's eyes displayed an emotion she couldn't define. Caution? Fear? She wasn't sure. Certainly mistrust. The lake folk were private people. Though most of them knew she was Henry's wife by sight, she was still considered an outsider, even after all this time.

"What you want him for?" Sander stepped further back on his boat and Ann followed.

"Well–" It was best to be truthful. He seemed the kind of man who'd appreciate that. "You know, I work for the Klamath Falls Journal and Sam called the office yesterday morning with some information he thought we might be interested in. I'm here to interview him. He's sort of expecting me."

"Really? That's awful strange, then. I don't know where he is and I'm getting mighty worried. Last I saw him or his boat was yesterday afternoon and, come to think about it, he was acting pretty squirrelly to boot, if I do say so, even for him." His bushy eyebrows shot up, the cynical look returned.

"He was acting squirrelly?" A tiny smile curled Ann's lips.

Sander snorted, gesturing dismissively. "Ah, Sam's been obsessing about some weird creature in the lake for weeks. Said it'd been dogging his boat, playing with and taunting him. Said it only came out at night and was as big as two houses put together, that's his exact words, and it had a long neck, huge teeth and was strong as hell."

He paused, as if to measure Ann's response, then, seeing encouragement in her manner, went on,

"He was scared of the damn thing, but wanted to capture it something dreadful, like it was a damn trophy or something." He grunted. "That's why he never told the rangers. He wanted to bag it for himself. Make a load of money."

"You didn't believe him?"

Willie chuckled. "Do I look like a nut to you? Nah. I thought he'd been hitting the sauce a little too hard. Started doing that a few months ago. He's gone on some real binges. Not like him at all. I told him he shouldn't be on a boat, much less captain one with people in his care, if he was going to drink like that and was seeing things to boot. He got furious at me and went off in a huff. The old coot. Now I wish I would've taken his problem a little more seriously. I feel something's terrible wrong." Regret softened his words.

He yanked off his cap, wiped his brow, and leveled his eyes at her. "I haven't seen him since yesterday. Which is unusual because he always comes in every morning to pick up passengers. Not like him to miss a beautiful day like this." The cap went back on his head and he sent his gaze away and out over the rippling water. "I'm beginning to worry. I didn't see him anywhere out on the lake today. Nor did anybody else I asked. Mighty peculiar that. There are lots of boats and we get around, but no one's seen him."

Ann stared at the grizzled captain. The first flicker of doubt awakened. She could sometimes sense when something wasn't right with a situation. At that moment, her inner voice was getting louder.

"Could he have packed up and left? Gone on

vacation and not told anyone?" Modern day adventurers, the captains and their boats came and went on the lake. They got tired of the same waters or the tourists and moved on. That's just the way it was.

"Not likely. Sam doesn't take time off, says being here in the park is like an everyday vacation. He's been here going on sixteen years now, longer than me. He loved it…until about three weeks ago."

"Let me guess," she interjected, "that's when he started seeing the creature in the lake?"

"Yep. You got it."

Her obvious concern about the missing captain and the way she was smiling so friendly like must have made him want to confide in her further. "Like I said, I thought he was imagining things. Stress as well as the booze. Ya know, his only son died last spring." He hesitated.

"I'm sorry, I didn't know."

"Ah, yep. The boy lived down in Illinois. Sam had a lot of guilt over that kid seeing as he divorced the boy's mama years ago and never got around to being the kind of daddy he'd wanted to be. Then time was up and he was grieving."

"So you think this 'monster' of his was a figment of his stress? Like his guilt chasing after and tormenting him?"

Sander hesitated long enough to make Ann wonder. "Colorful way of putting it, but yes. No such things as monsters, lady. We all know that. I even know that and I'm not a clever man. There ain't nothing in this lake but water and fish. Take my word for it."

After that he didn't want to talk any more. Clammed up. She thanked him for his help, handed him her card in case he remembered anything else or if Sam Cutler reappeared, and left. Looked like Zeke would keep his twenty bucks.

Ann made her way up to the rim and along the path to where she'd left Henry and Justin earlier, digging around in the dirt like two ecstatic kids.

"You got a whole dinosaur yet?" she kidded as she snuck up behind them.

"Three of them. Each as big as a baseball field." Henry, dirty-faced, played along, winking. He lifted one of his muddy hands to swipe his hair back. When he grinned, there was dirt on his teeth.

Justin looked as bad. Mudballs both.

"We're not disturbing the bones, though," Justin said, his face respectfully awed. "That wouldn't be right. They're fragile. Priceless. We're just chipping away the matrix, dirt and rocks they're embedded in so we can see what we've got, and taking pictures. This is a bonanza."

He pointed to a hunk of white sticking out of the ground. "Looks like this particular beast was caught in a landslide. Mud. Or snow and ice. Maybe glaciers displaced by lava underneath. Violent but instant deaths. That's why the specimens are so well preserved. It's remarkable."

Ann bobbed her head, trying to stash away everything he talked about in her memory, thinking about how she could use it in her articles.

Henry motioned at the scientist. "Justin, will you look at this?"

Ann sat down on a large flat rock and watched.

"Get your story, honey?" Henry looked over his shoulder at her.

"No."

"No?"

"Sam Cutler's nowhere to be found. No one's seen him or his boat since yesterday. Kind of unusual. I called him yesterday and he knew I was coming to talk. It was all set up, at least I thought so. Willie Sander thinks he went off looking for that creature in the lake. He wanted it for a trophy."

Henry's back stiffened. Ann could feel the change in his mood; see it, even from where she sat.

Justin's fingers stopped moving along a ledge of white bone.

Henry turned and looked at her. "Has a missing person's report been filed?"

"No. Not that I know of. Not yet." She recounted everything Willie Sander had told her.

"Hmm." Henry had risen to a standing position as she talked, wiping his hands on his jeans. "Maybe I had better do some sleuthing myself. I don't like the sound of it." Always the Chief Park Ranger.

Justin had been observing and listening to them, silently. An uneasiness in his stance. His eyes were on the bones in the earth wall and she didn't need to guess what he was thinking. *Perhaps the creature in the lake got him.*

"You know," the scientist said, "maybe there is something in the lake. Why not now? The caldera below us is realigning, heaving, shoving up things that haven't seen the light of day for eons. Could be it's uncovered something…alive?" He let out a low whistle.

Henry exchanged a look with him that spoke more than words. “Justin, I’m leaving now. Got something I have to do. See you later for supper?”

Justin nodded. “Sure thing.” He waved, as she and Henry, hand in hand, headed towards the jeep parked at the bottom of the trail.

“Did you invite him to supper?” She asked once they were out of earshot.

Henry seemed preoccupied. “Oh,” he replied after a few seconds, “I didn’t think you’d mind. Since you’re the one who’s playing matchmaker and I figured Laura might show up again. Besides he’s a nice young man. I like him. We have a lot in common.

“What are we having for supper?”

“Meatloaf. Mashed potatoes and gravy. Buttered corn. Chocolate pudding with Cool Whip for dessert.” Ann knew better than to ask him outright what was really on his mind. He’d tell her when he was ready.

“Sounds great.”

“Glad you approve.”

He squeezed her hand as they walked toward the jeep.

***

Henry stopped at the ranger station after he’d dropped Ann off at the cabin. George Redcrow was on duty so he took him along with him. They searched the lake in one of the park’s boats. Eventually they found the wreckage of the Seabird strewn along the more isolated eastern shore of Wizard’s Island like beached trash.

No sign of Sam Cutler.

Henry hauled in pieces of the destroyed boat bobbing around on the water and stuffed them into clear bags with George's help. Evidence.

"What happened to Sam Cutler and his boat?" George mumbled at one point, a haunted glint in his eyes as he handled a splinter of boat wood, turning it around in his hands in the receding sunlight. "It was a big boat. What could have done this to it?" A breeze skimmed the water and his hair ruffled around his ranger's hat. The gray of his uniform appeared black in the dimming light.

"I don't know, George."

"An explosion?"

Henry's eyes raked the shifting waters around their boat. He remembered the mauled animals George had been finding near the lake. "I don't think so. The boat's been thoroughly smashed by something very powerful, by the looks of it."

"What could do that?"

"I don't know." Henry stared out over the water. "No sense in dragging for the body. The lake's too deep. If it hasn't floated to the surface, I have a feeling we won't find it."

"But," George supplied, "we can assume that Sam Cutler's probably dead?"

"Most likely."

Both men fell quiet for a moment. The water lapped against their boat's hull.

"We'd better get back to shore, George, and start filling out the report, or we'll be all night. I'm officially opening up an investigation into what might have happened to Sam Cutler and his boat."

"You going to call in the local police for help?" George questioned. He often needled Henry about having been a big city cop. George thought of big city cops like other people thought of aliens.

"Not yet. We'll handle this ourselves for now until we see what we're up against. Keep it on the down low. If we need more assistance later on, I'll ask the Park Service for back-up and establish an Incident Command System." As Chief Ranger, he had the option of putting more men on to cover any emergency situation, setting up an ICS, if there was a dangerous problem in the park. "As of now, George," he added dryly, "I'm making you Assistant Chief Ranger. Congratulations."

"Thanks a lot." George didn't seem happy about the promotion. He knew what it meant. Henry was worried. Trouble was coming.

"But for now, let's get off this lake before it gets dark." Henry recalled what Cutler had been reported as saying: *It only comes out at night. Big as two houses, a long neck, huge teeth and as strong as hell.*

Henry's hand automatically fell onto the butt of his holstered weapon, a .40 caliber semi-automatic SigSauer, for comfort. Most of his men, including George, carried the 9 mm Sig, but Henry preferred the .40 caliber because of the larger, heavier bullets it shot. If he had to bring something down he wanted to be sure it didn't get up again.

"Anything you say, boss," George agreed. He worked his way to the boat's controls, plopped down into the captain's chair, and steered them towards land. He wanted to get off the lake as badly as Henry did. The low-flying gulls and the fish jumping alongside the boat apparently weren't the only things out on the water.

Wizard Island dwindled to a tiny lump on the horizon as they left it behind. Henry's mind was tumbling in circles looking for answers. Someone, or something, had demolished a tour boat and perhaps murdered Sam Cutler. There hadn't been a murder in the park since he'd arrived.

The Park Service wasn't going to like this at all.

His sense of duty and excitement triumphant over the fear, and because Cutler said it only came out at night, he decided he'd return after dark to see if something uninvited really lurked in the lake. Unless he knew what the problem was, how would he know how to handle it?

***

After supper, Justin persuaded Henry into sharing the night's adventure with him; and Henry was grateful for the company. In fact, he'd intended all along to take Justin with him. If some belligerent creature was in the water it'd be safer not to be alone, especially after seeing what had become of Sam Cutler's boat.

Still, beneath it all, the notion some beast lurked in Crater Lake waiting to waylay and destroy the unwary was too ridiculous to take seriously. Going out on the water that night was Henry's way of whistling in the dark. He couldn't allow himself to be afraid of the unknown. A pragmatic man, he was merely tracking down whatever leads he could uncover because Sam Cutler was missing and had last been seen on the lake. No big deal. It was his job.

To keep Ann from worrying, he said they were going to do a little night fishing, which he often did in the warmer weather. He didn't mention the Seabird's fate. She'd find out sooner or later, and later would be better because he didn't want it all over the newspaper yet.

He knew she suspected he was up to something, but being the good wife that she was, she didn't question him further. Just gave him a hug and a kiss goodbye and told him to be careful.

***

Although Henry and Justin patrolled the lake most of the night, and the next two nights as well, they saw nothing unusual. Henry talked himself into believing there wasn't anything strange in the water, and that Sam Cutler's disappearance and boat wreck had another cause. He just had to discover what it was.

Time went by and nothing else happened. The lake, as the park, was eerily quiet.

***

Eventually, Henry confided to Ann the fate of Sam Cutler's boat, calling it an accident. Cause unknown. Sam Cutler was missing and had not, as yet, resurfaced. She was shocked and, for once, speechless. She wrote up the story and Zeke ran it on the second page, per Henry's request. He didn't want a panic.

And Justin reluctantly divulged the fossil discovery to John Day's.

Henry was afraid it'd only take a few days until the park was swarming with more paleontologists and the curious. He wasn't looking forward to it, but on the other hand, he was curious about what the experts and the world would say. Just like a kid on his birthday waited to see under the wrapping of his presents, he wondered what the dig would ultimately unearth.

It wasn't until a week or so later, long after the Seabird's loss had been reported and investigated with no results that Willie Sander's boat also went missing. As with the Seabird, Willie Sander had been alone on the water after dark when he and his boat disappeared.

Henry and his rangers scoured the lake, filed more reports and expressed growing concern over the situation. But, as before, they found nothing except bits of floating debris. Henry still resisted initiating an ICS Team, which would have meant calling in specialists to help him investigate the situation, because he wasn't sure what the problem was. But he knew one more incident would moot that line of thinking altogether. Something was wrong in his park and he couldn't allow things to go on as they were if it meant people would keep vanishing.

The Klamath Falls Journal ran a front-page story on the two boats, their destruction, and their missing captains.

Henry notified the proper park authorities of the situation. He made public what Sam Cutler had been saying about a covert creature in the lake; what had been reported to Ann and Zeke; about the dead animals the rangers had found. Henry didn't think the National Park Service believed most of it, which didn't surprise him.

In the worst way, he wanted to admit his own suspicions about the bizarre animal tracks and the other sightings; but liked his job too much to take the chance. He wasn't a fool. They'd think he was certifiable if he started yakking about monsters in the lake. So he said nothing.

Justin hung around, pestering Ann and him and spending more time with Laura. He told everyone he was staying in the park so he could monitor the dig. He wanted to be there when history was uncovered. He wanted to protect the find.

Ann thought he also wanted to be with Laura.

Henry knew another reason Justin was staying–their night patrols on Crater Lake had resumed.

CHAPTER 5

Henry, as the other park rangers, was licensed to carry a firearm. After all, they were commissioned law officers; not just friendly tour guides. But since his police days, he hadn't felt comfortable carrying a gun. He'd never meant to kill the child who'd shot him in the projects. It'd been a horrible accident and he'd lived with the guilt ever since. Only human monsters, his guilt haunted him, would kill a child.

Each day it was difficult for him to strap the gun on his hip. But knowing he'd probably only use it on some maddened animal, not a person, had kept his head on straight. In all his years at the park he'd never had to draw the thing out of its holster once.

"Much good that gun will do you if we come across a prehistoric monster with teeth and an attitude," Justin remarked sarcastically, his eyes skimming the dark water around them. "Since I found those prints in the mud I've been doing some more reading. I just finished the most recent treatise on what my fellow experts now believe to be true about certain dinosaurs, known and unknown. Your Sig there wouldn't even have nicked their tough hides, much less stopped them from attacking you."

They were out on another of their evening

patrols, but as with the other nights, nothing except the voices of the night insects and park animals had marred the tranquil summer darkness.

"So what you're saying is if we did come across a live dinosaur, or any other prehistoric beast, then, we couldn't just shoot it?" Henry pressed.

"No. It'd take a lot more firepower than you have.

"And, aside from that, if such a creature exists we'd have to *protect* it, not try to *kill* it. Man has never laid eyes on a living dinosaur…except in those Jurassic Park movies." Justin tried to lighten the mood. "It'd be the greatest wonder of the world. I'd rather have you close the lake area, heck, the whole park forever if you had to, rather than harm such a magnificent animal. And I'm sure the National Park Service would agree. If it exists, I want to find it. Get a look at it. Get *pictures*."

"Magnificent animal? You're a little naive about the *terrible lizards*, aren't you?" Henry commented carefully. "I hadn't planned on harming it in any way, either. But if there is a dinosaur swimming around in this lake that's developed, perhaps, a taste for human flesh, as opposed to say, fish or plants, then we'd best be prepared to defend ourselves if we have to. The magnificent animal won't want to be friends, I can tell you that. Remember the damage done to both those boats? And what really happened to those two missing men? Were they snacks?"

Justin appeared distressed; obviously he'd been brooding on the problem, too. And, as the authority on the subject, his opinion on what should be done if they were dealing with something unnatural unsettled Henry. *They should just let it run free in the park? Fence it in and charge admission?* He'd never heard of anything so naïve.

Suddenly the night and the water seemed filled with danger.

"But, all that aside, you want my honest assessment of what we should do right now?" Justin whispered, as if he were afraid something was listening to them.

"Of course."

"After what I've gleaned from my research, I think we should get off this lake and not get back on again until we have either a faster boat or a bigger weapon, just in case."

Henry couldn't help but laugh. Softly. "In case what?"

"In case the creature finds us."

Exasperated, Henry exclaimed, "Being a little premature, aren't we? Thinking that there is actually something in the lake is still wild speculation on our part, isn't it? I mean, let's face it, we don't really *believe* there's some prehistoric monster in the lake, now do we?"

"Don't we?" a weak reply. "Then what are we doing out here in the middle of the night, puttering around in circles, freezing to death?"

"You got a point there. And if we do discover it exists. What, exactly, are we going to do about it? Worse yet, what if we discover it attacked those boats on purpose, maybe ate those men? And what if it keeps on attacking humans? Goes in search of them as a viable food source? If it leaves the lake and we can't stop it?" Henry said what he'd been thinking.

"Then, unfortunately," the scientist replied, "something will have to be done about it."

"Like what?"

"I don't know. I hadn't thought that far ahead."

"Maybe we should," Henry remarked.

Justin inhaled. "I wish now that I hadn't made the bones public knowledge and that your wife's newspaper wasn't doing that article on it Monday, along with a second story on the destroyed boats and the missing men…illustrated with her drawings of a mythical lake monster."

"Yep, and those stories are going to bring out a flock of the curious. Then there are your colleagues from John Day coming out next week to begin excavating the paleontological site. Long dead dinosaur bones in a place where people and boats have been mysteriously disappearing? Fertile ground for strange rumors and speculation." Henry shook his head in the dark.

"Your park's going to become a zoo." Justin's cynical laugh echoed across the cool night.

Henry didn't laugh.

"We released that information before the second boat disappeared. We thought the park was safe," Justin reminded Henry. "Sorry."

"Nah, you're not to blame." Henry's voice broke the hush that had covered the lake all night. "You were doing your job. But–" His voice stopped abruptly because he thought he'd heard something. They weren't alone. His gut told him so. He shushed Justin but no further sounds came.

Beneath it all, he felt bad he was still fibbing to his wife about the true reason he and Justin were out on the lake so much, even though he was sure she'd already guessed. Ann was a smart woman and she'd interviewed Willie Sander before he'd disappeared. She knew two boats, two men, were missing. She knew something weird was going on.

And Henry didn't usually do quite so much night fishing.

Ann had kissed him every night at the door with concern in her eyes and made him promise to be careful, not take any chances he didn't need to take, and to get the hell off the lake if trouble reared its head. But she hadn't once asked what was going on. She would, though, eventually.

"Don't be a hero, Henry," was all she'd said, and she'd meant it.

After a little longer silence, Henry yawned. "Maybe we should call it a night?"

"Sounds good to me," Justin croaked.

It was close to midnight and they were sitting in the front of the boat, shivering in their coats and life-jackets. The temperature rise in the lower depths of the lake hadn't made a measureable difference yet, except to create the growing mist that was rising over everything more densely each night. Mist as thick and eerie as any seen on Loch Ness.

By now Henry knew the young scientist better. Talking and hours spent chugging back and forth across the lake, the boat's bright headlights cutting through the fog that hung about them like a shroud, their hand-held flashlights crisscrossing the murkiness consuming the boat, had given them time to get to know each other.

Henry's first impression of the scientist had never wavered. Justin was dedicated and single-minded in everything he did, perhaps too much. The young man was over-compensating for something, carrying a chip of some kind on his shoulder. He did a fine job of hiding it most of the time, but he couldn't fool Henry. Henry had been a cop for too long.

Henry was waiting for Justin to fess up on his own. Sooner or later, he would, and Henry could wait. He wasn't one to pry into other peoples' lives, even if that person was dating his only daughter.

Justin stifled a yawn, and Henry repeated, "About ready to call it a night, Mr. Wizard?"

Justin's head came up, the lights reflected off his glasses into the inky gloom nudging in around them.

"More than ready."

They were exhausted from the cruises, staying up half the night, and weary of searching for something that might not exist. Henry had his regular job and Justin had been spending his days at the dig or with Laura and Phoebe.

It was time to pack it in. Justin could be right. They needed to do some more planning, to be more prepared, in case.

"We're heading home." Henry directed the boat towards Cleetwood Cove at medium speed. The night had turned chilly and he'd be glad to plop down before a blazing fire next to his wife.

***

Justin heard the commotion first. In the stillness of the night a loud swishing of powerfully churning water came from far away, moving closer. On the air trembled a soft cry, the sound filling the caldera as an echo filled a canyon.

Something rose up underneath the boat. Henry would remember later that in the horror of the moment, as they were lifted high into the air, that Sam Cutler had been right, it was bigger than two houses.

The boat plopped back down onto the lake, the whirling engines grinding, water splashing everywhere, soaking both of them. Another bounce like that, Henry thought frantically, and the boat would capsize.

"My god," Justin yelped. "It really is a monster!" He sounded like someone who'd just watched the sun explode up in the sky.

"I'll be damned," Henry mumbled, attempting to swallow. His body was frozen. Only his eyes could move, but they were glued to the creature's steep side. He couldn't believe what he was seeing, though in the dark and the chaos of the attack, all he could actually make out was a mass of dark scaly skin as the boat slid down along side of the creature.

He captured a flash of a thick neck, a huge blob of a head, two glaring crimson eyes and a wicked slash of sharp whiteness that had to be teeth as big as a man's hand. All in all, their attacker was a nightmare that froze him and Justin to the boat's rail, holding on for dear life as the boat beneath them bucked and rocked.

The thing was moving fast.

Justin's head lifted upwards on his neck, his eyes gawking up at the thing. He screamed.

The beast replied with a deep-throated gurgling rattle of a roar.

Justin stammered under his breath, "Forgot to mention, I hate the water. And I can't swim!"

"Now you tell me," Henry tossed back. "Don't worry, your life preserver will keep you afloat. If you go over, paddle like hell!"

The boat repeated its jump. The fiberglass creaked tortuously beneath them.

"If we go in the water will it try to eat us?" Henry voice was a hoarse whisper.

"I'm not sure. No way of knowing. If it's a descendent or a mutant of a species like Pliosaur, its ancestors were flesh-eaters. They ate anything they bumped into."

The boat was lifted a second time, bouncing it high into the air, then it came down violently, nearly capsizing.

"It's trying to sink us," Henry cried above the din. The bullets he'd taken in the line of duty hadn't scared him half as much as what he was feeling now. But he'd never seen the bullets coming. This was different. He couldn't miss the monstrosity slamming against the boat, playing with them as if they were a child's toy.

Then as swiftly as the water beast had appeared, it was gone.

The lake beneath and around them became calm. The boat lunged forward, the engines loud on the night air.

Long seconds went by.

Shuddering, on his knees, Justin whispered, "It's gone."

Henry crouched by the rail, listening. It was hard to hear anything over the loud thumping of his heart. "That was close."

"I've daydreamed about when dinosaurs walked the earth," Justin's voice was ragged. "I always thought it'd be neat to see one. I don't think so now. The shock alone could give a person a heart attack."

The paleontologist came off his knees to lean against the rail beside Henry. He wiped the water from his face, in the faint light, his eyes wide and glazed. "Ha, imagine, and I didn't want us to hurt it–as if we could have." An acid laugh escaped his lips. "That thing must be gigantic, by what we glimpsed of it. That tail and head went on forever. And did you hear that awful sound it was making, a rumbling snoring roar? It sounded as if we were under a waterfall."

"Yes," was Henry's only reply. He was still listening.

"What are we going to do, Mr. Ranger? Should we make a run for the shore or what?"

Henry stood up slowly, moved over to the controls and shoved the throttle full open. He put out the other hand to grip Justin's shoulder. "We get out of here as fast as we can."

They heard the water and the roaring noises resume around them.

"It's coming back!"

"I know," moaned Justin.

The boat began to rock harder. The beast was near.

Later Henry believed Justin's inspiration and quick thinking were the only things that saved them. "Noise! It's attacking the noise from the engines…and it sees the lights."

"Then we turn off the engines and the lights! If we play dead, it might leave us alone.

"And I've got a gun," Henry added, a hand on the Sig in his holster. "I can shoot it."

"Forget that," Justin hollered. "That pin prick would probably just make it madder and it'd come after us for sure."

Henry shut down the engines and switched off the power.

"Flashlights off, too," Justin breathed.

They blinked into darkness. It'd been a moonless, overcast night, with creeping fog to help hide them. Henry felt as if he were floating in outer space, no stars, no other light source, just endless eternal blackness.

"Justin–"

"Shhh," Justin hissed, yanking the ranger down next to him.

The wild pitching of the boat ceased but Henry's stomach remained in turmoil.

They waited for a long time for the creature to make its next move. Nothing. It was as if the disturbance had never happened.

They huddled on the wood of the deck, silent, barely breathing, their craft dead in the water, for what seemed like an eternity, the rest of the night. It wasn't until the first rays of sunlight filtered through the mist that Henry restarted the engines and gratefully took them home.

"I want to thank you, Justin," Henry said after the boat had resumed chugging along. "You probably saved our lives. I was ready to shoot at the thing. I think you were right–it would have just angered it more."

Peering at Henry through water-speckled glasses, Justin gave him a weary grin. "No need to thank me. I was saving my skin, too."

"Well, thanks anyway, quick thinker. You didn't panic as most people would have."

"Ha, I was too scared to panic." Justin released a shudder. "And I only used common sense.

"I thought I'd never say this, but as unique a creature as it might be, it doesn't belong here in our world. Here, it's a nightmare. You're right, it belongs to the ancient past."

"That it does."

"Henry, since you know the park and the lake area so well, where do you think it hides during the day?"

"Let's see…underneath the lake there's a honeycomb of caverns and caves formed thousands of years ago by lava streams when the volcano originally erupted. An amphibious beast could live, hide, down there in the connected waterway caverns forever."

"I don't like caves. They make me claustrophobic."

"And you don't like the water, either."

"I hate caves more."

"How did you ever become a paleontologist then?"

"I figured I'd be excavating mostly on dry

higher land. Most paleontological sites are up in the mountains or in deserts. So far I haven't had to dig underwater or in caves."

"That's too bad because after what happened last night, what we saw, if it keeps destroying boats and people keep popping up missing, we might have to search for the creature. Might have to find out where it's hiding, or living; maybe even explore the underground caves."

"You'd want me to accompany you?"

"If you would. You're the only paleontologist I know. I could use your expertise in dealing with the, er, dinosaur, if that's what you think it is."

Justin's face was ashen as he nodded. In the dawn's light he looked a hell of a lot older than he'd looked the day before.

"It, they," Justin muttered, "could live down in the caves."

"You mean there could be more than one of those things?"

"Why not?" Justin replied as their boat pulled up to the dock. "Heaven knows how long the creature we saw has been living in the lake. There could be more."

"Why has it only become a problem lately, then?"

"I have a theory. The earthquakes could have roused it out, opened new underground entrances allowing it access to the lake. And, remember, the water temperatures have been rising steadily. The lava flow deep under the earth could have incubated and hatched ancient eggs the earthquakes have unearthed as well as lured a full grown specimen out into the caldera. Hell, there could be a whole prehistoric world uncovered down there. All I know is that that water beast we saw last night was real. Wasn't it?" he asked as if he expected Henry to deny the experience they'd been through.

Henry didn't deny it. "Yes, it was all too real. And this creature's existence–whatever it is–is about to cause more havoc. If it keeps attacking I'll have to restrict people from the lake. Until the, er, problem is taken care of."

"What do we do if it's aggressively hostile and it leaves the lake?"

"Then we'll have to close the park or ask for help to deal with it." Henry's eyes met Justin's. "One way or another we're going to have to make sure the lake, the park, is safe."

"If I can help, count me in." Justin's faint grin was sincere. "If you need me, but I warn you now, I don't do underwater caves."

The ranger laughed softly and shook the scientist's hand. "You got a deal."

As they collected their things and hiked to the lodge, Henry's mind kept seeing frightening images from the night before. He was more than aware they could have died as horribly as the two missing men probably had. They'd been lucky.

Thinking about it was bad enough, but accepting he was going to have to tell people about the thing in the lake was worse. He'd be laughed at, ridiculed. But he had no choice. As a ranger he was sworn to protect the people in the park. It was his duty.

Worse, he was sure the lake was dangerous, at least at night.

"What species of dinosaur did that thing look like to you?" Henry inquired as they walked; hoping Justin had seen it clearer than he had. To him it'd just been a huge blur in the water.

"Not sure. It was too dark and foggy and I was too scared."

"It was big, though. Wasn't it?"

"Yes, it was…big…and loud and as quick as a laser in the water."

Henry sighed. "I can't wait to see the monster Ann draws from *that* description."

They both laughed and it felt good after what they'd been through.

CHAPTER 6

Henry dropped Justin off at the lodge and headed home. He wanted to clean up, eat something, and talk to George Redcrow about what should be done. He felt too keyed up to sleep anyway.

The park was serene and lovely at that time of morning, a footstep behind dawn. A nip in the air from the chilly night lingered, yet the sun was warm on Henry's back. He drove his jeep slowly along the asphalt road past the campgrounds and through Rim Village, his mind whirling over what had happened the night before.

Not many people were up and stirring, not even park visitors. Too early. But the season was only beginning and the visitors weren't many yet. In a few more weeks it'd be so crowded one wouldn't be able to move anywhere in the park and not bump into another person, except in the wilds of the back country. A fact that weighed heavily on his mind, because as much as he joshed with George about the pesky visitors, as all the rangers did, he never meant any of it. Visitors were the park's bread and butter. His job, as he knew it, wouldn't exist without them.

Henry sucked in the fresh air and rubbed his tired eyes with one hand as the other turned the wheel.

Golden squirrels and hares scurried across the road before his car's wheels; and he drove carefully so he wouldn't accidently hit one of them. Birds sang in the trees like any other morning. So deceptive, the normalcy. Henry knew the creature was about to change his little world as he knew it forever. And he didn't want it changed.

He loved the park, and wanted to protect it from the hectic outside world. How was he going to do that when the news got out? *Real dinosaur in the Lake! Come one, come all!*

It was too late to get Ann and Zeke to kill the upcoming newspaper articles. Knowing what he knew now, it would have been a good idea if the stories had never been written. They didn't need any more people in the park, hiking to gawk at the fossils up on the rim and peering into the lake searching for possible monsters. Too close. Way too close.

The park would be overrun with nosy reporters and the thrill-seeking curious. People trying to make a buck, or steal a buck; people who wouldn't care about the park's delicate natural balance and who'd trample over everything, throwing cigarette butts around like confetti and dumping litter over everything in sight. They wouldn't be there for the natural beauty of the land, as the usual visitors were, but for the hoopla surrounding a water monster in Crater Lake.

Henry was thinking about those strange tracks

George had discovered weeks back on Wizard Island around those animal carcasses. On land. If those tracks had belonged to the thing in the lake, and it'd located the only way in and out at Cleetwood Cove, did that mean the beast could come out of the water and crawl around on dry ground?

A shiver of dread spread through Henry's body.

He couldn't get that look of terror he'd seen on Justin's face, before they'd doused the boat lights, out of his mind. He couldn't erase his own horror as the creature was lifting their boat up. It lingered like a foul taste in his mouth. If not for Justin's quick thinking, and pure luck, would he even be here now to recall the experience? Probably not.

He pulled into his driveway, got out, entered the house and went into the kitchen. A note from Ann was propped on the table next to the summer bouquet centerpiece of silk yellow roses in a straw basket.

Honey, couldn't wait any longer, it read. *Went into town. I'll be at the paper. Call me when you get in. Love Ann.*

Henry made coffee and slumped into a kitchen chair. The previous night, a lead suit, collapsed on him. Feeling the exhaustion, he wished he could crawl into bed and sleep, as Justin had; lose himself in black oblivion. Better yet, he wished last night had never happened because now something would have to be done about the beast in the lake.

He stared out the window at the sunny day and tried to wipe his mind clean. But pretty soon he was back worrying over the next step to take. Worried about getting help with the situation and what he was going to say to Redcrow, without coming across as being plumb nuts.

When the coffee was ready he poured a cup, black, and drank it. Then another. He figured a good meal and a shower would revive him; keep him awake for seeing George and the long drive into town. So he fried some bacon and five eggs, plus toast with butter. Once he took that first bite, he realized he was hungrier than a starved bear.

Stark terror must do that to a person.

After cleaning up the dishes, he stood under a hot shower and afterwards put on civilian clothes, a pair of gray slacks and a casual shirt. At least he wasn't going to look like a crazy.

Henry drove the speed limit to headquarters. George's car was parked outside along with a couple of others. Shift change. Taking a deep breath, the Chief Park Ranger strode in.

Redcrow was heading out the door. They nearly collided.

"Just the man I came to see," Henry said.

"Thought this was your day off, Boss?"

"It is."

George took one look at his face and, gripping his arm, guided him outside into the sunlight.

"Let's take a walk," George suggested. "I need to work off those crullers I just gobbled down."

They walked.

"You were right, George."

"About what?"

"There's something, some huge water creature, in the lake. Maybe it's the explanation for the wrecked boats and those missing men. Could be it's what's been butchering the animals on Wizard Island as well."

George leveled Indian-black eyes at him. "I knew that. I'm the one who was with you when we found the remnants of Sam Cutler's boat."

"I remember." Henry kept walking. His face was turned away from George's, his shoulders slumping a little.

George understood. "You found it, then?"

Henry slid a look at his friend. "It found us. Last night. Justin Maltin, the paleontologist sent up here from John Day's, was with me. We were patrolling the lake after dark, as we have been on and off since the first boat disappeared. Looking for…something. Anything. We found it. It came up under our boat. I thought we were dead men."

"You should have been. You were protected. The water spirits were watching over you and your passenger. You're a charmed man, Henry. I've always told you that."

Henry threw Redcrow an amused look.

"What did it look like?" George's troubled eyes glinted ebony, as if he already knew what Henry was going to tell him.

"It was hard to see. But the creature, whatever it was, was enormous. It either had a long neck or a real long body and it appeared to be a dark color. Not really sure. But it did have lots of big white teeth because they gleamed in the dark."

George's shaggy eyebrows rose. "Even though I've seen the mutilated animals, seen the tracks, I'm still flabbergasted," his lips pulled back away from his teeth as he inhaled, "and frightened. If it's as aggressive and as big as you say it is we have a hell of a problem."

"Tell me about it. A huge problem. It's an immediate threat to anyone on the lake."

"Yes, it is." George whistled softly, dodging a tree.

"I thought it was going to belly flop right on top of us. I froze like a scared kid. Just gawked, dumbstruck, at it. Wasn't for Justin, who made me cut the lights, the engine and play dead in the fog, I might not be alive to be talking about it. The beast went away."

Henry stopped walking and leaned tiredly against a tree. In as few words as possible he described the night he'd had and everything he could remember about the leviathan.

"What do we do now? It's not going to stay gone, is it, Boss?"

"Imagine not. I'm going to need anyone who'll believe me. I thought you might fill the bill."

"I might," George replied with a reserved smile. "What are your orders?"

"We'll need to keep everyone off the lake, make it off-limits, for now, I'm afraid. Don't see any other alternative."

Henry fell silent as a group of chattering visitors swept by and went into a souvenir shop. He had the urge to run after and warn them not to go near the water because a monster would get them. But he didn't.

"You're going to report *this* sighting to the National Park Service, aren't you?" George's voice had that same sarcastic humor it usually had when he knew the answer.

"Again I don't have any choice, the way I see it, George. That creature is dangerous. We're going to have to do something."

"Capture or kill it?" George inquired curiously.

"Well, those are possibilities, if we can find it. Or, we can leave it alone."

"That last one's not an option. It's a threat to humans. It's proven that. And we both know it won't leave us alone," George murmured in a troubled tone. "Gonna close the park?"

"Nah, not yet. Just the lake area."

George grimaced.

"I know. I don't like the idea any more than you, but it's better than losing more lives. We'll close the lake, shut down the boat tours, and see what happens. I'm hoping it'll be enough for now."

"If the beast behaves and stays in the lake, right?"

"You got it."

"And if it doesn't stay where it's supposed to?"

"Let's face one nightmare at a time, please."

George shook his head and scratched the scar along his left cheek. He'd gotten it a couple years before in the deep woods during a terrible storm. A tree fell on him and he was trapped, with night coming on. Henry had refused to halt the search until they found him which had probably saved his life. A whole night out in the sub-zero weather, wounded, beneath that tree and George might have been a frozen dead Indian.

Ever since that day, George believed he owed

Henry his life. Since then, George, a hunter, often anonymously left gifts of fresh meat, rabbit or deer, at Henry and Ann's cabin. The two men never talked about the incident, though. It made Henry uncomfortable being on the receiving end of so much gratefulness.

Henry shoved himself away from the tree and they meandered back towards headquarters.

As they parted, George said, "Give my best to Ann, Henry. Tell her I enjoyed that story she did last week on the old fur trappers of the area. Good writing."

"I'll relay the compliment. Come on by for supper tonight, if you can. Usual time. We're having your favorite: liver and onions."

"I just may do that. You know me, I'd never turn down one of Ann's home cooked meals. Thanks."

Henry saluted his goodbye, as George drove off to make his rounds, then climbed into his vehicle and aimed it in the direction of town.

The ride into Klamath Falls was soothing. A lovely sunny day for early July, for a change he didn't need a jacket.

He'd gotten his second wind and could count on a couple more hours of feeling almost normal before the weariness would shut him down. But he was restless. The memory of what had occurred the night before ticked away, a tiny bomb, inside him.

Twice on the road he passed a park tour bus. One was loaded with people coming from Klamath Falls and one was empty speeding towards town. The visitors kept streaming in.

Klamath Falls was a tourist town, heart and soul, anchored on the south side of Klamath Lake, the deepest natural lake in the state. A large part of the city was subsidized by tourism, as the park was. People flocked to see the dressed-up rugged cowboys, Indians, and loggers strutting along the streets, just like in the old days. They came to gaze in awe at the beauty of Mother Nature as they ate steak and flown-in chilled lobster, as they overlooked the marinas, or had picnics in a lakeside park. Like the park, without tourists Klamath Falls would cease to exist.

***

Henry strolled into the cluttered building to the sound of his wife's voice.

Ann was busy checking the layout of the new weekly shopper, an advertising circular, she'd finally talked Zeke into doing. It was the only survival tactic the old publisher would accept to keep the paper afloat. The only one. The shopper would bring in desperately needed revenue, Ann told him; it already had four times the subscription of the paper itself. Her idea. Though she still couldn't get Zeke to take on commercial printing of business cards, fliers, and brochures, she hadn't given up trying to persuade him because they had to do something to save the paper.

"Better enjoy the extra revenue while we can," she was saying, "I hear the Schnucks store is going to close next year."

"Uh, huh, I've been hearing the same thing for months. Rumors, I say. Merely rumors." But Zeke's tone wasn't hopeful.

Henry, as Ann, knew the three town grocery stores were the last life supports of the expiring newspaper, and if one of them shut its doors, the paper would lose money it couldn't afford. Food stores paid good money and advertised year-round.

"Postal rates are going up again, too, Zeke."

"Always something going up…except our circulation," Zeke lamented.

"Maybe these stories about the missing boats and the dinosaur bones, plus more feature stories once the scientists begin excavating, will boost the weekly numbers," Ann offered.

"We'll need it, once that story on the annual Spring Fest's salmonella-infected barbecued chicken runs, if the local businessmen don't lynch us first. Then we won't have to worry about the paper at all." But the editor's tone held humor. "We'll really catch hell on the street tomorrow, Ann, when this story comes out."

Ann sighed, "Don't I know it. I'm not going in to Freddy's for lunch for at least a month, until the hubbub dies down. He'd probably poison me on purpose."

"Only a month?" Zeke snickered. "That's what you think, girl. Freddy will *never* forget."

"Well, then, I guess I'll just go to the Corner Cafe from now on. Except I'll miss Freddy's barbecue chicken." Ann was smiling mischievously.

"After the Spring Fest, I and about twenty-five others sure won't."

Ann laughed. Zeke had been one of the unfortunate ones who'd ended up at the hospital. So he'd experienced the story first-hand. Yet revenge had nothing whatsoever to do with Zeke running the story. After all, it was news and he had to print it.

Ann turned and saw him watching her from the doorway.

"Husband, what a surprise. What are you doing in town?" Pleasure on her face as she walked over, which quickly faded when she caught the concern in his eyes.

"Thought maybe you'd like to go out to lunch with me."

The ploy wouldn't fool her. His tired and glum expression would tip her off something was bothering him.

"Got something to tell me, huh?" she whispered up at him. "Something's wrong?" Then, nearly in the same breath, "You've figured out what happened to those missing boats, haven't you?"

He nodded. "I believe so. I'll tell you about it over lunch."

"Hi, Zeke," Henry hailed over her head at the older man.

"Hi, Henry. Out of your jurisdiction a little, aren't you?"

"My day off."

"Some people have all the luck," the editor grumbled good-naturedly. "I bet you even got a pension plan, too."

"A modest one." Henry's laugh echoed in the small room.

He chatted with Zeke as Ann shut off her computer and gathered her purse and sweater. After giving him their goodbyes, they walked into the bright sunlight.

"Are you okay? You look terrible," was the first thing out of her mouth as she eyed him. She gave him a quick, hard hug. "Looks like you haven't slept at all. No great mystery because you never came home last night."

"No, I didn't."

The Corner Cafe was a few doors down from the newspaper office and they were nearly there. It served sandwiches and soup, great pies and cobblers, but no barbecued chicken.

Henry took Ann's hand in his and tucked it close to his side. "I'm fine now that I'm here with you."

"You and Justin were on the lake all night again, weren't you?"

"Yep. Squatting dead in the water like two scared turkeys the day before Thanksgiving."

She stopped and studied his face. "You saw something, didn't you? There *is* something in that lake, isn't there?" She sounded both vindicated and stunned.

"Yes, we saw something and, yes, there is some sort of creature swimming around in Crater Lake and probably living below the water in the caves. Or so Justin thinks. Killing animals around Wizard Island. We ran into it last night. It attacked our boat. And it was *big*."

He heard his wife's gasp, saw her body tighten. "Animals and…people…have been killed?"

Henry nodded. "Possibly people. Right now they're still classified as missing people."

"My god, you and Justin could have been hurt. Killed."

"But we weren't. We're alive and kicking. Well, I am anyway. Justin's sleeping at the lodge. So you can stop fretting."

A bell rang announcing their entry as he opened the café door and steered her towards a rear booth. They sat down. The waiter, a skinny high school kid with shorn hair and an earring in one ear, dropped off menus and dashed off.

Over lunch Henry recounted the night's adventure.

Ann remained quiet, but her expression, at different times, displayed incredulousness, excitement, or apprehension. Then fear.

When Henry finished, her hand squeezing his, she said, "What a story! What a scoop. Wait until I tell Zeke."

"No, you can't tell him about this yet. You can't tell anyone."

She began to protest but Henry shushed her. "Don't you see, you can't tell anyone about this right now. It could unleash a mob of people on the park. Monster seekers, newspaper reporters, camera crews and the curious. They'd camp out everywhere. It'd be a circus. Worse. It could be a disaster. Justin and I feel the creature, whatever it is, is extremely dangerous, especially if it, as we suspect, can leave the water."

He told her about the dead animals they'd found around the Island, the missing boat people, and the tracks Justin had discovered going into the water.

Ann understood. "No, I guess it wouldn't be wise to advertise this yet." She smiled softly, holding his hand across the table. She hadn't let go of him since he'd told her of his close call the night before.

"I'm going to close the lake area down. You can print that. We'll just have to invent some other reason for it. Dock or road repairs or something. It's going to be hard enough emptying the lake area this time of year, especially after that story of yours runs tomorrow. But I promise you, honey, soon as it's safe and we figure out how to handle the situation, you and the paper can run the full account, exclusively. But first, one way or another, the problem will have to be solved. Park Service won't like keeping the lake closed for long, it's a large tourist draw and with that last round of budget-cutting the Forest Service did on us, we need the revenue."

Money, it always comes down to money, he thought.

"Now I'm sorry those stories are coming out tomorrow, Henry. I'd try to stop them, if I could, but the paper's already printed, bundled and on its way to the readers."

"Not your fault, sweetheart. Can't be helped, so don't worry about it. My men and I can keep the lake off limits, no problem." Or so he hoped.

He ordered more coffee and when the waiter left, he leaned against the booth. The orange plastic was cold against the small of his back. He was suddenly so tired he could have fallen asleep right there. Sensing his frustration, his exhaustion, Ann ran her hand down the side of his face and smiled understandingly.

"I'll finish my pie and we'll go home. You need

some sleep."

"That I do."

"What did the creature look like?" she wanted to know.

"Off the record." Then he did his darnest to quench her curiosity.

After he was finished, she asked about the progress of one of George's pet projects, a homeless camp inside the park set up by the Forest Service and funded by the county. A kind of tent city. Campers who'd come, stayed and had never left. She planned to write their story, hoping to gain public support. There were so many homeless these days. They needed somewhere to go. Help.

"The Forest Service got extra funding for them," Henry revealed. "They can stay for a while. George told me how grateful those families are, not to be charged fees, or evicted and moved on again. They're tired, beaten down. The board voted to let them stay until they get on their feet. George starts installing chemical toilets and setting up fire circles tomorrow. Several of the other rangers have agreed to help by reinforcing and rain proofing their homemade tents. And George is going to teach to fish those who don't know how. Heaven knows how much he's spent on the groceries he's already taken out there."

"George's a good man," Ann said. "Heart of gold."

"That he is. I haven't been out to the camp yet, but George says the conditions are pitiful. A dozen families live out there with their kids."

George wasn't the only one who cared about the

homeless. Ann was passionate about helping them, in and out of the park. How could people become homeless in the wealthiest nation on earth, she often asked him, and he knew she experienced guilt every time she bought a new blouse or ate a good meal when so many others wore rags and were hungry.

"George says those at the camp are mostly people who've lost their jobs. Blue collar workers who'd been living from paycheck to paycheck. They lost everything and foreclosures forced them to leave their homes. The poorest of them are living in tents propped up by tree limbs, patched with taped together plastic trash bags, and warmed with propane heaters. They're not bad people, just desperate. To survive, they're self-teaching their children and trying to live off the land like mountain folks. Nowhere else to go. I'm glad the park is letting them stay. Getting them aid and the necessary paperwork, so they can.

"Except," Henry paused, "I'm worried. That camp's near the quarry and that's awful close to the lake."

Ann's eyebrows lifted. "Could that be a problem? I thought you said the creature lives in the lake?"

"It does. Most of the time, we believe. Maybe, to be absolutely safe, we should relocate the camp farther away from the caldera. After all we have two-hundred and fifty thousand acres of valleys and forest out there to choose from. No sense in taking chances." He yawned, his eyes suddenly heavy.

Ann stood up, and put her purse over her shoulder. "Maybe we should pay the bill and get you home to bed? You look like a zombie."

"You're coming home with me?" He perked up, rising, as well, and fished out the wallet from his pocket.

"I could. I'm done at the paper. I was finishing up when you walked in."

"Good. I'll take care of the bill and you go ahead. I'll be right behind and will meet you at home, hon. Drive carefully."

"I will. See you there." His wife gave him a quick kiss and walked out the door.

He wasn't far behind.

***

Henry slept the rest of the day. Ann didn't disturb him. He awoke that evening and they had supper with George. The hot dinner topic being, of course, the mysterious beast haunting Crater Lake.

Later, alone, Henry and Ann watched a little television and turned in early. Justin had telephoned after dinner and arranged to have breakfast the next morning with him before he went on duty; said he wanted to talk about their adventure of the night before. Henry wondered what Justin really wanted.

By eleven they were asleep.

CHAPTER 7

Henry was awakened minutes before dawn by the telephone's ringing on the headboard's shelf. Half-asleep, he fumbled the phone, dropped it, and finally got it to his ear.

The conversation was brief.

"Chief, can you get into headquarters right away?" George's voice sounded strained.

As groggy as he was, Henry knew something was up. "What is it?"

"Superintendent Sorrelson's here. He wants to talk to you about our dilemma."

"Our what?"

"You know, closing the lake area. And there's another problem. Don't want to discuss it on the telephone, though. Big brother could be listening."

"I won't be long," Henry said and hung up.

Waking Ann, who could sleep through an earthquake, Henry made her aware of George's call. He climbed out of bed and put on a clean uniform and drove to headquarters with the rising sun in his eyes. It was around six o'clock. Usually he went in at eight, so it was only two hours early.

The ranger's station was abuzz with a lot of activity for such an early hour. Sorrelson, the Park's

Superintendent, was waiting for him in his office, sitting in Henry's chair, along with a grim George Redcrow sulking in the corner. Henry rarely saw the superintendent unless there was a problem. The man was usually busy with meetings and glad-handing state politicians.

"Heard about your close call the other night, Henry," Sorrelson grumbled, his plump lips barely smiling.

"It was close, that's for sure." Henry met the other man's flat gaze.

"Went fishing and caught something you weren't expecting, huh? Got any idea what you saw? Wasn't some giant fish, was it, now? Like they spotted a few years back at Culler's Lake? Or could it have been one of those inflatable dragon toys? You know how the city kids like to play tricks on us during tourist season."

"No, Sir, it wasn't a fish or a toy."

"What was it?"

Here goes nothing, Henry thought, *here goes my job*. "Now, don't laugh, but the paleontologist they sent us from John Day's–he was with me the other night–thinks it's some sort of dinosaur throwback. Maybe even an off-shoot of an ancient Pleiosaur. Or a mutant hybrid never seen before, but a live one and bigger than a whale. And it's here in the lake. Has been, most likely, for the last year or more. Only now, perhaps because it's become large enough, it's making its presence known."

Sorrelson didn't laugh, but stared at him as if he were waiting for the punch line, his eyes hard. He didn't wait long.

"In the lake you say?"

"Yes, in the lake." Henry walked over to the chair beside George and sat down. He yearned for a cup of coffee and his eyes glanced through the window towards the coffee pot in the adjoining room. The other men in the office had coffee, and he was jealous. Sorrelson caught him looking at George's cup. "Get yourself some coffee, Henry."

When Henry returned to his office, Sorrelson coaxed, "You sure, the thing in the lake couldn't have been anything else? A large log or something?"

Hell, Henry thought, *I knew it would be like this. He thinks I'm nuts.*

"Well," Henry fought a caustic smile, "it was dark and the fog was thick. But I'm sure it was alive, damn big, and viciously aggressive; it tried to capsize us, whatever it was. If it was a fish, it was the biggest fish I've ever seen. If it was a log, it was a mighty active log. It attacked our boat. Plain and simple."

"Bigger than a whale, you say?" Sorrelson's eyebrows were questioning curves. A beefy hand glided along the side of a fleshy jaw. A short, heavy set man he was also going bald. He wore glasses, but being vain, left them off most of the time, which made him squint a lot. He didn't reside in the park, preferring the town. Henry often wondered how he'd ever gotten to be superintendent of a national park. Connections, no doubt. But he was a wheeler-dealer and knew whose hand to shake, whose donation box to fill, to get what he wanted.

"Bigger."

Sorrelson glared at him. “Redcrow here says you want to close down the lake area; stop the boat tours for a while until we can decide if this *creature* is dangerous?”

“That’s my plan.”

The Superintendent didn’t say anything for a minute or two, as Henry and George waited. The room was hushed. From earlier experiences Henry knew Sorrelson was mulling things over in that steel trap of a mind of his, trying to find a way for the park to keep operating. It couldn’t bring in money if its prime attraction was gated off. Most people came to see the lake.

The silence broke. “I’d say that was too hasty. Let’s give it a bit more time, Henry. After all, tourist season is just coming into full swing. I hate to tell you this, but they’ve ordered me to cut back further on your funds this year. You might have to lay off a couple more rangers. If you close down the lake they might see that as justification for even more layoffs. Humph. A monster in the lake might be good for us. Bring more tourists. Budget needs the income.”

Layoff more rangers? They were short-handed already, and with some sort of giant predator prowling the lake on top of it all, what was the man thinking? Henry’s disbelief flushed his cheeks, anger showed in his eyes; but, with a warning look from George, he kept his irritation to himself. Sorrelson wouldn’t listen anyway. Once he decided something he rarely changed his mind.

The Superintendent grilled Henry, “Where do you think this thing in the lake–if there is something in the lake–might have come from?"

"Dr. Maltin, the paleontologist I mentioned before, believes it may live in the caves beneath the caldera." Henry cradled the Styrofoam cup in his hands and stared at the wet indentation the bottom had made on his pants leg. The cup was leaking, so he drank the rest of the coffee. It felt strange with someone else sitting at his desk, drinking coffee out of his cup. He didn't like it much.

"The caldera is honeycombed with underground caves. All of them uncharted and probably unstable." Henry met Sorrelson's eyes. "You called me in two hours before my shift, Sir, to ask about what I saw two nights ago in the water and to tell me not to close the lake area for now–is there anything else?"

Sorrelson's gaze shifted to George. "Well, there was something else. George can explain. He was on duty last night."

George Redcrow's head had been slumped on his chest, but when spoken to, he raised it. Henry recognized distress in his friend's face. "Yesterday there was an incident in that homeless camp near the old rock quarry."

"An incident?" echoed Henry.

"Late in the day, around eight or eight-thirty, close to sundown. You know, Henry, how gloomy it can be in the woods by that time of day?"

Henry nodded, waiting for George to continue.

"Seems they had a visitor. Some enormous, noisy animal, by their account. It scared the bejesus out of them as it crashed through the woods behind their camp." George produced a hand-sized notebook and flipped it open to the middle. "Two men, Gregory Black and a Leonard Morrison, were sent out to investigate the racket. Black was a vet and an experienced woodsman, who knew his way around the forest. He'd been out of a job, too, for a while, suffered from battle-related flashbacks, a chronic medical condition, but could take care of himself in the wild, according to the others. Morrison got laid off six months before from the mill in Medford and when the money ran out he and his family were evicted from their home. He's got three kids and a wife, Jane."

"What happened to him and his friend?" Henry cut to the point.

"Seems they never returned. They were officially reported missing as soon as the sun came up. Camp people were too scared to risk coming into headquarters before then, afraid the thing was still lurking in the woods waiting. They've asked for help to find the missing men."

Henry experienced a cold creeping dread.

"One of Morrison's children, a girl name Nikki, claims she saw a monster–her exact words–said it was about a thousand feet tall. Says it ate her daddy. She'd snuck off after him and Black when they went out looking."

George put the notebook away. "But I don't think we can count on her as a reliable witness."

"Why not?"

"She's seven years old and in shock. I tried to get her mother to take her to the hospital in town so a doctor could check her out, but none of them have medical coverage of any kind. And no money. Just a lot of misplaced pride. So I couldn't persuade her. The girl's mother isn't taking it well, either. She insists her husband's not coming back. That he's dead. That both men are dead. She believes her daughter. The situation is unsettling."

George seemed to be done talking.

"We need to get some rangers out to the camp and search for those missing men. Now." Henry looked over to Sorrelson, who had closed up his briefcase and was preparing to leave.

"I'm sure you'll find them, Henry. Unless a monster has truly devoured them," Sorrelson muttered sarcastically. He wasn't as worried about the missing homeless as Henry thought he should have been. He bet it would have been different if they'd been politicians. "I leave the matter in your capable hands. Keep me informed. And those other matters? Keep the lake open and let me know which two rangers you've decided to cut. Your choice. I'll try to get them the best severance package I can, under the circumstances.

"You can leave messages with my secretary. Tomorrow I'm flying out to Los Angeles for a golf tournament. Won't be back for a week or two, at least."

Henry was relieved when the Superintendent went out the door. The man couldn't get away fast enough.

"Okay, George," Henry exhaled, sentried at the window, watching the Superintendent's car leave behind a trail of dust. "Let's gather some rangers and go out to the camp. Find out what's happened to those two men. This whole thing's starting to spook me," he swore under his breath, slapping on his hat.

***

The homeless camp was less than half-mile from the lake. Henry had already asked himself if the lake beast was the same *monster* that had terrorized the camp. He was afraid it was. Either way, moving those people was a good idea, especially if there was something prowling the lake area.

But the camp people weren't the only ones in the line of danger. It depended on how far afield the creature could roam from its lair. Rim Village and the park's main campground were two miles from the caldera. Not that far. Most of the people, over two-hundred, who worked in the park lived in the Rim Village dormitories. Good Lord. Henry prayed the mysterious predator stayed near the water. Only what they discovered at the camp and time would tell.

Henry, George, Matthew Kiley and another ranger, Peter Gillian, arrived a short while later at the camp. It was early but the place was alive with activity. Henry could hear someone crying.

A rag-tag collection of children spotted them and came running.

"We need to talk to Mrs. Jane Morrison," Henry told the children. A small boy dressed in oversized clothes stepped forward. Henry noticed that though his clothes were threadbare, they were clean. A baseball was clutched in one grimy hand. A baseball cap sat cockeyed on his head.

"That's my mom. I'm Stevie Morrison. She's in our tent with Nikki and Mona, my sisters. I'll show ya."

"All right, son," Henry said. "You lead, we'll follow."

"A monster ate my dad," the kid blurted out so matter-of-factly he could have been reciting baseball scores.

Henry glanced sideways at George. The man's face was stone.

They followed the boy to a tarp-covered tent tucked between other tents; some small, some larger. Some appeared to be homemade and some were store bought. The one they found themselves in front of was made of different sized taped patches, old canvas peeking through. All different colored tape. Must leak when it rained.

Henry had driven past the camp many times since they'd set up weeks ago, but, though he'd meant to, he hadn't had the time to stop. There were many campers scattered throughout the park. Maybe the camp reminded him too much of the homeless back in the streets and empty lots of New York. Like a rampant disease, homelessness had spread over the last few decades until it had even encroached into the park. At least a camp ground was better than living in a cardboard box on the sidewalks of New York.

George Redcrow apparently had visited the camp many times. People waved at him as they strode by. The Morrison boy seemed to know and trust him.

Standing before the tent, Henry caught, out of

the corner of his eye, George handing the boy and his friends packages of Twinkies taken from a brown paper bag, and he smiled. Soft-hearted George. He should have had kids of his own. He had a way with them.

The boy scooted through the entrance flap and into the tent.

There was no place to knock, so Henry called out, "Mrs. Morrison, can we speak to you about your missing husband and his friend?"

From inside a woman's voice, between coughs, responded, "Come on in."

Inside it was gloomy. The green canvas filtered the sunlight into a greenish twilight and the space smelled of mud and damp. Henry hadn't ever seen anything like it. There was a folding table with a couple of rickety chairs surrounding it, covered with the basic necessities needed for tent life: boxes of cereal, cans of evaporated milk, paper cups and plates, lanterns and paper towels. Stacked to the right of the food were scuffed and lidded Tupperware bowls full of heaven-knew-what. Bundles of clothes and stacks of canned goods were piled around the sides of the tent. The wooden poles propping up the center had nails in them from which hung jackets, sweaters, and more lanterns. There were sleeping bags rolled up and stacked in a corner with blankets and pillows on top. The tent's floor was a layer of scuffed plastic.

Henry and George exchanged somber looks. Henry had seen poverty before, but there, in the middle of the forest beauty, it was somehow worse than the usual dilapidated town shacks.

"About time someone came out." The woman was seated at the table. She had long drab hair pulled into a ponytail; wore faded blue jeans and a Grateful Dead T-shirt. Possessing plain features and wet eyes full of misery, she cradled a child in her lap whose face was pressed against her chest. Another skinny blond-headed girl, about ten years old or so, in an oversized black sweatshirt, hid behind them. In the darkened tent, the girl's eyes reminded Henry of a deer's glimpsed at the forest edge at night from his porch. The boy, Stevie, plunked down in a lawn chair to their right.

"Mrs. Morrison," Henry spoke, "I'm Chief Park Ranger Henry Shore and these are three of my men, Ranger Redcrow, Ranger Kiley and Ranger Gillian." Gillian hung back at the entrance, aware how cramped the inside was. "We're here to see if there's anything we can do to help find your husband. Do you think there's something suspicious with his disappearance; maybe a crime's been committed?"

"Well, could be there's been a crime committed," she retorted hotly. "But I'm afraid you're going to have a hard time arresting the perpetrator. My Nikki here," she patted the girl in her arms on the head, "says it was some king of monster as tall as the trees. Something similar to a…dinosaur. She's an expert on them, loves them. Used to love them anyway. She says it ate her daddy, my husband, as well as our friend, Gregory." Her voice was chilling.

As the woman talked, it occurred to Henry she was educated. It was the way she met his eyes and phrased her thoughts. Her looks and circumstances were deceiving. Henry wondered what her story was.

"Can the child speak to us?" Henry stepped forward and bent down on one knee so he was at the same level as the girl.

"You can try. She wouldn't say much yesterday after it happened. It really scared her, but she's doing better now. Nikki, sweetie?" The woman hugged the child gently. "Can you speak to the ranger here? He won't hurt you." As if other men in uniform in other places might have. Perhaps, they'd been pushed on from one place to another by uniforms. No one wanted homeless people squatting in their manicured towns.

The child mumbled something, but she didn't come out of hiding.

The woman fought off another coughing fit, then cajoled, "Nikki, please, for Momma. It's important. What you have to say to this gentleman might help someone else."

"Okay, Momma," a tiny voice whispered, and the child turned to look at them. She wasn't pretty. Her hair wasn't shiny. Yet there was something so knowing, so resigned, in her melancholy eyes Henry knew she'd left childhood long behind.

He offered a friendly smile, but the child refused to return it. "Your name's Nikki, right?" He laid a hand on her shoulder in a fatherly gesture. She nodded. "Nikki, I know this is hard for you. For your mom, sister and brother, too. But we need your help. You saw something yesterday evening out in the woods, when you followed after your dad. What was it?"

"I saw a…monster," the girl stuttered. She bent her head upwards to an impossibly steep angle and pointed straight up. "Bigger than this tent, bigger than a mountain. It made lots of noise in the woods while we were trying to eat supper, growling and stuff. So Daddy and Mr. Black went to see what it was. I wanted to see, too, so I followed 'em. Even though Daddy told me not to. I'm not a 'fraidy cat like my brother thinks," she huffed proudly before her eyes turned fearful. "But the monster scared me real bad." Clutching her mother tightly, shaking her head, the words stopped.

"Nikki," Henry encouraged, "what happened then?"

"The monster came and ate my daddy and Mr. Black. Picked them up like raggedy-dolls. Daddy was screaming…and…and…I ran away fast as I could. I'm so scared, Momma, I'm so scared it's going to come and get me, too. I want to leave. Leave now. Momma. *Please?*" She was reduced to whimpering, as she retreated into a safer place, her eyes going empty. Reliving her father's death had been too much for her.

"Nikki?" Henry was anxious to get the answers to a few last questions.

"That's enough," her mother interrupted firmly, drawing the child deeper into her arms. "She didn't see anything else, Ranger. Didn't see where the monster went, can't describe it any better than she has. She's only a child. She raced back here, terrified it was going to come after her next. There, you know everything she does. Now leave her alone. She's sick with it all and hasn't slept a wink since."

Henry straightened up, frowning. His thoughts touched on his granddaughter, Phoebe, and he didn't have the heart to interrogate the child any more.

In a lower voice he asked, "Mrs. Morrison, does Nikki ever invent stories? I mean, is she an overly imaginative child?"

Anger glittered in the woman's eyes. "What you mean is, does Nikki lie? Did she make up this *monster?*"

"Sometimes children make up stories. They don't think of them as lies." Henry attempted to soften his meaning. It didn't work.

"No, Nikki doesn't make up stories and she doesn't lie." The woman released a sigh. "She's an honest child. If she says something happened, it happened. And she's a smart child. She's seen pictures of dinosaurs in books and on TV and she knows what they look like. So if she swears some kind of dinosaur-monster ate her daddy, that's probably pretty close to the truth, no matter how outrageous it sounds." Leveling eyes at him, she went on, "My husband and Greg aren't coming back. They're both dead. There's a bunch of the men out looking for them now, but they won't find anything, except maybe left behind pieces. It's a waste of time. So, Chief Ranger, listen to me. You'd be better off trying to find some way to track and kill that thing, than looking for two dead men."

She lowered her mouth into her hand and coughed. Stared at the blood with dull eyes and wiped it on her sleeve. The little girl was crying again, muffled sobs of anguish.

Sympathy for the woman's plight stabbed Henry. He didn't know what to say in reply to her advice. He saw the pain she and her daughter were in, and that she wasn't well. Her husband was missing. Conceivably dead. Being homeless was bad enough but being a sick homeless widow with three kids was even worse. He pitied her and her children.

The thing was, Henry believed the child. He'd seen the creature. He would have liked the girl to show them where it had happened, but thought better of it. Obviously, the child wasn't in any condition to go anywhere, or show anyone anything.

They were on their own.

"That's all we need from you and the girl, Ma'am, for now. If I think of anything else, I'll be back and you can tell me then. Thank you for your help. Thank you, too, Nikki." He reached out and patted the small head.

The woman remained silent in response, rocking her child in her arms protectively, her eyes closed, as the men exited the tent.

On the way out, Henry had caught George slipping a wad of money to the woman. "For you and the young ones. Go see a doctor for that cough, too," he'd told her, "and have him send me the bill."

Henry felt bad. He didn't have any extra money on him to give. He and Ann lived close to the bone these days, but they had a roof over their heads and food in their bellies. With luck Ann's newspaper story would raise money for the camp people. He'd have to be sure to ask her about its progress when he got home. Later he'd ask George what else he could do to help the camp's residents. There had to be something.

"Let's scout behind here in the woods," Henry ordered, once he and his men were outside. "If something as big as what Nikki says the creature was has rampaged through here, we're sure to see signs of it easily enough." He still couldn't admit out loud to the others that what they were searching for was really a monster. The word itself made him cringe. His men respected him and he didn't want to risk losing that.

Morrison's boy trailed them outside. "I can show you the direction my dad and the other man went last night, if you want me to. I saw them go this way." His finger gestured to their left.

"Lead on, son," George said. The boy took the Indian ranger's hand and led the men past the tents towards the woods and Crater Lake.

"That way, through there." The boy stopped at the fringe of the forest, refusing to go any further. "Walk straight between those two trees and keep going, then all you have to do is follow the path of smashed trees and stuff. Can't miss it."

George thanked him and the boy trotted back to camp, baseball clutched in a dirty hand, arm swinging.

"So, what are we waiting for?" Henry stormed into the bush, the others behind him.

The men worked their way through the sparse woods in the direction the boy had indicated. They saw a great swath of damaged, torn aside trees and trampled down foliage before them as if a giant scythe had cut through the woods.

"Good god," George exclaimed. "Looks like something pretty big crashed through here. Look at this, will you?"

Henry's expression was glum as they followed the obvious route. George was walking carefully along the path of destruction, examining the ground when he knelt down. "Look at this," he whispered over his shoulder as the others caught up with him. Twisting his upper body, George held a hand up. It was covered in dark crimson.

Henry's voice was soft. "Blood."

"And lots of it."

"You're right. Blood's all over around here." Ranger Kiley bent down and picked up a piece of a bloodied shirt.

Henry inspected the nearby area, trying not to let his panic show. It was one thing to imagine that thing swimming around in the lake, playing tag with and attacking boats. People could stay off the water and remain safe. But it was another thing altogether to accept it was actually foraging out into the park hunting for human hors d'oeuvres.

Stalking through the bushes, past Redcrow, Kiley and Gillian, Henry prayed he wouldn't find a dead body; that what he feared the most wouldn't come to pass.

What he found was just as bad. A large chunk of chewed-up flesh, gnawed by flies, lay on the ground in front of him. He pushed at it with his shoe. The flies scattered in a hundred directions before they re-landed. Henry backed away.

Ranger Gillian hunkered above the grisly find, studying it, hand over his mouth, a sickened expression on his face. He uncovered his mouth long enough to ask, "Animal or human?" He was a bookish man, with a weak stomach. A fairly new recruit, he'd only been a park ranger for two years.

"I'm afraid it's human." In his years as a cop Henry had seen plenty of human remains in various stages of decomposition. He'd recognize a human body part anywhere.

George agreed. He was staring at the carcass, too, with thoughtful eyes. As a hunter and ex-marine, dead flesh didn't bother him. It was what had done this that did. "Whatever tore this guy up had god awful big teeth," he concluded. "See these grooves in the flesh. We're talking one heck of a carnivore."

Kiley had nothing to say. He lifted his hat and wiped off his sweating face with the handkerchief he kept in his pocket. Kiley had been a ranger for longer than Henry had, but he'd never seen anything like what he was seeing now. And Henry could tell it upset him.

"Over there." Henry pointed a couple of feet beyond their discovery. "There's another piece of him, or his friend. Appears to be a leg."

Kiley and Gillain both looked sick.

The rangers didn't stay much longer, didn't follow the trail as far as they could have. It wouldn't have served any purpose. Henry would have bet a month's pay that it ended somewhere on the edge of the lake, probably in Cleetwood Cove.

He didn't need to check that out, he was sure of it. And so was George.

"Let's get busy, men," Henry said. "I'm going to rope off this area as a crime scene. I don't want anyone else stumbling upon these remains. While I do that, Kiley, go back to the car and radio headquarters to send someone out here to tag and bag these body parts for forensics and the coroner in Medford. Leave a message for the Superintendent of what we've found. Tell him I have to talk to him. Real soon."

Kiley left.

George volunteered to scout a little more around the area for other remains and Henry let him. But he didn't find anything else. The remainder of the two men had vanished. Not even another shoe was located.

Henry stooped down, and drawing out a hunting knife from his duty-belt, he cut away a section of the cloth covering what was left of the human leg; dropped the scrap and the piece of bloodied shirt in a plastic bag supplied by Gillian.

"Show these to Mrs. Morrison, Gillian, and see if she recognizes either one as something her husband or his friend might have been wearing." Henry met the other man's eyes. "Break the news to her gently, would you? Don't frighten them more than they already are. If these are Morrison or Black's remains, give her my condolences and tell her I'll be talking to her soon. Also alert the people in the camp we're going to move them out to another location. Today. Tell them to start packing it up. I'll be sending more rangers out with vehicles to help relocate them. I want them out of here by nightfall. Take them to the outskirts of the Last Creek Campground and resettle them there. I don't care if the other campers bellyache about it. I'll take the heat. I want the camp residents where I can keep an eye on them, protect them, if need be. Then hustle back to headquarters. I'll meet you there later to give you further instructions."

Gillain nodded, and tramped briskly back the way they'd come as if he couldn't wait to escape the scene.

Henry wrapped yellow plastic warning tape around the nearby trees, connecting them in a closed uneven shape.

When George returned, Henry was looking out through the trees with a frown on his face. "I'm going to recommend to the Park Service we close the park for a while. All of it. Until we know exactly what we're facing."

"Not just the lake?"

"Yep, all of it."

"Sounds like a brilliant idea to me," George replied. "I support the decision. But they're going to fight it. Sorrelson will go ballistic. He doesn't even want you to close the lake area. It's high visitor season, remember?"

"Then I'll go over his head. People are missing and dead. We don't have a choice." Henry examined the woods around them, his mind working. The forest was quiet, not a bird chirping or a rustle of animal noise. Not normal. Not at all. He stared at the blood on the grass. Well, if Sorrelson needed an undeniable reason to close the park, he had it now. Henry had little doubt the two missing men were dead. Body parts don't lie.

In silence George and Henry returned to headquarters. Henry unable to stop thinking about Jane Morrison and those kids in that awful tent village and the other homeless in their leaky makeshift abodes. Not only was it chilly at night, but patched plastic wouldn't keep out a chipmunk, much less a monster.

He didn't know what he was going to tell his wife. They lived in the park, so did their daughter and granddaughter, and he wasn't sure any of them were safe. His house was five miles away from the lake; before five miles had sounded fairly safe. Not any longer. And Laura and Phoebe were closer than that. If he were smart, he'd convince them to move into town. Today.

He'd never forgive himself if something happened to them.

As soon as he was able, he telephoned Ann at work and explained what was going on. As always, she drug the entire story out of him before he was ready to give it. He'd wanted to do it face to face, but it was tough keeping secrets from her. While on the phone, he strongly suggested she round up their daughter and granddaughter and move into town.

"Zeke has a large, empty house and I'm sure he'd let you all stay for a while," Henry wheedled. "At least I'd know everyone was safe."

Ann would have nothing to do with his plan. "Where you are is where I'm going to be." She was firm. "And no way am I leaving all this excitement. What a story."

Nothing he said changed her mind. But, if things got worse, he'd have to even if he had to tie her up and personally deposit her at Zeke's. She wasn't taking the threat serious enough. He recalled he hadn't at first, either, but there wasn't anything he could do about it until later. He was on duty.

At headquarters he called the off-duty rangers and asked them to report in by nine o'clock. After he got off the phone, he brooded over which two he could afford to lose. There were only six rangers he could pick from. Not George. His job was his life. Not Kiley, he'd been a ranger longer than any of the others. Gillian had three kids. Problem was, the others were good rangers, too. He couldn't afford to lose them, especially now. So, he wasn't going to lay off any of them, no matter what Sorrelson said.

He had to close the lake area. The entire park and knew he'd answer to Sorrelson and the Park Board about it later. Right now it'd take every ranger he had to do the evacuation. They couldn't risk people being anywhere in the vicinity of the lake after what he'd seen that morning.

Those decisions made, he finished at headquarters and drove over to the lodge to meet Justin for breakfast. His wristwatch said it was a tad after nine. Unbelievable it was still so early and so much had already happened.

Justin was sitting at the usual table sipping coffee and eating eggs when Henry slipped into the chair across from him.

"You're late. What's going on?" Justin leaned towards him as Henry sat down.

"I'm going to shut down the park."

"I thought so. I saw the activity at park headquarters on my way over." Justin's eyes were somber behind his spectacles. "It struck again, didn't it? This time on land?"

"Unfortunately, yes." In between ordering coffee (he decided he couldn't stomach breakfast yet after what he'd seen) he updated Justin. "This has changed everything. Quickly. I'm afraid the creature has developed a taste for human flesh."

"It never actually crossed my mind on the lake the other night," Justin said, "it was seeking us–human beings–to *eat*. I think it is and we have to stop it. If it's as clever as I suspect, we'll need to capture or, as much as I hate the thought being a scientist and all, kill it."

"I'm glad you agree because that's what I believe should be done, too. Because if it's preying on people, that destroys any awe, concern or pity I might have had for it." Henry kept seeing Jane Morrison's face and those ragamuffin kids, fatherless now; kept seeing those hunks of bloody flesh among the leaves. "If I could protect it," he muttered, "I'd shut down the whole park forever, but that won't guarantee the creature wouldn't escape and go on further killing sprees, butchering more people somewhere else."

"And if it craves human flesh, *nothing* could keep it inside the park if it can't get what it wants here."

"So the question is: How do we find it, contain it, or, if it turns out to be necessary, how do we kill it?"

"I don't know," Justin responded. "I've never

had to catch, contain or kill a renegade leviathan before. To be truthful, I've never been much of a hunter."

"I've hunted my share, but never anything this large. No dinosaurs, for sure."

"Perhaps we'd better find an expert hunter because something tells me we're going to need one before this is over."

"You have a good point there." Henry played with his spoon, stirring his coffee slowly. "I'll begin looking for somebody who has experience hunting large animals. Don't know anyone off hand, but I'll put out feelers."

"Oh, by the way, I've rented one of the cabins in Rim Village for the rest of the summer."

"With all that's going on, you want to remain in the park?" Henry eyed him over his cup, but wasn't surprised. The young man had more than one reason to stick close.

"Well, I wanted to spend time at the dig and, now, help you with the beast in the lake. Also," the scientist went on softly, "I want to be close to Laura. Sir, I'm crazy about your daughter. I've never felt this way about anyone. Ever."

"I thought so." Henry grinned for the first time in days, but behind it he was worried. "I would sure feel better if she and Phoebe were out of the park right now, though. It isn't safe. But the girl's independent like her mother. I know she won't leave unless I drag her out, especially now with you here," Henry predicted, his hand gathering the empty sugar packets up.

"Being her father, you know her better than I.

But I'll do my best to convince her to move out of the park until we know it's safe. Honest I will."

"Thanks. But you don't know my daughter, do you? She'll swear she can take care of herself. Just like my wife. Those kind of women don't believe in monsters unless they actually see them. And they won't run from something they don't believe in."

"Well, if they stick around here long enough, they'll see it, and believe it."

"That's what I'm afraid of."

Henry watched a gaggle of park visitors pay their tab. After today the visitors would be gone. He'd miss them. Never thought he'd feel that way, but he did. Never know what you had until it was gone.

"And you, Justin, you sure you want to stay here after what happened to those men? This isn't fun and games any more. We're in real danger. If you weren't such an authority on dinosaurs and their habits, I'd send you packing, as well."

"I know. But I'm staying. I'm frightened, but ambitious. To study and hunt a real dinosaur is an adventure of a lifetime. Something I can tell my grandkids about. Not to mention, get photographs of, write scientific articles on, and become famous for."

"If you live through it," Henry retorted cynically. "I have to get back to headquarters and meet up with my rangers. There's so much to do, moving the homeless camp and closing down the park."

"Oh, there's one more thing," Justin added after Henry had requested the breakfast bill. "My colleagues from John Day have arrived. They're at the dig site now, going crazy over the dinosaur bones. The group leader is Dr. Harris. He appears capable, his credentials are impeccable, but I know him, and, let me tell you, he's a fanatic. I couldn't get him to shut up or get out of the dirt for a second. We're going to have trouble with him. If he's that crazy about our dead specimens, heaven knows how he'll react to a live one."

Henry grunted. "So they're not going to listen when we tell them, for their own safety, they have to go?"

"No, they're not going to listen. Harris believes this fossil bed could be the scientific discovery of all time. The group is settling in near the fossil wall. Last time I looked there were ten scientists, three tents and a couple of RVs. More coming. The word's gone out."

"Damn," Henry swore as he slapped down some money on the table for his coffee. "Now I got them to worry about, as well, until I can chase them away."

"Good luck with that. Dr. Harris has high-up, influential friends. If he wants to stay, he'll stay."

"We'll see." Henry shrugged. "Right now I got to go. Catch you later." Brushing by the young man, he strode out the door.

He was going to have to talk to Sorrelson about the paleontologists, among other things. They couldn't be allowed to stay, especially so near to the lake. They'd be the creature's next meal–and there was no way they'd be able to cover up *that* story. Missing homeless were one thing, but missing or partially eaten high-up muckety-muck scientists were another.

Rushing to headquarters, Henry knew he had no authority over the John Day scientists. They could ask permission to stay from the Park Service and get it. But he was still going to try to run them off. It was too risky, them being on the lake's rim. The body count was too high already.

When he arrived at his office, Kiley informed him Sorrelson hadn't been reachable, his phone turned off; his secretary wasn't sure exactly where he was, but eventually, she'd promised, he'd be in touch.

Gillian reported Mrs. Morrison took the bad news about being relocated in stride, and the camp was on the move.

Henry and his men got to work, preparing to shut down the park.

CHAPTER 8

The family had spent the day on Phantom Ship Island, brought out early by a tour boat. They snuck off against park policy to explore the small island by themselves and time had slipped away.

They didn't see the ranger patrols stopping and boarding the other tour boats and they didn't know the park was being evacuated.

Instead, they spent the day scuttling across the island, searching for wild flowers in the nooks and crannies of the steep rocks and collecting unusual stones; they spread blankets and ate their picnic lunch with gusto, happy with the lovely summer day and the beauty of their surroundings. The sun burned their skin and sun-dried their hair, but they didn't care.

It was the family's first vacation in five years. They were having so much fun, laughing, chattering among themselves and snacking on the lodge's sandwiches and lukewarm cokes from the picnic basket, that they were totally unaware of the activity on shore.

Marcy, the youngest girl, didn't want to return to Cleetwood Cove when the tour boat was loading up to return. She'd fallen in love with the picturesque isle. Since it was her birthday, her father and mother agreed they'd stay behind on Phantom Ship and catch a later boat. They hadn't heard their park ranger saying earlier that all boats were to be off the lake by twilight. They didn't know there wouldn't be another boat docking at the Island that afternoon or for the foreseeable future and they were stranded.

The sun dipped into the horizon beyond the scrap of land covered in trees and wildflowers before they began to get worried. The spires of volcanic rock rose up from the island's base and looked ebony against the setting sun. It was getting cooler. The woman made the girls put on their sweaters as the mist heavily blanketed the surrounding water. They seemed to be the only people left out on the lake.

"I wonder where all the boats are. It's getting late," the woman voiced aloud when the night shadows danced in. She'd forgotten to bring their cell phones and now she regretted it.

Only the radio they'd brought along, playing an old Beatle's song, broke the peacefulness of the place.

"Maybe I should swim for help," her husband suggested, studying the mist on the darkening water. He was an associate vice-president at a New England brokerage firm. The youngest one they'd ever had. He wasn't a good swimmer and his wife knew it. He was prone to colds, too.

"The water's too chilly. You'd freeze. The ranger said no one swims in the lake unless they're polar bears."

The two of them laughed, trying to cover their growing uneasiness over coming nightfall, the spooky fog and their isolation.

After waiting another hour and seeing the full arrival of night, the man said softly, "Well, it looks like we might be spending the night here, girls. I wish I'd found us a safe cave or a hole or something to spend the night in, but I was so sure there'd be another boat. Now, without a flashlight, it's impossible to find or see anything. I should have come more prepared," he chided himself. "Gosh, it's dark out here in the wilderness."

His wife hugged him to show support as well as to get warm. The night was cold and all they had on were sweaters. They hadn't planned to spend the night. "It's all right, Jerry. How were we to know we'd be marooned here for the night? The park brochure said the tour boats ran between the Cove and the islands until eight o'clock. I don't understand why there hasn't been another boat."

Jerry nodded and pulled his girls tightly into their circle. Strange noises bellowed over the misty water and the lake churned, the sounds rising on the night wind as if it were crying.

"What is that?" his wife whispered in a trembling voice.

"I don't know," he whispered back.

"It's a water-spook," the youngest girl, Rebecca, murmured. At eight she had a vivid imagination having had read most of the R.L. Stine books for her age group. Too many, her father thought. "It's coming to get us!"

"Nonsense, Becky, there's no such thing as a–"

A horrendous shriek split the night air and none of the humans uttered another syllable.

Eight eyes stared out over the gloomy water, searching for bobbing lights or for any other sign of help coming. Blackness covered everything. Not a sliver of moonlight or a tiny ray of light reflected from anywhere.

"Let's move away from the lake, behind the rocks over there," the man proposed, not knowing what else to do.

They were almost to the rocks when something broke the water behind them and rose up swiftly. Something out of a nightmare, with a gargantuan head and gaping jaws filled with serrated teeth. The head lunged back and the hooked snout canted upwards.

At first they gawked in horror, struggling to see what was coming at them in the darkness. A limb with claws at the end swiped viciously downward, slashing the air. A snake-like tail lashed out and slammed against the ground at their feet. The island shook.

The four humans fled into the rocks, stumbling in the dark.

Not quick enough and not nearly fast enough.

The leviathan slid from the water; crawled onto the land. It moved swiftly for its huge size.

Malignant eyes fixed on them and the mouth yawned wide, closing in like a descending crane with teeth from the sky above as they tried to hide behind the rocks.

A child screamed. The woman grabbed the hand of one girl and the man grabbed the hand of the other.

If we can get to higher ground, the man thought frantically as they ran, *we might be able to escape.* But it was so dark, he kept running into trees; they kept falling over the rocks beneath their feet.

The monster moved faster, coming in for the kill. It smelled the scent of the creatures it craved. And it was hungry.

The man and the youngest girl found themselves falling through the air and into the cold water. They'd somehow crossed the island and had reached the lake again.

The creature dove into the frigid water behind them and the weight of its body hitting it caused such a suction that the two people were pulled down into the whirlpool. A wicked fin the length of its back the last thing seen as it, too, submerged.

The humans never resurfaced. The mist so thick it swallowed them all, beast and human alike.

An ear deafening roar filled the watery world and soon the beast was on land again, hunting for the two survivors it knew were there. With its night eyes and acute sense of smell, it didn't take long until it found them as they huddled, hiding, among the rocks.

Her daughter had fainted, and the woman lifted the small body into her arms and lurched for the rock spires in the center of the island. A protection from the monstrosity chasing them. If they could wedge deep enough between the stones and crouch low enough, they might be able to escape the creature's reach…then wait it out until morning and help arrived.

But as the woman cowered in the dark between the towering volcanic pinnacles, child now awake and weeping in her arms, the monster lumbered over the land like a bulldozer and came for them. Amazingly quick on short, powerful legs ending in wickedly clawed feet it rose above them, blacking out the sky it was a shadow panting and slobbering with hunger, flashing bloody teeth, whipping its tail through the air.

It'd found them.

No time to scream, the woman and child ran.

It found them again. They couldn't get away.

The beast had demon's eyes to be able to see so well in the dark.

Out of breath, her chest ready to explode, her legs rubber beneath the weight of her and her daughter, she scurried around a sharp spire, playing a deadly game of hide and seek. The child heavier than anything she'd ever had to carry. Run. Hide. It did no good. The creature reached out with its long neck and the mouth enveloped her and the girl.

The mist swirled around the shadows on the island, hiding the crime. The muffled screams didn't last long.

The monster, its hunger sated for a while, slid into the murky water and disappeared, heading towards the subterranean caves it called home. It was still young and needed a lot of sleep, just as it needed to feed often. It was always hungry and had discovered the perfect food source. Tiny, stick-like things that hopped about and made much noise; they were abundant, sweet and tasty–once they were caught. Oh, they could run, they could hide, but it could smell them a mile away, it was faster, and they didn't have a chance. Not a chance.

CHAPTER 9

"We've had reporters from as far away as St. Louis nosing around the paper, pressing to get the real story of why the park's been closed down and locked up tight in the middle of tourist season. Seems some of them don't buy that prediction of a major earthquake excuse you're giving out, not with all the other juicier rumors flying around," Ann told Henry days later as they sat on the porch swing.

He'd been off duty less than an hour and was still in uniform. Supper was simmering in the kitchen and bread baked in the oven. Ann had come home early from work with the urge to bake, which she often did when she was worried about something.

She'd stayed away from the park and their home for three days at his insistence, but as the days had gone by and the lake creature hadn't made any more appearances, she'd slowly begun sneaking back in to pick up more clothes, clean the house, or to make supper for him. The next thing Henry knew she was spending the night. She'd glacially informed him that morning she wasn't going back to Zeke's anymore. This was her home and this was where she planned to stay. Said she didn't believe the creature was a threat to them this far away from the lake. And she wanted to follow the *story of the century* up close because she suspected, sooner or later, the lake creature would be sighted again somewhere.

Henry, missing her, unsure she wasn't right about the distance being a deterrent, and lulled into a false sense of security because the creature hadn't been seen since the park had been emptied, was perhaps too easily persuaded. It was hard to believe in monsters when the normalcy of daily life intruded.

"Rumors have gotten that far, huh?" Henry shifted on the swing. Disquieted and restless all day, his sixth sense for trouble was simmering beneath his calm. Things were way too quiet.

Under the circumstances his apprehension wasn't a surprise. Dr. Harris, the head paleontologist in residence at the paleontological dig, had been dynamiting the underside of the rim. Henry could hear the ruckus even down here. It made him nervous. Shaking the hell out of the area surrounding the caldera, he was afraid it'd lure the creature from its watery lair.

He was shocked when he first learned Harris was using dynamite to dislodge the under layer of earth beneath the fossils. Justin had explained it was done all the time. Experts laid the explosives in selected places so the bones wouldn't be damaged. Paleontologists sometimes had to remove excess rock, or overburden, as it was called, from around the buried fossils and there was enough overburden in this case to warrant blasting. The scientists were anxious to get to the concentrated fossils. It still made too much noise.

"I think James Bradley is the one leaking information," Ann told him. "He's the brother of that woman who vanished with her family last week somewhere around the lake. He's been asking questions everywhere. Making trouble. He was on vacation with them, but was sightseeing elsewhere the day they all vanished. They were supposed to meet him for supper that last night at the lodge, but they never showed. He's been looking for them ever since."

"George brought me up to speed on that situation. Bradley was in to see him, too, when he filed the missing persons' report. Asked about these monster stories going around in the park. He swore he'd blow the whistle. Go on television, go to all the big newspapers if he had to. He's staying in Klamath Falls, won't go home, he swears, until he's found his sister and her family. Just what we need. It's been hard enough evacuating the park and keeping the curious out, especially since those scientists swarmed in and started their excavating and blabbing."

Ann was looking at him. "They come into town all the time to eat at the restaurants and buy supplies. And the word is spreading like wildfire they're probably unearthing the most significant dinosaur fossil bed ever found and what they're going to exhume will rock the world. Everyone in town is talking about it. Justin mentioned they're considering a press conference to let the world know of the find–in town, of course, because you won't let the press into the park."

Henry almost made another comment about that's where she should be–in town–but they'd been arguing about it for days and she'd worn him out on the subject. She reminded him every time she was a reporter and there was no way she was running out on the greatest story ever to hit Klamath Falls. Heaven help me, Henry thought, gazing at her, she *wants* to see the monster. She wants to take pictures of the damn thing.

She was like a child looking for buried treasure and she wasn't about to give up her dream of being a famous reporter, either.

Excluding the missing vacationers (and there was no proof they'd actually disappeared in the park…maybe they'd gone into town and something had happened there), there'd been no further trouble since they'd moved the homeless camp. No attacks. No sightings. Henry would have preferred to get everyone out of the park, no exceptions, but the homeless had nowhere to go. The investigation into the missing camp men hadn't uncovered anything new, except the mauled torso had been Morrison's and the leg, Black's. Jane Morrison identified both the shirt and the trouser material as having belonged to the missing men.

The coroner had reported an unknown large animal, a mountain lion or a bear, had killed and partially eaten the men. The pathologists were still debating that one. They were not going to admit that the teeth and claw marks had been made by something they'd never seen before. Medical men didn't acknowledge the unexplained, particularly if it would scare the locals.

And the dig scientists hadn't heard or seen anything out of the ordinary since their arrival, or so they'd assured Henry. When he'd gone out there that first day to warn them they could be in jeopardy and might consider, for safety purposes, to vacate the area for a while, they'd hid their skeptical smiles behind excitement over what they'd already exposed: bones never before seen by any scientist and certainly of an unknown hybrid species of Plesiosaur or mutant Kronosaurus…or even a totally new breed of dinosaur never heard of. They'd raved on and on about what it could be.

Justin had pegged Harris right. He was a fanatic. He lived and breathed dinosaur, wallowed in the prehistoric past like a pig in warm mud. He and the others with him had no interest or time for fanciful stories about skulking, live prehistoric predators that only a child would believe in. They were men of science. Dried prehistoric bones were all they knew.

In the beginning Henry tried to force them from the area, but Harris made a few phone calls and somehow got permission to stay. Henry hated it when his decisions were superseded, but didn't have the power to kick them out. Sorrelson had been upset enough over having to close the park; he'd ranted and raged and even now was working behind Henry's back to get it reopened. No one believed in the existence of the monster.

Only he and Justin had seen the creature that night, and lived, anyway. Only they knew it was dangerous. Even Ann wasn't taking the monster seriously, or she'd be hiding in Zeke's house in town, as far away from the lake as she could get.

There were also times when Henry questioned his own sanity for remaining in the park, except staying was his job. He could have asked for a transfer, but he loved Crater Lake. It was his home. And he'd never walked away from his duty before and wasn't about to now.

Yet it was more than duty that kept him there. The creature was a killer, and he had to protect the people left in the park. But along with Justin, he feared sooner or later, if the creature wanted food badly enough, it would again leave the water.

It was enough the park and the concessions and campgrounds within were closed; the tours canceled. The boats were tied up at the dock. This didn't make the people who worked and lived in the park happy. Most of them had moved into town. Henry hadn't the final authority to force everyone to leave, and some, in the dorms and the houses, hadn't, but he'd warned those who'd stayed behind that something was prowling the area and killing people. As if they'd listen.

The lake itself was different. Henry allowed no one around the water or to be on their boats at night at the dock…might as well ring the dinner bell for the beast. Of course, there were those hard-headed types who disobeyed that order, as well, for one reason or another. So he made his rangers check the boats each evening and chase off anyone they found.

The park was emptier than Henry had ever seen it. No visitors, no campers besides the homeless, which he was thinking of moving out of the park soon as it could be arranged; no giggling hikers or bird watchers. The souvenir shops and restaurants, except for one in the lodge, were closed down. It was depressing.

At first Laura had taken the baby and moved into Zeke's place. Henry had told her the truth about the predator in the lake. He wasn't sure she believed him.

Henry suspected Laura hadn't gone to Zeke's the night before, either. It was hard for her to drive back and forth every day to see Justin. The two had to be together. Love. Any other time, he'd have been overjoyed she'd found someone as decent as Justin, but it made him nervous to have her and his granddaughter in the park. Just more for him to worry about, that's all. But his daughter, as his wife, was a headstrong woman and did what she wanted. She kept sneaking back in and he couldn't babysit her and Ann every moment of the day.

Four days now and not a glimpse of the monster. Where the hell was it hiding? What was it eating? Henry worried about the answers as he sat on the porch with his wife and watched the sun go down.

"I've scheduled another meeting tomorrow morning at headquarters," he said. "So we can plan what to do next." Rangers had been scouring the area around the lake for days searching for signs of the renegade carnivore. So far nothing.

"Sorrelson, still off playing golf, called me today. He's furious I closed the park, but, so far away, he can't do much about it. Yet, anyway."

"You'll be in deep water when he gets back," Ann quipped.

"I know. But I'll face that problem when it comes. I'm responsible for people's lives and I'll fight him on reopening it, if he forces my hand. I'll threaten to go to the press. That'll shut him up quick enough."

"It probably would. Even if you wouldn't do it."

"I might. If I have to. Meanwhile Justin's been studying up on different dinosaur species' known habits. The information is pretty sketchy though. We don't know if this thing is related to a known species of any kind or a completely new one. No one's really seen the creature up close and survived to give us a detailed description and it was too dark to see much when Justin and I ran into it. Right now, we'll only guessing what it might be. Besides, known or unknown genus, not much is known about how a live dinosaur behaves. Only theories."

"Can I be at the meeting?"

"Can I keep you away?"

"No."

"Then you can be there," he replied begrudgingly. "Just keep a low profile."

"You mean lurk in the rear of the room and pretend I stumbled in by accident?"

"Very funny."

Henry heard a car and glanced up. Justin, Laura and Phoebe had pulled into the driveway.

"Company," Henry announced, forgetting about their difficulties. He could only be scared so many hours a day and at that moment he was tired of it.

"Ann, we have to convince Laura and the baby to go back to Zeke's. She shouldn't be staying here so much. I'm not sure it's safe. We need to talk to her again." The car door slammed and the three walked up.

"After supper, honey. I've missed them. The lake is so far away and no one's seen hide or hair of the dragon in a long time. It can't hurt to let the kids visit for a bit, can it?" she pleaded.

She'd begun calling the creature a dragon. Henry wasn't amused. Beneath it all, no matter what he'd said, she still didn't believe it existed. Like a lot of people.

Seeing the baby's smiling face, he surrendered. Ann was right, it couldn't hurt to let them stay for supper. They were a long ways from the lake.

They greeted their guests with plastered smiles on their faces.

"Hello, you three. Just in time for stew. There's plenty. Can I talk you into staying?" Ann opened her arms to a giggling Phoebe and the child climbed into them.

"Mom, you know I love your stew." Laura stole a glance at him, knowing how he felt about her being in the park. When he nodded in resignation, she accepted, "Sure, we'll stay for supper. You got homemade bread to go with it, too?"

"What do you think?" Ann hugged Phoebe tightly.

Phoebe held her arms out to him as he sat on the porch swing. He took the child and cuddled her as the swing gently swayed back and forth. Phoebe loved the swing.

The women went into the house to dish out supper and Justin plopped down on the top step of the porch below Henry and Phoebe.

"Justin, I thought you were going to talk to Laura about her staying at Zeke's? She and the baby are in danger here, you know that."

"I tried. Honestly." Justin silently crossed his heart. "No go. I keep sending her back to town but she keeps coming back. You're right; she is one mule-headed woman."

"You don't have to tell me about these Shore women," Henry groused, resting his chin on top of his granddaughter's silky head. Phoebe was already asleep in his lap.

"But I'll keep trying to get her back to Zeke's, Henry, I promise, after supper."

"Thanks."

"I was down by the lake today getting readings," the young man said quietly so he wouldn't wake Phoebe. "It seems as if your public excuse for closing down the park might turn out to be prophetic. My readings jive with what I've been told by John Day's. There is another earthquake coming. A big one, I'm afraid."

Henry contemplated the growing twilight around his home. He didn't have to respond to Justin's announcement. Both men knew it complicated things immensely.

"And," Justin tacked on, "I thought you'd like to know there're a couple of reporters camping on the west side of the lake. Hiding out. Waiting to get a look at our monster, I imagine. Get photos."

Henry ceased swinging. "Reporters?"

"Yep." Justin tilted his head to avoid the glare of the fading sun. "I'd bet ten bucks they are. They were taking videos of the lake and the surrounding area, jotting down notes, acting goofy. All the signs. They're reporters."

"How many were there?"

"Three. Could be more, but three were all I saw."

"Trouble." Henry released a deep breath. "Now it starts. I wonder how many more reporters and monster hunters will be slipping in if these get away with it? Waiting for the creature to show itself and if they're real lucky getting photographs of the thing gobbling down a person or two."

"Yeah, if they're not careful, it could be them. How did they find out?"

"Well, first there was Ann's newspaper story. Then I reckon they talked to the brother of that woman and her family who went missing around the lake or maybe to someone in the homeless camp. The scientists at the dig go into town all the time, too. And they talk. Rumors of the creature in the lake are everywhere, Ann says. Someone must have listened."

"Don't they realize, under the circumstances," Justin said, "they're at risk? Camping so close to the water. What happens if–"

"If it craves a midnight nibble and comes ashore?" Henry shook his head. They both knew what would happen. The sun was descending and night was coming. "I'd better take a hike down there right now before it gets dark, supper can wait, and escort them out of the park." Henry stood up with Phoebe sleeping in his arms. He carried her inside, and headed for his jeep.

Justin fell in behind. "I'm coming, too."

Henry shrugged. "Sure, I could use the back-up. Come on."

"I need to let Laura know I'm going."

"I already did," Henry explained as they got in his jeep. "Ann promised they'd save us stew. We shouldn't be gone long. I don't want to be anywhere near that lake after it gets dark."

He peered at the sky. "Two hours, possibly three before total nightfall." More than enough time to locate the trespassers and kick their butts out of the park.

Justin described where he'd seen the campers.

"I know the place," Henry admitted.

They drove back roads down to Cleetwood Cove, parked the jeep, and hiked the rest of the way. They heard the journalists long before they spied their camouflaged tents, tucked away behind some rocks, which blended in so well with the surroundings they couldn't easily be seen from the rim of the caldera.

Two men and a woman were sitting and chatting before a campfire, eating supper from tin cans.

They looked up as Henry and Justin approached.

"Oh, oh," the woman said, wiping her hands on her blue jeans. "The law's found us."

She was tall with sharp features, questioning eyes and a tough expression. Her dark hair was tied back in a ponytail. To Henry, she looked like a big city reporter. She didn't seem upset over their arrival. Smiling at them, and afterwards, reading their intent, her face went sullen and determined.

One of the men looked to be in his mid-thirties with curly hair and a broad face. He wore dress slacks and tucked-in white shirt. An expensive state-of-the-art Minolta camera with a zoom lens hung around his neck. They'd certainly come prepared, Henry thought.

The other man was young, had long hair, a bandana rakishly tied around his head, and a gold loop earring. Dressed in black, he was a modern day pirate. Probably a cub reporter, or a photographer, learning from the pros how to sneak in where they weren't supposed to be, break the law, get the story, win the prize.

Be something's supper.

"You folks aren't supposed to be here," Henry led off. "The park's officially closed." He stood there watching the three come to their feet, guilty looks spreading over their faces. The game was up. They'd been caught.

"Because of the coming earthquake, huh? Really worried about it, aren't you?" The woman's tone was sarcastic. "We heard it was something else entirely you're worried about."

Henry didn't rise to the bait. "What are you three doing out here?"

"We're reporters. I'm Selby Merriweather. This is David Gates and Earl Laurence." She put out a hand for Henry to shake.

He shook their hands one at a time. He couldn't treat them as criminals. They were doing their jobs, as he was. Being married to a newspaper woman had taught him that much. "What newspaper you with?"

The younger man replied, "*The National Inquirer.*"

Henry couldn't help himself from laughing. Ann was forever making jokes about the Inquirer. She and Zeke called it the biggest trash rag in the country, although both would have killed for a fraction of its circulation.

That laugh broke the ice. The three reporters invited Henry and Justin to have a cup of coffee. Discuss their unwanted eviction. See if they could talk him out of it.

Henry's eyes scanned the lake in the late afternoon light. It seemed strange not to see a boat on it; to see them, empty, moored silently at the dock in a line. To hear no human voices or laughter echoing along the caldera. The night mist was drifting in and settling across the water, the land and the trees.

He shivered. The lake was noiseless and serene at the moment; no sign of any dragons anywhere. There was time. The sun was bright yet in the skies, illuminating everything. The birds were singing and the breezes were cooling.

"Sure, we'll have a cup of coffee, and then you three will have to pack up and move on out of here. Before dark." Half the reason he accepted their offer was out of curiosity, half for his wife. Ann would be interested to know what they were up to…what they'd learned. What kind of a husband would he be if he didn't help Ann protect her biggest story ever?

"You know why we're here, don't you?" the

woman asked once Henry and Justin had settled down cross-legged on the ground across from them. They were handed cups of steaming liquid. Some of that fancy expensive coffee Ann liked so much.

"The fossils up on the rim, I'd guess." Henry smiled broadly, playing their game.

"No." The woman shook her head. "Oh, that's a good story, too. We've already sent it in to our editor. Headline's gonna run something like: NEW DEADLY SPECIES OF DINOSAURS FOUND BURIED ALIVE. No, it's the other story here that we're digging for." She grinned, the coffee cup poised in her hands as her arresting blue-colored eyes met Justin's. They glowed with an inner light. With flashy crimson nail polish on lily white hands, the woman made sure Justin saw there was no ring. She was flirting with the paleontologist.

"What other story?" Justin pretended not to notice and Henry was relieved to see he wasn't returning the young woman's attentions.

"Oh, you know…the monster in your lake here."

Henry could have lied, but couldn't bring himself to do that anymore, especially under the circumstances. This woman sensed, knew, something was in the lake, but they needed to understand how perilous the situation was. Sooner or later the creature would emerge and strike again. Only a matter of time.

Could be the truth would scare them off, save their lives, which was more important than keeping the lie alive. "It's true, everything you've heard," Henry confessed. "There is some sort of unidentified creature in the lake here." But he didn't say anything more. His loyalty to Ann and all. "That's why you're in danger. It's aggressive."

"I told you it wasn't the earthquake," the girl exclaimed to the older man. Her eyes lit up, and she moved closer to Henry. "Is it a dinosaur-like creature similar to the one in Loch Ness? A real monster?"

"We're not sure what it is. It's a wild marine animal, that's all, trying to survive." Just a half lie.

"The rumors are it's predatory and very large. That true, ranger?" the younger man questioned, standing up.

"Yes to both."

"Anyone seen it?"

Henry cocked his head at Justin who was staring at the placid lake with uneasy eyes. "We've seen it."

The girl whipped out a notebook and a pen. "Where? When? Can you describe it? When would be the best time for us to catch a glimpse of it?"

Henry shrugged eloquently, remembering his promise to Ann. "I'm not at liberty to go into that. And you three aren't sticking around to get a look at it. The evacuation is to protect people. You have to go. Now. As I said…you're in extreme danger."

The girl frowned, but her excitement didn't abate. She was going to be a hard sell.

"The park, especially the lake area, is closed to visitors. By being here you're breaking the law. I could fine you, and the fines can be stiff." Henry paused to stress what he was going to say next, aware that, finally, he'd seen doubt in their eyes.

"And I'm going to ask you not to release the story yet. Or, at least, don't pinpoint which lake the creature is in. I can't make you, but I'm asking you. For the safety of all the curious who'll come looking for it if you do. They'll sneak into the park just as you've done trying to see it, and maybe end up missing or hurt for their trouble. No matter what you think, it's not like Nessie. It's nothing to mess with. So take my advice and clear out. While you still have the chance. It likes the night, but it's been known to show itself in the late daylight hours." He wanted to add so badly, *And it's big, has lots of sharp teeth, is quick as the devil, and it's already killed many times. You won't know it's coming until it's got you. Most frightening, it seems to be highly intelligent.* But knew if he did they'd never leave. He'd recognized that obsessive gleam in the woman's eyes.

Her face a shade whiter, she started to say something, but stopped.

"So you see, it'd be foolishness to stay out here tonight. Making yourself a target." Henry finished his coffee and rose to his feet as the three reporters stared at him. Justin stood up beside him.

He'd shook them up. He could tell. Good. Maybe they'd go and stay gone.

"If this creature's so menacing, what is the Park Service doing about it?" The woman was on her feet, too.

The crickets and frogs were singing, accompanying the coming night. The sunlight appeared dustier, the mist heavier; its tendrils creeping around the humans' shoes like cats slinking along the ground. The sound of the water lapping at the rocks lulled.

"We're working on it. That's why we emptied the park. We haven't exactly decided how to handle the situation. Yet. But we will. We know what we're doing," Henry said, though he wasn't sure of that at all. He'd been fretting over what should be done with their unwanted leviathan since the deaths at the homeless camp. In the end, though, he feared it would be out of his hands. There were a lot of other people involved now.

"So we see," the older man articulated with a touch of irony. Henry couldn't tell if he'd convinced him they were in jeopardy if they remained, but the man jumped at every noise.

"It's been nice meeting you." Henry flashed him his sternest official look. "But I'm insisting you pack up and leave the park before it gets dark."

"Okay, Chief Ranger, we're going. For now we got what we needed here." The man, who acted as if he were in charge, raised an eyebrow at his silent comrades. His shoulders had fallen in stoic acceptance. He turned to his companions, "We'll regroup someplace safer, in town, at that Cafe we ate at last night? Rethink this assignment. I'll call Hodge. We'll interview some of the people who've left the park to flesh out the story. There's no guarantee, even if we camp out here for weeks that we'd see the creature anyway. Might as well leave."

He directed his next comment to Henry. "Thank you for coming all the way down here to warn us. I appreciate it. We'll pack up now and go. Won't take long."

"By nightfall," Henry repeated one last time. "Don't make me come back here again. I'll have to cite you for sure."

Henry and Justin walked away. Henry could hear the three arguing behind him. They'd better come to an agreement quickly and get packing. Another hour and night would fall.

"You think they'll really leave?" Justin asked from behind as they hiked up the trail towards the jeep.

"They'd better. I shook them up a little. Did you see the look on that young guy's face? He was scared, all right." Henry snickered. "We could have waited and escorted them to the gate, but I'm treating them like adults and trusting them. Now I hope to god they behave like adults and leave. Mistrustful as most reporters are, they probably think we'll be hiding in the bushes watching them until they do depart."

Justin's eyes flicked behind him at the three reporters, the woman smiled and waved, and then he hurried to catch up with Henry.

"I hope you're right about that and they don't slink back in somewhere else along the lake as soon as they think it's safe."

"Naw, I don't think they will. Not tonight, anyway. If they're smart, they'll want to discuss the situation before they do anything rash. They must realize there's a good reason we came all the way out here to chase them off. Or, at least, that's what I'm counting on.

"Now what they do tomorrow," Henry grinned, "that's another matter."

"You know, there's going to be more like them," Justin told him as they got into the jeep. "You can't stop the flood of publicity seekers with only a handful of rangers. The town's seething with gossip about the thing in the lake and the wall of bones. People can't resist paranormal mysteries and there's good money in lake monsters. They'll all be trying to get pictures of the American Loch Ness Monster."

"Appropriate name for it, I guess. But Nessie hasn't killed anyone, that's ever been reported anyway. Not like this creature. And I know there'll be more gawkers. I'll handle them as they come." He started the vehicle, but instead of going home, he maneuvered it along the narrow drive that wound its way along the top of the rim, and parked.

"I have to make another stop," he disclosed, getting out of the jeep.

"The dig, right?"

"You got it." He knew Justin had been there every day unearthing, packaging and tagging the fossil imprints for transport, but that the young man hadn't tempted fate by staying past dusk. He'd been there so much, and with Laura in the evenings, Henry had hardly seen him since their breakfast four days earlier, though, they'd talked by phone several times. "I have some bones to pick with Harris."

Justin's lips curved up a moment at Henry's pun.

"And, you want to warn them one more time about taking precautions, even if they don't believe in the lake creature?"

"Yeah, but fat good it'll do. As you pointed out, Justin, there's money in them bones. But they've been dynamiting too much. Dr. Harris promised it'd only last a day or two. Well, it's been three."

"Harris won't listen. He's dynamiting because he needs to, so he can uncover more fossils, quicker. He doesn't believe in our monster. He thinks we invented it to scare them away and keep this paleontological discovery to ourselves."

"What an idiot," growled Henry.

"Yes, but a brilliant, well-connected idiot."

They hiked down the rim's trail and entered a village of tents and RVs. Some of the scientists and their assistants were staying below at the lodge, but about a third were camping out around the excavation site so they could be close to and protect the place.

Henry spotted Dr. Harris. He was relaxing in a lawn chair in front of his RV, chatting with a couple of colleagues. A bottle of root beer balanced in one hand, a dog-eared notebook in the other. The man looked perplexed. His face was sunburned around his beard, across his high forehead and the bald spot on top of his head.

Henry also recognized Dr. Daniel Alonso, and Tony Bracco, Dr. Harris's assistants, from an earlier visit, but had no idea who the older gray-haired woman in the khaki top, shorts and wide-brimmed straw hat was. The woman stalked off as Henry and Justin arrived.

Dr. Harris shaded his eyes with a hand, smiling as they stood above him. He remembered him from his previous visits.

Working the dig together Justin had become friendly with Harris. After all, they were both respected paleontologists. There were only forty or so of them in the world in Justin and Harris's league, and most of them knew each other. Just like Justin, Dr. Harris had been all over the planet. China, Canada, England. Wherever they uncovered buried dinosaur fossils. But unlike Justin, who was amiably humble, Henry had found Harris to be an arrogant stuffed peacock.

"What's she mad about?" Henry inquired, indicating the retreating woman with a jab of his thumb.

"The new procedures." Dr. Harris closed the notebook in his lap. "The guards I've posted since your last visit and other safety precautions. She doesn't feel they're necessary and resents the intrusion into her privacy."

Dr. Harris' colleagues stood up after acknowledging their arrival and wandered away.

Dr. Harris motioned for him and Justin to have a seat beside him. They did.

"Better safe than dead, I always say." Henry stretched out his legs and took note of how low the sun was getting. He removed his hat and placed it in his lap.

"Well, in part I agree with you, and in respect for your concern, and for the well-being of my associates here, I'm insisting all but a few–to guard the dig, you understand–spend the nights at the lodge below, to be safe. They can work the dig during the day, but at twilight, I want them to leave. I was just getting ready to scoot them all out of here for the night."

The lodge wasn't much safer than the rim, but Henry let that slide. Surprised at the change of strategy, he inquired, "Has something happened?"

Justin listened, his expression troubled.

"Well, not exactly." Harris reneged on his denial when his eyes locked with the ranger's. "All right. Yes, something has. Nothing truly horrific, though. We've been hearing some mighty peculiar noises coming in off the lake at night. That's all. As you said, better safe than sorry."

"Noises, huh? Care to elaborate?"

"Oh, you're probably thinking it's that mysterious monster of yours," Dr. Harris' tone was somehow unsure, and without half the sarcasm that had been there days before. He made a reticent gesture with the hand holding the root beer.

"I'm sure it was just some normal park critter. Unhappy, perhaps, or in pain. But it's spooked some of my people, so I'm being cautious. A rabid bear or a rogue cougar could wreak untold damage on our expedition here."

Henry glowered at the man. He still believed he and Justin had invented (for whatever reason) the lake creature. "You could stop dynamiting." Henry snorted. "Maybe that'd shut up the lake creature. Could be it doesn't like that noise."

Justin hid his grin behind a hand.

"We have to break up the rock. It's the only way to get the fossils out." Dr. Harris raised his other hand, palm towards Henry. "But after tomorrow, no more dynamiting. We'll be finished for a while."

"Good," Henry said. Tomorrow was better than

next week, and not worth pulling rank over, but was it soon enough? He almost said something else to Harris, then thought better of it. The man was insufferable. He'd do what he wanted anyway. By the time Henry had permission to shut the dynamiting down it'd be tomorrow.

"What about the strange animal noises? Can you tell me anything more about them?"

Harris complied. "They began last night and continued on and off until early this morning. The best way I can describe them, they were a sort of a roaring sound. Maddeningly persistent and exceptionally loud. Amplified, no doubt, by the caldera's echoes. They were unusually unnatural sounds altogether. Quite extraordinary, in fact. I've never heard anything like them." His voice lowered, "It almost makes me believe in that lake monster of yours." He laughed.

Henry and Justin didn't.

"Of course, no offense to what you and Maltin here thought you saw in the lake last week. I'm not saying you're lying, Ranger Shore. I respect you and my fellow paleontologist. I'm merely saying that you couldn't have seen what you claim to have seen. It was the night and the fog inciting your imaginations. Who can hold credence that there's a live prehistoric creature paddling around in the water below us? Preposterous. Not that I'm saying I wouldn't love to see a real dinosaur myself. Don't get me wrong. What an astounding opportunity it would be. What a treasure. A live, breathing dinosaur!" Harris's eyes shone like any zealot's and gave Henry a dark glimpse into the man's mind.

At that moment he had a sinking feeling.

Harris was the type who'd want to capture the damn thing, cage it, probe and prod it. Run tests and try to clone it. Exactly what Henry would have wanted to do before he'd had the run in with it, and had seen those men's bloody body parts in the woods. Now Henry was sure such an anachronistic bloodthirsty creature couldn't coexist with them in their world. It'd be like trapping a malignant virus in a test tube and putting it on display, one if ever released could kill countless people. The risk wasn't worth it.

"Yeah, and wouldn't it be an astounding opportunity if the creature turned out to be a deadly predator dinosaur with uncanny intelligence that loved to hunt, kill and gobble up human beings and was extremely good at it? How would you fight such a creature?" Henry couldn't help but pose the scenario, to see how Harris would respond.

"Fight it?" Dr. Harris's voice shook. "If there truly was a *live* dinosaur in the lake, Ranger Shore, we couldn't hurt it. We'd have to capture it. Study it. It would be incredible to have a breathing one in captivity! Think of all the things we could learn."

Henry turned his head, rolling his eyes at the heavens. That'd be all they'd need, someone with political pull wanting to save the creature. Bag it alive. Put it in a cage somewhere on display like a cuddly panda bear. But then, Harris hadn't seen it or its handiwork. He'd sing a different tune if he ever came face to fang with it.

Dr. Harris' look of shock relaxed into a sly smile. "You almost had me going again, Ranger.

No, it's impossible. There are no live dinosaurs. They died off millions of years ago. It must be some other large animal making the ruckus and the lake's caldera, like I said, is distorting its cries. That's what it is."

He avoided Henry's gaze and Henry wondered what, exactly, the doctor wasn't admitting. That even he was afraid?

"And Justin," Harris spoke to his associate, "if you did see something out on the lake that night, well, surely it's all a grand hoax, a joke you've been subjected to, a humorous gag or something that some prankster is giggling over at this very moment. A live dinosaur, please!"

Henry was getting angry, but Justin sent him a smile, as if to say, *don't worry about what he says, we know the truth.* Let it lie.

Harris looked at the tents and the people bustling back and forth from the plots they were sectioning out of the earth. The wall of fossils, once fifteen feet tall in some places, was crumbling, being eaten away by digging tools. There were hunks of dirt, and white plaster bundles of packaged fossils ready for shipping, littering the ground.

"Someone," Harris was saying, eyes blazing, "perhaps, may even be trying to make us leave. As if we would abandon such a monumental paleontological find because we were frightened of monster rumors. Ha! This discovery is far too important. *Nothing* would make me pack this camp up and leave now, I promise you. Come here." Harris abruptly jumped out of his chair and headed for the fossil wall.

Henry and Justin followed.

The site didn't look the same as when Henry had first seen it. Cordoned off, it was dug up like a terraced farm around and through the hill that contained the fossils. There were fresh strips of dirt and rock stretching away in every direction. People knelt in the earth scraping gently around objects dirt-embedded and scooping bits and pieces of fossilized stone into crate boxes resting on the ground besides them.

Dr. Harris stood above his workers and directed his attention to Henry. "We'll gently chisel the ground away in pieces around the more delicate artifacts and ship the whole chunk back to John Day's, or to another University, for further examination and cataloging. There's already interest in this find all over the country. Ten universities have contacted us and offered support and financial backing for a part of the haul. I've never seen such interest before. These fossils are going to set the scientific world on its ear." The scientist's expression was jubilant.

A few of the workers waved as Dr. Harris ambled by with his guests, but most of them were too intent on beating the going light and didn't look up. There was a tangible enthusiasm among the workers, but Henry also sensed anxiety. Some of the diggers glanced too often at the setting sun, their lips drawn tight. The light was receding.

Their skittishness reminded Henry night was coming quickly; that he and Justin should return to the cabin. Ann and Laura would be worrying, and the thought of supper made his stomach growl.

Any other time Henry would have been overjoyed at Harris's personal tour of an active paleontological site and to see the scientists digging out the precious fossils with their own hands, but his mind was on other things.

It seemed strange he should fear the night. Something he'd always been so fond of, especially in the park, with its velvet calmness. The darkness brought out the night animals, brought rest to the land, and renewed the forest for another day. In the years since he'd come to live there, he'd grown to love taking night walks close by his cabin. Yet, shading his eyes at the falling sun, he was intensely aware of the ominous silence that had fallen over everything. Wasn't normal. Not a bird was squawking or a squirrel chattering. The rising wind was heavy with unspoken threats.

Dr. Harris, still lecturing, paused in front of a sea of lumpy white bundles laid out on the ground around his feet.

"The fossils we've found so far have been wrapped in cheesecloth and strips of burlap dipped in plaster, in preparation for shipping to their destinations," he explained, his tone full of reverence, as he spread his hands in the air above them. "From what we've dug out so far I believe we've only touched the surface. No saying what we'll discover on the lower levels."

To Henry the white bundles looked like Christmas presents or huge smooth white rocks. The dynamiting had uncovered many treasures.

Harris scrutinized the wall honeycombed with fantastic impressions. "There's an entire dinosaur in there. I feel it. The skull, too, I pray, and that's extremely rare. The world-wide Dinosaur Society, as well as every scientific journal in the world, will want an account. They'll be fighting to get the story."

Dr. Harris knelt down and dusted the last bits of dirt off a very large and well-preserved fossil which hadn't been packed for travel yet.

"My associates are certain we've unearthed an entirely new genus of dinosaur, Ranger Shore. Some of these bones are similar, but not quite like, the species of Nothosaur, which was a group of predatory marine reptiles that flourished in late Triassic times. More like a mutant Nothosaur; one we didn't know existed. Perhaps, the highest evolution of another branch of the species. An advanced creature that roamed the earth for only a brief span of time before the end of the dinosaurs came. That's why we've never heard of them."

He tapped the piece beneath his hand. "This specimen is from one of those missing links. In its day it was possibly a voracious predator…over forty feet in length, had a rear fin and clawed feet."

"Could it, also," Justin broke in, "have been more intelligent than its predecessors?"

"Intelligent? A Nothosaur offshoot? I doubt it. Theory goes none of the Nothosaur family was very bright." His face broke into a grin as he looked at the wall. "Most dinosaurs had tiny brains, you know that, Dr. Maltin. We've talked about it many times over the years."

Justin said nothing, but his frown showed skepticism.

Harris went on, not noticing Justin's reaction. "This whole section here is a concentrated graveyard of dinosaur parts. Some I recognize but many I don't. Complete skeletons might be hidden within it. We've found shell fragments and fossilized eggs." His feverish eyes gloated over the scenery and the freshly retrieved fossils and wrapped parcels. He wiped the sweat off his bald spot with one hand and sighed aloud with pleasure. "And if we exhume baby bones, too, that would be a monumental find."

"Herds of these beasts must have roamed this area eons ago," Justin interjected, "to have left such a huge fossil graveyard. I'm thinking a flash flood, an earthquake or a mud slide caught and killed them all at once and left their carcasses imprisoned here along the crater's rim."

"Herds?" Dr. Harris gave him a disdainful look. "Don't tell me you're one of those heretics who believe all that herd nonsense? Have I taught you nothing over the years? There's no evidence to substantiate that hypothesis. I've never accepted it."

"Yes, I recall us discussing it," Justin said, "but the new research supports the theory that most dinosaurs ran in herds; were very social animals, and possessed a higher level of intelligence than previously believed. They were warm-blooded and nurtured their young, as most mammals."

"Interesting hypotheses," snapped Harris, "though I'm not sure I'd go so far as to carve them in stone. There are as many schools of thought on the matter of what the dinosaurs were really like as there are scientists. You're aware of that, Dr.

Maltin. All we do know is that these dinosaurs died here. Some great catastrophic event trapped them in this hill for all time. I would accept it'd been an earthquake, or, as the Alvarez theory proposes, a huge meteor, or asteroid that hit the planet. Maybe this mass extermination occurred at the precise time the meteor fell. The impact changed the atmosphere, blanketing the earth in debris and dust and killed these creatures, as well as the other dinosaurs and most of the earth's plant life. Eventually, without their food source, the rest of the plant-eaters died off, and later, the carnivores, because their food sources were also gone. The plummeting temperatures underneath the umbrella of dust did the rest."

Dr. Harris then seemed to think of something else. "Dr. Maltin, don't tell me you believe your monster down in the lake might be an offshoot of one of these?" He pointed down at the fossils around them. "A mutant species of Nothosaur? But alive?"

Henry thought Harris was mocking the younger man. Justin didn't seem to get it.

"Exactly! Yes. But I disagree that the thing in the lake might be of the same species as these. It could be something entirely different. Something completely new."

"Surely you're not serious?"

"I am! You still don't believe we saw what we saw, do you?"

"Do I look crazy as well?" Harris shook his head.

The two men glared at each other. Henry hadn't

seen Justin angry before, but he was now.

"You've got a right to what you believe but so do I." Justin smoothed things over, his irritation dissolving as he inspected the lengthening shadows dogging their feet. "But I know what I saw. Experienced. I *know* there's something in the lake."

Dr. Harris just shook his head. "Been working too hard, Maltin. You need a rest."

"Well, thanks for the guided tour Dr. Harris." Henry wrapped up their visit. "But I strongly suggest you get everyone down to the lodge, if that's what you've decided, and it's time Justin and I get home for supper; my wife's been keeping it warm for us. It'll be dark real quick." Henry glanced down at the lake, his eyes scanning the water. They were too close.

"Don't you worry, Ranger, we can take care of ourselves. We're not cub scouts out here, you know."

"Goodnight, Dr. Harris," Henry said. *Good luck.*

Justin nodded his farewell, his eyes, too, on the lake.

In the blue twilight, they moved at a brisk pace along the trail towards the jeep.

Justin scurried after Henry, running to keep up. He barely made it into the seat before Henry shoved the car into drive and took off in a cloud of dust.

Henry's expression was grim. He didn't like leaving those people behind. He could have stayed and escorted them down to the lodge, but that would have been admitting he didn't trust them and Dr. Harris was offended enough the way it was. Henry couldn't babysit everyone. It was getting dark.

A revolver and a rifle was what Henry had with him and he didn't think that would stop the beast if it decided to show itself. He'd put a request in for heavier artillery, but he didn't know if he'd get it or not. Sorrelson didn't believe in the monster, either.

Halfway down the dirt road leading to the lodge they heard the screams in the distance, but it was hard to tell where they were coming from.

Henry slammed on the brakes. "Did you hear that?"

"Yes," Justin's voice was watery thin.

"Let's pray it isn't our hungry friend. We're not ready for him, yet. All I have on me is a pistol and a rifle."

They waited for more screams, so they could pinpoint the origin. The minutes ticked away as the light faded. Someone was shouting and then came the bellowing roar of something hideously inhuman–and from the roar's magnitude, something extremely large.

The unnerving call chilled the blood in Henry's veins, momentarily incapacitating him with terror. The experience didn't feel real, he kept waiting for the sounds to subside, so he could forget them. If they continued he'd have to do something and he didn't know what. His hands were sweating on the steering wheel.

The beast bellowed again.

"It's down by the lake." Justin swiveled in his seat to look behind them.

"The reporters," Henry mouthed in a flat tone. "My God, it's after the reporters."

Another shriek from the monster. Another

human cry.

Someone desperately needed help.

Henry wrenched the wheel, spinning the car around, and backtracked to where they'd last seen the reporters. Taking short cuts, he forced the jeep over rough terrain, threading the vehicle through trees and rocks; barely making it through a couple of tight places.

He drove as close as he could to the commotion, and when the jeep came to two boulders it couldn't squeeze through, he yanked out the keys, grabbed his rifle from the rear seat and handed Justin his pistol.

"Know how to use one of these?"

"Sure. I think. Just aim and pull the trigger?"

"That'll do. Take the safety off first, though."

Cursing the fading light and the trail that was practically gone, Henry hoofed the rest of the way on foot, with Justin reluctantly trailing behind him. The evening had cooled and the mist rising from the warmer water, a gray steam, made it difficult to see ahead even twenty feet.

He loped through the woods, along the lake's edge and toward the human cries, aware Justin, younger or not, was having a hard time keeping up.

"Using these weapons will be as useless as using sticks," Justin yelled breathlessly, "against a mad bear!"

"It's better than nothing," Henry yelled back, as he brushed aside the whipping limbs. The forest had become gloomy with barely a trace of residual light. Shadows were everywhere…ghosts waiting to ambush them.

"I hope you're a good shot!" Justin shouted.

"Expert."

"Then aim for the head or an eye if you can."

"I'll try."

The tents were smashed flat and wreckage littered the ground around them. There were no humans anywhere.

"They didn't leave quick enough, did they?" Justin breathed, short-winded from their run.

"No, I guess they didn't." Guilt hit him. "I should have handcuffed the three of them and taken them out."

"You didn't know the beast would strike so soon, Henry. It isn't your fault."

Along the caldera's rim where the incline to the water wasn't too steep, they heard a woman's screams.

Henry sprinted towards them. Justin hadn't abandoned him. He was panting along behind.

The woman was howling now.

Henry tripped over something. He looked down. By its shape and size, it was a video camcorder. Banged up, but still in one piece. They'd been trying to film the creature instead of running for their lives. *Stupid. Stupid.*

Henry kept moving.

Then it was there, hulking above them in the shadows. The only thing that saved them, Henry realized later, was its back was to them. It was busy.

"Damn, it has to be fifty feet tall," Justin croaked, most likely too shocked to be afraid yet as his eyes traveled up the creature's height.

Henry didn't understand why Justin was

speaking in a hoarse whisper. The monster was making so much noise; it'd never hear them, even if they'd been screeching at each other.

"Where's the woman?"

"Over there, hiding behind those boulders. See." Henry tapped Justin's head some to the right with his free hand until Justin's eyes focused on her. The woman, a frenzied shadow, was dodging between the rocks trying to escape.

What was left of the faint light allowed them to see the creature in silhouette only because of its size. But that was enough. With its short, but powerful arms, it was picking up boulders and throwing them out into the water, or knocking them aside as if they were made of paper-mache, working its way to the woman.

Dr. Harris is so wrong, Henry thought. The creature was anything but dim-witted, or slow. It moved like quicksilver for its size on strong legs. Its steps quaked the earth. Its strong-necked head tilted downward, its tail balanced on the ground to support its bulk. An eerie low-throated growling erupted from its massive chest. Its head was large for its body, and the neck wasn't nearly as long as Henry would have figured, yet its movements were graceful. The eyes, in the dark twilight, were beady hunks of obsidian glass.

Henry had never seen anything like the beast in any movie or book. Justin was correct, it must be a more highly evolved strain of one of the known species, or some completely new one. Where in the world had it come from?

Henry gulped, his throat so dry it'd closed up. It

was as if he'd been transported into one of those dinosaur horror movies he'd loved to watch as a kid. But this was real. That titan beast snarling ahead of them, chasing that poor woman, would kill and devour her if it could.

Henry and Justin chased the creature. It moved so fast.

"Where are the other reporters?" Henry growled aloud. A memory flickered behind his eyes: a mauled and half eaten body out in the woods beyond the homeless camp. A leg.

"Dead. The creature probably killed them," Justin hissed between roars." I can't imagine them deserting her if they were alive."

"I can't either." But Henry knew men did funny things when they were scared. They might be dead or they might be hiding somewhere. For their sakes, he hoped they were hiding or running.

The woman was screaming again. The creature had her trapped between the rocks, in a corner below a steep cliff she couldn't climb.

"Come on, Justin, if we're going to save her we've got to draw its attention away from her."

"How?"

"We'll edge closer and shoot it. Might not hurt it much, but maybe it'll distract it enough for her to get away."

"Shoot it? You've got to be kidding!"

"Does it sound like I'm kidding?"

"It'll come after us."

"Yep."

Justin grumbled something under his breath, as they scuttled in closer. Henry knew he was frightened, his body was shaking as if it were twenty below. But he wasn't a coward, he wasn't running away. He lifted the pistol and pulled the trigger.

Henry raised the rifle and also fired at the beast. Even in the dark, the monster was so huge it was hard to miss. The bullets bounced off as if they were made of rubber. Must be covered in plate-like scales or its hide was so thick the bullets couldn't penetrate, Henry thought, as he fired again and again.

Just as he'd feared, to fight the creature they'd have to have something with a lot more firepower.

"Good god! The bullets don't faze it." Justin screamed, as the monster swung its bulk around and roared down at them.

Rearing up on its hind quarters, the last of the day's light glinted off narrow, reptilian yellow eyes and glowed off bared, jagged teeth. The head was bigger than a man. A monstrous fin followed the curve of its back. Its arms tapered to webbed claws. As it swiped at them with one, Henry could hear the wind whistle from the power of the stroke. It drove them backwards.

Justin's teeth were clattering like castanets. Henry could hear him making the strangest whimpering sounds in between shots.

Yet instead of coming after them, the creature swiveled around to its cornered quarry and went in for the kill.

"I'll be damned," Henry gasped. "It's too smart to be drawn away from a sure thing."

"Aim for the head!" Justin yelped. "The eyes.

Stop it!"

Henry kept firing, but the beast cleverly hid its face, protecting its eyes from its attackers, and the bullets continued to bounce off. Nothing deterred the creature from getting to the woman.

"I have to get closer!" Henry shouted.

He yanked Justin along with him, hunching over as he ran, holding the rifle up high. "I just have two shots left, so we'll have to get around to the other side, if we're going to save her I have to make both shots count. It's got to have an Achilles' heel somewhere."

He had extra ammunition on him, but he didn't believe he'd have the time to reload the rifle before the creature would have the woman. He got positioned and got off his last two shots. He missed the eyes, it was moving too much. The creature was untouched.

Henry bent down, and with trembling fingers reloaded his rifle as quickly as he could.

It wasn't quick enough.

The monster scooped up the woman reporter.

It was over in seconds. One moment the woman was there in the beast's claws, and the next she was gone. Her final scream haunted the air.

Justin doubled over and retched.

Reloaded, and angry beyond reason, Henry scrambled in closer and, while the thing was busy, he got off as many shots to its head as he could. The bullets were like throwing pebbles. The creature was too swift for him. Henry found himself cursing at the thing, shaking his fist, an insane rage gripping him strong enough that it overrode the fear. He continued firing at the leathery skin until most of his bullets were gone. Useless, as well.

Justin, cognizant of their sudden danger now the woman was gone, had to drag him away while the monster was occupied, which wasn't for long.

The beast's head swung about and glittering eyes fixed on them, really seeing them for the first time. More food.

Facing them, it roared, its jaws yawning wide to reveal blood-stained teeth. That snapped Henry out of his defiant, senseless rage. Justin no longer had to pull at him to get him to leave.

"We got to get the hell out of here!" Justin yelled. "Now!"

They ran toward where they'd left the jeep, slipping in the dark over tree limbs and rocks.

It was a good thing Henry knew the area as well as he did or they wouldn't have gotten away at all.

They were almost at the vehicle when they heard the brute crashing behind them. Still hungry. *Hell, we're not going to be its dessert.*

"It's right behind us!" Justin yelled as Henry leaped into the jeep. The tires threw rocks as they raced off. Henry deliberated over switching the headlights on, and then did. The monster knew they were there. Its eyes must be keenly adapted to the darkness. No use trying to hide. Speed was the only advantage they'd have.

That brute could move.

Henry hadn't used his police academy Emergency-and-Evasive Driving experience for years but hadn't forgotten any of it. It returned easily, second nature. He drove the jeep harder than he'd ever done, dodging trees and boulders, spinning its wheels on the narrow pathway and ramming the accelerator to the floor.

An expert driver, he was familiar with the terrain, the trail; the woods. His car had great traction. Still, the monster was breathing down their necks. The route wasn't always clear and fragments of limbs and rocks rocketed everywhere as they hit them.

The jeep bucked like a wild horse, crashing through brush and sliding along the rocky path. Justin was holding on for dear life, praying. Out loud.

"I think we gave it the slip," Justin exhaled a while later with relief. Except for their heavy breathing, the crunch of the rolling tires on the ground, and the racing of the engine, there were no other sounds.

The snarling and booming footfalls behind them had ceased a ways back.

But Henry didn't stop. He didn't drive as crazily as before, but he didn't slow down much, either. It was too quiet.

He didn't trust the damn thing. It was up to something.

They raced through the night. All Henry could think about was getting Ann, Laura and Phoebe safely out of the park and away from the monster. He'd been a fool to think the creature would stay forever in or around the lake…a fool to allow his family to return.

No telling where the monster would go now. It traveled as easily on land as it did in the water. Now

Henry knew that for certain. He'd seen it. Could no longer deny it.

"I can't believe we got away," Justin breathed, slumped against the inside of the door. "Can't believe we're safe. In one piece. Alive. Sheesh, that was close. That poor woman."

"Yes." Henry felt so awful, he couldn't say anything more.

They heard a bellowing roar and looked up. The monster was looming above them in the night, ahead of them…right in the middle of the road. Waiting.

It bent down, claws reaching. Bloodied saliva churned in a yawning mouth full of wicked looking incisors and dripped down in its drool. A powerful stench of carnage hung about it.

Henry had a split second to evade the mouth. He wrenched the wheel savagely to the left and hurtled the jeep into the blackness of the nocturnal woods–into the unknown that could have been a tiny gully, or a steep cliff of rocks or an endless plummet into a chasm of empty air.

But any death would have been better than the monster's fangs and claws.

The jeep disappeared into the darkness amidst a screeching ruckus of twisting metal and breaking tree limbs. It flew through the air and before it rolled, Henry shouted at Justin, "*Jump!*"

Henry's body rolled down the steep hillside and landed in a bed of branches and leaves, enough to soften his fall. His fingers reached up and touched scratches that burned along his face. His shirt and pants were ripped, but he was fairly sure he hadn't broken anything; there was no howling pain anywhere in his bruised body. Just a general aching.

As he sat up, rubbing his side where something sharp had poked him, he heard Justin's moaning. Dizzy-headed, Henry crawled past the upside-down jeep toward the scientist. The jeep's tires spun in the silence.

"You okay?" Henry's voice was hushed. He didn't hear the monster anywhere, but wasn't taking any chances. It'd already proven smarter than they'd ever imagined. So much for Dr. Harris's dumb-dinosaur theory.

"Breathing," Justin answered. "I hit a tree coming down. I'm going to have a hell of a head bump and something inside my chest hurts. But, otherwise, I think I'm okay. And," he chuckled, relieving the tension, "imagine that? My glasses are still on my face, unbroken. You?"

"I'm going to be as sore as hell, scratched up like a cat post, but I'm in one piece, too."

"We're lucky. Someone's watching over us.

"Where is it?" he asked.

"Don't know," Henry whispered. "We went a good distance before we crashed. We left our nemesis up there somewhere." He waved a hand upwards in the darkness and prayed to god the beast wasn't looking for them. Without a car they wouldn't have a chance in hell to get away.

It was cold in the deep woods. A faint moon was rising to their left and provided just the tiniest bit of light to see by. Better than nothing. Henry had no idea where they were.

"That was close," Justin groaned. "I thought I

was dinosaur chow. I still hear those poor woman's screams echoing in my head and my heart's still doing a rain dance."

Henry struggled to his feet and carefully helped Justin to his. The boy could hardly stand.

"I had a cell phone in the car but there's no way I'm going to find it now," he said. "Darn thing rarely worked out here anyway, so no big loss. So we have to get to a telephone, and warn Ann and Laura to get out of the park, if we can't get them out ourselves. Alert those scientists at the dig. Ranger Headquarters is the closest telephone I can think of. I also had a flashlight in the jeep, darn it. We're going to have to hoof it in the dark. As silently as we can."

"We couldn't have used a flashlight anyway, Henry. Too risky. It'd be like sending out a beacon on us. We don't know where that bastard is."

"You got a good point there." Henry was standing beside Justin and reached out to steady him. "We need to be in stealth mode. No lights. No noise." He was listening to the woods. Shivering. "And my rifle bounced out somewhere on the flight down the hillside, too. It's gone. We're defenseless."

"As much good as it did us anyway. It didn't seem to affect the creature at all. Just made it madder." Justin swayed in the chilly air. Henry wondered if he was in shock or hurt worse than he was letting on. "I still have the pistol you gave me. Here." Justin handed him the gun and Henry slid it into the empty holster around his waist.

"Thanks. Are you really all right?"

"Sure," Justin sighed, "I'm fine. Just a tad shaky, that's all. Let's go."

They climbed in the direction they believed they'd come from. Feeling with their hands…using trees as railings…cursing the darkness. Wishing the moon would rise quicker and give more light.

They located a road and trudged in what Henry thought was the right direction for headquarters. Every step treading on eggshells because they weren't sure where the monster was, if it'd come after them again, or if it was rampaging at that moment where their loved ones were.

Panicked human cries shattered the night about a half hour later. They stopped to listen, trying to tell where the shouts were coming from.

"It's your friends at the dig," Henry declared with a horrible certainty. "They stayed too long."

"When it couldn't get us, it went after them."

"I have to see if I can help, it's my job, Justin, but I can send you in the right direction to get you to park headquarters. You tell them where I am and that I need reinforcements pronto. Tell them to bring the biggest guns we have. Can you do that for me?"

Not a hint of fear, not a word of excuse. The young man didn't hesitate. "I can."

"By the noise, if the dig is that way," Henry turned to his right, "then headquarters is that way." He pointed in another direction.

"On second thought, no," Justin blurted out. "I'm coming with you. I know them and I want to help. If I know Harris they'll have some sort of weapons we can use."

Henry didn't have to think about it. There wasn't time. "Okay. Let's go."

As exhausted and battered as they were they broke into a scrambling run, fighting through the trees in the direction of the shouting…and gunshots. It wasn't hard to locate the site.

Human cries mingled with the monster's roars as it thundered through the woods, its jaws snapping. And they heard other awful sounds long before they arrived.

They burst into what had once been a paleontological dig, but the only way they could tell that now was by the crushed tents and knocked-over shadowy RVs around them in the spreading moonlight. There were no lights. The scientists were gone, most likely scurrying or hiding for their lives–if they'd been lucky.

A steely stench of fresh blood clung to the place, it reeked of it, and Henry feared there'd be bodies or partial bodies strewn in the wreckage when daylight broke. The creature hadn't stopped to feast on its kills, perhaps still chasing some unlucky scientist or expecting to return later and finish its smorgasbord. It, too, was gone.

Henry and Justin stood in the middle of the destruction, until they heard the cries deeper in the woods and followed them. There were survivors and Henry was relieved; then appalled as he and Justin thrashed through the dark trees, the bedlam forever seeming somewhere just ahead of them, to their right, or to their left. Always somewhere else.

The human wails rose to a crescendo and dwindled into the night air. There was nothing the two men could do to save any of them. Henry felt helpless. It was a feeling he wasn't used to.

They found no one.

In time silence came.

Justin halted Henry's movement by restraining him. "It isn't going to do any good, us crashing through the woods like this in the dark. We're not going to find them. They've all scattered. They're hiding, dead, or trying to get to the lodge. We'll never find them in the dark without shouting. That's not such a hot idea. We don't know if the monster's moved on or not. Let's pray most of them escaped. And we need to get to headquarters, don't we?"

"We do," Henry agreed. "We have to get out of these woods and alert everyone to what's happened. I need to call Ann. We have to get to the lodge."

He had a terrifying image of the monster approaching the lodge or his cabin and tearing the roof off the buildings to get to the people huddled inside. He could barely dwell on it because it sickened him beyond words.

"Feels like we've been running for hours," Justin moaned. "To me everything looks the same out here. I sure hope you know where we are, Mr. Ranger, cause I'm lost."

The moon, higher in the sky, was brighter now as Henry peered around. "I think I do. Follow me."

"Okay. Lead on. I'm behind you."

They began walking, looking for a pathway or the road, each apprehensive the monster would show up again, hot on their trail.

It didn't. The night remained empty.

It was Justin who first spotted the headlights in

the distance on their left. They ran, yelling and waving their hands like madmen, forgetting their fear.

In minutes they'd flagged down a park service jeep with one of Henry's rangers in it and he drove them to headquarters. The ranger, Peter Thompson, said he'd heard screams on the night air from below while on normal rounds and came up to investigate. Taking a chance, he checked the paleontological dig, knowing people were there; had driven through the shambles, finding no one. He was on his way to report what he'd found when they'd flagged him down.

After Henry explained what had happened, the ranger stared strangely at him, but kept his mouth shut. Henry was his boss, and the man knew he wasn't a liar or a storyteller. Thompson had been briefed about the creature in the lake as all the rangers had been. Evidently, like a lot of others, he hadn't put much stock in the story, couldn't swallow the whole thing yet.

Boy, is he going to be surprised, Henry thought.

Thompson drove them to headquarters. Henry was amazed to discover it was only ten o'clock. It felt as if they'd been running in the woods half the night.

He didn't have to worry about being believed any longer, either, because the surviving dig scientists had trickled in with their accounts. Dr. Alonso and Tony Bracco were missing, presumed dead as well as many others. Dr. Harris was among the survivors and sat in a corner, mumbling and talking to himself, his head bowed. Henry walked over. The man gaped up at him when he was spoken to, answered questions, but was clearly in shock. That insane glint in his eyes was stronger than ever though. *Oops, that's got to mean trouble, somehow, sometime.* Henry finished talking to the man, offered his sympathy for his lost colleagues, and walked away.

He borrowed a car so he and Justin could drive to the cabin.

Against Ann and Laura's protests, he and Justin bundled the women out of the park immediately, taking them to Zeke's. They were given orders this time to stay away until it was safe again, whenever that'd be. Henry refused to listen to Ann's pleas about her duty to get the story for the newspaper. He told her about the woman reporter and her fate, sparing no details. She shut up after that and went along quietly.

Afterwards he and Justin returned to headquarters so he could fill out reports from what was left of Dr. Harris' people.

He put in a call to Sorrelson, who'd finally returned from vacation, brought him up to speed on what had been happening, and laid down the law.

"I'm evacuating all the remaining scientists," he firmly informed him, "people left at the lodge and anywhere else in the park. No one but me, my rangers and Justin are to remain in the park. No exceptions. Somehow we'll find a place in town for the homeless. Relocate them as well. It's too dangerous for any of them to stay here. Not now.

"And I'm establishing an ICS at Headquarters. We're going to assemble a team of specialists who'll help us track down this monster. We need professional help. I'm requesting the Forest Service send us the right people to deal with the situation." And he left no doubt in his boss's mind what he'd meant by the *right people*. People who could rid the park of the creature.

Sorrelson was angry, still disbelieving, but Henry didn't give him a choice to object.

"If this thing really exists…and if it's actually a living, breathing dinosaur…you can't hurt it," Sorrelson tried to dictate. "Dr. Harris has already put in calls to his influential political friends guaranteeing protection of the creature. He says it's a national monument. The eighth wonder of the world. Hell, he wants the park sectioned off as an off-limits protected game preserve to house the beast. Shut it down to the public. String eighty-foot electrical fences or something to keep it in–like that movie *Jurassic Park*, I suppose. As long as that thing's alive."

"That's not feasible," Henry snarled back. "The creature has already killed at least eleven people that we know of. That changes everything. It's proven it not only can come out of the lake to hunt, but can navigate the land as easily as water. Worst of all, it's highly *intelligent*. It can *think. Scheme*. It's diabolical. It'll never stay in the park if we take away its favorite food source, which is human, no matter how high you string a fence. It'll go hunting for them wherever it has to. I'm not even sure it wouldn't find a way to get through the barriers and run amok into the nearby towns if it gets hungry enough.

"Sorrelson, I've seen it in action. Believe me, as much as I hate to say it, it needs to be disposed of–put down–for the safety of humanity. It's too damn clever." Henry didn't utter a word about his other fear: If there was one creature living in the caldera, were there more?

"We could capture it and let someone else worry about it," his boss stated.

He would have loved to see Sorrelson on *that* expedition. But the Superintendent was not only his superior the man had no sense of humor whatsoever, so it was a thought not spoken.

"You mean like King Kong?" Henry scoffed. "And you recall what happened in that little tale, don't you?"

"That was a movie, Henry. Fiction."

"Well, this monster, whatever it is, isn't fiction. Good luck to any fool who tries to catch it. You haven't seen it. I wouldn't like to be the one lowering the net on its head, not with all those teeth, let me tell you. I think we just need to find a way to kill it."

"We don't want it hurt," Sorrelson reiterated sternly, "remember that."

"Sorry, sir, but too many people have died. I'll do what I have to do. Whichever way that falls. People's safety is more important than that creature."

Then he hung up and put in the call that would begin the creation of his ICS Team.

CHAPTER 10

Ex-FBI agent Dylan Greer sat straight in his chair, his eyes flint colored like his bushy eyebrows and thin mustache, and in striking contrast to his snow-white hair. Even though he'd been retired for two years, he still wore the dark suit and conservative tie and scribbled everything down in a small notebook. Yet he was nothing like any FBI agent Henry had ever met. He had an air of authority about him, a detached coolness that in the situation, struck Henry as unnatural. There was also something in the set of his jaw, his sardonic manner, which labeled him, more than anything, a rebel and a strong-minded man. A hint perhaps to why he left the agency to strike out on his own.

He'd been recommended, with high praise by someone Henry trusted, to be his second-in-command on the ICS Team. A man who could get things done, they'd said. A man with connections and old friends in the Bureau. A man with hidden talents. Only later would Henry recall that phrase and understand what they'd truly meant.

Unlike other federal agents Henry had known, Greer had long hair, even if it was combed straight back on his head. Must hairspray it like crazy to keep it so perfect, Henry mused as he ran his hand through his own shaggy mop before he could stop himself. The obsessive neatness of the retired FBI agent made him painfully aware of how he must appear, with his unruly hair, unshaven face and tattered, dirty clothes. He'd been awake all night bringing his team together, planning strategies, brooding over what he had to do, and hadn't taken time to change or clean up after his flight through the night woods.

Agent Greer's associate, who he insisted be included on the team because of his experience, couldn't have been more of an opposite. Scott Patterson, who'd served with Greer, was a pudgy man in an ill-fitting brown suit; taller than his friend, and the most fidgety, nervous-acting man Henry had ever met. His large hands couldn't seem to hold on to a pen for the life of him, nor could they stop tapping across things on the desk. Patterson had a broad, eager-to-please face, a crew-cut, and brown puppy-dog eyes that reminded Henry of an Irish Setter he'd had as a boy. That dog, lovable as he'd been, had been stupid. Henry hoped Patterson would turn out to be smarter. He needed good people on his team. People's lives could depend on it.

Henry lounged in his chair, across a table covered with Styrofoam cups and overflowing ashtrays, half-asleep, and observed the odd pair in action. He'd marveled at how quickly they'd arrived, barely hours after the phone calls. The Forest Service had made contact and flown them in. Since then he'd been briefing them on the situation.

Not that Greer or Patterson believed the story of a real live dinosaur, hungry and on the prowl in the park. They didn't, of course. Henry could tell by the incredulous glances between them as they asked their questions and wrote down the bizarre answers, shaking their heads all the while.

So far it was a joke to them. Henry couldn't wait until the first time they bumped into the park's giant predator. Wouldn't that leave them laughing.

More of his team were on their way. The Forest Service had called in an aquatic biologist, Jim Francis, and his partner, Mark Lassen, an oceanographer; both retired Navy, who were bringing a one-man sub to search the lake's depths for the creature if they needed to. Francis and Lassen would arrive sometime the following day.

Henry chose Justin as the team's paleontologist, though he suspected Harris would kill to get on it so he could try to protect the monster. Wouldn't do him any good. Henry wanted Justin.

So far Greer and Patterson were the first arrivals. Justin was having the ribs he was afraid he'd broken in their car crash checked out. One of the other rangers had taken him to the hospital in town for x-rays. And Henry had never left.

Outside the window the sun was rising. Another day. The world was still there. He was still there. But there were some who no longer were and it made him feel blessed, guilty and frightened.

Henry spotted his friend George chatting to another ranger by the door. He'd also picked him for his team, the best outdoorsman and tracker he knew. George caught Henry's eye and tipped his hat. Henry saluted back. As suited the occasion, George's expression was solemn.

Henry now had six men on his team. Those six plus his other four rangers could probably handle anything, including this monster predicament. Besides, ten men were all he was going to get and he was lucky to have them.

In the meantime, the creature had apparently crept back to its lair and the birds were singing in the blue skies. As had happened that night on the lake when Justin and he had first come into contact with the monster, the horror of the night before seemed an unreal nightmare. But Henry knew it wasn't and his mind kept replaying bits and pieces of it, a DVR stuck in reverse-replay, reverse-replay, over and over. Usually the same two worn spots to catch on: that woman reporter and her last seconds on earth when he'd been so desperate to save her, but couldn't, or when the creature surprised them in the middle of the road before their daring jeep flight into the velvet black woods. How had it gotten ahead of them so quickly?

He focused on the jeep, to keep from thinking about the monster's unexpected cunning. The vehicle was most likely totaled. It'd been in excellent shape for its age and paid for. He'd kept it immaculate. The insurance would never cover what it'd been worth to him. He consoled himself that they'd walked away from the crash without serious injuries; were both lucky to be alive and not in the creature's stomach. He was grateful for that.

Soon he'd take the others to the scenes of the crimes, the dig and the reporters' camp, to glean any clues from what was left. Henry didn't really want to go, but he was in charge and it was his job.

Dr. Harris would accompany them to the dig. It'd been his encampment and his people, after all. He'd been there when his comrades and friends had been mauled and eaten alive. Had seen their nemesis face to face and experienced its vicious destructiveness. According to him he'd escaped by the skin of his teeth. *More like the skin of his backside as he was running away.*

So how could Harris promote ensnaring and sheltering that monster? Anger boiled beneath Henry's skin. Harris had no idea what he was asking for. If Henry was any other sort of man, he'd step aside and let Harris and his sycophants have their way. But he couldn't. It was his park, his job, his very way of life at stake. And as sure as men and women had already died by the jaws of that flesh-eating carnivore, Henry knew attempting to capture the thing would only result in more carnage. No beast, no matter how rare, was worth the loss of so many human lives.

He shifted in his chair, grousing under his breath, as he answered Greer's endless questions. His body ached from the crash landing and his eyes burned from cigarette smoke and no sleep. Yet he didn't feel as bad as he should have. He was coasting on the adrenaline surge. It'd catch up to him sooner or later.

Greer was thorough and had a no-nonsense interrogation manner. Henry had to give him that. It was easy to see he was used to being in command. That could be a problem. Everyone on the team would be equals, with the power of the final decision resting with Henry.

Gazing over at Greer's stone face or Patterson's mocking eyes Henry wished he was home with Ann sleeping peacefully in their bed and none of this was happening.

But Ann and Laura were at Zeke's and he was here. So was the monster.

This was no time for daydreaming. He needed his wits about him, and the help of these men before him, to find and exterminate the park's little problem.

"You have any idea where your friend Godzilla might be now?" Patterson's question seemed amiable but Henry caught a whiff of thinly veiled contempt.

Henry smiled. Hadn't he called the beast that once himself, as if it was a joke? Patterson was a non-believer, not that he blamed him. In the beginning he hadn't believed, either.

"Not really. The Paleontologist on our team, Dr. Justin Maltin, speculates it might live somewhere down in the subterranean caves and tunnels below the lake. But that's only a theory."

"That it lives in the caves and tunnels below a long dead volcano? In a lake that has no other channels to another body of water, that you know of, anyway?"

"Caves and tunnels created thousands of years ago by lava flows. And, yes, no other outlets…that we know of."

"Oh, I see." Yet it didn't seem as if the man did. There was an annoying ridicule in his expression.

Henry had known a lot of law enforcement types in his career. They were good at procedures, details, investigations, and crime, but not much else. Most of them weren't open to the unnatural or the fantastic. Cardboard people with Mister Potato Head brains. Henry hoped Patterson and Greer wouldn't turn out to be of that breed. He needed men with open minds.

Or the creature would defeat them.

George Redcrow moseyed over and reported the park had been effectively emptied, except for them. Some of the park workers were still in the dormitories packing, and a few older residents who had nowhere else to go were still refusing to go. In the meantime, George had ordered the park's perimeters patrolled and guarded to keep reporters and other people out.

Once more Henry wished he had more help. The park was vast.

"Why do you think Godzilla is attacking and killing humans now?" Patterson questioned, watching Henry as if he were an outpatient from a psychiatric ward. "Why has it left the water?"

"I closed down the lake area when the first boats and their captains came up missing. Took away its food supply. It's hungry, so it comes out of the lake looking for more food. Maybe it's depleted the fish supply in its hunting ground, or the warming water has killed them off. I don't know. Now that we've evacuated the park, I'm afraid it's going to increase its hunting perimeters."

"Sounds as if there's no way to contain it, other than to seek it out and destroy it," Greer spoke up.

"Especially if it's developed a taste for human flesh."

Well, I'll be, Henry thought with mild surprise, *a man who gets right to the heart of the matter. Hmm, we're going to get along just fine, after all.*

"How long has this creature been giving you problems?" Greer asked.

"It began killing animals a few weeks ago and people soon after. But there were unofficial sightings of it going back to last year. In the water."

"And you didn't alert the authorities until just recently?" Greer's dark eyebrows rose, as he leaned towards Henry and gave him an intent stare.

"It never bothered anyone at first. Just swam around and minded its own business. Then a boat and its captain disappears one day, body never recovered, then another boat and another. Suddenly all hell breaks loose, and Godzilla, as your partner there has christened it, is chasing and taking bites of people all over the place. Obviously we're the tastiest thing on its food list right now and, for its growing size, the most filling. Easy to catch, too." Henry's smile was weary.

Greer didn't return the smile. Henry couldn't figure him out. In some ways, Greer reminded him of his friend, George. Unreadable.

Henry shut his eyes. Starving and exhausted, he craved a hot meal, a gallon of coffee and about twelve hours of sleep in a warm bed. It'd be easier to cope with everything if he'd gotten those things first. His mind was wrapped in cotton candy.

"I've talked to Professor Harris over there," Greer's voice was hypnotically soft. "He maintains the creature isn't all that smart and it was acting out of pure animal instinct, but you believe it's extremely clever, don't you? That it can actually think ahead and plan?"

Henry stared at Greer. "Before last night I might have agreed with the good Doctor Harris that the creature was merely a dumb, hungry beast…but not now. Not after the way it behaved. I was there. I saw it with my own eyes. It out-thought us and was always one step ahead. Unbelievable how smart it was. Now," Henry slid a sideways glance towards where Harris was holding court across the room, "that's *my* opinion, and I'm no dinosaur authority. I'm just an ex-cop and a forest ranger."

Henry stood up to his full six-four and bent over, bringing his hands to rest on the edges of the table as he looked down at Greer and Patterson. "All I know is that monstrous anachronism refused to be sidetracked by our bullets or distracted by the noise my friend, Justin, and I made, and ate that woman reporter right in front of us. To get at us it took a short-cut and got somewhere on the road in front of us. Was waiting for us. Trapped us. Now, I don't care what anyone else says, that's *smart.*"

Greer lifted his head, lowered his eyes, as if he were thinking something over, but didn't respond.

Henry had had enough of talk. They could sit and talk until the cows came home and it wouldn't change what had to be done.

"I've had a hell of a night. So before I fall asleep on my feet, Mr. Greer and Mr. Patterson, let's get a move on. I'll show you where the damage was done so you can see for yourself. Then I'm going to steal a break, get some food and some much needed rest before we do anything else. By then, the remainder of our team should be here."

"Okay." Greer shut his notebook, slid it into his suit coat's inside vest pocket next to the antique watch on a chain, and stood up, too. He came to Henry's shoulder. "I have a quick phone call to make first and I'll be with you. Then we'll do it."

Henry tipped his head and Greer marched away.

"Why did he come?" Henry asked Patterson. "He doesn't seem happy to be here."

"Well, let's say he has special talents. Over the years in the Bureau he acquired a reputation for the unusual cases. The unexplained spooky stuff, if you know what I mean." Patterson pursed his lips and refused to divulge anything else about his friend.

Greer *was* like George. Enigmatic. "You mean cases involving things like UFO's? That kind of stuff? Like Fox Mulder on the X-Files or on Fringe?" Henry voiced with a nervous grin.

"Sort of. He'll tell you about it when it's time. I can't speak for him. All I can tell you is he can see, accept things most people can't. He brings a different perspective to his cases."

Oh, great, Henry mulled tiredly, *I have a spook seer on my team.* No wonder Greer was ex-FBI. The Bureau frowned on people who could see things others couldn't. At least, Greer would be more open to believing in lake monsters than the normal man.

"I'll tell you another thing, Chief Ranger, if I had to choose one man to guard my back in any situation, I'd pick Greer. He's a remarkable individual. A quick thinker and cool under pressure.

You'll see."

It was all Patterson was able to say because Greer rejoined them and they accompanied Henry to the door.

Dr. Harris appeared out of nowhere, pale and frantic-eyed, and attached himself to the group like a parasite.

"I heard you're going up there. Of course I'm coming with you. I have to see what's left at the site, if any of the equipment can be salvaged. John Day wants a detailed account of what has been lost. Perhaps there are footprints we can get impressions of or some other proof of the dinosaur's existence lying about the campsite. The newspapers and scientific journals are crying for pictures. Any evidence at all."

Henry felt disgust. Harris didn't want to see if anyone had survived, were perhaps hiding, wounded, in the brush somewhere. He only wanted proof the dinosaur existed. The image of the reporter's camcorder plagued Henry. He'd have to retrieve it. No way, if he could help it, was Harris going to get his hands on that video and profit from those poor people's deaths.

Henry halted before the door, Greer and Patterson observing, and glared at Harris. He didn't like the man. He didn't like him at all. He seemed the mad professor, his clothes stained and rumpled, his face etched with a fanaticism that only made his wild eyes look wilder. What hair he had around the bald spot was going every which way like one of those troll doll's his daughter had loved so much as a kid.

Harris turned his attention to Patterson and Greer and was zealously attempting to convince them they mustn't hurt the creature, but capture and safeguard it for humanity.

"Yeah," Greer quipped with a perfectly straight face, "you can feed it with spare body parts and teach it to do cute tricks for the people. Until it breaks out of the cage and eats them." He slipped out the door without a glance back.

As Harris stood there with open mouth, Henry chuckled. The sarcasm had gone over the doctor's head. Zealots had one track minds and no sense of humor.

But in the end, Harris joined them. As Henry thought he should, if for no other reason than to remind the man how vicious the beast had been.

George was outside waiting behind the wheel of one of the park's four-wheel drive vehicles. The five of them crammed into it. Henry propped himself in the front with George, and fought to stay awake. In the rear, Harris rattled on endlessly about how fantastic discovering a live dinosaur was and all the plans he had for it. What the world would say when they learned of it. Saw it. Henry wanted to reach back and knock him on his troll head, or, at least, kick him. Must be lack of sleep, he told himself. He wasn't usually vindictive.

Henry had George drive them to the remnants of the reporter's camp first and he walked and talked the group through a brief scenario of what had occurred there the night before, his stomach queasy the whole time. But he wanted Redcrow and Greer to know everything. He recounted how Justin and he had vainly fought to save the woman reporter and described the way the monster had behaved. The blood stained rocks around them illustrated the horror. He couldn't let the others see him as weak and tried not to let the memories get to him. It wasn't easy.

The others spread out and began their investigation by stuffing bits and pieces of material and flesh into plastic bags. Henry tried not to look. He didn't want to look.

Then they visited what was left of the paleontological camp site.

They found no traces of anyone, dead or alive, though the men shouted for survivors to show themselves. No one responded. Trash skittered across the earth, bits and pieces of the place and the people that had once been there, but were no more. A section of a wrecked RV lay on its side, gleaming in the sunlight. The creature had demolished most of the tents and campers and there was twisted metal everywhere. Personal belongings were strewn along the ground as if a hurricane had vandalized the site. Empty soda cans stuck in the dirt. The meticulously plaster-packed bundles of fossils were smashed to flattened lumps of white powder and the neatly cultivated mound of bones was trampled.

Henry returned to the vehicle after the initial scouting, and slumped against the fender as his men combed what was left of the dig. Harris darted around like a maniac raving about the damage and the money it'd take to replace everything; how many fossils had been destroyed. Not a tear for his dead and missing comrades.

Henry's eyes took in the mess, heartsick. It looked worse in the daylight. The stench of blood and fear was a pall hanging over everything.

Patterson sent up a yell when he discovered the body.

Henry strode heavy-legged towards the shouting. He knew what the mutilated body would look like, so wasn't as shocked as the others when he saw the bloody corpse. Patterson's face had gone a funny shade, but Greer wasn't affected by the half-eaten carcass. Obviously, he'd seen mauled bodies before.

"You have any idea who this is…was?" Henry asked Harris.

Harris barely looked at the thing. "No idea at all. It's too mangled. Sorry. Could be Lawrence Sanders or Earl McCarthy. They're both missing. I'm not sure."

The entire time they dealt with wrapping up the body for later retrieval, Dr. Harris continued to avidly lobby for preservation of the monster. He drooled over every claw impression and every sign the monster had left behind, no matter how small.

As Patterson and Redcrow did some final scouting, Henry sat in the car, closed his eyelids and listened to the familiar and comfortable noises of the one place in the world where he'd been happy for the first time in his life since childhood. Now nothing would ever be the same. Not unless they got rid of the intruder.

"So what do you think, Ranger Shore? You believe the creature that chased you and your friend, demolished this place, and killed those people, will be back?" Greer had snuck up and was eying him through the car's window, his fingers caressing the chain to his watch. The notebook nowhere in sight. Henry took one look at the man's face and knew Greer felt as he did. Mass devastation, missing people, and mutilated dead bodies were not good.

"That's a foolish question, Greer."

Greer waited.

"Of course it's going to come back. It'll come for food," Henry snapped bluntly. "Like any predator that has no fear of its prey, or of anything." The sun shone in his eyes and he lifted a hand up to shade them. "The monster isn't out to get us, Greer. It isn't evil or anything like that. It's just hungry, that's all. And, like our cattle, it sees us as its food. Nothing more, nothing less."

"Except this predator isn't like anything you've ever come up against, is it, Shore? It's huge and it's crafty and it eats people. It enjoys it. That's what makes it so dangerous. You don't consider that evil? You don't believe there are entities in this world that are pure evil, do you?" Greer's tone had changed and it gave Henry a spooky feeling.

"Not really. I'm a realist, after all. In nature, nothing's truly evil. Predators hunt and feed on prey to survive. That's life."

"I think you're wrong. There is evil in the world. Yes, even in nature. The trick is recognizing it when you see it. Because the creatures touched with evil cannot be salvaged, they must be destroyed *at all costs*, no matter how unique or valuable they are."

Henry met the other man's eyes and wondered

exactly what he was trying to tell him. That animals could be evil and if they were they had to be killed? Strange belief.

"And we can't count on it to come out only at night anymore, can we?"

"No." Henry sighed. "It knows by now we can't hurt it. We don't scare it. It's learning new tricks. Coming out in the daytime, if it's hungry and desperate enough, could be the next one. Scavenging further afield, widening its territory. It's coming into its own. Growing bigger and smarter. We have to be prepared for that."

Henry's gaze swept past Greer's shoulders to the woods beyond.

"It could be out there watching us at this very moment," Greer spoke Henry's fears aloud. "A scary thought."

"Very. Especially if Godzilla's hungry again. We'd both make yummy appetizers."

Greer broke out a grin for the first time. So the man could smile. "Here's something else to be afraid of. As soon as it gets out that those newspaper reporters were eaten by a prehistoric beast, the Inquirer and every other gossip rag in the country will be sending out a flock more of them reporters to find out what really happened. They'll be sneaking in left and right like rats scenting fresh carrion. You said there were miles of back roads and paths into the park and that anyone, if they really wanted to, could get in."

"True. We don't have enough men to guard every back road."

"A battalion of armed men won't be able to

keep out the reporters and television crews we're going to have out here. It'll be a free-for-all. The beast will have plenty of fresh prey. So, the way I see it, we don't have much time to take care of this problem."

Henry leveled his eyes at the man framed in the sunlight.

"And we're wasting it," Greer finished.

"You know, you're right. We'll discuss this further at a later time."

Greer smiled again. "I'll be there."

"Are we about done here? I need to wash the stink of death off me and go into town, that's where my wife and daughter are. Then go home, get some food and rest."

"We're done, Shore. But I'd like to hang around a bit longer with Patterson and your ranger, Redcrow, to wrap up a few loose ends."

"Good. I'll send Redcrow back after he drops Dr. Harris and I off at headquarters. He'll drive you anywhere else you want to go."

"Thanks."

Henry's eyelids were as heavy as lead. The surrounding scenery appeared fuzzy and unreal. He kept hearing the monster's growl on the breezes. Boy, did he need sleep.

"Shore, I want you to know, I think you were a brave man, trying to help that woman reporter, whether you succeeded or not. It took courage. You must have been a damn fine police officer."

"Thanks, but I did what anyone would have done, or thought they would have done. Someone needed help and I tried to help, that's all. Only wish

I could have succeeded."

"You know, the Governor wants us to capture alive whatever is in the lake. If it is a prehistoric throwback, all the more reason not to harm it, he claims."

"You called the Governor?" Henry experienced a hint of irritation.

"No, Harris did, but I happened to be nearby and he put me on the phone after him, demanding I listen to what the Governor had to say."

Henry whispered an obscenity, his eyes stormy.

"The Governor wants us to take it alive. In fact, he insists."

"And how many more innocent people will we have to lose," Henry's voice was sharp, "before he changes his mind, I wonder?"

Greer shrugged his shoulders. "Myself, I've always thought most politicians are clueless. They have too much damn money, don't live in the real world and care more about publicity and what things look like than the people they're supposed to represent. Just my opinion, mind you."

"You're going to get along great with my wife, Ann. She feels the same way about politicians, politics and the government.

"And what did you say to the Governor?" Henry had to know.

"Not much. I stalled. I knew nothing about the situation at the time and I never make a decision on anything until I know what I've gotten myself into."

"And now?"

"Off the record, I say we find the thing and kill it, no matter what the Governor wants."

"I agree, wholeheartedly, but rifles and guns don't stop it and this creature isn't something we want to play games with. Justin Maltin, that paleontologist I mentioned before, might have an idea of what kind of weapons would affect it. Won't be small artillery, I'd wager."

"Well, when he figures out what weapons will kill it I'll make sure we acquire them. I have old friends at the Bureau who'll help us."

"Don't forget, we're going to need a mountain of luck, too, to find that thing before it kills again. Ask your friends at the Bureau where we can get some of that," Henry added. "But now, I want to see my wife and catch some sleep before I drop. Won't be of any use to anyone if I can't think straight or keep my eyes open."

"Can't help you with that luck, but I'll get back to work so you can do what you need to do," Greer said, smoothing his hair, which didn't look so neat any longer, off his forehead.

"I hope you know not to stay up here past dark?" Henry warned. "Not to be out in the woods at all after dark?"

"I know that. I'm no martyr."

"We'll meet at headquarters later tonight. I'll call you."

"I'll be waiting for it, Ranger Shore." Greer spun on his heels and rejoined the others.

Henry laid his head on the back of the seat, closed his eyes and didn't open them again, even when George slid behind the wheel and asked him where he wanted to go.

"To Zeke's first, my friend, to check up on Ann

and then home," Henry muttered and promptly fell asleep to dream the monster caught him and ate him–in one gulp.

CHAPTER 11

That evening Justin was waiting on Henry's porch swing when he returned from town and a stop at headquarters. He'd conferred with Greer and the team on their plans for the next morning when Lassen and Francis were due to arrive.

It was seven o'clock and twilight fingers were creeping down across the forest behind them. The park had a strangely alluring, primeval ambience with the whispering trees and empty sky, deserted as it was, not a park visitor in sight; the way it must have been eons ago before the forest had ever heard man's voice or cradled his footsteps. The park had become a fit stage for the dinosaur that reigned over it. Henry and George had lingered on their return trip longer than they'd intended. Driving slowly to his cabin over roads covered in shady trees, Henry's mind tried to make sense of things that didn't lend themselves to making sense, such as monsters and fighting them.

Sorrelson had left a message at headquarters. Henry hadn't had to guess what that message was, either. He knew before he read it. Sorrelson ordered him to capture the monster alive for delivery to the federal government, which was showing great interest in the creature for scientific purposes. Of course they would. Henry hadn't answered Sorrelson's summons as yet and wasn't about to. And since Sorrelson wouldn't show up in person as long as the monster was loose in the park, later Henry could plead ignorance saying he never got the message.

But he wasn't happy. Now he had Harris, the Governor and Sorrelson working against him. They wanted the damn beast alive. Hell, let them bring it in then, he'd griped to George, who'd sat silently listening to his friend.

George dropped him off at his doorstep, saying he'd pick him up again bright and early the next morning and transport him to headquarters, and Henry went to meet the man lounging on his porch.

"So the hospital didn't keep you, huh?"

"Nope, I didn't let them. They bandaged up my bruised, not broken, ribs," Justin lightly tapped his chest, "and I packed up and left."

"Good. We're going to need your expertise, so I'm relieved to see you're fit for duty." Henry settled on the porch swing beside him. He'd gotten a little sleep at Zeke's house, but it hadn't been enough, and his body and mind were still tired.

"You think I'm going to let a couple of sore ribs keep me away from the greatest event of the new millennium? No way."

Henry regarded the scratches on Justin's face and the bandage on the left side of his temple. "Looks like you've been in a scuffle."

"That I have." The young man grinned.

Henry had been lucky, too. He'd escaped their accident with just aching muscles and scrapes. He leaned against the swing, his sore back reminding him.

"I knew you'd come home sooner or later. So

I've been waiting."

"You were right. I could have stayed at the lodge, but what the heck, this place has all the comforts of home and it's probably safer than the lodge or headquarters anyway. I can get in quick enough if they need me."

Henry noticed how Justin flinched when the swing moved. "You sure you should have left that hospital?"

"I'm sure. Besides there were reporters nosing around at the nurse's desk. I don't know how, but they got word of something big happening out here. So I opted to leave while the leaving was good. I made sure I wasn't followed, either."

"Nothing's going to keep them out, I'm afraid. Harris has been blabbing about the monster to the whole world. He's probably waiting at the gate for the first tour group to arrive."

Justin snickered, scratching his cheek. "I can see him doing just that. Maybe putting up a billboard announcing: *This is the home of the famous Oregon lake dinosaur. The American Loch Ness Monster. Beware: Dinosaur may be hungry.*"

Henry found that amusing and chuckled softly. It sounded like Harris.

"Speaking of our dinosaur. You think we're safe here?" Justin asked. He was looking around as if he expected the creature to appear any second.

"Safer than if we were at the lake, not as safe as if we were a hundred miles away. But if the thing shows up I'm sure we'll hear it coming."

"No doubt."

"So keep your ears and eyes open."

"They are."

"You see Laura and Phoebe before you came out here?"

"I did. I've come from Zeke's. Saw them there. Must have just missed you. Ann said you'd been there all day eating and sleeping." Justin grinned again, his gold-rimmed glasses glinting in the tawny light, his hair wisping around his thin face. "Ann mentioned you'd gone in to headquarters, but you'd be here later on.

"You feel better now?" It was Justin's turn to ask.

"Somewhat better. I needed the sleep and the food. At least my brain doesn't feel like wet cotton anymore."

"I know what you mean. I caught some rest in the hospital. Woke up and realized I wasn't hurting that bad; that I'd rather be here where all the action was and where I can help. Your wife, bless her heart, fed me leftovers." Justin patted his stomach. "She's a sweet lady, your wife. Not to mention that Zeke, boy, can that old man talk your arm off." Justin shook his head but there was fondness in his voice.

"Zeke's got stories to tell, all right. Working on that small paper brought him into contact with some strange tales and stranger humanity."

"You know, your wife hates this arrangement even more than Laura…us here in the park and them in town."

"I know. Ann feels as if she's let me and the newspaper down, that she's run away. She takes being a reporter seriously and can't stand letting the greatest story of her career, as she tags it, slip through her fingers. But they're safer there. I can't be worrying about them every minute on top of everything else. It'd drive me nuts."

"I know it would. I recall how upset you were last night when you thought the monster was heading towards Rim Village and the cabin. I know how you felt because I felt the same fear for Laura and Phoebe's safety. But you're right, we need less to worry about, not more."

Ann had consented to stay put at Zeke's this time, but made him promise he'd keep her updated on everything and get pictures if he could. She wanted an exclusive. She'd shoved her camera at him when he'd left and expected him to keep it in his car, and use it. Yeah, fat chance. He'd have a lot more on his mind if a photo opportunity like that arrived than snapping a picture. He hadn't forgotten the reporters' camcorder. George had stumbled upon it on their expedition that morning, scuffed up and dirty, but the video inside intact. Henry made a mental note to save it for Ann, and if it had anything on it, maybe she'd forgive him for sending her away.

"Ann's worried about you," Justin said, wincing again as he shifted on the swing. "She bribed me with food and chocolate cake so I'd keep an eye on you. Though, I would think it'd be the other way around. I'm no Indiana Jones, that's for sure."

"Neither am I."

The two men sat there for a while as the gloom captured the sunlight, both lost in thought. Thinking about the night before. It was there between them, ghosts: the dead ones they hadn't been able to save.

"I didn't know those reporters long," Justin confessed, "though I felt sorry for them. But I'd gotten to know those people at the dig really well. I liked them; they were my colleagues, too. Some of them were friends. There's this empty hole here now." Justin's hand was on the space above his heart. "I can't seem to find any amazement or mercy for that dinosaur after last night.

"Do you happen to know if Dr. Alonso and Tony Bracco have been found yet? They were still missing when I'd left for the hospital."

"Sorry, they're still unaccounted for. My men searched the area around the dig this morning and no sign of them, and they haven't made it to the lodge or headquarters. We're still looking, in case they're alive."

"God," Justin lowered his face into his hand, "they were good men. Had families waiting for them. They didn't deserve to die like that. None of them did."

Henry would have loved to take a walk in the woods to clear his head. It usually helped. But, under the circumstances, that was impossible. He had to remain at the cabin. It had a basement. A better defense than climbing up a tree or firing off a pistol.

"Greer said he can get us any heavy artillery we need," he said to Justin. "All we have to do is put in an order. As our dinosaur expert, how big a gun do you think we'll need?"

"I've been thinking about that. You and Greer give me a list and what each weapon is capable of killing and I'll tell you if I think it'll do the trick."

"Sounds plausible to me. We'll do that."

"Sooner the better."

"Couldn't agree more."

The two were quiet for a while, listening to the sounds of the woods. From far off came the call of a hawk and behind them the limbs of the trees knocked against each other in the breeze. No dinosaur sounds.

"This might not be the perfect time to tell you, with all that's happened, people dying and all, but I have to. Now while I have the chance," Justin's voice had softened. "I want to marry Laura, when this is over. As soon as her divorce is final, that is."

Henry's mouth spread into a wide grin. Wait until he told Ann. "I thought so. You guys have been spending a great deal of time together. She's happier than I've ever seen her, and Phoebe adores you, too."

"Well, how do you feel about getting me as a son-in-law? I'm more than aware your daughter recently got out of an abusive relationship and I know it's awfully soon, but I love her. I really do." There was hesitation in the younger man's words and the eyes behind the glasses were closely observing him.

He gently patted Justin on the back, not wanting to jar the boy's ribs. "I say welcome to the family, young man. I heartily approve. You're going to make a fine son-in-law. Especially after that weasel, Chad. There's no comparison."

"She deserves better than me, truthfully, but I'll be the best husband I can be. I promise. She's younger than me, but sensitive, smart. She has great potential if she'd put her mind to it. She could be, do anything. She's one in a million."

There, that self-modesty again.

"Yes she is, though I'm prejudiced, being her father." It seemed odd, in the midst of the horror to receive such happy news. And Justin's excitement touched him. Finally his Laura would have a chance at happiness–if he could keep Justin alive.

"Oh, Ann will be ecstatic. She's been hoping you two would fall in love and get married from the beginning. You know that, don't you?"

Justin smiled. "That was fairly obvious. Laura and I never minded. You see, I knew Laura was the one the moment I met her that first night at supper. Funny thing was, I never believed in all that nonsense, love at first sight, until I met her. Never had much time for relationships or love to be honest. I've always been too busy working, making something out of myself."

His voice was serious as he said, "Too busy running away from my past."

So Ann had been right about that, too. The boy *was* hiding something.

"You got skeletons in your closet?"

"Sort of. Family problems. I've been wanting to tell you about it for a long time, since family is so important to you and Ann."

"Trying to prove something to someone, huh?"

Justin met his sharp gaze. "I'm that transparent?"

"To Ann you were."

"You've got an insightful wife."

"Not telling me anything I don't know. She thought you were running away from something or someone. And while we're on the subject, who were you trying to prove something to anyway?"

Justin didn't answer immediately. Then in one breath, "My father. Nothing I ever did was right. He hated me. I mean hated. I never knew why, he'd never tell me, but he did."

"Oh." The pieces fell into place. Henry had had the same uneasy childhood and father. Nothing had ever pleased his, either. No matter what he'd done, it'd never been enough. Henry had spent half of his life trying to make his old man proud, until the old man had died.

"Where's your father now?" Henry asked.

"I'm not sure. I haven't spoken or seen him or my mother in over ten years, not even a phone call, since I ran away from home at seventeen."

"That's a long time to stay away from your family, son. Don't you think your parents have been worried sick about you? Wondering how you're doing or if you're alive or dead?"

"Yes, a decade is a long time." Justin stared off into the dark forest. Night had fully fallen. His shoulders slumped in that certain way Henry had come to recognize. "I know what I must have put them both through, too. My mother loved me, even if my father didn't."

"Your father probably loved you, too. Probably just couldn't show it." Henry remembered the bad times they'd had with Laura. What would he and Ann have done if their daughter had disappeared during that time and never come back? It would have broken their hearts.

"I don't think my father loved me. I don't think he knows how to love." Justin paused thoughtfully. "He only loved money and what it could buy. Power it could bring. He worked constantly; was rarely home and when he was, we fought. I was supposed to do what he wanted me to do, not what I wanted. He expected me to become a lawyer! I'd rather be a trash collector.

"The way he was, the way our lives were, drove my mother into depression and she took a lot of prescription pills. She wasn't there for me most of the time, either. She'd given up her life, you see, for him and there was never time for her in his. She lived in this fantasy world. And there wasn't any room in it for anyone else. I can look back now and understand how lonely she must have been, how lonely I was. It underscored everything I did."

Classic story. Henry had heard it many times when he'd been a cop. Uncaring, absent father and a pill, or other drug, addicted mother. "You were an only child, weren't you?"

"I was an only spoiled-brat, stubborn-minded child. I wanted to get through to them in some way, hurt them. Running away was the ultimate punishment. I was immature. Cruel. Foolish. I never understood they had problems of their own and couldn't see mine. As soon as I could, I got out. Changed my name so they couldn't track me. Justin's my real name, but not Maltin. It's Stockdale. I had it changed legally when I turned eighteen. After months of drifting and acting like a bum, I got tired of my aimless life. I guess I'd already started growing up.

"I got a job, my GED, and later secured grants and put myself through college. I made something out of myself, what I wanted to be, and did it on my own. At first, to get back at them, but later, for myself.

"I've never gone home since. Afraid they'd shut the door in my face if I did. Lately, I've been thinking about them and about maybe calling them to start with."

"What's changed now?"

"I don't know." Justin was tapping the swing arm with his fingers. "I've grown up. Being here, meeting you and Ann, Laura and Phoebe and seeing what a good family could be like.

"And there is what's happened the last couple weeks…the creature…the killings…it's made me see how fragile and short life can be. Death, whether we want to face it or not, is around every corner. We need people to love and be loved by, we need friends, family. Not someday, but now, for we might not have tomorrow." He released a held-in breath.

"It's strange," Justin said, "but I realized, after all these years, I'd become my father. All work and nothing else. I never reached out to anyone. Until now. Now I have Laura and Phoebe. I'm learning the responsibility of love and I suspect, perhaps, it wasn't entirely my father's fault. I wasn't exactly a lovable kid. Heck, as a teenager I was horrid. I wish I could get back those years. Wish I had my family. Wish I had the guts to call them."

"Well," Henry proposed, "if you can't manage

that first phone call why don't you send your father and mother a letter? That's a start. If you know where they are."

"Oh, I know where they are. They live in the same town, same house, but my father's not in politics anymore. He's got a regular nine to five job. I also learned they've been looking for me since I left, and I have a younger sister, Mary, who's eight years old now." He rubbed his eyes. "Both revelations shocked me." He shook his head slowly. "The time I've wasted. But I'm scared to death to see them. What will they think of me after all these years? Do they hate me? Will they even want me to be part of the family again?"

Henry didn't know what to say to him, so he said something he'd wanted to say since they'd escaped the creature the night before. "They'll be proud of you, Justin, as I was last night. As terrified as you were, you were brave. Didn't lose your head. They've got quite a son. A PHD and a hero, too. What more could parents want?"

Justin mumbled something and swung his head away. Then said, "I was too scared to do anything else but what I did. Did it without thinking. I couldn't leave you to face that monster alone."

"You're just being humble. You were courageous, is what you were. I want to thank you for sticking with me."

"You're welcome." Justin stopped talking as a plane flew overhead and shattered the silence of the evening.

There was a sudden noise behind them somewhere in the woods and Justin jerked around to look. "Did you hear that?"

"No. What did it sound like?"

"I don't know. Something moving among the trees."

They were silent for a while, anxiously listening. No further suspicious sounds came. Only the usual night's chatterings.

"I guess it's okay," Henry concluded. "The monster isn't coming for us. Not yet anyway."

"You talked to your superintendent yet? Told him we're not going to take the creature alive?"

"Not yet," he hesitated, his irritation showing, "Harris and all of them are insane if they believe we can bag it, tag it and take it home like some cuddly overgrown koala bear."

"What about his powerful politician friends?"

"Too bad. I don't take orders from the Governor or his friends. I have to do what's best for my park and my people."

"Ah, but you don't know what a plum for Harris's career it'd be if he could bring the beast in alive. It'd make him famous. Wealthy. Two things he craves above all else. And I'm sure his politician friends think he'd then donate a fair share of that wealth to their reelection funds."

"It isn't going to happen," Henry said. "Too many people have already died. We can't fool around any longer. It's either us or that monster."

"Men like Harris don't care how many lives are lost. Human beings are nothing compared to a live prehistoric specimen."

"Not to me. Humans trump monsters every time. Besides, that creature is too damn intelligent.

It won't be easy to kill, much less capture. It has to die. End of debate."

"I never thought I'd say I'd agree to that before. But I can't stop thinking of those victims last night. That woman reporter. One moment she's flirting with me and the next she's dead. I've never seen anyone die like that." His body shuddered, his eyes appraising the darkness, a grim curve on his lips. "So…just how are you planning on killing the monster?"

"In my life, I've done my share of hunting. Spent weekends with my friend, Redcrow, out in the back woods. He's taught me so much. He's tracked large animals and brought down mountain lions and grizzly bears or so he says. And there're other hunters on our team. This beast, after all, is nothing more than an animal. Clever as it is. It can be put down with the right weapons."

"If it lives beneath the lake how are we going to find it?"

"That's where Jim Francis and Mark Lassen come in. We'll have access to their aquatic biologist friends, and their submersible craft tomorrow."

"Oh, Lord," Justin blurted out. "Those things are nothing but claw-sized tin cans. Has this plan been thought out?"

"Yes, that could be a draw back. I never thought of it that way. A tin can," Henry repeated. "But it beats going down in wet suits. We'd have no protection at all in them except, perhaps, spear guns. Though, Lassen and Francis claim their Deep Rover, that's what they call it, is the swiftest craft around and it can out maneuver or out run anything in the water. Anything."

"Or so they say."

"It's going to be a dangerous hunt, Justin, no matter which way we approach it. But we have to find the beast before we can destroy it, don't we?"

"If it doesn't find us first."

A little bit later, Henry said, "Justin, there's no sense in you going back to your cabin alone tonight. Not with that monster on the loose. You can bunk here. Got a spare room. And up in the hallway closet, top shelf, I have books on military weaponry; we can take a look at them."

"Sounds good to me. To tell you the truth, I really didn't look forward to traipsing back to that cabin through the woods alone anyway. With Laura and Phoebe in town, it'd be too empty. Not to mention, our nemesis could be anywhere. Wouldn't want to bump into it in the dark."

"No you wouldn't."

The two of them went in to look at the weapon books.

As outside the forest suddenly hushed for the night.

***

Ann inspected the cluttered newspaper room. Jeff had fled hours ago and Zeke was in the storage area putting away supplies. She could hear him singing, off-key, as usual. With no husband to hurry home to she'd stayed late to finish her articles and to keep Zeke company.

She didn't need to be anywhere until eight. That was when Laura had her GED classes at the high school and she'd babysit Phoebe. So, in that sense, being in town was convenient. She didn't mind babysitting. She was proud her daughter was following through on her promise to get her high school diploma.

Ann wrapped up what she was working on, her mind far away with Henry and with the park's newest inhabitant. She'd sell her soul to have that story with pictures. But overriding that desire was the prayer her husband and Justin would emerge from the situation unscathed. Safe.

Outside the dusty windows the sun hung low in the sky, embedded in fleecy clouds and the breath-taking colors of an Oregon sunset. The town around her was lighting up like twinkling lights on a Christmas tree.

Staying with Zeke was hard. Oh, not because Zeke wasn't a sweetheart, he was. He loved having her and the girls there and spoiled them to death. He'd been lonely a long time and loved the company. Going to a lot of trouble, he'd fixed up two of the upstairs rooms. And he insisted on cooking for them, trying different kinds of exotic dishes he thought they'd enjoy. And he wasn't all that bad of a cook. It was nice to have someone else doing the cooking, besides her. It was like a holiday.

But she missed Henry and her home. She didn't like living in town, snuggled in between a row of houses, with all the town noises. She missed the woods and the animals behind their cabin. Henry's daily telephone calls didn't make her feel less lonely, only more. Her body ached for his strong arms to be wrapped around her, for his cold feet to tickle her in bed. They hadn't been separated like this, nights, since his police force days.

She switched off and covered her computer, then turned off the desk lamp.

Zeke was behind her. "Ready to call it a night?" He had his jacket and her sweater hanging on his arm, her purse in his hand.

She stood up, her middle-aged muscles protesting. "More than ready." She took the purse. Her boss, always the gentleman, helped her put on the sweater.

Zeke knew about the trouble in the park. She'd confessed everything. He'd been astonished, then worried as she'd disclosed the complete story. Worried because so many people were missing or dead. She asked him not to print the story yet and he'd consented saying he understood. Though it was the kind of spectacular feature that could have saved the ailing newspaper, Zeke wouldn't jeopardize people's lives. He knew the story would only send curious people running to the park, where they'd be in danger, too.

But he couldn't wait until he could run it and talked about it constantly. What perspective to write it from, how to lay it and the photos out on the front page to gain the most effect, how long they could ride on the series.

Ann stood on the dusk-darkened sidewalk and watched Zeke lock the door. They strolled through town past the shops on the way to his house, a tall rambling structure that cried for fresh paint and tons of work. Not that it was ever going to see either.

"Ann, been meaning to tell you something, but

I've been a coward, I guess."

She paused in front of a book store, slid a sideways glance at him, a sense of sadness settling, a heavy shawl, upon her shoulders. She knew what he was going to say and didn't want to hear it. He'd been subdued all day.

"After next week I'm shutting down the newspaper. I can't make payroll anymore. Can't pay the rent, the electric bill. I've gone through most of my personal savings and, well, now I have to admit defeat. Throw in the towel. I'm real sorry. I know how hard you've worked to keep it going. You've loved it nearly as much as I have," his voice was choked.

Ann didn't know what to say. She wanted to cry, but that'd only make it harder for Zeke, who looked as if he felt bad enough. "I'm sorry." She touched his hand sympathetically. "Really sorry."

They continued walking in sad, draggy steps.

The paper had been Zeke's life for so long, it was inconceivable to think of him being anywhere else but in that building down the street working on the following week's edition.

"What are you going to do now?"

"Well, I imagine I'll retire. I should have long ago. My son wants me to come live with him in Los Angeles. Says I can work part time on the paper there."

Ann was surprised. Zeke had lived his whole life in Klamath Falls and sworn he'd never leave, except in a box. But, times, as well as people, do change. "Are you going to?"

The old man seemed to be taking in the last of

the sunset, drinking in the misty pastel colors and the distant border of the park's woods with hungry eyes. "Nope, I could never live anywhere else but here. But I think I'll go up and spend the remainder of the summer with them. Get to know my son, my grandchild, a little better. It's the right thing to do. Haven't seen any of them in a couple of years. Always too busy. Now I'll have the time, I guess."

Ann didn't know what to say. She was experiencing guilt in the pit of her stomach. That dinosaur in the lake story would have saved the paper, could still save the paper. If only it was safe to print it. If only.

"How about you? What will you do," he could barely get the words out, "once the paper closes down?"

She smiled. "Get another job, I suppose. Unlike you, I'm too young to retire." Her and Laura both would be looking for new jobs. Even Henry, if he couldn't get rid of that interloper in the park. "Besides, we can't afford to live without my paycheck."

"Sorry, Ann," he repeated spiritlessly. "I sure tried to keep it all going. But the rising costs and the declining circulations finally did me in."

"Ah, don't think you have to explain anything to me. Worry about me. I know, better than anyone, how hard you've worked. I'll do fine." She patted his back in a daughterly fashion.

"Oh, I know you will. You have Henry, Laura and Phoebe. You're so lucky." The man's face, in the fading light, seemed to crumple. "None of this would bother me so if Ethel was still alive. We'd had such plans for retirement. Together. We were going to see America in a R.V. Now I'll go see Los Angeles. Alone."

He looked at her over his shoulder. "Don't ever take your Henry for granted. Life has a way of dealing us unexpected blows when we least expect them. I thought I'd have Ethel forever. We'd be old together. Die together. I miss her so much. It's lonely in the world without the one you love."

They were in front of Zeke's house and she gave him a quick hug. Over the years, he'd become like a father to her. So she wasn't just losing a job. She was losing a mentor and a cherished friend.

They went in.

Breaded pork steaks, corn, and mashed potatoes were on the table waiting for them. Since Zeke had made supper the night before, Laura was paying him back. Her daughter, baby in her arms, was smiling as they sat down to eat.

"What's up?" Ann asked.

"I got a job today. In town."

"Good for you," she congratulated her daughter. "How about Phoebe?"

Laura sat down with the child, sleepy-eyed, in her lap. They'd already eaten. "That's what I want to talk to you about. The job is at Freddy's Diner. Night shift. Ten until six in the morning. So I can still take the G.E.D. classes at night. I thought, well, I'd hoped that as long as we were staying here at Zeke's you might watch Phoebe for me. She'd be sleeping, and you'd be here sleeping anyway, too."

Ann gazed at her granddaughter. Phoebe was a good child. She went to bed at eight and usually slept the night through. And Laura, like her, was only filling the time they found on their hands with the men camped out in the park waiting for their monster to show up again. Then again Laura needed a job. One thing Ann could say about her daughter, she wasn't lazy.

"All right." Ann nodded. "As long as I'm here. Just don't count on it forever. I'll be moving back home any day now."

Laura gave her mother an understanding look. They missed their men. "Well, who knows, my plans might be drastically changing after that." Laura offered a secretive smile, and wouldn't say anything else. But it was easy to see she was in love and she had a secret. It showed.

"Freddy's?" Zeke huffed after a bite of mashed potatoes. "Does he know who your mother is, who she works for?" Freddy was the one who'd cooked the contaminated chicken for the Spring Fest.

"Sure he does." Laura's eyes sparkled. "Don't worry, you two, he's not holding a grudge anymore for that article the newspaper did on the bad chicken." Laura waved her hand. "He claims he got over that a long time ago."

"Good," Ann said. "We never meant to hurt him or his business. We published the facts. The truth, nothing more. That weekend his bad chicken just happened to be news."

"Oh, he knows. He told me to tell both of you you can start coming back for lunch again any time. No hard feelings. In fact, he thanks you for making him aware of the bad meat. He changed his meat supplier and he's more careful now."

Zeke and Ann exchanged subdued looks. When working, Freddy's had been one of their favorite lunch places, but without the newspaper, there'd be no lunches to go to.

They ate supper and talked about everything, except the newspaper. Laura went to her classes. Ann and Zeke cleaned the kitchen. Afterwards Zeke, despondent from the events of the day, went up to sleep. Ann played with her granddaughter until it was time to tuck her into bed.

Afterwards she tried to call Henry's cell phone, but the park, in certain areas, had terrible reception and the call didn't go through. All she'd gotten was cut off. Then she tried their cabin. If he was there, which he should be, she should have been able to reach him. No answer.

As she was waiting, she thought about what closing the newspaper would mean to Zeke, her, the town. She couldn't let that happen. Not if she could change it. She remembered how the paper's circulation jumped after the fossil story had come out. Zeke had told her if they'd just had had access to updates on the dig site (which they hadn't), or another story, a series of them, as good as that one, the paper would have made it. *Would have made it.*

Ann had been a journalist most of her working life. It was everything she'd ever dreamed of, except winning a Pulitzer. Yet how could she save the best little newspaper she'd ever worked on and help the old man who'd come to mean so much to her?

Only one way. She had to get that story. She *needed* pictures of that dinosaur. But how was she going to steal into the park and get them without blowing the whistle on the cover-up or breaking her solemn promise to her husband?

No way…unless…if she got the pictures and wrote the story anyway, but didn't say where the exact location, or the lake, was. Kept it secret. There were many lakes in the area covered by the newspaper. All she had to do was make sure none of the background was recognizable as Crater Lake or the park land. Hard, but not impossible. Generic pictures with the monster in them. That'd work.

She'd have Henry to contend with. Oh, well, she smiled in the dim living room, the telephone in her hand, she didn't have to tell him now, did she? And once it was done, the story printed, well, what could he do about it then?

Nothing.

The phone was finally picked up on the other end and she spent the next twenty-minutes talking with her husband. It was comforting to hear his voice. To know he and Justin were okay. She made sure the questions she asked about the park and the creature sounded innocent. Which wasn't hard to do. Henry was so trusting. Then she went to bed.

Making that decision to sneak into the park had taken everything out of her.

CHAPTER 12

Aquatic biologists Jim Francis, and his partner, Mark Lassen, had been piloting the gray one-man submersible called the Deep Rover for many years. They'd used it most often in the oceans, exploring sunken ships, searching for antiquities and lost treasure, but they'd also taken it into deep lakes to recover bodies or evidence that would have been impossible to retrieve any other way.

They'd logged in over fifty rescue missions. Last year they'd been responsible for freeing eight men who'd been trapped in a crippled submarine near the Florida Keys. They'd had to make eight trips, taking turns piloting, and pick up one man at a time; squeeze him in. They'd been in the area, nearby, when the emergency had happened and they'd agreed to help. There hadn't been time to wait for a larger rescue vessel before the submarine's life-support systems would have given out. All eight servicemen were alive today because they'd gone down and gotten them.

They were proud of what they did, and were good at it. They enjoyed their wandering life, the excitement, and the good pay. They were professionals.

They often teamed up with police departments or local authorities when their services were needed. But this was only the second time they'd been called in by the National Park Service to be part of an ICS Team. Not much call for a submersible in most parks.

The Deep Rover's pressurized hull was a sphere, with one viewing port in front and three more ahead and down, at various angles. The external propulsion machinery and other equipment were aft, blocking any possible viewports in the astern direction. In length the sub was twenty-two feet, with fifteen of it consisting of a conical attachment on the seven foot sphere that terminated in a swiveling propeller used for propulsion and steering. The one drawback was the Deep Rover was meant to carry only one person comfortably at a time. He and Lassen took turns going down. The other stayed on shore and monitored the mission with the latest in photographic technology which not only allowed the voyage to be followed up close, but provided a permanent record.

He and Lassen had arrived at Park Headquarters soon after dawn two mornings earlier and the ICS Team leader, Chief Ranger Shore, had given them permission to enter Crater Lake and begin the search. And they did.

They'd been cruising the darkness of the lake's deepest regions, 1,032 feet beneath the surface, for the last two days. Looking for some huge lake creature everyone said was down there somewhere. A giant animal that reportedly had so far had killed eleven people or more…if any of that tall tale could be believed. But, what the heck, Francis thought as he maneuvered the craft through the underwater world, they were getting highly paid for the wild goose chase, so why not? It was an interesting job. Like treasure hunting…except for something alive. It'd do until he and Lassen could find something better.

Not that he was able to see much of anything beneath the water with the sub's high-powered floodlights and cameras. It was murky in the lake.

And as of yet…he'd seen nothing unusual. No water monster. Small or large. Nada.

He'd had orders from Ranger Shore not only to locate the so-called creature, if possible, but to get an idea of where it might be hiding or nesting. But he wasn't to engage the animal in any way and was not to stick around under any circumstances if the creature saw him. He'd been warned to keep as much distance between them as he could because it was hostile to humans.

"Of course it's *hostile* to humans, if it attacks, kills and eats them, for God's sake," Mark Lassen had pointed out. "According to Ranger Shore this isn't the Cookie Monster we're going after, Jim. And, to be truthful, if any of this stuff we've been told about the creature is true, I'm not sure we should even be out here."

In fact, the whole assignment had disturbed Lassen so much he hadn't wanted to accept it in the first place, but Francis had over ruled him, saying humorously, "Most potential water monsters, imaginary or not, like Nessie, are shy creatures. They don't want to be on the nightly news or have their pictures taken. They flee, avoid, humanity. I don't see how this creature could be as dangerous as they say. Something else must have taken those people or killed them. Don't worry so." Not that either of them had ever gotten close to any so-called water monster before. Oh, they'd spotted a fin once of some unusual sea inhabitant off the coast of Florida. Another time they'd seen a big blur on their sonar in a deep loch in Sweden. Nothing had been real. Nothing they could have proven existed with concrete evidence. Most "monsters" turned out to be an exceedingly large fish, shark, octopus or whale.

Francis didn't believe in monsters and viewed each of these hunting expeditions as jokes, although well-paying ones. But Lassen wanted to believe and actually found this particular case intriguing mainly because a ranger and a paleontologist both claimed to have seen the water beast up close. In the flesh. Seen it kill someone.

But Ranger Shore was concerned about the body count; afraid their submersible would be the creature's next target. Francis had to reassure him that the Deep Rover could out-maneuver or outrun anything in the water. "No matter how fast the animal is," he said, "we're faster. The Deep Rover's too big to eat. Too tough to tear open. She's equipped with outside television cameras, so we can see everything around us, and she has mechanical arms capable of picking up a dime on the lake's floor. There's a direct radio link-up to home base that can be set up on any boat or dock, keeping the sub in touch with the shore no matter where she is. She's indestructible.

"The only thing our sub is missing is weapons, but we don't need them. Besides her speed and agility, when the Deep Rover sits immobile on an ocean or lake floor, her color makes her nearly invisible. Most marine creatures we come into contact with think she's a big rock.

"So, you see, all things considered, we're safe when we're in the Rover. Take my word for it."

Ranger Shore, his face grim, hadn't been convinced. "I know you think you'll be safe in your submersible, but let me make this clear. I'm giving you strict instructions not to hang around if you find yourselves in the beast's path. No matter how much you'll want to gawk. It's damn big, damn fast and incredibly sneaky, as unbelievable as that sounds. So don't. I'm not as sure the beast won't recognize your sub for what it is and go after it." Francis knew the ranger had had second thoughts about calling them in, but it'd been the only way of finding the creature's home. It'd be too risky to send a diving team down.

"For an animal that'd be genius level thinking," Francis had mocked.

Ranger Shore had replied with a solemn frown. "Then you don't know this animal. It can *think*. Strategize. Don't underestimate it, is all I'm saying."

Funny thing was, Francis had later mulled over what the man, who didn't come across as nuts in any other way, had said. Maltin, the paleontologist, hadn't seemed crazy either. Just leery and a little frightened. Their astounding account of their earlier run-ins with the creature and the other rangers' healthy caution had made Lassen uneasy; but had made Francis want to search for it even more.

So here they were.

And the Deep Rover dove, hunting for something that probably didn't exist.

It was when Lassen was in the sub, third day down, that the cave lair was discovered.

***

The Rover's headlights skimmed across patches of yellow and orange bacteria that Francis, who waited with Ranger Shore, Dr. Harris and Maltin, Greer and Patterson on a boat at Cleetwood Dock and who was in constant radio and visual contact with it, claimed lived on minerals rather than photosynthetic products of sunlight. He loved to lecture to anyone who'd listen about his field of expertise. The screen showed them everything Lassen was seeing below.

"These particular bacteria are everywhere down here," Lassen voiced over the sub's radio, aware Francis wasn't the only one listening. "They're real pretty."

Lassen seemed delighted at the variety of plant life he was seeing.

"They're growing in puffy masses. Some as large as fifty feet across. They resemble loose mattress stuffing. So weird looking. I'd love to touch them. Wonder if they're soft or hard. Hmm."

"That type?" Francis said. "Probably soft like mushrooms." He laughed. Always amazed at how childlike Lassen could be when it came to what lived on the water's floor.

Francis, short and wizened, looked older than his fifty years, and liked to dress in shades of gray. Casual wear. Bulky sweaters and Dockers. His hair of the same color was tied in a ponytail; he often wore a cowboy hat and was considered an eccentric individual who kept to himself. Best at what he did, he knew oceans and lakes and the creatures that lived in them.

Lassen could have been his brother, most people said, they looked that much alike, except Lassen had no ponytail and was taller than Francis. He wore his hair medium length and shaggy; had pale blue eyes like ice. He enjoyed people and was the more sociable of the two.

Lassen was the mechanical expert. He kept the Deep Rover running safe. He was also the married one of the two, having a wife and two chubby kids waiting for him in Vancouver, while Francis was a lifelong bachelor. Yet they were staunch friends and had been for over ten years, as long as they'd been partners.

The day before, Francis had piloted the sub along the lake's bottom and discovered what the paleontologist, Maltin, had previously discovered, that the water was being heated by subterranean volcanic eruptions. He'd also told him they'd done the necessary tests, had recorded the results and found the water was nearly eighty-five degrees along the crater floor, although the deep-water temperature of the lake was supposed to average somewhere around fifty-five degrees. Francis had been disturbed, but intrigued by the temperature aberration.

His search had also found radon, the radioactive decay product of radium, at levels nearly two thousand times higher than at the lake's upper levels, and unusually large amounts of the light element helium-3, a component of the hot viscous rock called magma that flowed upwards from the mantle beneath the earth's crust.

"There are also signs there's been extensive earthquake activity, perhaps going way back to prehistoric times, down there. Astonishing," Francis had exclaimed the day before.

"Still is earthquake activity," Henry had commented.

Francis thought about the earthquakes as the engines of the submersible purred through the radio and it picked up speed to cut through the cloudy water.

Through the sub's mechanical eyes the men watched above as the Deep Rover passed rocky basins which resembled small volcano craters. These, like the ones Francis had seen the day before, were filled with dense water rich in salts that appeared vividly blue in the bright headlights and contrasted sharply with the gloom of the surrounding water.

"Wow," Lassen remarked from below. "See these spires of silicate rocks on the cameras up there? Some of them must be thirty feet tall." He was referring to the pointed spires rising around him from the bed of the lake like a stone garden. "They're similar to those black smokers we found along the upwelling heat sources of that ocean ridge near Hawaii, remember those, Jim?"

He and Lassen had charted the depths of the Pacific and seen the lush plant life six-thousand feet down. Yet the bottom of Crater Lake still held unique sights. "Must be the volcano's influence and the molten lava that created these formations. Lovely."

"We see them," the answer bounced back across the miles after a short pause. "They're awesome. But, Mark, watch your way between them, looks like it's going to be a tight fit."

"It is," Lassen responded. "But I'm a good driver." He chuckled.

"You getting tired down there, Mark?"

"No. Doesn't take much energy to shove around a joystick and aim the sub in the right direction. So far so good. Not tired at all. I can stay down a bit longer. Got another six hours of air. By the way, the scenery down here is exquisite. For a lake, extraordinary."

Lassen had been searching the east curve of the caldera for hidden caves the last two hours.

"Well, put in another hour, buddy, then surface." Francis didn't want him under too long. The tense work rapidly wearied a person, and tired pilots made careless mistakes.

If Shore was right, his partner couldn't afford mistakes if the mystery creature showed up.

"I hear ya," Lassen responded. "But I haven't found anything yet. No so-called water monsters. In fact, strangely enough, I haven't seen any fish. None at all. If, as they say, they stock this lake every two years, and there aren't any inlets or outlets with the sea, then something's depleting the supply big time."

Francis noticed the ranger listening to the conversation and didn't seem surprised at the news. Greer's colleague, Patterson, was listening, too.

"I'm in full throttle and retracing my route to the other side of the lake to a place I passed earlier,"

Lassen told him. "By the time I saw it, I'd passed it. I'd like to check it out. I thought I saw tunnels branching off and burrowing down away from the bottom. Huge mothers. Must be the lake's plumbing system. If I explore, could be I can figure out where all the heat's coming from."

"I didn't see any large tunnels yesterday when I was down there," Francis said. "Just small caves."

"You were on the other side of the lake most of the day, remember, Jim?"

"I was, wasn't I? Okay, check them out, but be careful. The tunnels could be unstable with the recent earthquakes and since we don't know where the magma flows are originating, even more so. And if that's where the heat's coming from, even the Deep Rover's thick hull might not keep you from turning into a crispy critter."

Lassen snickered from the cockpit. "Yes, mother, I'll be careful." Francis could almost feel the sub shifting slightly to the right and gliding through the dark liquid, so often had he driven it and so attuned was he to the machine. The headlights would be roaming the rocky floor like a hungry eye as the swishing gurgle of the water coursed up through the radio.

"Yep, you can sure tell there's been earthquakes down here," Lassen kept up the chatter, a link to the land as the men above observed the scenery through the Rover's eyes. "It's a mess in this section. The crustal plates are cracked and have shifted up and onto each other. The sediment's a mile thick in some places. There's rising steam everywhere."

"We're getting clear photos of it up here.

Fascinating what nature can create, isn't it? The view's even got Greer's attention. Made him put that notebook of his down and he hasn't checked that pocket watch of his for the last ten minutes at least, either."

More chuckles.

Greer, in his neat suit, was hovering behind him at the make-shift base in the abandoned boat chained to the dock. Dr. Harris was next to the man, making faces at the video screen; waiting for the elusive creature to make an appearance so he could coo over it.

Justin Maltin, scribbling something on a notepad a few feet away, was getting ready to return to John Day's to do some more research.

Francis liked the young paleontologist, having found him not only affable but highly intelligent. He even appreciated Greer, rough and enigmatic as the man was on the outside, he was probably a decent guy beneath the steely exterior.

But that Harris fellow. Francis wasn't sure he was for real. Such a pompous ass, a nuisance. Always underfoot. Always hatching schemes to make money, gain fame off the situation.

"There!" From the boat, as he watched the sub's progress, Francis directed his friend in the submersible. "Veer directly to your left. Sharp. That's it.

"See that crater to your right, Mark? It looks like a miniature volcano in a volcano?"

"They're all over. There's a truly impressive one below me now."

"We see it. Watch those silicate columns

starboard, buddy. Cutting it awfully close, aren't you?"

Lassen was weaving in and out of the columns with the submersible, a pinball in a giant pinball game. He was scaring his friend.

"Don't worry, I know what I'm doing, Jim. This is fun. Great stress reliever, dodging around these rocks. Like bumper cars but underwater. Whoopee!"

"Not like bumper cars. You don't want to *hit* them." Francis put his fingers over his eyes, shaking his head. "And I thought you were a sane man."

Lassen played around a little longer and then said, "Stop nagging me. I'm heading towards those caverns now. I know my time's running out."

Francis wished he was below in the lake and Lassen was on top with Harris and his whining. The man was driving him nuts. He never shut up. Always making plans for what he'd do if the creature showed up, if they caught it. Blah, blah, blah. Another half hour of Harris's babbling and he'd knock the guy senseless just for some peace and quiet.

The Rover was skirting along a series of cave openings, all of them too small to take it. Lassen was describing and reporting what he saw as he went. He'd moved halfway around the arc of the lake when he exclaimed, "There's this large cavern down here, behind the rocks. I mean big. The entrance opens in an o shape. Don't know how I ever missed it before."

He gave his GPS coordinates, pinpointing his exact location for the ones listening above.

"Something's hiding in it. Something….

"I'm going in."

Francis watched through the view screen as the Rover glided into the opening.

"The cave appears to have been well-used, and recently," Lassen continued the commentary. "The stone around the opening is freshly scratched and there's loose debris and rocks everywhere."

"Watch yourself, Mark," Francis advised, his eyes glued to the story the cameras were sending back. It was difficult to see much beyond the sub's lights, the water was so misty. "This could be the hiding place we've been searching for."

"Could be," the pilot's answer crackled across the space through the radio channel. "I'll keep my eyes open for any unfriendly monster cave dwellers."

Only Patterson laughed. Evidently, he didn't believe in the monster either.

Dr. Maltin, from a chair in front of the console, gave him a dirty look.

Greer and Ranger Shore had been discussing other caves they'd known, but fell silent, as they hulked anxiously over the radio set. He'd overheard Shore say he'd done some cave climbing when he'd been a teenager. But, it turned out, Greer was the expert spelunker. He'd been in over a hundred caves.

"Caves," Greer announced, "are one of my obsessions. And the only variety of cave I haven't explored is precisely the type of cave I'd bet Lassen is in now…an underwater lava cave."

"An underwater lava cave?" Shore asked.

"Yes, and they're often treacherous and unpredictable."

"Ha, any cave is treacherous and unpredictable," Maltin snapped. "Things can fall on your head any time." He whispered, "I hate caves."

Francis wasn't listening to them, instead he was fretting over his friend in the caves below. He had an uneasy premonition something wasn't right.

"It's a maze of passageways," Lassen was describing in an echo of a voice that seemed far away. "It keeps twisting, and turning one way and then another…a true labyrinth. Magnificent! Some tunnels are too narrow to navigate through….I'm backing up, going another way. Now I'm in a much larger one. Good, there's more room to maneuver."

"Jim, all of you up there, you ought to see this! I mean the full up-close effect, not just what the cameras are picking up. It's breathtaking. Wait a minute, there's light directly above me. I'm going up."

The sub moved upwards at a steep angle. The eerie light grew brighter. Warm glowing crimsons and whitish oranges. It kept getting closer.

The Deep Rover surfaced from the water into what looked like an above water cavern full of wreathing bluish smoke and watery air. The walls were covered with dripping stone and lime formations. "Wow, this cavern is something," Lassen murmured. "Looks real old. Prehistoric even. There's multicolored lava rocks glittering along the walls, rising in spirals from the floor. They're so delicate looking. Can you see them? And look at those rocks embedded in the ceiling.

What fantastic shapes and colors. A rainbow."

"We see all of it, Mark," Francis sent back. "It's on camera now. Even from here it looks spectacular."

"It is. See the live lava river?"

Along one side of the cavern there was a moving stream of sluggish lava creeping its way into the adjoining tunnels and pillowing into the water less than fifty feet from the submersible.

It meant the cavern and the nearby water's heat would be extreme. It also meant the warm cave could be a home to a living creature. The men on shore realized that.

"With all that active lava," Francis spoke into the mike, "it must be hot in there."

"It is. The instruments are recording a steep jump in temperature. It isn't a dangerous heat level…yet. But it could be if it keeps building. See the steam?"

"I see it," Shore spoke up.

"This chamber probably leads to another exit," Lassen reported. "To my right. See? I wish I had the time to explore this place more thoroughly. It's truly unique."

"Not by yourself, mate," Francis told him. "Too dangerous. We were only to locate a possible lair, not toddle around in it, peeking behind rocks, twists and turns."

He didn't have to explain that what he'd meant was they weren't to take any chances like that *not without weapons*. Weapons that hadn't arrived yet. Weapons the Rover didn't have.

"I know. I'm going back down. Get out of here.

It's getting a little spooky. Shadows all over the place. Strange noises."

"Yeah, better safe than monster chow." Patterson snorted.

Francis gave the man a dirty look. He was uneasy enough.

"I'm leaving the cavern now," Lassen's voice sounded strained. "Those shadows are creeping me out. They're…moving."

His audience was holding their breath until the craft submerged again, leaving the fiery chamber behind, and wound its way through the tunnels towards the cave's entrance.

"That explains why the water temperature's been rising. The earthquake must have opened those old caverns and released the magma flows," the pilot was speaking as the sub descended. "That cavern deserves further study. It could ruin the delicate ecology of the park if enough lava is pumped into the lake."

"I agree," Francis said. "You returning to base now?"

"Sure am. I'm hungry. What's for lunch?"

"Whatever they're having on special at the closest restaurant in town. My treat."

"Sounds good to me." They could see Lassen was exiting the mouth of the underwater cave, the Rover gaining speed. The rear cameras were giving a wide view of all behind him.

Greer was stepping away from the monitors to inquire something of Dr. Harris when Shore cried out. He'd been studying something on the edge of the screen. "Lassen, behind you! It's behind you!

Get the hell out of there!"

The following seconds were chaos. Dr. Harris and Greer scrambled back to watch what was happening on the cameras.

"Oh, my god," Lassen could be heard exclaiming from inside the sub.

Dr. Maltin, who'd left his chair and moved over to the screen, cried, "Oh, my god, there it is!"

For what seemed like an unbelievable amount of suspended time the men stared at the *thing* outside the sub's portals.

"It really exists," Patterson gasped, as a scaly wall of emerald skin filled the portals of the Rover, trapping the wide-eyed Lassen inside. The creature pulled away and everyone could see it clearly framed in the windows. "Well, I'll be damned. An honest to god dinosaur. Would you look at that thing!"

Francis, along with the other men, were. He was as shocked as Patterson. He hadn't believed in the creature, either.

Outside in the inky water they caught patchwork glimpses of the monster: a belligerent eye peering in, a spiked tail swimming by a window. Teeth when the thing snarled.

Lassen was trying hard to hide his panic, but his trembling voice gave him away. "It does looks like some kind of dinosaur, Ranger Shore, just as you and Dr. Maltin said. I've never seen anything like it in my life or in any of my sea explorations. Oh, Lord…*it's so big.*"

All the men around the screen found they couldn't take their eyes off the apparition.

Ranger Shore took the microphone from Francis. "What are you going to do?" he demanded softly of the man in the sub, knowing what he was feeling–absolute terror–because he'd been there. Felt it.

"N..n..nothing. I don't think it even notices me."

"Don't underestimate it, Lassen. It sees you all right. Get out of there. Now, while you can."

Lassen moved the submersible away, forgetting completely their big rock-on-the-bottom-of-the-lake strategy. Apparently all Lassen wanted to do at that moment was get as far away from the creature as he could.

Francis didn't blame him one bit.

Stationary, the monster examined the metal craft with glittering eyes. Then it opened its tooth-filled mouth and silently roared. Bubbles exploding from its mouth. Its claws came up to its chest and flailed in the water. It almost seemed to the men watching that it was waving at Lassen.

"How long can *it* stay underwater before it has to go up for air?" Lassen voiced meekly.

"I don't know." Dr. Maltin's face had a stricken look on it. "Just tell him to get away."

"I'm increasing speed."

Dr. Harris's eyes were glued to the screens, too, but the glint in them was one of greedy excitement.

The submersible sped faster through the dark water.

The beast became smaller in the sub's windows as the distance grew between them.

Faster. Faster.

Francis was breathing again when the monster

begun to move, churning the water like a giant paddle wheel, neck stretching out, tail pushing it along. Francis had never seen an underwater creature move that quickly. Not even a shark or a Great White. It was eating up the water.

It was coming after the sub. After Lassen.

"Gonna try to outrun it," Lassen under toned, his demeanor still calm.

Not for long though. His friend must be so afraid, Francis thought, putting his hand to his brow. They never should have put the submersible in the water, but how were they to have known the monster was *real*? Or so gigantic…and curious?

By the instruments he could tell the Rover had ratcheted up to its top speed. The monster easily caught up with it as if it were idling in the water. Through the radio lines there was the sickening sound of claws scrapping metal as the beast reached out and captured the sub in its embrace, holding it prisoner.

By then Lassen's coolness had evaporated and he was groaning loudly as the giant tail encircled his metal sanctuary. There were more scraping, scratching noises. Now the sub was motionless. Lassen was screeching something but none of the men above could make out the words, there was so much background noise.

The creature seemed to be amusing itself with the submersible. Playing with it.

"Why can't he get away from it?" Greer's hands were clenched before him, his expression flat.

"It's too strong," Ranger Shore sighed.

"It can't get to him in that sub." Francis

swallowed. "The hull's too thick. Made of the best, strongest metals. It's–"

Lassen's shaky voice haunted the speakers, "My god, it's trying to break in. Why won't it just leave me alone and go away? What the hell does it want?"

You, Francis answered silently, meeting the panicked gazes of the men around him.

"He's not going to make it," Shore said. "And it's my fault. I knew what the creature was like. I knew it was real. Deadly. I never should have let him, anyone, go down there…without weapons to protect themselves."

"How can you blame yourself, Henry?" Greer tried to ease the ranger's guilt. "He was only doing his job. He knew the risks."

Dr. Harris snapped, "And he's not dead yet. He'll get away. That creature is not that smart, I keep telling you. A human surely should be able to outsmart the thing."

"I hope you're right." Francis regarded the monitors, his jaw clenched. He found himself praying for his partner's safety deep below in the lake.

Suddenly, the beast released the sub and the machine pulled away. It was chugging ahead, leaving the monster behind.

The men on the boat cheered.

The Rover slowly increased its speed, as if Lassen was afraid to recapture the creature's attention. Then it was a gray bullet flying through the water.

The monster waited for a while and began to follow. Gaining. Gaining.

The submersible ceased moving, falling dead in the water.

"Mark!" Francis cried. "What's wrong? Why aren't you getting the hell out of there?"

"I don't know! She won't accelerate. She's dead in the water." Lassen could be heard panting, pure terror in his words.

The leviathan had caught up to the Deep Rover and was slowly circling it.

"Maybe something's wrong with the engine…I don't know. I've checked everything. Everything was fine this morning."

Then Lassen was screaming.

The screaming made Francis's blood freeze.

The pictures on the camera were going crazy, one moment a view of the lake bottom and the next of nothing but water churning.

"It's got me again! Got the Rover…tearing at us…" the man inside the sub rasped breathlessly, his utter terror painful to hear. His words were now gibberish and his shrill shrieks, and pitiful pleas for help, were lost among tearing metal. The microphone and cameras giving a gruesome account of what was occurring, up to the moment Lassen was taken from the Deep Rover.

The beast had him. Like a can-opener, it'd pried the sub open and popped the human out.

The others watched, mouths open in horror, their faces registering shock, as the man in the submersible was ripped from his sardine can and disappeared from view. They watched the screen until it went dead and there was nothing else to watch or to hear but the pounding of their own hearts.

"Oh, god, we've got to do something," Francis cried. "We've got to save him!" The others had to restrain him or he would have started the boat and gone to rescue his friend. Hopeless. There was no way he could have saved him. Lassen was gone.

"It's too late." Greer's eyes were glued to the screen but there was nothing left to see. "It's over."

Under his feet Francis could feel the sway of the boat, moored to the dock. Outside it was broad daylight. But he didn't feel safe. As long as he was on the water, he wouldn't feel safe.

The monster, and that was what it was, had come out early to feed. It wasn't even dark. Which meant either it was getting bolder, or hungrier. Or both.

Francis stared at the other men. Everyone but Dr. Harris was in shock. Even Patterson.

He collapsed into the chair Maltin had just vacated, his distress a live coal in his gut. He'd really cared about Lassen. He'd been his partner, his friend, for so many years. The man had a family. How was he going to tell them? He felt sick.

How could this have happened? What were they going to do now? He couldn't think about that, his revulsion, his grief was too fresh.

"Sending that sub into the lake was like sending out a bright fishing lure on the end of a line. Come and get me, monster," Ranger Shore gritted through clenched teeth. "We as good as sent that man to his death. It's my fault, I should have known how dangerous the mission was; never sent him. I'm so sorry, Jim."

Jim Francis, who'd been quiet since his outburst, jerked his eyes towards Shore. "It wasn't your fault. You didn't know this would happen."

Shore lowered his eyes but said nothing more.

"At least he didn't suffer long." Francis laid his head on his folded arms and Dr. Maltin put a comforting hand on his shoulder.

"No, not long," Henry Shore said gently.

And no one disputed that.

***

The horror of what had taken place was so palpable Henry could have reached out and touched it. No one said or did anything for a long time, not even Harris.

Then Greer began scribbling notes and Dr. Harris, back to his old self, began gushing over the size and power of the monster.

"Did you see it?" Harris kept asking. "I know what just happened was a terrible thing, poor Lassen and all, but, that creature is an astounding anachronism…a prehistoric live, *breathing* dinosaur! Colossal. Did you see the tail, the claws on it? Not webbed feet, like a normal Nothosaur, but claws on appendages that could grip? Evolution at its highest level. Definitely not the Nothosaur we are familiar with, but many steps up on the evolutionary chain, or even an entirely new species never before seen on the earth. Distant kin, but not similar, to those fossils we found at the site. Did you see the fin?"

Jim Francis raised his head from his arms and glared at Harris with hatred. "Shut up, will you? A good man has died horribly. A lot of people have died. And all you can do is rave about that butchering evil creature. It should die, hear me! *Die!* Before it kills anyone else."

"What's one human's life, a thousand lives, against the greatest discovery of the millennia?" Harris declared.

Henry stormed off the boat. If he'd have stayed a moment longer he would have decked that idiot Harris who felt no sorrow over the man who'd just died in front of them. All he cared about was that damn monster…that dinosaur.

Sending the Deep Rover into the lake had been foolish, he brooded, as he stared out over the lake, the sun shining brightly above it. It was a lovely early August day. Warm. Clear. Great weather for hiking the rim, cruising the waters, or picnicking in the woods. Except there were no one on the lake and no one in the park. The visitors were gone. Everyone but them.

Henry studied the line of bobbing, empty vessels and the placid lake covered with that creepy mist which lately hovered everywhere all the time. Ironically, the heat from below the caldera meeting the cooler air above was creating a prehistoric environment. The monster must feel right at home.

Children's laughter and the salty jabs of the boats' absent captains whispered like phantoms on the warm air.

He thought he heard Justin's voice. But Justin, seconds after the tragedy, had muttered a few trembling words of sympathy and had gotten off the boat as if it were on fire. Henry saw him on the dock about thirty feet away hunched over the water.

Throwing up.

Standing there, the earth quivered under his boots. For a moment he was afraid they were having another earthquake. But then nothing. The earth calmed. He breathed a sigh of relief.

Great.

So not only did he have the lake monster to worry about, he also had the unstable earth. What else could go wrong?

He squeezed his fists at his side and fought dark thoughts.

The beast was down there devouring Lassen, but soon it'd be up there with them again looking around for more appetizers. The park now belonged to it. Not the humans.

And here they all were sitting on a docked boat on the water, easy pickings.

Henry ran back to the boat and scrambled inside.

"Everyone get out. Now. Unless you want to be the monster's second course."

They obeyed, and dragging Harris with them, they piled into the park vehicle Henry had borrowed for the day and he aimed it for park headquarters.

Reality had sunk in. The creature could emerge from the water any time and attack. One human snack wouldn't be enough, if, as Lassen had inferred, the lake's fish were gone, and it was starving. They'd seen the creature's immense body, its head with the gigantic fanged mouth; its glowing hungry eyes, through the sub's cameras. It'd take a lot more to fill that beast's belly.

Henry glanced at Patterson in the back seat. As

tightly as he clutched them in his lap, Patterson's hands wouldn't stop shaking.

Greer's hair was mussed, and he hadn't checked his pocket watch once since the incident, yet he kept peering behind the moving jeep towards the lake.

"Can't this thing go any faster?" Dr. Harris demanded, looking behind them, too.

They were going fast enough. The scenery speeding by like in the movies. Henry slowed down for a sharp curve.

"So now, at last, you're scared?" Henry snapped at Harris, sitting up front with him and Justin. Harris grunted, keeping watch.

Patterson was mumbling in the back seat, "I didn't think *it* really existed. Until it got Lassen. Never believed in monsters under the bed, as a kid, either." The man was shook up. "Lord, that thing was big. Fast. And Ranger, you say it can travel just as well on land as it does in the water?"

Henry swung his head around to look at the man, and before he could stop it, he laughed. It wasn't funny. A fine man had died, right in front of their eyes. But the way the usually taciturn Patterson had said what he'd just said forced it out of him. It was only a release of tension, but it still felt disrespectful. But a human being could only take so much horror then it had to be disposed of somehow. Humor did that. It was either that or cry. Henry knew crying was a waste of time and energy. Lassen was dead. Nothing would change that. They had to take care of themselves.

"It can."

"My, my, my," Patterson was moaning behind

him. "We're in trouble now."

Henry got them miles away before he slowed down. Just a little.

Behind him Greer leaned forward and said loud enough to be heard, "When I was still FBI, I had a macabre case, oh, about a year ago. Serial killer. Loathsome. He stalked and meticulously butchered young women. All his victims had to like classical music. All had to be short, with dark hair and blue eyes. They had to be good girls. No whores. Most of them honor roll students. Talented. Young women who might have been impressive adults." In the rearview mirror, there was a look on Greer's face that Henry couldn't place or describe. Rancor, perhaps.

"I won't go into details of what he did to those girls when he caught them, it was bad. Real bad. He liked to see them suffer. He was a monster. Pure and simple. Malignant to his roots. Like most serial killers.

"I tracked that bastard for months and months. He was so damn smart. Used to send me packages with body pieces in them. Dirty letters. Taunting me; telling me what he planned to do next. Sometimes, even where. Just never gave me much time to get there. I had to beat him to the location or a girl died.

"No matter how hard I tried, I never made it in time. As the months went on, and I didn't catch him, I couldn't sleep, couldn't eat. I became obsessed. I had to find him. Rid the world of his bloodthirsty evil. But," Greer confessed, "I couldn't stop him. Or the killings. He got eight girls before I cornered him in Utah. I only caught him, in the end, because of an anonymous tip and pure dumb luck. I was close by. He'd planned on killing two at once, changing things up I guess, and had finished with one young woman already. Her remains were still warm when I found her. He quickly killed the other woman, when he sensed I was closing in. I missed saving that one by seconds, I think. Seconds. I'd been so close. So near. He'd mocked me with those girls. Calling me up and saying vile things to get a rise out of me. To make me doubt myself." Greer's eyes were diamond chips in the mirror as he looked at Henry, his smile self-hating.

Dr. Harris was listening closely to what Greer was saying. Henry could see the little weasel in the corner of his eyes.

Jim Francis was staring out into the woods, his expression unreadable. Patterson acted as if he'd heard the story before and knew the ending.

Then Greer leaned even closer to Henry's ear so only he could hear what he said next. "But I made sure I was in the house first when we finally cornered and caught him months later, before the police closed in…and I shot him in cold-blood as he grinned at me over another poor girl's mutilated body. I won't lie. His hands were empty and held up in surrender, the knife on the floor next to him. I shot him eight times, for every girl he'd murdered, and I shot not to kill until the final bullet. He screamed a lot. I put the final one dead center in his brain. And later, I claimed it was self-defense. It wasn't. I executed him, and I was glad I did, for all those girls.

"Because I'd be damned if some fancy lawyer was going to get him off on a technicality, or plead him insane. That man was never going to walk the earth another day or be allowed to ever kill again. That human monster had to die. I had to rid the world of him forever. Because that's what you do when something is so maliciously evil. You exterminate it."

Henry glanced behind at Greer as if he'd never seen him before. Most people wouldn't have understood or approved of what the ex-FBI agent had done. Henry didn't one-hundred percent, either, but he understood. Fully. And he understood what Greer was telling him.

Greer didn't always follow the rules. And the guilty, the evil, must pay for what they did.

"Sounds like he deserved it," Henry offered simply.

Greer smiled, as he reclined back against the seat, and Henry returned it. He was starting to really like the man.

He slowed the vehicle down even more. He was sure they'd put enough distance between them and the lake. For now.

"You know, though, this case is different, the perpetrator isn't human," Greer went on. "I've dealt with some strange cases, but this is the first one dealing with a…dinosaur. Because, that's what my eyes tell me we saw in the water back there. Or something like it.

"I'll tell you something, Shore, I never liked going to the zoo when I was a kid, either…and those creatures were all in cages."

"And they weren't as big," Henry tossed in.

"No, they weren't. This is going to be a pickle to deal with. We're going to need really big guns for this one."

"You're telling me," Henry shot back. "Can you and your friends get us any hand-held missiles? That's what Maltin here thinks we'll need to kill it."

"I can get you anything we need."

"Good. Bigger the better. Sooner the better."

"I'm working on it."

Dr. Harris had stopped listening and with squinty eyes was avidly searching the road and forest around them.

"You hear something?" he kept insisting of anyone and everyone. "I thought I heard something."

Henry speeded up again.

CHAPTER 13

That morning Laura had taken Phoebe to the doctor's because the baby had a cold and needed medicine. So the coast was clear. Good thing, Laura would have known what she was up to and would have stopped her. No doubt about it.

Ann told Zeke she was going shopping and left him, unsuspecting, at the kitchen table pouring over the open newspaper and munching from his bowl of Rice Krispies.

She caught a glimpse of him through the kitchen window as she drove away. He was shaking his head, probably over some typo he'd found in the copy. She made sure he couldn't see her before she turned down an alley and went the other way towards the park.

She checked to be sure she had her note tablet and her digital camcorder. It was an older model; she'd given Henry her new one. Her acceptance in leaving the park and staying out had had to look good. Her husband wouldn't have fallen for anything less than a perfect performance.

But darn it, there was only one way she could save the newspaper and her job. She *had* to get a photo of that creature in the lake, whatever it was, any way she could. Or she had to find that dead reporter's digital camcorder that Henry had mentioned the night he and Justin had crashed the jeep. She was sure, if she could find it, that it held film–if it wasn't smashed up so badly there was nothing left to salvage. She was going to look for it and find it, too. Oh, not just for the Pulitzer the pictures would probably bring when they were published all over the world, and not just for the money (they could make her and Henry rich) but for Zeke and the newspaper.

Ann couldn't let the paper close; couldn't let Zeke down. She loved her job and the newspaper too much to lose them. To lose Zeke. He'd wither away if he didn't have his beloved paper to live for.

Oh, she respected Henry's theories on how conniving the creature was, and it was terrible how many people had died, so she would be *so* careful getting her proof. But in the newspaper business sometimes taking risks was a part of the job. You either got used to it or you gave your press card away.

Henry would kill her if he knew what she was planning, yet she shrugged that thought away. She understood why he didn't want her in the park. It was dangerous; he loved her, and didn't want her to get hurt.

But she was a smart woman, smarter than any old overgrown fish, and she could take care of herself. She had a car and she had her eyes, ears and wits. She'd be safe enough.

She needed that exclusive, before the newspaper shut its doors, or all the other newspapers horned in, which wouldn't be long according to the rumors she'd been hearing. Now that those reporters were officially missing it was only a matter of days or even hours before the tabloids and other newspapers, or television crews, would send in their commando teams. Then she'd be left out in the cold. A second hand story wouldn't save the Klamath Falls Journal.

So, anticipating the story of a lifetime and all the good things that'd come from it, Ann was grinning as the car bumped over the country road and took one of the lesser used rear entrances into the park. It was a lovely sunny day. She didn't need a sweater. Summer was brief in Oregon, but it was sweet.

Winding through the park's narrow highways she reflected on how beautiful the forest was in its new silence. The only noises those of nature's. While in town, she had missed the solitude more than she'd admit. All those years living in big noisy New York had made her appreciate the woods even more. And as nice as Zeke had been to them she wanted so badly to be back at home with Henry. That's where she belonged. She prayed he'd take care of the creature problem soon so they all could go home.

After she got pictures of the demolished paleontological dig, she'd go to the lake, search for that lost camcorder; keeping her eyes and ears open so the creature couldn't surprise her, and if it did, well, she'd get photos before she fled. How fast could something that big move?

Besides, from what she'd heard about the monster, it preferred darkness. She was safe in the sunshine.

Henry had described the location of the reporters' camp well enough for her to know where it was. It was easy to get to. She knew the lake area well after exploring around it as much as she had, so it shouldn't be hard to find.

She parked the car in a circle of bushes and trees, for camouflage, and hiked down to the lake, her camcorder slung on her shoulder and a lunch of ham sandwich, an apple, and a bottle of water stuffed in her over-sized purse in case she got hungry. Careful to be quiet and as inconspicuous as possible, not only because of the monster, but because if Henry or his rangers caught her, they'd escort her to the entrance and boot her out. She couldn't have that, not until she'd taken those pictures and found that camcorder.

She took photos at the dig site, astonished and frightened at the devastation she found. As she swept her eyes over the crushed RVs she almost lost her nerve and hightailed it back to town. Anything that could do so much damage must be huge. Vicious. Then her reporter's hard headedness kicked in and she set her jaw.

So what if she was a woman and a grandmother. She'd get her story. She wasn't a fraidy cat. Death was too far away to worry about. Or maybe because she'd never seen the creature, a part of her doubted its existence.

Once she'd climbed below to and passed Cleetwood Cove she began her search, eyes on the ground, bent low. The sun blazing warmly above her. She couldn't have felt safer. It seemed like any summer day in the park, except for the peculiar silence, the empty lake and abandoned boats bobbing along the shore.

For hours she hunted for the camera in the shrubbery and along the rocky shoreline, losing track of time until her stomach protested. Then she sat on a grassy spot higher up overlooking Cleetwood Dock, so she'd have a better view, and settled down to eat her lunch and rest a little. She hadn't found the camcorder and the sun was beginning its decent towards the other horizon. She didn't want to be in the park after dark. She wasn't that stupid.

Where could that damn camera be?

As she ate, she thought about the creature many of the rangers had jokingly started calling Godzilla. Not that Henry did. He had other more colorful names for the beast. She remembered those whimsical drawings she'd made that day on the lake as she'd waited for a Sam Cutler who'd never return. The drawings had been done and published only weeks ago, but it seemed years. According to Henry and Justin, who'd seen her drawings and the real thing, her sketches looked nothing like the monster. Nothing.

Ann gazed at the serene lake and listened. She heard little but the wind sighing through the trees. Not even birds. Strange.

All those weeks Henry and Justin had been seeking the creature, she hadn't believed in its existence. What sane person would? In the beginning, oh, she'd accepted there might be *something* in the water bothering boats and people, something large. Maybe someone had dumped a shark or a huge squid in the lake. Possible. But not a real monster. When Henry had seen the beast that first night, she'd been as surprised as anyone. And if it had been anyone but Henry she wouldn't have believed it in a New York second. But Henry would never have made that sort of thing up. Henry didn't lie.

Ann shook her head, brushed the crumbs off her clothes, and crunched her teeth into the apple, her eyes sharply scanning the lake and the area around her. On the lookout. The lake was so placid, peaceful. How could it hold such a deadly creature.

After Henry's sighting, the disappearances and sudden deaths, the fear had come, fear for Henry and Justin, fear for the people in the park, as well as for her daughter, granddaughter and herself. But along with the fear had come a voracious curiosity that had fed on itself until she could no longer stay away.

She had to see the monster. Just once. She mulled over the serendipity of that happening. Fat chance. It was daytime. The monster didn't come out in the bright sunlight. She frowned slightly. Henry had worried that it might begin to emerge during daylight hours…if its hunger were great enough. She quickly pushed that thought out of her mind. It was too scary to dwell on now that she was back in the park.

It was so quiet. Spooky. *I shouldn't be here doing this dumb stunt. People have died. Do I want to die? No.* Her hands were quivering slightly. Her mind seemed a little fuzzy, as if she were in a dream.

But she couldn't leave until she had some kind of proof of the creature's existence; not until she had her story for Zeke. She'd come this far, worked this hard. No, she wasn't leaving until she'd accomplished her task.

It was as she was getting ready to resume the search, that she heard the commotion below and was startled to see her husband pacing on the dock. Justin, bent over the water, a short ways from him. As far away as she was, she could tell Henry was furious. It was in his hunched over walk and his angry clenched-fists. The way he rocked his head back and forth in obvious frustration. She knew that gesture. He was upset. Real upset.

Where had he come from? Her eyes followed as he climbed back down onto one of the bigger boats and disappeared below deck.

Oh, so that was their headquarters for the submarine launch? Henry had told her about the Deep Rover and the scientists who were piloting it, and he'd vented his concerns of the whole scheme. He was afraid it was too dangerous. For the pilots.

Ann's reporter's sixth sense kicked in. Something had happened. Something was wrong.

A few minutes later a group of men exited from the boat. Justin joined them. Huddled in a tight group with frantic eyes, they hurried towards a park vehicle, practically dragging some man who couldn't seem to walk. Henry driving, the car started up and went careening wildly up Cleetwood Road. Coming her way.

Grabbing her things, she ducked behind some bushes and the car screeched by her so close she could see the horror in her husband's face.

They were speeding in the direction of Ranger Headquarters.

Time to get out of here. Ann raced to her car.

She was on the road when she heard the noise. At first it was water splashing and then a sort of roaring sound. Her foot automatically hit the brake and the car came to a grinding halt in the middle of the road. She glanced over her shoulder at the water.

And she looked up…up…up.

"Oh, my god," she whispered, lips trembling.

She'd seen dinosaurs in books and movies before. But nothing had prepared her for what she was seeing at that moment. With the bright sun backlighting it, it was the biggest damn thing she'd ever seen. Alive anyway. And it was definitely alive. Breathing. Snarling. Advancing.

"It's got to be at least fifty-sixty feet tall," she breathed, oddly calm, because she wasn't believing what her eyes were seeing.

The creature had climbed out of the water at Cleetwood Cove and was posed glaring up at the sky. It was an ugly greenish-brown color and possessed a mammoth body, a strong neck and a gigantic head that swiveled around gracefully for its size. The creature had short front arms that it held up before it as a Tyrannosaurus Rex might have, but the arms seemed powerful and ended in webbed wicked-looking claws.

It flexed its neck and yawned open its jaws and she spied the jagged teeth and slimy narrow tongue that licked lips that weren't really lips. The long, long tail drug half in the lake, thumping and spraying water everywhere. There were no spikes on the tail, it was smooth.

Ann squinted, shading her eyes. The water beast

reminded her of some dinosaur she'd seen in a text book, but not really. It was unlike any drawing she'd ever seen. Must be a new species of dinosaur. Amazing. Unlike the dumb stare the book dinosaurs usually had, this dinosaur had a strange, fierce glimmer in its reptilian orbs as its glare roamed along the abandoned boats tied up at the dock. The beast was hunting for something.

The determined way it was behaving scared her. This creature before her was aware.

Ann felt with her fingers along the seat beside her and brought the camcorder up to eye level. She filmed a short video quicker than she'd ever had before as she held her breath, her heart slamming in her chest.

The dinosaur rose the rest of the way out of the water, strong hind legs, moving it along.

Its head began to tilt downwards and its eyes riveted on her.

Oh, oh.

Ann dropped the camcorder in her lap, turned her head around, and pushed the gas pedal down. Hard.

She didn't look back to check if it was chasing her, figuring she didn't have the time, she knew it would. If she could get to Ranger Headquarters she'd be safe. Henry would protect her; know what to do. He always did. They'd surely have guns there. She hoped they had big ones.

The gas pedal was to the floor and she kept busy by watching the road. Afraid to look back even once.

She was just a curve away from the long low

building she was racing towards when the monster's foot came down on the front of her car and smashed it dead.

Ann scrambled out of what was left, leaving everything but the camcorder, she fled into the woods. Her heart was screaming as she ran, but her vocal cords were frozen. She hurdled her body towards the welcoming building and the people down the path in front of her as the monster finished demolishing her vehicle. She could hear the awful crunching sounds behind her.

Headquarters was directly ahead. She was nearly there.

She didn't look behind her. She knew if she did, and the monster was too close, she'd faint, and the thing would have her for lunch.

A tall man in dark green pants, gray shirt and a wide-brimmed brown hat was suddenly standing in front of her, arms outspread as if to catch her. A ranger. Someone she knew, but she wasn't sure. Her mind wasn't working right.

"George!" Ann found her voice and her mind. "It's coming! The monster's behind me!"

George didn't hesitate, didn't ask any questions. Her terror-stricken face must have convinced him what she said was true.

He grabbed her hand and they sprinted for the building down the road. George yelling a warning and screaming for back-up as they went. He didn't bother to use the gun he had on his hip, it wouldn't hurt the monster anyway, Henry had told her that, but those ex-FBI agents might have a more lethal arsenal. She prayed they did, or they were all dead people.

***

Henry and the others had arrived at headquarters and heard someone shouting outside that the monster was coming. For a heartbeat, he was taken off guard, and then demanded of Greer, standing beside him, "I don't suppose you and Patterson brought any larger weapons?"

"Nothing major, we have those on order, should be coming in any minute. All we brought was my personal arsenal, HK PDW's, and a few TMP's machine pistols. All state of the art Personal Defense Weapons which offer accurate semi and full-auto fire at a rate of 900 rounds per minute. I stashed them in the back room.

"Those weapons might not kill it but could make it think twice or chase it off."

"A Russian RPG with rocket propelled grenades might kill it," Henry suggested. "Got one of those?"

"Sorry, we don't have any RPGs," Greer said. "Yet."

Henry sighed. The commotion was getting closer. "We'll give the HK PDW's and TMP's a chance. Pray they do the trick and send the thing running."

Greer ran for the back room.

"Wait a minute, your orders are to bring it in alive, remember?" Dr. Harris, eavesdropping, growled. His face was red, his eyes blazing. "Not blow it to kingdom come!"

"All righty, Dr. Harris, what do you propose we do if it attacks us? Let it eat us? We hadn't planned for it to follow us from the lake, come in this far, and if it poses a direct threat I'm sure as hell going to try to get rid of it. I don't care what anyone says. We'll protect ourselves."

Outside they could hear the thunderous growling. Roaring. The ground was thumping like a herd of elephants was coming.

It must have sunk into Harris's head that the monster was outside the door because the expression on his face morphed into one of panic. "Y-e-s, I guess we should protect ourselves…if we're in immediate danger. I see your point."

"Glad you feel that way, Harris," Henry said. "Because the monster's here and survival is our top priority at the moment. Don't you agree?"

Harris glared at him. Nodded his head.

Jim Francis was still red-eyed from the loss of his friend. "We'd better stop standing here yakking like idiots and get down to business or it'll get us, too." It was the first thing he'd said since they'd arrived.

Henry rubbed his eyes, fighting to think. But the noise outside was too much competition. Time had run out. Greer reappeared with an armful of guns and quickly handed them out.

Henry looked at Greer and Patterson, then the building around them. "If we're not sure about our weapons, we should evacuate everyone now before the creature stamps us out like ants. This building is little more than a trap. It wasn't built to withstand a rampaging dinosaur."

"You're saying we haven't got a chance if we attempt to fight it?" Patterson stuttered. He'd dealt with human monsters most of his career, but real monsters were a different game than rapists and serial killers. He must be wondering, how did one fight a nightmare?

"Me? Truthfully? I don't think so. It's come hungry, we're its prey and it'll do what it has to do to get to us. It's already surprised me a few times with its cunning. I wouldn't put anything past it. Retreat is our safest option."

Greer nodded. "I second that."

Henry heard the monster's bellowing and the thundering noises outside. Much louder. It was close. Too close.

His men were scurrying about, yanking weapons from their holsters, and looking to him for orders. With frightened expressions they tried to conceal, they crowded around him.

"We're in for it, I'm afraid," Henry reported to Greer. "I'm going to need your help."

Greer nodded, swung around, and began giving orders to some of the rangers. Henry caught him reassuring the men as he directed them, and his standing in Henry's eyes went up yet another notch.

The human screaming outside had increased, and the voice became recognizable.

"That's George out there," Henry cried.

Alarmed, he peered through the window and saw two figures staggering towards them and, in the same instant, he saw the monster looming over them.

In the daylight the creature appeared even more unreal, if that was possible. For the first time Henry could see in detail what it looked like. Its head was high above the trees and cocked to the left, its eyes liquid granite as they locked onto the escaping people far below. It threw up its ugly, scaly head and its roar shattered the afternoon's stillness, and revealed a mouth full of drooling, dagger-sharp teeth. With a grace that belied its size, it picked up a tree, wrenched it from the ground by the roots and tossed it at the running figures.

The earth shook when the tree hit close, too close, to the people.

One of the figures lost their balance as a thick limb brushed it. It tripped and sprawled in the middle of the road. A woman screamed, and Henry's blood tingled hot in his veins.

He tore his eyes away from the beast and looked down.

"It's Ann…what the hell is she doing here!"

Then Henry growled at Greer, "It's here. Get everybody out right now. I'm putting you in charge. Tell them not to fight it, just run, get out of its way. Fighting it will make it angrier and more will die."

Henry was out the door before Greer could reply or object. The only thing on his mind was Ann and that she was in danger. He had to save her.

Bursting out the door, he sprinted past the cars on the parking lot. The place was pandemonium. Everyone was pouring out of the building, running everywhere, raising their weapons, taking positions or hiding.

A person would have to be a fool not to want to run from it. But Henry's men were well-trained. They hid their terror behind strained faces and did what they were supposed to do.

Henry sprinted towards the two figures in the web of leaves. His anger at Ann's hair-brained stunt of sneaking into the park in the first place snuffed out as he grasped the danger she and George were in. For it was George who was with her. He'd recognized him as he got closer.

The monster was before him, hulking above his wife and his friend who hadn't made it to the building. The beast had them trapped.

Ann had ceased shrieking and was trying to extricate George from beneath the tree limbs.

A bullet zipped past Henry's head and another exploded feet away from Ann. Bullets, angry wasps, were filling the air; their target, the creature.

The other rangers were trying to divert the monster's attention to save Ann and George. They were hiding behind trees shooting at it, and the rounds were bouncing off the creature's hide, which must have made it angry because it was howling.

It advanced on the two humans. George, with Ann's help, had untangled himself from the downed tree and had come to a standing position.

After that everything happened so swiftly Henry couldn't move fast enough.

Oblivious to the gunfire, the beast grabbed for Ann and in those final moments before the monster's claws reached her, George flung himself in front of her and rushed into the thing's arms, sacrificing himself instead.

"George! No!" Henry screamed, as Ann ran into his arms. But George couldn't hear him.

For the rest of his life Henry would never forget the way his friend died. The images. They'd haunt him forever. In the movies they always made a death look so quick and clean. It wasn't. Not the kind of death George had.

With tears in his eyes, Henry took his wife by the shoulders and propelled her to the nearest hiding place. The crawlspace beneath headquarters porch. He shoved her under and scuttled in behind while the monster was busy. It was their only chance of survival, unless the dinosaur trampled the building.

From beneath the porch, among the dirt, bugs, and spiders, Henry and Ann watched the slaughter. His men were shooting at the intruder to keep it away from them, but, again, that only seemed to make it madder. The men scattered as the beast clamored after them, slavering, swiping and mauling everyone it captured, before it tossed the ragdoll-like bodies aside.

Men stumbled, crawled or fled for their lives. Some made it, some didn't. Henry was powerless to help them. The pistol in his hands was useless.

He spotted Greer, firing at the monster from behind a tree with one of his PDW's. He wasn't hiding or running, but was keeping the beast away from the others. Firing the automatic like he knew what he was doing, he hit the creature dead target every time, but his weapon was as ineffectual as Henry's Sig and Greer eventually fell back to save his own skin.

Henry wondered what kind of weapon it'd take to defeat it. An A bomb?

Patterson was on the edge of the woods over to Henry's right, aiding a wounded ranger. Gillian it looked like. Patterson, too, had given up fighting and was attempting to help the injured. A brief thought wisped through Henry's mind. Patterson had finally gotten to see his Godzilla up close. God only knew what the man was thinking.

The air had filled with anguished cries and moans as the monster fed. Some men had tried to reach their cars and few had made it. Their vehicles were smashed on top of them or the beast had picked up and thrown them like toys into the woods.

Henry had never seen anything so strong or so aggressively lethal.

It seemed to relish maiming and killing, stopping to eat little of its kills. Cowering under the crawlspace as far back as they could scoot, Henry watched in horror as Ann hid her eyes and sobbed silently into his chest. He stroked her head and hushed her. If she made too much noise it'd come for them, too. There was nothing he could do to save the men who'd died or were wounded, not now, and it made him as sick as George's death.

Ann peeked up when the yelling stopped. The creature was charging towards the building. "It's coming this way," she gasped. "*Oh, my God!*"

"We have to get out of here! Crawl backwards and to the right. That's it. We'll sneak out on the side."

He slithered in reverse dragging Ann with him. They slipped out from under the crawlspace and scrambled into the woods as the monster, growling and roaring, stomped on the building.

Henry prayed everyone had gotten out.

From behind a cluster of large rocks, they stared as the monster demolished headquarters until it was a pile of flattened timber. Then the beast crashed back into the forest, leaving behind a battleground of strewn bleeding body parts, crushed cars and a heap of splintered wood. The whole attack, from beginning to end, had taken less than ten minutes.

"Thank God it's leaving," Ann wept, clinging to his arm.

"It's not leaving, it's heading towards Rim Village," Henry's voice was hoarse. "And there are still people there." The ones who'd stayed behind to take care of the buildings and the properties. A few of the student workers who hadn't left yet. Die-hard, hard to roust out, residents who didn't believe in the lake monster. Were they in for a surprise.

"Stay here, honey," he told Ann who'd collapsed on the ground. "I'll be back for you."

"You're not going after it, are you?" Panicked. "You can't." Her hand reached up and grasped his.

"Not to fight it. To warn anyone left in Rim Village that it's coming." He released her hand. "I'll be careful, but I have to go. They're unprepared. They don't know what's coming."

Before she could protest he was gone. He left Greer in charge and shouted for willing survivors to accompany him. Kiley and another ranger, a newer man called Cummings, fell in with him and the twilight woods swallowed them up. A short cut he knew through the woods would be faster than using a car.

As they ran, the whole time all Henry could think about was George. The brave look on his face as he'd faced the monster, protecting Ann. His muffled screams as he'd died. And he ran faster.

***

They got to Rim Village as the monster was finishing up and evening was claiming the day. In the remnants of the light they could see it had decimated over half the buildings in the small community. The restaurant and several of the shops had been destroyed and it had ripped apart most of what was left. Water was running somewhere from broken pipes, and a few of the structures were haloed in electrical sparks, which faintly lit up the area.

Henry stood at the edge of the forest and took in the damage. It crossed his mind: Had the creature been so vindictively destructive because they'd retaliated? Shot at it? Because they'd angered it? Henry believed that to be true, but no one else would. Well, maybe Justin would.

There weren't any fatalities, though, thank God. The smashed buildings had been empty. Pure luck.

"It's a good thing we evacuated days ago," Kiley panted. "We already have one bloodbath back at headquarters."

"Yes, good thing." Henry was surveying the mess. One of the buildings was on fire.

He asked Cummings to return to headquarters and have someone call into Klamath Falls on a car phone, if they couldn't get a cell phone to work, for firefighting equipment. He was sure Greer had already put in a call for medical assistance.

The pre-historic encroacher was nowhere in sight, but they could hear its bellowing voice as it moved away through the park. The air was filled by the snapping of trees and foliage crushed beneath giant feet.

"Where do you think it's heading now, Henry?" Kiley stood propped up against a tree, his face and clothes filthy. His head hung hopelessly in the fading light, as if he were so weary he couldn't hold it up.

"Back to the lake, I pray to god, and good riddance, and not towards another populated area, like a town. We'd have a real problem if it decides to leave the park."

"Wouldn't we? I don't even want to think about that possibility."

"Me, neither." Yet Henry had already thought about it and it filled him with despair. If that happened he'd have to call the local law enforcement authorities, the Feds and the media. The public had to be warned.

Walking towards the shattered buildings that had once been Rim Village, he gestured for the others to follow. "Anyone have another flashlight?" Though he had his, he wanted more light for their search.

The other two men switched theirs on and they advanced on the ghost village with the beams leading the way. There was only the sound of settling wood and leaking water pipes, the crackle of the fire. If anyone had been in any of the buildings, they were gone now, escaped into the forest or hiding somewhere. Henry prayed they wouldn't find any bodies buried in the rubble.

"Before we leave, let's check everything out. Make sure there's nobody trapped in any of these buildings. Nobody in need of help or medical attention."

The rangers trailed after him in the gloom as they shifted through the wreckage, their eyes nervous, their movements jerky, as if they were poised to run any second. Henry didn't blame them for being frightened. They'd seen what the creature could do. But Henry had to be sure there wasn't anyone who needed help before he and his men could leave.

Later, finding no one, they returned to headquarters and joined the others.

"Come on, Ann," Henry murmured when he found her sitting, dazed in the dark, on what was left of headquarters' steps. Those left behind had been afraid to call attention to themselves with lights. "I'll take you back to Zeke's."

He pulled her to her feet and brushed the dirt off her jeans and shirt. He didn't say a word about George; didn't question her on why she'd been in the park in the first place. He'd noticed the camera but hadn't said anything. She was feeling bad enough the way it was. They'd talk about everything later when she could handle it better. He was more concerned about the present whereabouts of the creature and what destruction it was wreaking at the moment.

Ann didn't inquire about Rim Village, too overwhelmed with what had happened earlier. And helping with the wounded had numbed her the rest of the way.

He'd sent one of his rangers to update Greer, so he didn't seek him out. All he had to do was get Ann someplace safe, someplace where she could rest and begin recovering from her ordeal. He'd never seen her in the state she was in. Her eyes were darkened with torment over what she'd seen that day and guilt over George's death.

She inclined her head, and followed him, silently; clutching her camera and her purse like a security blanket. She wouldn't meet his gaze. There was dried blood on her face, blood in her short hair. George's blood. Henry pulled her into his arms and rocked her, but still the tears refused to come.

Men were moving around, searching for their missing friends or partners, checking the damage and the dead; shuffling around like zombies.

Dr. Harris was nowhere to be found. Probably still hiding somewhere, plotting ways to capture and cage the monster. Maybe he was chasing it through the woods, like a hound dog on a rabbit, so he wouldn't lose sight of it.

As they were leaving, Henry saw Greer over a mangled body. He glanced up, recognized Henry, and signaled him to come over.

Ann insisted on coming with him and they walked over. Henry had overheard Patterson that morning talking about how Greer was a decorated Marine veteran. How he'd served three tours of duty overseas and had been a crack-shot sniper. Greer's long white hair was wild, his face and suit dirty. A bent and smashed MP5K clutched in one hand. He threw the broken weapon against a tree.

"How about Rim Village?" he asked Henry.

Henry slid a glance at Ann, her eyes closed as she leaned against him. He never was one to lie, so told the truth. "Demolished. The beast leveled practically everything. Just like here."

"Anyone else hurt?"

"Not that we could find. We checked the ruins. No one. Maybe some ran off. I hope so. Good thing we made everyone who could leave, evacuate days ago."

"Lucky for them." Greer rubbed his jaw with a shaking hand. He studied Henry. "Thanks to you. Park authorities wouldn't have pushed the park evacuation at all. But you went over their heads and did it anyway." The ex-agent paused, his shoulders falling. "There were enough deaths and injuries here."

Henry was surprised at the emotion he sensed in the man. Greer had feelings after all. And by the way he was behaving; he now had a quest as well.

"You were right, Chief Ranger, in one way," Greer added with determination in his eyes. "That monster needs to be *dead.* That's all. Not brought in alive. Not put in a cage like some tamed zoo animal.

"But in another way, you're wrong. You don't believe that creature is evil. And, maybe, it isn't really all evil. But as far as I'm concerned, if it keeps on killing–and I believe it will, until someone stops it–that's my definition of evil, whether it's intentional evil or not, human or animal. So damn the world and the creature's right to live in it because it's one of a kind. Damn Harris and his wealthy friends. Damn the Governor.

"We have to track the S.O.B. down and exterminate it as soon as possible."

Henry smiled at the man, and remembered the story he'd recounted about that serial killer. The man believed in retribution. "My way of thinking exactly, Greer."

He looked down at the woman huddled in his arms. "You seem to have everything in control and before anything else happens, I'm taking my wife to town so she'll be safe. When I return we can discuss what we're going to do next. I have some ideas I need to pass by you."

"I'll be here." Greer was staring around at the wounded that had been gathered. The dead. Some were covered, some weren't. Henry couldn't bear to look at them any longer. They'd been friends. There were at least four dead, three rangers, including George, and one maintenance man who'd been in headquarters that day repairing the plumbing, and two wounded, whose groans filled the evening. There was only one dead body, though, because the creature had completely consumed George and two others of its victims.

"I'm sorry about your friend, George," Greer whispered. "I saw the whole thing. He was a courageous man."

A lump caught in Henry's throat, but he managed to answer, "That he was."

"Get your wife out of here." Greer's voice was normal again. "She looks like she needs a quiet place to recuperate."

"How will we get to Zeke's?" Ann said, suddenly seeming to be back with them. "My car was destroyed. It's up the road a ways."

Henry glanced at the smashed vehicle he'd been using the last few days. The beast had danced on it, too.

Greer was looking at the same thing.

"Here." He handed Henry a set of keys. "Use my car. The black Chevy over there. It's in one piece and I won't be needing it for a while."

"Thanks." Henry took the keys. "I'll return it after I've dropped Ann off in town. I won't be gone long. I just want her someplace safe."

"Don't worry, Ranger, I'll hold down the fort here until you get back. I don't think our visitor from a horror film will return tonight, but I'm not sure, and we have to get these wounded out of here in case it does."

"And we still don't have those bigger weapons."

"About the weapons, I'll be making a call to someone concerning that soon as the ambulance picks our wounded up. I'm tired of waiting for what we've ordered through proper channels. I have a special friend, who I'm sure will help us–without questions and right away."

"Great. That takes one worry off my mind."

Henry steered Ann towards the car, helped her in, got in himself, and drove into the dark. He fought the desperation, the fear, in his gut, aware that his headlights could be seen for a long distance, and tried not to speed too much. It was hard. He wanted to be back with Greer and the others. There was work to do and they might not have much time before another assault came.

He and Ann talked little on the way. She was so sorry she hadn't listened to him and came back into the park. So sorry George was dead. But she couldn't bear to really talk about it yet, as if by not talking about him would change what had happened. She cried. Henry consoled her, driving one-handed, fighting his own grief, as well. He couldn't afford tears or they'd end up in a ditch somewhere. Not a good idea. He had no clue where the monster was.

But during the drive all he could think about was when the creature would reappear. Where? Who would it butcher next? And how in the world were they going to stop it, before Harris brought in reinforcements to protect the damn thing?

For it was a certainty that if Harris wasn't dead, he was off somewhere bending someone's ear, trying to safe guard the monster.

Over my dead body, Henry swore. And meant every word.

***

The creature stalked the forest searching for more of the funny, puny two-legged critters that tasted so good. Though the critters did make an awful racket when it caught them. Its belly was full, but it was an eating machine. It'd eat until there was nothing else to eat. Then it would root out more. It was smart enough to know that its supply of food had been dwindling. First the tasty swimming things in the lake and now the critters…they were getting harder and harder to find. It had to search further out. Even in the daylight. If it was to stay alive, it must eat.

It was bored, too.

Lonely. Deep in its brain it knew there should be others like it. A herd of others like it. Running and playing, feeding, together. Swimming the caves under the lake. Who would be its mate when the time came? Who would help it raise the little ones coming? It'd never seen another one like itself, but in its genetic memories it sensed they must exist. Somewhere. It was looking. Forever looking.

It looked up at the dark sky, growled at the tiny sparkling pieces of fire embedded in the black velvet. The call of the peaceful, warm water; the safety of the caves, its home, was too strong to resist and it returned to the lake. Dived deep and swam hard. It was a powerful swimmer. But it would become stronger as it grew.

It was young. Still growing and learning. It needed more food.

Entering the large underwater cave that was its home, it remembered when those peculiar floating things that chirped and flashed with pretty lights, putted across the lake's surface like big bugs. It had loved to play with them. Chase them. They had been creatures nearer to its size. Strange companions, but still companions. Now they were gone, they'd all died, it seemed, and now were empty shells beached along the shore which no longer had the spark of life.

It missed them. It'd pretended they were its own kind. But they were never strong. It always beat them. They fell apart, when it nudged them. It hadn't been able to eat them, either. They hadn't tasted good. Hadn't filled its belly. Whereas the small critters, at least, did that.

It entered the subterranean cavern and swam back into its world. A world of stone, water, and molten lava, of darkness and bones. Of long past whispers. A world of dead skeletons that stared out of the rocks at it, but never stirred. Just bones. Lifeless.

But it was a world where there weren't any of those queer tiny beings shouting and running, throwing things that sometimes stung. They made it angry hurting it as they had. It had come to enjoy hurting them back and smashing their frail hiding places made of wood and stone.

It scooted into its cave, its world of warmth and safety.

Its home and once the home of all its family. Brethren now long gone but for whom it was forever searching. Someday it'd find them. Someday there'd be more like it. It sensed that.

CHAPTER 14

Ann needed a sedative that night to sleep. Zeke had some mild pills he deemed were safe enough for her to take and gave her two.

Henry tucked her into bed and closed the door quietly behind him, leaving Laura hovering over her mother, playing the worried nurse. He couldn't bear to hear Ann crying any more.

Ann had confessed what she'd been doing in the park; explained about how Zeke was going to shut down the newspaper, and that was why she'd risked reentering–for the pictures and the story. She'd told him about the camcorder she'd been looking for and that's when Henry divulged he'd had it all along. The realization had made both of them feel worse. If only he'd told her. If only she'd asked. It made George's death seem more unnecessary.

"There are forests, miles and miles of woods and other lakes around here. I wouldn't have given away the precise location of where the creature was, Henry," she'd confided in a guilty voice. "That would have put other people in danger. All I needed was the pictures."

He wasn't angry at her for George's death. Ann could have, should have died that day, and he was relieved beyond thankfulness she was still alive. George had selflessly given up his life for her as he would have for any number of people he'd cared about. The park, the safety of its visitors had been important to him. Henry would have done the same.

Ann claimed the blame for George's death

anyway. It'd take her a long time, if ever, to forgive herself. George hadn't been just a man who'd worked with him, she'd known George, had been his friend, had laughed at his jokes, lame as they'd usually been; served him her best meals and homemade pies, for the time they'd lived in the park. Because George and her husband had become fast friends the minute they'd met when Henry had first arrived

"None of this was your fault," Henry said, trying to console her. "It's that monster out in the woods that killed George and the others."

He hadn't breathed a word about the doomed Deep Rover and Mark Lassen's death to her, but as he gulped down a cup of coffee in the kitchen, he told Zeke about it and the attack at Ranger Headquarters and Rim Village.

Zeke listened, somber faced, and didn't once ask if he could print the story, though Henry knew as well as the old man that it would have saved his dying newspaper. And the thought came to Henry that Zeke might in part blame himself for Ann's misadventure, and perhaps, indirectly, even George's death, because she'd done it for him and the newspaper.

Zeke offered him a tuna fish sandwich, but Henry wasn't hungry. He needed to return to the park and prepare for the creature's next onslaught, make a few difficult phone calls and help Greer fend off the press. Because there'd be questions to answer; questions they wouldn't be able to avoid this time. Henry couldn't hide the bodies or what had happened to them once the ambulances made their way back to the hospital. And then there'd be hell to pay.

"Tell me something, son," Zeke asked Henry. "That monster going to stay in your park, or do we here in town have something to worry about?"

Henry had never seen Zeke so disconcerted, troubled. "Zeke, I'm not going to lie. I don't know. So far it's remained in the park, close to the lake, but I don't know if it'll stay there. It's already surprised us a couple of times. It's so unpredictable."

"What are you going to do about it then?"

"Me?"

"Yes, you? I can tell you're plotting something by the way you're acting. Got that, *I'm going to take care of it* air about you."

Henry met Zeke's eyes. The old man looked tired and older than the last time he'd seen him. According to Ann, his wife's death and now losing his business was prematurely aging him.

"If I tell you, you have to keep it to yourself. Off the record?"

"That goes without question."

"Against orders, a team of us are going after *it*. And when we find it we're going to destroy it."

"I imagine, under the circumstances, that's the best thing. Good luck, then."

"Thanks, we'll need it."

As he left, the last thing Henry saw was Ann's camera on the kitchen table. He must have been in a state of grief over his friend's death because he didn't mash it into pieces.

The drive into the park helped clear his mind.

He had private time to grieve. Tears glistened in his eyes as he let the good memories of his dead friend slowly overlay the horrific images of his last minutes on earth. George must have thought he owed him something for that time he'd saved his life out in the woods. Poor George. What a terrible way to die.

At that moment, Henry despised that creature more than anything in the world. He wanted to kill it as it had killed George. Nothing else mattered. All his earlier awe and love of prehistoric creatures, dead or alive, had evaporated.

By the time he arrived at what was left of headquarters he was almost himself again. With the absence of lights from the buildings now gone or shuttered in darkness, night, a solid velvet blanket, had settled on the park.

Dim lanterns were in use, hanging from trees, glowing like weak fireflies and softly highlighting the wreckage. Just enough to see by.

No one wanted to draw the monster back to finish what it'd begun.

There were three silent ambulances without lights. People, not saying much, milled around searching for the missing, or parts of them. Outside authorities had been tipped off and officers were everywhere filling out reports while the nearby local newspapers were snapping pictures and asking uncomfortable questions. Everything was being conducted in an orderly fashion and as swiftly and inconspicuously as possible. They'd all been warned not to make noise or call attention to themselves and had been told why. Of course, no one believed them.

Greer had done well, taking George's place as smoothly as if he'd always been Henry's second in command.

Henry helped load up a mauled body shrouded in a blood-stained sheet. Greer turned away from the ambulance after the doors closed and said, "We're having a hell of a time keeping a lid on this with the news media slobbering over us. The ambulances from town lured them out here like flies to carrion. We've been fighting them off since you left. Keeping them quiet as to what happened here isn't an option, either. I'm afraid our cover is blown. The monster will soon be famous." In the faint light Greer even cracked a sarcastic smile.

"We've had to escort at least three newspaper reporters off the premises and one television crew. They were making too much noise and were flashing lights everywhere. One of the television crew, I'm afraid, got film of the carnage. They got away before we could confiscate it. Slippery little devils, aren't they?" The last thing they wanted was people to panic.

"The media. Most of them aren't any better than rabid dogs once they get the scent of a disaster."

"And those Inquirer reporters you talked about have definitely been missed. Their backup is arriving in force."

"And we thought," Henry sighed glumly, "we had trouble before."

"Ain't seen nothing yet, I reckon."

"Well, it can't be helped. Publicity. It was only a matter of time. Too many people disappearing and too many unexplained deaths to keep it a secret now. Let's just get these people cleared out of here before that monster comes back for dessert. We've got to move quickly now."

"You got it, Ranger," Greer said. "But first, can I talk to you in private?"

Henry nodded and they stepped away from the crowd to stand behind a mound of wooden debris; all that was left of Park Headquarters. Greer kept shifting his eyes behind and around him, watching and listening. He was a trained soldier beneath his polished ways, always on alert.

"I don't think it'll come back here tonight," Henry tried to ease the man's fear. "It's too shrewd for that. It knows we might be ready for it next time."

"You think it's that smart, huh?"

"Yes, I do."

"Oh." Greer leaned against a section of wall that didn't look too sturdy but where there was no light. Shadows hid the two men as they talked. The barrier muffled their voices.

It'd been warm that day but the night had brought a distinct chill. There was the scent of rain in the air. Maybe it'd wash away the cloying stench of fresh blood, Henry brooded.

"There's going to be a next time, Ranger, isn't there? Real soon."

"Yes, but on our terms. We're going to locate that thing's lair and exterminate it before it slaughters anyone else. It's killed too many people. Some were good men, with families. I'm going to have to face those families and I can't unless I've gotten rid of that abomination once and for all."

"I second that. It's time to go on the offensive. Go after it. We can't keep letting it make the rules and butcher more people." Greer gazed off towards the distant trees. Watching. "Because what's to keep it in the park now? There are people and towns out there." The man, his silhouette in the gloom stooped, wiped his face with his hand.

A moon was rising and Greer's predatory eyes gleamed in its soft glow as he tilted his face towards Henry's.

The two men stood there, listening. The night animals were chattering. The winds were whispering. A light splattering of rain caressed their faces. For now it was safe. All was normal. But for how long?

"I've been talking to Jim Francis," Greer said. "He has an idea how to solve our problem."

"So Francis made it through the attack? Good." Henry liked the older man, ponytail, cowboy hat and all.

"He wants vengeance for his friend's death also."

Out in the black woods Henry thought he heard George's ghost laughing. Finally free of human form, George's Indian spirit was wandering the forest he'd loved. That mental picture, at least, brought a smile to Henry's lips. It was better to think of George that way than decomposing in some beast's belly. Around them the wind rustled the summer leaves high up in the trees. Henry imagined it was ghosts, all the humans who'd ever died in the park over all the years, talking among themselves;

George now with them.

"Francis is getting another submersible down here. He pulled some big strings and got a four-seater this time called the Big Rover. He's piloted it before. This sub is not only bigger, faster, but possesses formidable weaponry. He believes it'll be more than a match for the creature. He'll bring the sub down from Vancouver in a couple of days, after he informs Lassen's widow of the man's death and attends the funeral…well, a memorial, at least, because there's no body to bury. He's flying there tonight. He's already left.

"When he returns, he'll study the video tapes of Lassen's exploration of that underwater lava cave. Francis is positive we'll find the monster in there somewhere. He's sure that's why Lassen motored into it."

"Justin believes our target's living in one of those caves, too," Henry recalled. "Humph, exploring that submerged cave isn't something I'm looking forward to, but Justin's sure the monster lives in one of its tunnels. I've never been in an underwater lava cave before."

"Me neither. Not an active one like that anyway.

"Okay, Ranger, so we're going hunting for the creature. If we find it, we have to be sure we can kill it," Greer's tone was serious. "So I made that special phone call when you were gone. I think I have the weapons on their way that'll do the job. A couple of grenade launchers and some other goodies. Should be here tomorrow."

"You're a man of many hidden talents, Greer."

"Thanks, I aim to please."

Henry thought Greer grinned in the dark, but he couldn't be sure, the man's face was in shadow.

An owl mourned for the dead from the tree behind them and brought Henry back to the painful present. For some reason the sound made him nervous. The woods and everything in them seemed alien and threatening all of a sudden. The moon had slipped behind clouds and shadowed the earth. Henry couldn't shake his growing disquiet.

"You know how to operate a grenade launcher?" Henry grilled Greer.

"Of course. I was in the service. Marines."

"So was I," Henry disclosed. "Iraq."

"Me, too, very beginning of it. But I learned how to use a L.A.W.S. Rocket and grenade launchers. That's one thing you have to give our armed forces. They teach you how to kill pretty well. The bigger, the more destructive weapons, the better.

"I figure a RPG-7 Grenade Launcher will make a dent in that thing's tough hide. Hopefully stop it dead in its tracks. Blow it to pieces. And I know some tricks that'll guarantee it. Bet you do, too."

Henry didn't need to answer. He'd been in a war zone and knew the tricks just as well as Greer. Now Greer knew he knew it, too.

Greer went into a crouch then and Henry followed, down to the other man's level.

"We can doctor up the grenade rockets…fill them with white phosphorus," Greer said. "When the rocket explodes it'll burn everything it touches, inside and out, until there's nothing left. It'll burn even when submerged in water."

"Sounds right to me. Should do the trick." Henry whistled low under his breath. "Good plan, Greer. Couldn't of done better myself."

Greer made a noise that might have been a polite grunt. "We better conclude our business, though, before Dr. Harris gets the Governor to send the army in here. They'll lock up the park tight as a jail and launch an all-out search to seize, capture, the valuable *specimen*." He stressed the last word. "Harris is probably on the phone with the Governor right now."

"Damn," Henry swore. "I'd hoped the monster had gotten him. No such luck, huh?"

Greer laughed, restrained, but still a laugh. Everyone knew how he felt about Dr. Harris.

"I think we have maybe two days before the troops arrive," Henry warned. "If Harris can talk the governor into it."

"Oh, he can. If there's notoriety or money to be made, a politician will move a mountain to acquire it. I know the Governor personally and he's as greedy and crooked as they come."

Henry and Greer stood up. Someone was calling their names, looking for them.

Henry recognized the voice. "It's Maltin, back from John Day's."

The two men went to meet the paleontologist.

"What the heck happened here?" was the first thing out of Justin's mouth.

"The creature followed us from the lake and attacked us," Henry replied. "You had already left."

"Oh, god, I was afraid of that. It's extending its hunting territory seeking food. Three miles from the lake, though, heaven knows how far out it can travel. Even into town."

"Even into town," Henry echoed softly.

The three of them spoke quietly in the fluttering lantern light about what had happened when Justin had been gone. The scientist was shocked to learn George was dead. He'd liked him, too. He felt awful about his death, yet was relieved to hear Ann was okay. He agreed wholeheartedly with Henry and Greer that they *had* to go after the monster. They no longer had a choice. It was either the creature or them.

They discussed what they'd do when the submersible arrived. None of them spoke of how dangerous their unauthorized expedition would be. They didn't need to. It was something they all just understood, accepted.

They'd get some food, sleep and reconnect at dawn. Henry wanted to sift through the debris of Rim Village for bodies in the daylight.

Henry and Justin left Greer, who was staying at the lodge, and returned to Henry's cabin. Greer again loaning Henry his car since he was only a short walk from the lodge.

The whole drive, Henry's nerves were on edge, afraid the headlights would spotlight their nemesis. If it showed up now, before they got their weapons, he knew they wouldn't have a chance.

Henry breathed with relief when they pulled into the driveway and he shut off the car's lights and motor.

"There's steaks in the freezer, Justin. I'm not sure I'll eat much myself, but we need to keep our strength up, so I'll force myself. Can I interest you in a steak, with all the fixings?"

"Sure," the young man answered. "You know I can never turn down a free meal. I haven't eaten all day. Been on the road. I wanted to get back and didn't stop for anything, not even food. I've discovered more than I bargained for and wanted to share it with you."

"Good. You can tell me about it when we get inside. Right now, we'll grab the steaks from the freezer and take them to Zeke's. I want to check on Ann. She was pretty upset when I left her earlier." And he wanted to be with her, Laura and Phoebe one more time before they went after the monster. In case, like Lassen, he never made it back.

"That's an even better idea," Justin exclaimed as they got out of the car and he trailed Henry into the cabin. "I need to see Laura and Phoebe, too."

"I thought you might."

Inside, they gathered the supplies for their meal as they caught each other up on things.

Justin told Henry he wanted to come along on their dinosaur hunt.

"Are you sure you want to come along? You don't have to, you know." Henry gave the kid a chance to back out. "Your ribs and all." Justin was moving as they still hurt him.

"No, I'm fine. They hardly hurt at anymore. Well, not much. I'm just tired mostly, that's all. I've come this far, might as well go in for the whole shebang. Besides, I have inside information about that creature that might help you to fight it."

"So you found out something more from those

expert friends of yours at John Day's about our enemy, hey?"

Justin had collaborated with some other paleontologists about the creature's possible origin and behavior patterns. Hoping to glean more information they could use to fight it.

"I did. The animals represented by the samples they'd been provided aren't exactly the same as the thing that's giving us what for, but my associates agree they're possibly a pre-ancestor. Between all of us we came up with a game plan on how we might defeat a live one."

"Great, you can tell me more on the way to town. I want to get out of here quick as we can. No dawdling."

"Oh, and Leon Vaughn, one of our new guys, talked to a friend of his at the Seismographic Center in Portland about our earthquake problem. Leon's friend said that the signs show we're probably due for a big one in the next few weeks. He'd stake his reputation on it. And, no surprise, the fault line that runs through this area goes right beneath the caldera."

"I wish your friend's friend could have given us an exact day and time, as well. Our trip can't wait until after the earthquake…if we have one."

"I knew you'd say that." They left the house and got into the car.

Justin wanted to see if his cabin, with all his personal stuff in it, in Rim Village was still there, so Henry, against his better judgment but caving into Justin's need, drove him by the destruction. The fire trucks had done their job and were long gone. The smoldering heaps of concrete and wood were deserted in the dark. His cabin was one of them.

"Well, I guess I'll have to buy new clothes. No one was hurt, though?"

"No, not here anyway, not that we could tell. Most had already left."

"Lucky for them," Justin murmured. They drove through the dark park on their way to town, alert to the slightest movement or noise that might herald the return of their nemesis.

The first tremors they didn't feel because they were in the car bumping along the road. But they felt the larger ones, which were violent enough that their vehicle swerved across the road and nearly ended up in a ditch.

Once Henry brought the car under control, he stopped beside a swaying tree, the ground rocking wildly. Justin was holding on to the dash.

Neither of them said anything until the earth grew calm again.

"That was fun." Henry glanced over at his passenger.

"I'd estimate that was about a four pointer," Justin muttered. His eyes were on the shadowy night world outside the windows. "About as bad as the one they recorded here this morning around dawn. All just warm-ups for the big one."

Henry got the car on the road again, grumbling under his breath all the way. Outside it began to rain, soft and light.

Voracious monsters, an empty park, his family miles away, dead friends, and earthquakes. How much worse could it get? Henry didn't want to think about it. What he cared about was seeing Ann and the girls and making sure they were okay.

The rest of it could wait until tomorrow.

***

And it did.

Justin, Greer, and Henry were inspecting what remained of Rim Village, as they waited for the submersible to arrive; jumpy every moment about the monster returning, when one of the other rangers down the street came jogging up.

There were bodies under the ruins.

The men, even Justin with his sore ribs, helped dig them out.

"Who do you think they were?" Justin stared at the corpses, his face a shade off color.

The three bodies were laid out in a row besides the demolished building, a Mexican restaurant that had served the best burritos in the park. Ann had sent Henry himself many nights for their carry-out because they'd used real cheese and the freshest lettuce and tomatoes.

"I don't know." Henry's eyes slid over the bloody bodies as one of the rangers covered them. The dead faces were dirty and mangled. They could have been under the monster's feet, they were that bad.

Greer was almost his old calm-faced self. A clean set of clothes, a blue shirt and blue jeans; not his usual suit, his hair neatly combed, but unsprayed. The man was loosening up, except for the notebook in his hand as he jotted things down. But there was a different look in his eyes now, a humble one, and he hadn't pulled out his fancy gold watch once.

"There was an apartment behind the restaurant," Henry filled in the blanks. "I guess these were three who hadn't left yet. Maybe were laying low." It didn't make him feel any better knowing the victims had stayed for whatever reason, and now were dead for it. He should have been firmer, more efficient, in his evacuation policy. Yet, a lesson had been learned and he'd ordered his men to clear everyone in a twenty miles radius surrounding the lake out of the park, cabin by cabin, door by door; no more excuses accepted.

"We'll need to track down their families." Greer had turned his gaze away from the covered lumps on the ground.

Patterson walked up. "More bad news. They've found two more bodies a couple of buildings down. Dead as cardboard, and just about as flat. The monster did a job on them, too." Henry noted that Patterson had stopped calling the monster Godzilla since he'd seen it in action.

Greer frowned slightly, his face fighting to stay emotionless.

"Damn," Henry swore. He didn't want to see, but he did anyway. The bodies resembled the others. Hardly recognizable as human. "Let's pray there aren't any more like these."

Overhead gulls were singing to each other beneath a gray sky. To Henry it looked and smelled like rain again.

"Well," Greer commented standing beside him. "We keep looking."

They spent half the day in the debris searching

and raking through the wreckage. They continued to find bodies. Henry despaired. There were too many of them. Why had they all stayed? Why hadn't he known they were hiding and gotten them to leave? His guilt bit at him.

Fear churned in the air around them. Someone jerked or jumped every time there was a strange noise; eyes probed the woods and peeked around building corners before the person followed. Henry put two rangers on guard duty. If they saw or heard anything that could be the creature coming, they were to alert the rest of them immediately and they'd all bug out. But they had to get the dead out first if they could.

At mid-day, Henry in his dusty uniform, Justin and Greer, sat down under a shady tree and ate the hamburgers and fries one of the men had brought them from town for lunch. The search was taking longer than they'd planned. They'd uncovered more dead.

It was overcast, warm, yet the rain hadn't materialized. Henry was glad of that. His men were having a bad enough day without getting soaked to boot.

Justin and Greer, who'd hit it off from the start, were scheming on how to find and kill the beast, but Henry was scrutinizing Rim Village. So much devastation in so little time. A bomb might have been dropped. The absent owners of the demolished stores and shops would be upset when they discovered their buildings were gone. He knew many of the businessmen; known how hard they'd scrimped, saved, to have their shops. How loved some of the crushed cabins and cottages had been by their owners. The owners who were still alive, that is.

Greer and he discussed if the absent businessmen should be told their places were gone.

"We could let them know." Henry had eaten as much of his hamburger as he could, but couldn't finish it. In his mind, he kept seeing the corpses on the ground. "Don't know what good it'd do. Anyway, it's too dangerous to allow them to reenter the park to assess damages."

"They deserve to be informed," Justin joined the conversation as he wrapped up what food he had left. He, too, hadn't eaten much. No one had. Half of it was left for the garbage can.

"You're right." Another unwanted duty to perform.

"I say we don't tell them quite yet," Greer counseled. "They'd swamp the park, wanting to see, rebuild, demanding to be told what happened here. It's not safe. Better to keep them out until the creature is taken care of."

So that's how it ended. Henry would report the destruction to Superintendent Sorrelson sometime that day, he had to, but Sorrelson was as far as the news was going for now.

They finished at Rim Village and packed it in for the day. Henry growing more nervous every minute. Where was the monster and why hadn't it shown itself all day? What was it up to now? When would it strike again? He had no answers.

He sent his men to safety and invited Greer and Justin over for supper, telling Greer he'd pick him up at the lodge at six, before the daylight went; after he and Justin checked in on Ann and Laura again. They were still using Greer's car.

Jim Francis had called Greer earlier saying he'd be bringing down the new submersible the following day. He'd said he couldn't wait to go after the evil creature.

Not Henry. He wasn't eager to face the thing on its own turf. He knew it had to be done, but sure wasn't looking forward to it. Francis might believe the Big Rover was safer than the Deep Rover, but Henry couldn't forget what had happened to Lassen, and he'd believed in the safety of the submersible as well.

The men split and went their separate ways. The creature hadn't been sighted and, for some reason, that made Henry more anxious than he could say. He kept rehearing what Greer had whispered the night before: *There are people and towns out there.*

Henry kept expecting to hear about a monster attacking a heavily populated area any second. It gave him a sick sense of urgency that wouldn't be quieted.

Perhaps that was one of the reasons, after they left Greer and before they went into town that Henry spoke to Justin about watching over Ann if something were to happen to him. Somewhere deep in his mind, though he didn't want to admit it, he was preparing in case he didn't survive the underwater caves.

He told Justin where the camcorder was that Ann had been looking for and he made Justin promise to get it to her. Ann had risked her life looking for it in the first place and Henry could understand why. That video or pictures from the video of the creature, later when it was over, would fetch quite a sum of money. Not only would it save the Klamath Falls Journal, and Ann's job, but it'd help her, moneywise, if something happened to him. He worried about her. If he were dead she wouldn't be allowed to stay in the cabin; there was only a small life insurance policy through his job and they had little savings. The reality of living middleclass these days.

Justin had looked at him oddly when he'd talked about such things, but he'd agreed to do as asked. "Anything for you and Ann," he'd promised. "Whatever you want me to do, I'll do."

As they drove through the park towards the exit, Justin remarked on the growing mist everywhere. "I imagine the lake's completely covered in it. Bet, if we drive down there right now, we couldn't even see Phantom Ship or Wizard Island. It's eerie. Gives me the creeps."

"Worst I've ever seen it. And this early in the day," Henry commented. "The mist will get worse as evening and lower temperatures come in." The fog had curled up around their car, an invisible entity that made them feel as if they were driving through a cloud. They couldn't see the road. Could hardly see the trees looming above them. Just a strip of asphalt winding ahead of their headlights.

"I haven't had time in the last few days to take any readings, so it's more of a general observation, but temperatures under the lake must still be rising." Justin looked out over the swirling cloud. "And the rock below the caldera might still be shifting from the earthquakes. That means more lava coming up to the surface and heating the water. This mist is the result."

"If it keeps up," Henry snorted. "When we reopen the park, we'll have to advertise the lake as the amazing boiling lake. Cook your eggs in it for lunch! Hang your coffee thermos over the edge of your boat's side, and keep it warm. Jump in the water and take a hot bath!"

Justin chuckled.

So did Henry. It felt good after all the terror and sadness of the last two days.

Talking about hot baths reminded Henry of the homeless camp. He wondered how they were doing in town where they'd been relocated. If George were alive he would have known, would have cared enough to seek them out and make sure they were all right. Henry made a mental note to ask Ann to check up on them in the next couple of days. It might help take her mind off George's death, helping those he used to help.

Leaving the park, after a particularly long silence, Henry slid his eyes across to his passenger and smiled. In the front seat, against the foggy window, Justin had fallen asleep.

Henry didn't have the heart to wake him though they had so much more to discuss about Justin's recent fact-finding trip. But, Henry thought tiredly, it could wait until later. Let the young man get a small nap. He seemed to need it.

His foot pushed harder on the accelerator pedal. As the afternoon's shadows slipped in around him with the mist, he was aware they weren't alone. *It* was out there somewhere in the lake or the woods, and Henry felt like a painted target rumbling along in his borrowed car.

CHAPTER 15

As the Deep Rover before it, Jim Francis's friends brought the Big Rover down to Cleetwood Dock on a flatbed truck. It impressed Henry that Francis was able to secure another vehicle after what had happened to the last one.

The submersibles were worth a fortune, and after Lassen's death and the Deep Rover's destruction, Francis's benefactor had been cautious. He hadn't wanted to lend out the Big Rover. But Francis, in the end, had talked it out of him. It'd helped that the man was one of Francis's good friends and had known Lassen, too.

"Since the massacre at Ranger Headquarters and the leveling of Rim Village, the word there's some mysterious predator stalking the park is out of the bag," was the first thing Francis relayed to Henry when he met him and the others on the dock that morning.

"It was all over the news last night and this morning. You're going to be plagued from now on with television crews and newspaper reporters from all over, swarming into the park hoping to get a look at the *monster from the lake*. Danger or no danger. It'll be crazy."

"Damn, just what we need. Trespassers and gawkers. Well, we'll just have to keep them out, that's all."

"Good luck," Francis muttered. "I saw the curious gathering at the park's main entrance as I brought the Rover in. They're a pack of wild animals, let me tell you. They were all over me with questions and camcorders in my face."

Henry was relieved Francis was more himself since his return. He also seemed extremely determined to find what they were looking for and to deal with it.

The Big Rover was a different sort of craft than the smaller Rover had been. Francis confessed right off that it was an experimental model designed for much more than research. "It's brand new off the assembly line and bigger, sleeker, than the first Rover. It's also diesel-fueled, entirely computer controlled, and built for speed, with strong retractable jointed arms and claws for picking up objects. It can outrun anything in the water and resist any attack, its hull is that strong. It's made to defend itself, with limited missile ability, if need be.

"And, as you can see, it's a dull black, no shiny surfaces to attract the leviathan, with large portal windows circling the top, and is also equipped with underwater lights, television and cameras. It seats four people."

"Only four, huh?" Henry studied the machine as it was lowered from the truck into the water. The men who'd brought it were anxious to unload it and get away from the lake. He didn't blame them a bit. If he could, he'd run away, too.

Patterson posed the top question on everyone's mind. "Which four of us are going on its maiden voyage?"

Henry had decided on who should go the day before but until that moment hadn't talked about it. "I'm going. Greer, as my second-in-command.

Maltin, because he's the dinosaur expert, and, of course, we'll need Francis to operate it.

"The rest of my men will remain behind to keep people out of the park and keep things running, with Patterson in charge. He'll have my permission to alert the National Guard or the army if the creature reappears and heads for any park exit."

No one was surprised at the choices. Patterson was openly relieved he wasn't going below as did most of the other rangers. After what had happened to the Deep Rover none of them wanted to play Sea Hunt in the lake.

"I've been in helicopters and on boats of various kinds," Greer admitted. "No submarines, though. And I'm eager for the coming adventure."

"I haven't, either." Henry patted the man on the back. "So it'll be a new experience for both of us."

"The three of us, you mean?" Justin interjected. "I've never been on one, either. And I don't like closed in spaces. I'm sort of…claustrophobic."

Henry eyed the young scientist. "You don't like water and you hate caves. Now you're telling us you're afraid of tight places? You *sure* you want to come along, Maltin?"

Justin straightened up to his tallest height, his gaze steady. "You need me. I think I know the creature we're going after better than any of you. So I'm coming." But to Henry, with that unruly blond hair of his and round spectacles, he still seemed an innocent teenager.

Henry nodded, looking out over the lake in the early morning mist. Where was *it* now, he thought? *Where was it?*

The rain had not materialized, but the air was wet with moisture and made everything feel clammy. The clouds had blocked the sun's light, making it look more like early evening than morning.

Greer was busy checking out the Big Rover. He'd been intrigued from the first second he'd laid eyes on the contraption, asking questions of Francis on how it was operated and controlled. He'd started making conversation to bring Francis out of his lethargy brought on by Lassen's death. But once he'd got the man talking about his work and now the Big Rover, Francis had opened up. He'd even begun to smile again.

Once the Rover was in the water, Francis gave Greer, Justin and Henry a guided tour of its interior. Henry wanted to know everything about the control panel and what switches and dials ran what. Francis was happy to oblige.

"This doesn't look anything like the other one," Greer said to Jim Francis once they'd lowered themselves into the craft. "It's got so many windows."

"The two Rovers are light years apart, and yes, there's a reason for all the window area, Greer. It's so you can see more outside."

"With the sneakiness of our quarry, we're going to need that."

To Henry the Deep Rover had brought to mind a large suited-up space alien with a bubble head. Its basic design hadn't been very appealing. But the Big Rover looked more like a true submarine should. It reminded him of a very large, sleek ebony shark. Which might or might not be a good thing.

"You men ready for a trial run? I've been dying to try this baby out." Francis looked at them one at a time.

"I'm ready," Henry replied.

"Let's do it." Greer tipped a finger forward.

Justin gulped, but bobbed his head yes.

Henry marveled at the advanced technology and the maneuverability of the Big Rover once they were submerged. He tried a hand at piloting and caught on quickly as Francis explained the running sequence. Then Greer tried his hand at the wheel. Henry and Greer pestered Francis with questions about the machine and the pilot seemed happy to answer them.

"It wouldn't be such a bad idea," Francis proposed, "if you and Greer had a rough idea of how to handle this baby." In case, Henry thought, something happened to its pilot?

Justin didn't seem interested in driving lessons. He was more obsessed with the view from the windows and the smallness of the enclosure. His eyes never left the water beyond the glass, his fingers never stopped tapping nervously on one surface or another.

Francis took extra care explaining how the sub ran to Henry and Greer, though.

"There…that red toggle switch there, Shore…easy…easy…now you can accelerate. That's right, that pedal. You want to try reverse?"

"Sure. Which switch is that?"

Francis showed him as the Big Rover cleanly sped through the water. Suddenly the sub came to an abrupt stop and backtracked so quickly, Justin fell out of his seat.

"You seem to have a knack for it, Chief Ranger. You're a natural."

Greer chuckled. Justin buckled himself in like he should have done. Henry tried again. The ride was smoother the second time.

After a little more instruction Francis declared, "Shore, if you ever consider giving up bossing around these rangers of yours give me a call. I'll put you to work in one of these babies. Make you my new partner." Henry had done well on his maiden voyage, as had Greer, and Francis agreed to teach him more when they had the time. Then Francis took over the controls.

"Thanks. I'll remember that offer." Henry watched Francis maneuver the sub. "After this little escapade of ours, I might need a new job. And I always wanted to live in Canada. I hear the hunting's real good up there."

For the brief time they'd taken turns piloting the sleek submersible their predicament hadn't been the main topic. Their problems were set aside but not forgotten. Even Justin seemed to stop worrying about the monster lurking beyond the windows as they traded stories of old hunting trips and better times.

It was the break they needed.

"You heard right," Francis said. "Sometimes my brothers, I have three, and I go out camping in the wilderness for weeks. We pack up tents, warm sleeping bags, and live off the land. Sometimes I go alone. Last year I ran into a herd of moose and followed them for days, observing. Magnificent animals. Dumb, though. And the country's beautiful up there. No humans for as far as the eye can see, just forests and sky. Virgin territory."

"As beautiful as this?" Henry waved his hand to include the lake and the land beyond it.

"Almost." Francis grinned over the video screens in the sub's cockpit. "Except the bears are worse up there than here. We grow them bigger and meaner because the winters are harsher."

Greer gave Francis a doubting smile.

The sounds of the engines steady and strong were humming around them. Henry could feel the acceleration as the sub moved silently through the water.

"No winters are harsher than Oregon winters," Henry stated. "We're usually snowed in from September to May."

"Well, then." Francis chuckled. "We'd better catch this thing before September. I don't think Big Boy here can cut through ice."

"Why not? It appears capable of doing everything else."

"Doesn't make a difference anyway," Justin put his two cents in. "This lake is never going to freeze again. The water's too warm."

Greer seemed to tolerate them and their chatter. The second part of the trial run, after he'd put his time in at driving, he was busy with his notebook and intent on the murky outer scenery through the portals as they slid through the water back towards the dock. But Henry knew it was just a façade he presented to the world. The night before Henry had caught a glimpse of the caring man he was underneath all the stone, but that hadn't lasted long. Today the man was back to his old, professional self.

Though, in his own way, Greer was absorbed with the submersible and everything connected with their coming odyssey. And Henry was certain he was listening closely to everything Francis was saying; watching everything they were doing at the controls and most likely memorizing every move. Using that photographic memory of his, no doubt.

Justin, on the other hand, had disliked the submersible the minute they'd lowered themselves into its belly. Even if it was four times larger than the smaller Rover, it was still too cramped for Justin.

There was no place to go once you were in it, he complained. He hated contained spaces, hated the blackish water where you couldn't see five feet ahead, and hated the very thought of exploring the underwater cave. But he still wanted to come along.

He sat slumped in his chair peering out the portals most of the short trip, lost in reverie. Not that he could see anything outside, he couldn't. Oh, every once and a while a column of light-colored rock would loom up and then fade away, or a lone fish would slither by a portal. There wasn't much of the wildlife left. Their enemy's voracious appetite had seen to that.

They spent a couple of hours getting familiar with the submersible, scouring the lake's bottom and the lower walls, seeking Lassen's underwater cave until they found it, sensitive to the fact that every hour wasted brought them closer to outside intervention with their problem.

Yet they didn't enter the cave and didn't stick around longer than they had to, for fear the beast would show up, but made plans to return once they were fully prepared to enter and fight it.

Just the hours they'd been underwater had brought more people to the park. Greer, with his binoculars, sighted more illegal intruders, probably reporters, crawling around on the rim of the crater. Some Henry's rangers sent packing; some were too quick and scurried away into the woods before they could catch them.

"*Stupid reporters, stupid tourists,*" Greer groused under his breath when he spotted them. "Going to get themselves *killed.*"

Henry couldn't have agreed more. "So last night's ten o'clock news has released the genie from the bottle?"

"Looks like it."

But they were too busy after that to worry about the human trespassers. Their weapons had arrived and they made plans to submerge at dawn the following morning for the final time, not coming up until they'd taken care of their problem once and for all. They talked, packed and made plans.

There was no time to see Ann and Laura, no time to waste. But Henry stole a few minutes to write a last letter to his wife, full of the love he'd felt for her in their life together, and shorter letters for his daughter and granddaughter, and gave them to Patterson to deliver if they didn't return.

The four men packed as if they were going on a

hunting combination cave exploration trip with minimal supplies (because there wasn't much room in the submersible) and climbing paraphernalia–and, of course, the new weapons.

Henry left detailed instructions with Patterson and his rangers. This was when he missed George the most. George would have been the man to take his place. He could always count on George. But since George was gone, Patterson would have to do.

So it was early the next morning when Francis stared out of the front window of the sub and announced, "There's the cave's entrance off the starboard at approximately two o'clock."

No one uttered a word. All faces were tense. And Greer's eyes were hooded as he peered out at the yawning hole ahead of them.

They waited as Francis expertly steered their craft, careful to avoid the sharp rocks along the crater wall, into the opening. The Big Rover was tough, but not indestructible.

When the submersible entered the cave Justin's teeth could be heard softly chattering. "You don't think it's waiting for us right inside, do you?"

"Let's hope not," Henry couldn't help saying.

"And if it is," Francis whispered as he checked his instruments. "We'll shoot the bastard out of the water."

Justin piped up, "Sounds like a good plan to me."

The scientist remained visibly uneasy, but when nothing happened he did begrudgingly acknowledge it was a splendid and unusually rare, vast Lava Tube cave they were entering. "I wonder if we're the first ones to explore it, besides Lassen, I mean?"

"Possibly," Henry answered. "There's nothing whatsoever about it in any of the park's records. It was undiscovered, I imagine, until now."

Henry glanced at Justin and gave him a thumbs up sign in the artificial light. Justin's face was so pale it looked like it was painted white, but the young man smiled back, fighting hard not to show alarm. He was sure the monster was lying in wait somewhere, or would somehow corner them down in the depths of the cave. Ambush them. They'd have no way out. And what would be left of their mauled bodies would never be found, like Lassen and the others.

Henry was scared, too, but not as much since he'd learned the sub was equipped with defensive weapons of electrified probes set two feet apart across the hull.

"Anything tries to touch us, we'll fry it," Francis had declared.

The sub also carried the two precious grenade launchers Greer had procured and a large supply of rigged-up phosphorus rockets. And at that moment, Greer was inspecting one of the launchers as he sat up front with Francis. He was going to be ready if the beast showed up.

This time, Greer was positive, they'd be able to hurt and kill the creature.

A lot depended on where they found it as well as how effective their weapons were, in and out of the cave. And those were the unknown factors that made their journey so perilous. None of them were sure they would be victorious, but they had to do it anyway.

So they rationalized, grasping for hope. The fatal flaw in the smaller unarmed Rover's destruction had been engine trouble, Francis had concluded. "It wasn't up to evading the creature, wasn't powerful or fast enough, and, in the end, of escaping its clutches.

"That won't happen with the Big Rover. I know we can outrun or shoot the monster if we need to."

Henry only wished he could believe that. It sounded too easy. That was the problem. Go and find the monster and shoot it. Kill it. Way too easy.

Strangely enough, the beast hadn't shown itself or made an attack in days. No one knew where it was or when it was going to strike again. The submersible couldn't be everywhere in the lake at one time. What happened if they missed the creature and it got past them? If it was out of the water; out of the park already? That thought terrified them, though there were enough people sneaking through the woods and around the lake to keep it fat and happy.

They had to find it first. None of them wanted more people to die.

"You think we should really be doing this? Going after the thing into the cave? Puts us at a disadvantage, doesn't it? Maybe we should wait until it emerges onto land again," Justin grumbled to Greer. "I despise caves, especially one with a nasty surprise hiding in it."

"Too dangerous. Once it gets out on land again it'll just be a short run to the exits. Then the towns. And I'd think that as a paleontologist," Greer raised an eyebrow, "you'd have been in lots of caves?"

"You would think that, wouldn't you?" Justin replied meekly. "But no, I've stayed out of as many caves as I could manage. Always let someone else have those particular jobs, unless the discovery was monumental. That hadn't happened, until now. I hate caves," he repeated.

"Would you like to tell me why this cave is called a Lava Tube?" Greer was making conversation to ease Justin's discomfort. They'd entered the underwater cave and the walls were closing in.

"Sure, I'll tell you. Because immense flows of lava moving through drilled it out from the rock. And this particular cave, from what I see on the Deep Rover's camera, is even rarer," he added. "Since its main orifice originates in a volcanic caldera. There is even less known about volcanic Lava caves."

"Yeah, and, I bet, this sort of cave is highly treacherous, isn't it?"

"Of course. Lava Tubes can be real tricky. And sometimes, as in this one, there's active lava, and you never know how deep under your feet an active flow is still moving. So, if we leave the sub, be careful where you step." A small grunt escaped Justin's lips, and he directed his next remark to the three men around him, reiterating what he'd already said. "Hey, you guys, maybe we really should have waited for the thing to come to us?"

Greer turned around and playfully thumped Justin on the shoulder as Henry chuckled and said, "Too late now. We're here, and I wouldn't be surprised if Godzilla doesn't already know we are."

Greer even cracked a smile at Henry's off-handed reference to his partner Patterson's original nickname for the creature.

Peering out through the glass into the open cavern, Justin looked as afraid of the looming cave walls as he was of the monster.

The Big Rover glided into the immense cavern they'd seen through the other Rover's cameras, and it slowly surfaced into the main chamber. They'd accepted this cave was the most likely candidate to be the monster's escape route, its hiding place or even its home. Lassen had also believed that. So they'd explore it first.

"Well, here we are," Francis announced. "It was a little tight getting in, but it's not so bad now."

Unlike Justin, Henry adored caves. He'd studied them and had trekked through lots of them when he'd been a teenager. Many a weekend he'd spent crawling around in the caves in the woods behind his house. But he was only familiar with the more common limestone variety, not Lava Tubes. For him this was a new experience. And he thought the cave was beautiful, no matter what it sheltered. It wasn't the cave's fault it hid a predator.

The chamber they found themselves in was filled with stair-stepped rows of orange-red stalactites and large rim stone deposits formed of drip-deposited silicon dioxide. Thin grayish black stalactites of once molten lava hung above bulkier stalagmites built up drop by congealing drop, and could be traced to the slumping and dripping of glazed lava that thinly coated the tubes.

All along the stone on their left the glaze had formed spectacular patterns resembling clumps of gray toffee. The cave walls were grooved, deeply ridged, and ledges created long ago by various lava flows through the tunnels jutted out along the cave walls. Congealed lava tongues and frozen lava falls were everywhere as the crackling active lava lit the cavern into a soft golden twilight. Steam rose from the churning magma flow that meandered across the rear section of the chamber and as it met the colder air, it created a wraithlike fog that drifted head high through the tunnels. Henry had to squint through his portal to see anything. The cave's weird formations and stone were wreathed in the heavy fog and muted rainbow lighting.

"As dangerous as it is…it's still beautiful. The colors are so rich, vivid," Henry said. "And now we know where the mist on the lake is coming from."

"Yes, exquisite, isn't it? This cave's so primitive. Like something from another time." Greer's voice was tinged with awe.

"And was probably formed thousands and thousands of years ago, when the volcano blew its top off," Henry supplied, his park ranger spiel kicking in. "It hasn't changed much since, except for the gradual cooling of the lava, which allows us to enter it now. I'd wager only some of the chambers we'll be going through will house active lava; be hot. Most will be bearable."

"Hope you're right about that." Greer was still eying from the portals the cave they were traveling through. "Or our expedition might become very uncomfortable."

"Oh, I'm pretty sure I am. How long do you think we'll be in the cave?"

"We'll be in the cave as long as it takes to search it, on foot if the waterway runs out. We won't leave until we're sure it's empty or we locate our hungry friend."

"Oh, boy. Cave exploration with a voracious meat-eater Jack-in-the-Box hiding somewhere in the tunnels. I can't wait." Justin shook his head.

The sub had broken the surface of the water and come to a full stop. The water had run out. Ahead of them was nothing but cave.

Well," Greer swung around in the tight space and spoke to him and Justin. "Are you ready? Let's find out if this is the bastard's home."

Everyone looked at him. The certainty of what they were about to do had settled in. They were leaving the metal sanctuary of the submersible and going on foot into unknown territory.

"Justin," Henry reminded him, "don't forget the radio and the fire crackers."

Music and firecrackers had been Justin's idea. They'd use them to draw the creature out because they couldn't just sit around and wait for it to show up. That could take forever.

"When we see signs of recent habitation or believe the beast is near, we set off the fireworks, turn up the music loud as we can," Justin had said. "The more noise the better."

"Anything, but shoot off the real guns," Greer had advised. Henry and Greer were sporting revolvers on their hips. "The shells might ricochet off the rocks or walls of the cave and hurt one of us, or break through a lava seal, you did say they could be fragile, and flood the tunnel or chamber. And we'd be flooded in with water or fresh molten lava."

Justin had whistled. "Don't want that."

"No, we don't. We only use the weapons within the confines of the cave, especially the grenade launchers, if we absolutely have to. And when we have a target. The bigger the cavern we're in, the safer firing our weapons will be. So keep your heads about you, boys. Eyes open."

Justin had brought his own radio, an old battery powered Magnavox boom box. Ancient. Said he took it with him everywhere. It made Henry smile when he'd first laid eyes on it. It reminded him how young Justin was. The young always had to have their music. Laura was the same way.

Greer was watching Justin as he unloaded the radio from the sub.

"If we suspect our creature is anywhere in the vicinity," Justin said, "we'll leave it in the open, turn it up full blast; shout loud enough to wake the dead, and set off the fireworks then run like hell and hide. Wait. All the ruckus should attract the monster if it's anywhere nearby."

"Should. Sounds in a cave this deep can carry for miles, even through the water." Greer was struggling into his backpack. "If the monster's anywhere within that radius, it should hear the commotion."

"And when it shows up, we shoot it with the grenade launchers," Justin finished, grinning.

"If the launchers can pierce the thing's tough hide," Henry tossed in.

"And if our aim is true," Greer worried out loud. "That monster can move."

They'd discussed the plan many times, but now that they were actually in the cave, disembarking, it didn't sound as fool proof, clever, as before. There were a hundred things that could go wrong, and they were beginning to think of them.

For instance, it'd dawned on Henry as Greer had been giving his warning about firing off live rounds, that if live bullets in the cave could be hazardous, what would happen when they fired the RPG-7's? If they missed the monster, big as it was? He didn't want to think about that.

There were risks any way he looked at it.

"I hope the cave's not too hot," Justin had fretted as they exited the submersible.

"By the way, the lava in this cave can actually be cooled down enough for a man to enter and move around through," Greer cautioned, "but still be deadly because of lethal gases and places where the magma is still active. So appearances can be deceptive. If the lava is fiery and steaming, and moving, I don't have to tell you to stay away from it, we all know that. But if any of you detect something strange in the air, it could be noxious gas. So say something and put on those gas masks you have in your backpacks immediately.

"Be careful where you walk, scan your helmet lights downwards as much as ahead and upwards. There're bottomless pits and crevices where you can get so stuck you can't get out."

The other men trailed Greer, helping each other over the damp, slippery rocks to solid ground that led up into the cave. They'd unloaded the supplies and divided them between themselves to carry, and were stalking through the cave's above water chamber loaded down with their backpacks.

Making small talk among themselves to ease the growing tension, Greer entertained them with his spelunker horror stories.

"Ever hear of Floyd Collins?" Greer asked innocently.

"No," they chorused. Their footsteps were loud in the dark cave. The lights from their helmets tiny rays of brightness leading their way.

"Well, he was a man in 1925 who'd decided to explore this cave on his property. Don't know what they called it back then, but today it's called Kentucky's Onyx Cave. He got trapped in a tight corkscrew fissure so tightly locked in that he couldn't, for the life of him, get out. Sometimes it happens that way. Spelunking can be dangerous if you don't know what you're doing. You should never do it alone, I say. After a few days missing, his brother went looking for him, suspecting he'd gone down in the cave. Floyd was always exploring them. His brother found him, but couldn't get him out. The crevice was too narrow and too deep. The man's body, too tightly compressed, had swollen. He was wedged in that fissure for eighteen days as they tried to free him.

"People flocked to the place, like it was a circus, to wait, pray, and socialize while they tried to dig the poor man out. You have to remember there wasn't any television back in those days and this was a big deal. But, no matter what they did, they couldn't free him. The rock was too hard. They fought to keep him alive. Talked to him. Fed him. It was January, bitterly cold. And, though, they tried to keep him warm, they couldn't. The rocks holding him were like ice, and he was caught so tightly between them they couldn't even get a blanket around him.

"He died a horrible death. When he was dead they finally retrieved the body by cutting it into pieces."

"Oh, my," Justin moaned. "That's terrible."

"Cheery story to recount while cave exploring," Francis cracked, trudging along behind them. Greer was at the front, Justin behind him. Then Francis. Henry at the back. Henry had thought it best to put the two greenhorns in the middle.

"Oh, there's more," Greer went on happily. The man was becoming quite the clown of the troupe. As if by leaving his stuffy briefcase and suit behind he'd liberated the true Dylan Greer. "There's the well-known story of Lost John. Well, that wasn't his real name, no one knows his real name. That was the name given to the skeletal remains found pinned under a six ton boulder in Mammoth Cave."

"Sheesh," Justin exhaled, shuddering under his heavy backpack.

"So you see, people are hurt, lost, or die in caves all the time, if they don't know what they're doing."

"Thanks, mother." Henry laughed. "We're so glad we have you along then. Heck, you're not only entertaining us with you heartfelt tales of past cavers, you've warned us what to expect and even how to dress for caving. What would we have done without you?"

"A lot worse, I daresay," Greer said. "You're all newbies compared to me when it comes to exploring caves. Now let me tell you about this one cave I spent a week lost in–" And off he went on another cautionary tale, everyone groaning aloud.

Well, Henry mused, the guy was still as smug as ever. That hadn't changed.

Like most Lava Tubes, the walls had long ago been carved out of the rock by exploding lava, and were jagged and sharp, hard on clothes and human skin alike. Greer had advised them the night before to wear extra rugged clothing. He'd provided the special knee pads, gloves, and boots they were using, having taken their sizes and actually having one of the other rangers run him into town late the night before to purchase everything, as well as the tents and other supplies they'd be using on their journey.

Henry had been impressed by Greer foresightedness and touched by his thoughtfulness.

"Don't be too grateful, Chief Ranger," Greer had cracked, when he'd shown Henry the booty. "I put it all on your tab."

He'd brought back unbreakable flashlights, lifeline ropes to connect the four of them together for when they'd have to climb or descend, a sturdy inflatable raft in case they encountered a body of water, and caving helmets with carbide lamps attached to the front.

"Carbide is a gas and its light's a brilliant white, better than regular flashlights, though flashlights are an adequate back-up." Greer had wanted them prepared for anything.

Henry couldn't get used to Francis in a helmet instead of his cowboy hat. It'd protect his head good enough from falling rocks, but didn't go with the ponytail as well.

The four made a motley crew. Francis, a wiry old man, with as much spunk as a man twenty years younger. Greer, strange looking in marine fatigues instead of his usual meticulous suit and fancy watch. No notebook. Justin was in faded jeans and a plaid shirt, long stringy blond hair and those golden wire glasses of his. He hated the helmet he had to wear, said it was too clumsy, hot and uncomfortable. Henry sported worn hunting clothes and a three-day beard on his solemn face. The cover-everything clothing made the heat more intolerable, but it kept their skin from being scratched from the sharp protruding rocks.

Greer led the men through the tunnel, one of the grenade launchers on his back hanging from its straps; talking a blue streak in a low voice, which was also unlike him. But then, some men reacted differently to stress.

Henry, in the rear, lugged the other rocket launcher. Justin, besides his backpack, carried a compressed bundle that was the raft. Francis, as the old man of the group, toted the first aid kit, the firecrackers, and Justin's boom box.

Every man carried generous canteens of water. In a cave a person dehydrated quickly, and in an environment sometimes heated with steaming lava, even quicker.

The four of them explored. Two very tall men and two short with drawn faces and glittering, wary eyes.

"I've been thinking about if and when we have to use the RPG-7's." Henry moved ahead of Justin and Francis and broached the subject to Greer. "We'd better be sure we hit what we aim at, don't you think?"

"Don't see any problem with that. If I can't aim and hit something that big with this rocket, I'm a sorry hunter indeed." But, for the first time, Henry caught a flicker of doubt cross the other man's face as he glanced over his shoulder at him.

For Greer knew as well as Henry that it was possible to miss anything.

It was suddenly hot as blazes. Henry fell back to the rear of the group as they entered another cavern. Sweating, he felt it trickle down his back under his shirt.

"Heat's not too bad," Greer pronounced when they'd first exited the submersible, yet he was sweating now, too. "About eight-five degrees, I'd guess, right now in this cavern. Warming up, though. We can take it. As long as we remember to keep drinking water." He'd grinned in the glow radiating from his helmet, the gray of his long hair glinting in the light.

The next section they marched into was considerably hotter. The one after that, a little cooler. And that was the way it was. Some parts of the cave were almost unbearably hot, while others were normal, or even cool.

"This is one of the most breathtaking caves I've

ever seen," Henry admitted a short while later. "The limestone caves I've explored can't hold a candle to this. It's huge."

"Ah, breathtaking, but hazardous to people," Greer responded. For the rock they were treading on was wet and slippery, the fog pesky as it further hindered their progress. Even with the bright headlights, they had to watch every step or they'd end up sliding down into a black pit or a lava stream.

They had to look out for Justin. Though he kept swearing his banged up ribs weren't bothering him, it was easy to see they were. Henry had been a lot luckier, his sore muscles and bruises from the jeep accident had faded away in the time since. Yet soon after their trek through the cave had begun, he realized they shouldn't have let Justin come along. His ribs hadn't healed enough. But it was too late to turn back so they'd have to make the best of it. Under the guise of needed rest breaks for all of them, they halted often; stayed close together.

They couldn't become separated, no matter what.

Carefully working their way down the winding maze of stone capillaries and veins, it looked like it'd go on forever. Down, down, down. They used the ropes when they had to, to lower themselves to a ledge, or get up to another entrance. And as they descended further into the narrow twisting tunnels, they left a trail of red phosphorescent ribbon to mark their passage so they could find their way back later. Another one of Greer's excellent suggestions.

The heat was one of their worst enemies, sapping their strength. When the group came to pools or streams of churning lava, which was often, the temperatures soared. They walked guardedly on tip-toe across passages of what appeared to be thin crusts covering cooled lava and they burrowed through small connection tunnels dragging their packs and supplies behind them. They splashed through shallow lakes of water for hours and hours.

Finding no creature or even a sign of its passing.

The blackish walls and rock they moved past and across were sometimes unstable, and crumbly, and they took extra care to avoid brushing the ceilings or disturbing talus, an accumulation of rock debris. The mineral formations, stark white blooms of gypsum and Celestine, as they worked their way deeper into the cave, were delicate and it wouldn't have taken much to bring them down on their heads.

"Careful here," Greer would say. "No. Come this way. That ground won't hold your weight there."

Then there was the heart-squeezing fear that at any moment they'd come face to face with what they were seeking and that made every discomfort worse.

But they kept moving.

They walked in single file at times, peeking into dark corners and back tracking when they had to. Their conversation died as the going got rougher. They didn't stop to eat for a long time. If they were hungry they pulled snacks, candy bars, granola bars, or dried fruit, from their pockets and gnawed at them as they walked.

They overhanded across cliffs with the aid of the climbing ropes, waded through chest deep water and climbed endlessly, helping Justin when his injury acted up. As intense as their journey was, they still marveled over the flow stones created by centuries of coursing water, and at the left-behind and wedged lava balls, remnants of the lava flow that had once surged through, which plugged many of the corridors and made them almost and sometimes impassable. There were places they could barely squirm under, or climb above, but they managed somehow. Everyone was soon exhausted from the extreme exercise.

In the silence their hearts were as loud as drums. Henry knew they were all running scared. They'd seen the creature and what it could do to a human. Yet they couldn't give up and forged on.

Until their bodies told them in no uncertain terms it was time to rest.

"In caves there's no such thing as time," Greer said. "No days. No nights. It's dark all the time. Unchanging. It's easy to forget time completely. But the body still needs sustenance and sleep. To remain sane and healthy, we must continue to follow the outside world's time table. So it's time to pitch camp and get some real food in our bellies and some sleep while we can."

"Wise words, friend," Henry seconded. "Let's do it."

Tired and filthy, they set up camp that first night in a cool chamber. With sparse conversation, they ate their army MRE's (Meals Ready to Eat) hungrily. The meals were compact and, thus, had been easy to carry with their limited space; another one of Greer's ideas. Wrapped into a tiny bundle of dark brown plastic, all of it looked worse than it tasted. Justin had diced turkey with gravy, Henry had chicken a-la-king, Greer had beef stew, and Francis had meatballs with barbecue sauce. All of them had added entrees of dehydrated fruit, beverage powder for a cold and hot drink, a dessert, unsalted crackers and a cheese or peanut butter spread.

Justin had never eaten MRE's before. In the beginning, as he unwrapped his dinner, he made faces, then after the food had entered his mouth, he declared with surprise, "Other than my hunk of maple nut cake resembling a smashed heel of wheat bread, it isn't that bad. In fact, it's pretty good."

"That's because you're starving." Francis laughed.

"Well, the pears were good, even for a MRE," Greer concurred. "They've improved them considerably since I was in the service, I can tell you that. But," he handed a small package to Justin, "I've had enough peanut butter and crackers to last me a life time. Here, you want them?"

Justin did. They, too, were gone in seconds.

"There's no vegetables," Francis pointed out.

"Sorry," Greer muttered. "Maybe the next batch will have them."

They slept in their army sleeping bags. Nearby, a lantern was turned down low for light, and they took turns at guard duty through the eight hours. They couldn't take the chance of being unprepared if the creature showed up.

The following morning they resumed their search, tracing the dank tunnels through the earth. Still they found nothing. No tracks, no fossils, no human remains or animal leavings.

"What if it's not in the lake or the caves anymore at all," Justin worried out loud, "but out in the park, or, worse, in a town somewhere, wreaking havoc?"

"We can only do what we can do, one possible hiding place at a time." Henry's lips were drawn into a tight line. "We're only four. We're only men."

He locked eyes with Justin. "We continue on until we're sure it isn't in the cave. If we don't see evidence it's been here within the last couple of days, we'll consider returning to the lake and looking somewhere else. We can even sub through the water and see if we can't get the thing to come out after us."

"Ah, we'll be bait, huh?" Justin didn't seem happy with that proposal.

"I don't like that idea, either, but it might be one way to draw it out."

Justin fell silent and the men kept moving.

Greer believed there were other entrances to the cave. That it honeycombed around and came out somewhere else, maybe under the lake itself. He became more sure about it with every mile they chalked up.

"I know another exit is down here somewhere," he told Henry. "And I know the monster's in this cave, or has been recently. I feel it in my gut." He tapped his abdomen. "It'll be back. I promise you."

"You get these *feelings* very often, Greer?" Henry teased.

"Sometimes. I'm usually right."

"I bet you are." Henry recalled Patterson's warning about Greer. That he had special talents most people couldn't understand. Henry was beginning to. Greer's special talents had to do with intuitions and a sixth sense that frightened most people. Not Henry, he was open-minded.

By the second night, their bodies more used to the strenuous activity, they had the energy to sit around and talk before they went to sleep. Sitting on their sleeping bags, MRE's balanced in their laps, their faces and clothes caked in lava dirt, they speculated as to what the creature really was.

"Remember that picture I showed you in that one book, Henry? Of the Nothosaur?" Justin asked. "You thought it was so ugly?"

"It was."

"I believe our creature's a far advanced hybrid of the Nothosaur, no doubt about it, the next evolutionary rung up. Or two. The one that was never allowed to be born before the comet fell, or whatever it was that happened to plunge the world into dinosaur genocide.

"Somehow, this particular creature's egg was preserved and protected and remained viable. And it actually hatched. Astonishing. Certain circumstances, the earthquakes and the warmth of the lava, most likely, uncovered and incubated it." Justin reclined on his sleeping bag, propping his head on his backpack, wincing, reminding everyone his bruised ribs were still giving him discomfort.

"You mean this thing we're chasing hatched…from an egg?" Francis sputtered. Sitting cross-legged besides Greer, for being the old man of the group, he'd weathered the last two days better than any of them. He didn't appear tired and his eyes were alert. He'd begun to act as if he were enjoying their strange crusade. In the end, he'd accepted his friend's death quietly, though sometimes spoke affectionately of the missing man as if Lassen were still alive somewhere.

Henry sympathized with him about his absent friend. He couldn't think of George as dead, either. It was easier to pretend the Indian was just out wandering the woods, happy and free. That he'd see him again someday.

"That's where dinosaurs come from. Eggs." Justin had closed his eyes. He looked about twelve years old at that moment.

"Wait a minute," Greer interrupted, bending towards the paleontologist. "Then it's possible there are more eggs somewhere? Unhatched or ready to hatch?" His eyes gleamed blacker in the lantern's soft circle of light that separated them from the cave's outer darkness.

"You're correct. There could be more eggs or more…dinosaurs. None of us can say for sure there's only one of the creatures, can we?"

"Oh, boy. I'd never thought of that possibility. That there could be more than one," Henry growled in a low voice. "One's enough for me. Oh, boy."

"Not necessarily," Justin rationalized. "Our hostile antagonist has only been sighted for the last two years. Where was it before that? In an egg or living somewhere else where it didn't have easy access to humans?"

He shrugged. "Who knows? And if there are two or more of the beasts, why haven't we seen them together? Dinosaurs are herding animals. But, hey," he put his hands up in an apologetic gesture," that's only my opinion. A lot of paleontologists don't believe dinosaurs ran in herds and cared lovingly for their young. I do."

"But there could *still* be other eggs somewhere and someday there could be more of the creatures?" Greer wouldn't let it go.

Justin sighed, his face sleepy-looking. "There could be or this creature might be the only survivor." He yawned.

"We can only hope." Francis was studying the blackness beyond their camp. "We're having enough trouble tracking and trying to kill just one."

Greer was brooding. There was an odd expression on his face and his thoughts seemed elsewhere. Henry wondered what he was fixating on, thinking about; where his mind truly was.

After a while, Greer turned towards Henry, changing the subject. "How was your wife doing when you left her?"

"So, so." Henry fluttered his hand. "She's trying to cope." The sorrowful image of Ann's tear-stained face came back to him. "She blames herself for George's death and nothing I said changed her mind."

"It wasn't. It's the monster's fault George is dead, no one else's. From what I've heard of her, she's a strong woman. She'll get through this. Just give her time."

"I hope so." But in his heart, he, too, knew Ann would be okay. Greer was right, she was a strong woman.

And with the video Henry had found when he'd searched the dead reporters' camp site, Ann might be in a position to help save Zeke's newspaper and her job and that would give her some happiness. What she'd done hadn't been totally in vain. It wasn't getting George's life back, but it was something.

Henry found himself telling Greer about the video. How it showed the monster in all its glory. Close up. It played like a horror movie with great special effects. Frightening to watch.

"I hope Ann makes a bundle off it, writes the most sensational story ever to go with it and wins a Pulitzer. Any reporter, especially a woman, having the guts to chase a story the way she did, danger and all, deserves it."

"I hope so, too," Henry could only say.

Greer was attempting to be kind with his comments. But his words only reminded Henry of Ann's despair and those poor reporters' and George's awful deaths. All in all, the price for the video had been too high.

"Ann didn't want you coming down here, did she?" Greer pressed Henry.

"No, she didn't. But she knows catching this monster is necessary. It's my park, my responsibility, our lives. She understood."

"Remarkable woman. You're lucky to have her."

"I am, and I know it."

Ann hadn't understood him coming on this mission. She'd been terrified that he wasn't only reentering the park, but was going into the lake in a flimsy (as she'd put it) submersible to hunt for the creature. Too dangerous, she'd said. Far too dangerous.

She'd tried talking him out of it. Had cried. She hadn't done that before, not in all the years he'd been a cop. More than anything he'd wanted to stay with her, hold her in his arms and promise he wouldn't put himself in danger again, but couldn't. He had to do what he had to do.

When Ann had seen he was going to go, no matter what, she'd clung to him, told him how much she'd always loved him, would always love him.

"You're the best man I've ever known. The bravest. Come back to me, Henry," she'd whispered. "Please come back to me."

He'd never forget the love in his wife's touch, her smile or her sad eyes as he left Zeke's house. They'd held each other and she'd cried silently as he'd given her a final goodbye kiss.

He'd hated to hurt her. Hated to see her cry.

He'd never loved her more than that moment, except perhaps that other long ago morning when he'd awoken in a New York hospital after being shot and had found her head bowed on his bed. She'd slept nights in a chair by his side, refusing to leave. When he'd come out of the coma and she'd looked at him, well, he'd never forget that look, that smile ever, either.

The four men talked among themselves, of things only men liked to talk about. They expressed their fears of what lay ahead and went over their plan again on what they'd do when they finally confronted the leviathan.

Henry was touched by the camaraderie growing between them. He hadn't been this close to a bunch of guys since he'd been in the Marines. These men were his equals, his peers, while his rangers had always been like his children, George being the exception. He'd held himself back. But true danger sometimes brought people close in a way nothing else did and there'd never been any real danger being a park ranger–until now.

"You've never been married have you, Francis?" Henry was munching on a Hersey's bar. Dessert.

"Never have. Oh, there have been women. Some were good women. I've loved a few of them. But none of them could take me away from the sea, the water or my submersibles. My job has consumed me. My exploring. It's been my only passion, my obsession. If I stay out of the water too long, I get homesick." He smiled. "I'd always thought it'd be too cruel on a wife and family to be away as much as I am. Wouldn't be fair to never be home." He spread his hands in the gentle light, his face melancholy at what might have been, but never had.

"Lassen was married, though, wasn't he?"

"Yeah, and he was in love, really in love, with his wife, his family. It wasn't the same for him. He didn't love the job as I did. He went home often, while I kept working."

Everyone was quiet, Lassen on their minds.

"And you, Greer? You been married?" Now it was Francis's turn to ask.

For a long time there was no answer. The ex-FBI agent seemed lost in his own thoughts. Francis must have thought he'd hit a raw nerve and dropped the subject.

Henry swallowed the last piece of chocolate.

Then, "I was married. Once," Greer confessed.

Henry stared at the man. He wouldn't have guessed. Greer never seemed to need anyone but himself.

"Divorced, huh?"

Another silence.

"No," low voiced. "Her name was Amy. She was an artist. Beautiful. Loving. And she died a long time ago. Murdered by a serial killer."

He stopped talking, his dirty face blank, as if the memories could no longer bring pain, as if he'd accepted her death, the way she'd died. Unless you looked into his eyes.

Greer would reveal nothing more about his deceased wife, that's what his eyes said.

A slight jolt went through Henry. He'd received a sudden insight into the man of stone. Was his murdered wife the reason he'd initially joined the FBI, or was it the reason he left? Had his wife been one of that serial killer's victims…the man he'd killed in cold blood? Was it why he came across as an extremist, especially concerning killers? Hmmm. Perhaps, one day, Greer might tell him.

Justin asked, "Francis, with all your submersible time in the oceans, have you ever gone down looking for buried treasure?"

And the three of them listened in fascination as Francis launched into stories of his early treasure hunting days, until exhaustion claimed them.

Henry was about to nod off; Justin and Francis, Francis snoring softly, were asleep and Greer was sitting guard when he startled Henry by saying, "Ranger, remember when I said that this was the strangest situation I'd ever been involved with?"

Henry groaned. He was next in line for guard duty and had almost been asleep. Was walked and talked out. Yet something in the man's hushed tone brought him back.

"I remember." Henry shoved himself into a sitting position, rubbing his face. What he wouldn't have done for a shave, a bath. Putting on clean clothes tomorrow or brushing his teeth with water from a canteen wouldn't do it. Maybe they could find a shallow pool sometime tomorrow and take a quick dip. His tired thoughts touched on his wife. He missed her as she slept in her safe, clean bed at Zeke's.

"I lied."

Henry waited, wondering what this was leading to, and why Greer was telling him now.

"All right, you lied."

Greer's eyes turned to meet Henry's half-lidded ones. "You know, there're things in this world we can never understand. Oh, I didn't doubt you in the beginning when you told me about your monster in the lake. I've just learned to keep a low profile. Because, you see, I've come across things in my life I simply cannot explain away. Don't even want to anymore. Though, lord knows, I've tried."

Bingo, Henry thought. Perhaps he was going to learn why Patterson believed his partner, Greer, was so unusual.

The ex-agent gave him an unsettling smile, his voice a low rustle so that Henry had to scoot closer to hear him.

"Especially this one experience I had. A case from my earliest days in the bureau. Heck, I was a kid. Not even twenty-five. Only been in the agency for about a year. I was real green back then, never questioned anything they told me to do. Always followed orders, no matter how idiotic they seemed. Like I said, I was young. Later, as I grew older and smarter, I'd question things more. That was one of the reasons I eventually left the Bureau. I couldn't trust them anymore and couldn't, wouldn't, blindly obey."

"Go on, tell me about your experience," Henry encouraged. "I'm listening."

Greer took a deep uneven breath. "I've never talked about this before to anyone. No one knows this, except the men with me all those years ago. I believe they're dead now. Unexplained accidents and suicides, all. I guess it's time I tell someone. Someone else should know, in case it ever happens again. Though, I don't want to put you at risk, for knowing, that is."

"It's okay. I'm a big boy. I can take care of myself."

"All right, but don't say I didn't warn you." A pause.

"Do you believe we've been visited on earth by

aliens before?"

The bizarre question threw Henry off. "Greer, before this little adventure we're on now, I might have said: Hell, aliens? And thought you were probably nuts.

"But now, I don't know. If an extinct dinosaur can come back to life, anything is possible." Henry's eyes stared off into the endless pit beyond the lantern's glow. He could hear something, a shuffling, scratching noise, out there. He just wasn't sure what it was.

He shut his strained eyes, rubbing them with sooty fingers. He could hear Francis's snoring. Justin restless tossing in his sleep. Hear water dripping somewhere behind him in the cave. They were in a warmer cavern tonight than last night. Smaller. He wiped a trickle of sweat off his forehead. He'd taken his shirt off, leaving only a T-shirt.

"I believe we've been visited by aliens. Many times. As far as I know, it's still happening."

Now Greer had captured all of his attention. The thought of sleep was receding.

"These days, Ranger, it wouldn't surprise me one bit to learn my next door neighbors were aliens. Or that the world was populated with aliens and ghosts." He released the breath he'd been holding. "I'm open to anything. I'm a believer."

"That the reason you left the Bureau? Aliens and ghosts?" Henry couldn't help but ask.

"Some of the reasons."

"Well, are you going to finish your story or not?" Henry pushed.

"Oh, the story. Yes. It was twenty years ago and, as I said, I thought I knew everything. Smart-alecky young FBI agent. College graduate. No one could tell me anything. I imagine I was a real pain in the ass. Enough people told me so anyway."

Henry chuckled. Greer echoed it. They'd both been there. Everyone had.

"There was this little podunk town in Nevada. I won't tell you its name. Doesn't matter anyway. It doesn't exist any longer. The whole incident is high priority top secret. The bureaucrats have sealed the records tighter than a new soda bottle cap."

Henry shifted on his sleeping bag, the stone beneath was hard and his hip was killing him.

"You're not going to believe this, but we were called in to investigate the sinister disappearance of the whole town. Over two hundred people. Men, women, children. It was unbelievable. Everything was gone. Everything. The people, their houses, their possessions, cars, dogs, cats. Even the trash cans and mail boxes. There was nothing but the scooped out dirt holes where the houses had been and impressions of where their possessions had stood. Kind of like that old spooky episode of Twilight Zone, you know? Where a whole neighborhood is snatched up and taken to an alien planet and the people wake up to find themselves surrounded by…nothingness?"

Henry found he'd been holding his breath. He let it out. He remembered the story. His mouth fell open, but he shut it long enough to ask, "What happened to the people in the town? Anyone come forward with an explanation, anyone see anything?

Witnesses?"

Greer released a cynical laugh. "Oh, there were witnesses, all right. Three men who'd been on a camping trip that weekend and had, unknown to them, camped very close to the town. When, in the middle of the night, they said they were awoken by a horrendous ruckus of some kind and they went to get a look. Investigate. What they saw scared the hell out of them."

Greer stopped talking. He was peering past the perimeter of the light's circle again as if he expected someone or something to come walking into their camp.

"Well, what did they see?"

"They swore, I mean, swore on the bible, that when they got to the town there were these huge silver glowing spaceships all over the place, hovering right above the ground, and they were lifting the people and the houses; yanking them right from the earth like bad teeth and drawing them into their bellies. When there was nothing left of the town except fresh ovals of dirt, they zipped off into the atmosphere. Disappeared in a flash as if they'd never been there."

"What did the FBI do about it?" Though he already suspected the answer.

"Covered it up, of course. Pretended as if it never happened. Like they do with a lot of cases they can't explain. Are frightened of. For the public's peace of mind, they say. Ha. They think every man out here is a superstitious fool. Wouldn't, couldn't understand. Would panic. To this day, I don't know what they did with those three campers. Poor slobs. They whisked them off somewhere. Years later, out of remorseful curiosity I tried to run them down. They'd vaporized from the face of the earth. Even their birth certificates were gone."

"How about relatives of the people who'd lived in the town? Friends? People who'd visited or had done business there?"

"They told everyone the town had been hit by this virulent and very contagious virus. Everyone had died. No one was allowed to come near. That was why they had to bulldoze the town into oblivion and burn everything. The FBI quarantined the area for miles around. And as far as I know, it still is.

"Because there weren't any other witnesses, they were able to cover the whole thing up."

"Well," Henry huffed. "That's one thing they can't do here, can they? Cover this up. Too many people have seen too much. The story will be all over the world news as soon as the gag order's lifted. Which, as I see it, won't be much longer. It's already leaked out."

"Yes, it'll be pretty hard for them to cover what's happened up, won't it? Maybe, without Ann's video, and all the press nosing around, they might have been able to. But not now."

Greer was obviously finished.

"That incident in Nevada really shook you, didn't it?" Henry didn't know what to think about it. It was almost too much to grasp. Aliens taking complete towns. Cats and all. He shivered, even in the warmth of the cave. How many times in history had such things happened, and how many times had their government hidden them?

"At the time, no. I believed what the bureau told me to believe. After our job was done, I went on to another case and shoved that weird town out of my mind. Pretended it'd been some great practical joke. Ignored the facts right in front of my eyes. Denied what those campers had told me. Hell, one of them had been a bank president, the other two had been respectable, level-headed businessmen from a nearby town. They hadn't been some country yokels. Where was my brain? Why would men like that have lied? It made no sense.

"Over the years, that town and its missing population haunted me. More each year. Not that I wasn't part of lots of other shady situations when I was an agent, I was. But that cover up was one of the reasons I left the Bureau. I finally had to face the truth about that town or it would have driven me insane, you know? Dwelling on aliens abducting entire towns and taking off with them. To where? Why? What happened to those people? Were they subjects of some cruel alien experiments, as a lot of abductees say, or are they living high on the hog somewhere on some Eden of a planet? Fat, happy, and sassy, like in that movie Cocoon?

"And, my worst speculation of all was, were the aliens someday going to return and steal something bigger the next time…like New York? I figured if they could abduct a town, they could abduct a city. And we couldn't do a damn thing about it."

"Now that's a mind-boggling thought. New York nothing but a big earth-black pit." Henry didn't laugh. He could tell Greer was disturbed by the whole thing.

"I suppose that Nevada town vanishing into thin air could upset a person," he offered instead. "A sane person would've tried to forget it, but, as you did, probably wouldn't have been able to. I wouldn't have. The idea of being so helpless that any extraterrestrial could just zip us away would scare the hell out of any human."

"It scared, scares, me. I can't forget that place. Sometimes I want to believe it's a nightmare I dreamed, or the first blossoming of insanity. To accept that things like that can even happen in our safe little world. I hadn't been myself at that time to begin with. I'd recently lost Amy. Coming so swiftly after my loss, it pushed me to the edge."

Henry caught the reference to Greer's wife and another piece of the man's life fell into its slot.

"You believe me, don't you?"

"I have no reason not to. Though I don't know what to think about it. Heck, I don't want to think about it at all. I've got enough trouble of my own right here. This here's another one for the book of the unbelievable and strange."

Greer chuckled, scratched the side of his cheek. "Sorry, but I had to tell someone. After all these years. Someone who wouldn't laugh."

"Sure. You wanted me to go nuts, too, trying to figure out where in the hell those damn people went," said with such humorous sarcasm Greer laughed out loud.

"Get some sleep, Chief Ranger," Greer finished. "You stand guard next. I've already kept you up too long with my crazy story."

"Wasn't a crazy story. Interesting, actually. It gives me something to ponder on. But it does sound like our government, always making weighty decisions for the public, whether we want them to or not."

"That's our government, for sure."

"Goodnight, Greer."

"Henry, can you call me Dylan from now on? That's my name. All my friends call me Dylan."

"Sure thing." Henry smiled, secretly pleased, and laid his head down into the plumpness of the sleeping bag. "Wake me when your watch is over…Dylan."

"Will do. Oh, and about that serial killer who murdered my wife? He's the one I shot to death up in Utah."

"I'd figured that one out already."

"I thought you might have, Henry. You would have made a great agent."

"Thanks. See you in an hour and a half. Don't forget to get me up." It'd be like the man to take his shift, too. He didn't seem to need much sleep.

"I won't," Greer droned softly, and went back to checking the grenade launchers' mechanisms for at least the tenth time since they'd started their quest. He'd told Henry often enough they had to work perfectly, without a hitch, at the moment they were most needed. It could mean life or death for all of them.

Shaking his head over the enigma that was Dylan Greer, Henry shut his eyes and slept.

CHAPTER 16

Late the following day, after they'd crossed a tricky succession of connected chambers, they stumbled onto another of the cave's entrances and the evidence that something extremely large had been using it.

Justin had begun to behave nervously as they traveled deeper into the cave, but hadn't said anything to him or the others. Sensitive to what he was feeling through the soles of his booted feet as a few-time survivor of earthquakes; after the gloom and doom warning his seismologist friend had been feeding him for weeks about the big one coming, Henry thought he was extra sensitive to the earth quivering through a series of pre-earthquake tremors. But he felt them, as well. Not wanting to upset the others, he'd kept his mounting fears to himself. And if any of the others had noticed the shakiness beneath them at times, none of them had mentioned it. Could be, like him, they were afraid to. They were so deep into the caves, no matter what happened, they'd have a heck of a time getting out if the big one hit.

But Henry knew he couldn't remain silent much longer. The tremors were getting worse. If they didn't stop, they'd have to halt their search and get out or risk being underground when the earthquake came. He'd hate to be trapped underground when and if it did. The cave had been there for thousands of years, but if the quake was massive enough, all that could change in seconds. The cave could become their tomb.

Greer was the first one to see the other opening to the lake. He'd led them into the enormous cavern, which was almost the twin to the entrance they'd come through three days before, and where they'd left the submersible. Once they entered the chamber, there were no other tunnels leading anywhere. Just the water.

"End of the line, kids. By the way the current's flowing, I'd say down there somewhere," Greer pointed at the softly lapping water in front of them, "is another entrance to the lake. I suspected there were others."

The four men stood at the brink and stared down at the dark water.

Eventually Justin walked over to a nearby rock and sat down. His ribs must be bothering him, he seemed to be in pain, but complaining to the others would be the last thing he'd do. He was high on the adventure, so what was a little pain? He'd said that morning, "One day I'll probably look back at this summer as the highlight of my life. Fossil discovery, monster dinosaur, underwater cave spelunking and all. If I live through it, that is."

"Let's inspect the place," Henry said, "to see if our boy's been living in here."

He, Greer and Francis panned their helmet lights into the vast crannies and corners of the chamber. The illumination was inadequate, so they ended up climbing around with handheld flashlights to further dissolve the gloom.

"Here!" Henry yelled, and in moments the others were by his side. "Something big has been in here. Recently." He was studying where the stalactites had been knocked off to nubs, crushed or shoved to the side, rocks strewn everywhere. There were deep impressions in places where something heavy had tread and broken through the soft rock of the cave floor, leaving clear outlines of an animal's footprints and different sized puddles of cooling lava.

Henry bent down and lightly outlined one, not touching it, with a gloved hand, cocked an eyebrow up at Justin. They'd seen these before. "We're in the right place. It's been here. And by the amount of tracks, often.

"This way." They trailed him through the haze across the cavern.

"You smell that?" Greer pinched his nose shut with two of his fingers. Like the rest of them, he was drained from the heat they'd been trudging through all day, his eyes red-rimmed, his face bristly with beard and dirt from the volcanic ash that covered everything. They'd been dunked and soaked more times than he could count from wading through watery lakes which had looked shallow but hadn't been. Earlier, Greer had fallen over an unseen ledge and had scraped himself up. As much as he loved exploring caves, he'd confessed, this cave had about used him up. He said he was relieved they'd come to the end because it meant they'd be turning around and heading back to the submersible. Their underground journey was over.

Henry was also aware of the stench. "Smells like putrid meat. It's stronger over this way." He gestured towards the right and they went in that direction. He'd never seen a cave as large as the one they were in, though Francis remarked he had. It went on for what seemed like miles with the lake rippling on its left side like a yawning inky pit and lava bubbling through weak spots of the floor, so they had to jump the boiling liquid like obstacle fences.

They hiked across the unstable surface until Francis stepped on something. He dipped his flashlight, bent over and picked it up.

"A bone."

Henry looked at what Francis held in his hand. "A human bone."

They searched the black spaces around them until they found the source of the odor, a monstrous pile of bones, animal and human, with rancid flesh clinging to some of them. It was only one of many piles strewn along the rear of the chamber. The freshest kills were human. Henry felt nauseated.

"Now we know where the missing people ended up," he spoke softly, "or parts of them, anyway."

"Apparently the creature drags back a large portion of its prey to eat here. Its home," Justin said.

Francis cocked his head upwards so the helmet's light skimmed across the back wall of the chamber. His hand covered his mouth and then his nose. He froze, probably terrified he'd discover body parts of his dead friend among the refuse. He strode quickly away from the pile.

"Look at this!" he exclaimed over his shoulder.

The rest of them tore themselves away from the bones.

Henry, Greer and Justin moved up besides

Francis, who was standing beneath something, gawking up at it. A solid wall of embedded dinosaur fossils.

"I've never seen such complete, perfect, specimens. Never," Justin breathed. "Not even up above at the dig."

Heads, feet, all parts of the ancient monsters stuck out at them like a bizarre relief sculpture. The outlines so clear of the original animals Henry was afraid they'd come to life and jump out of the wall at them.

"Nothosaurs, I think. No, Kronosaurs, no," Justin stuttered in wonder. "No, neither of them." His voice turned grave with foreboding. "This is some fantastic creature no human has ever discovered or conceived of. It's a creature from hell, is what it is. Look at the size of the things! They're much larger than our creature. Much."

"For now, anyway," Henry supplied. "Maybe that's how big our beast is going to get."

Greer, staring up at the wall like a man in a nightmare, whistled. "We got to find it and destroy it before it gets this big then."

"We're trying, Dylan. We're trying," Henry sighed. Things were looking worse every day. Now this.

"Henry, this is most likely where the wall you found up above begins. Down here deep under the lake. Astounding," Justin mumbled, still in shock. "There must be hundreds of the animals captured in this rock."

"What happened to them?" Greer couldn't take his eyes off the fossils.

"Perhaps an earthquake millions of years before the one that blew the top off this volcano and created the caldera. The lava was so hot it melted the rock and embedded the creatures in it for eternity. Subsequent quakes, even the ones we've been experiencing lately, might have unearthed it."

"Wow!" Francis mouthed, inching close enough to touch a protruding white leg bone.

"They moved in herds, you know," Justin was rattling on, probably to hide his uneasiness. "They could have been migrating to some other place."

Henry's flashlight had caught something else and he moved away from the wall. That's when he saw the eggs, clustered near a pool of bubbling lava.

"Justin," he whispered, "you better get over here. You won't believe what's here."

Justin hobbled over, his aches and weariness forgotten, and with Henry, bent down to study the huge white-shelled ovals. The first moments he smiled like an enchanted child, then his face drew tight under the grime. "Oh, my god."

The others crowded around and stared at the ovals. There were twelve, nestled together in a lop-sided circle and partially covered in ash. They looked as if they'd just been left there. An hour, a week, a month ago. An impossibility.

"Are they still viable?" Greer quizzed Justin.

"I don't know," the scientist replied, lifting one up in his hands. It was heavy. Warm. He put it to his ear. "Something's moving around in there. I think this one's close to hatching. The lava's incubating them. Now we know where our monster came from." He looked up at Henry with dread in his eyes. "They've probably been down here somewhere for–who knows how long–thousands, millions of years, locked air-tight in a rock pocket, perhaps, or coated in hardened lava that the recent earthquakes uncovered and melted as the heat grew in the cave. It set them free." He caressed one of the eggs gently as if he were afraid it'd break.

"These eggs would be worth a fortune in the outside world. A monumental scientific discovery," Justin announced. "We'd all be filthy rich if we brought them back."

"You want to take them back? To civilization?"

Justin shook his head after just a slight hesitation. "No."

"No," Greer concurred solemnly. "Can you imagine more of those monsters roaming the earth? Eating every living creature in their path? Some men would think they could control them, outwit them…but I don't think they could."

"No," Francis sided with the others, gazing at Justin. "Your colleagues would try to hatch them, raise them as pets to put in zoos. As amazing as that'd be. We can't allow that to happen. They don't belong in our world anymore."

In a fleeting wisp of memory Henry recalled Ann's face as the monster had hulked over her. He saw the disbelief, the horror, that'd frozen her into a helpless rabbit in its path. George's death cries joined the memory. The cries of all the other victims. No!

"People wouldn't understand, wouldn't believe," Justin spoke, "how damn smart they are. People are so arrogant. And if there's money to be made–they'd be like lambs to the slaughter."

The men looked at each other. The same expression of fear on each face.

"We have to destroy them," Justin pronounced sentence. "Because if one of them hatched then others could. It's too dangerous to leave them. Intact."

The others watched Justin, a look of absolute loathing for what he had to do, pick the eggs up one by one, walk a ways into the chamber and throw them into a lava stream. The ovals quickly sunk, burning, into the fiery quicksand.

After he'd disposed of three the other men helped him finish the job.

This is for you, George, Henry thought as he dropped an egg into the lava. *None of these will ever hatch and grow into the thing that killed you.*

They uncovered other nests and dealt with them in the same manner.

As a devoted paleontologist, it was the hardest thing Justin had ever had to do. Henry caught tears in his eyes more than once.

Afterwards, exhausted in mind and body, they settled down to rest and plan. Time was running out and they knew it.

"Since this cavern appears to be the creature's home base, I'm hoping we can lure it back here." Justin propped his chin in his hands. His face was flushed.

"Whatever we do, we need to do it quick," Henry decided. "None of us can take much more of this heat."

The chamber the eggs had been in was like an

inferno, a giant incubator. The men had retired to the further corner, as far away from the lava as they could get. It wasn't far enough. They were all dripping in sweat.

Justin looked as if he was about to pass out. "There must be a large river of active lava somewhere not far beneath us."

"We can't leave," Greer reminded them of something they didn't want to hear, "until we try summoning the creature. This is its home."

The others groaned and grumbled, but knew Greer was right. They had to call the beast back to its lair. They'd come all this way for that reason.

"Let's rest first," Henry suggested. "Eat something. We're going to need our strength."

And they sat and talked among themselves for awhile, comrades now, to fight their growing fears of not ever returning.

"It's time," Henry finally announced, "Now or never. Let's do it."

Justin took the boom box and set it on the ground. Popped in a CD. Heavy metal. Volume up full blast, loudest it'd go. Francis pulled out the fire crackers and lit the tied together bundles.

Combined, the noise was horrendous.

They found hiding places nearby, staying close together, and doused their lights. Covered their ears. Greer mumbled, "I should have remembered ear plugs, too. Too late now."

They waited in the eerie reddish glow the live lava gave off, drenched in heat and fear sweat, their hearts beating as loud as the CD. Their launchers at the ready. Their eyes glued to the placid body of water before them. If it came, it'd probably come from the water. From the lake.

They waited. Hours.

The fire crackers were used up. The heat, the tension, and the increasing earth tremors that soon all of them could feel, finally wore their patience and courage down.

"Enough. It's not coming. We need to regroup and try another location." Greer had come up behind Henry and yelled in his ear.

A flashlight switched on and Francis rose up, stepped over to where Henry, Greer and Justin were crouched. "I guess it's not going to show today," he cupped his hands around his mouth and yelled in their direction.

Another flashlight and a helmet switched on. "I guess not." Justin stood up. There were rings around his eyes behind the glasses. Blond hair stuck out every which way from under his helmet. His skin coloring was awful. He'd spent too much time in the dark.

Greer winced, putting his hands to his forehead. "Somebody turn that damn music off," he yelped. "I never told you but I hate heavy metal. Classical's more my style."

Justin scooted over and shut the thing off, plunging the cavern into blessed silence.

Henry gave a shuddering sigh of relief. "Now I know why I stopped listening to rock music. My eardrums wouldn't take it anymore. Give me Vince Gill or Alabama any day."

Justin made a face, and turned to Greer. "But it sounded like such a good idea, lying in wait and making lots of noise. Should have worked."

"Nothing's easy, kiddo," Greer mouthed. "Don't take it to heart. It was a good idea. Just didn't work."

"Yeah, well, we need to leave the cave and the lake," Justin urged. "You feel that?" The ground rocked beneath their boots. "This *whole* cave could come tumbling down on our heads any minute. We can wait here forever, but it won't guarantee our dinosaur will come, especially if there's other ways in or out of the cave. But the earthquake is going to happen soon. It's too risky to remain here."

"And if we sweat away any more water, we'll dehydrate," Greer tossed his prognosis in. "Have heat strokes and then we'd never make it to the sub. It's a long walk."

"I say we move out now as well. I'm worried about the Big Rover," Francis said. "We've been away from it for three days. It'll take three more, at least, to get back. A long time to leave it unattended, unguarded, even with its electrical defenses on. I don't like leaving it this long."

He didn't have to remind them the submersible was their only way out. Unless they wanted to swim, unprotected, across the lake. They knew that well enough.

"Well, we'd better pack up and start hoofing it." Greer shifted the pack on his back into a more comfortable position. "We have little time and hard traveling ahead. Let's get going."

"So, Justin, you believe these tremors we're having are a prelude to the big one?" Greer asked as they gathered the rest of their equipment, getting ready to go.

"My seismologist friend does. He expects a full blown earthquake any time, now." Justin's face in the lantern light was anxiously grim.

"Let's move faster, boys," was all Greer said then.

No one had to voice the fear they might not make it back to civilization. It was on their minds as the earth shook violently below them.

"We never should have come down here," Henry muttered apologetically to Justin. "I knew an earthquake was coming. You warned me."

Justin flashed him an impatient look. "Don't be sorry for anything. I could have said no, you gave me lots of chances. Same with the others, too. We wanted to come. Can't change what's already been done. And we don't really know when the earthquake will come. No one really knows. The earth could rumble for days or weeks first." His eyes scanned the cave, as he strapped on his backpack. The others were ready, waiting for Henry and Justin to start moving.

"Now," Justin snapped, "let's get out of this cave before it falls on us."

"I'm with you. Let's get above ground and see what's happened in the park since we've been gone. See how many more people our hungry friend has trampled or eaten. Clever bastard. It probably knew we were down here all the time and it's been playing hide and go seek with us. We come seeking it, and it hides. Laughing at us the whole time."

The ground shuddered as they departed the cavern, single file, as rapidly as their tired legs and the unsteady ground would allow.

Henry didn't look forward to three more days of cave climbing, grueling heat, exhaustion and dirt. But they needed to get out of the cave. He was also dreading what might have taken place up above when they'd been away. That dread was a monkey on his back he couldn't shake.

They hiked in the direction of the submersible, following the phosphorescent bread crumb string of ribbon through the tunnels. It'd worked like a charm. But this time, in their desperate urgency, they rarely stopped and slept little. The cave began to disintegrate around them and Henry grew more fearful with each second they'd be entombed forever.

While Francis was worried that something had happened to the Big Rover.

Less than three days later they were reentering the entrance where they'd left the sub. Four walking half-dead men with dirty faces and nervous eyes. The earth had been calm for the last day but there was a strange feeling in the air, a feeling of destiny and finality. A feeling as thick and tangible as the churning mist that clung to the inside of the cave and kept them, at times, from seeing even the man in front of them.

The earth was still experiencing tremors, some worse than others.

So they were relieved their escape vehicle to dry land was waiting where they'd left it, bobbing in the water, unharmed, a beautiful sight. Getting ready to embark, Francis fussed over the machine as if it were his long lost child.

Slumped in their seats from weariness, groaning, Francis piloted the Rover out of the cavern, happy to be out of the furnace and motoring out of danger. It was the same way Henry felt when he left the dentist's office.

Out of danger, or so they thought.

The monster was waiting for them outside the mouth of the cave. It let them pass and putter along for quite a stretch then it swam in behind.

Henry was the first one to spot it because he'd been looking for it. He'd had a sickening premonition it'd be out there somewhere…waiting.

His eyes stared out the glass portal at it. He wondered how long it'd been waiting. It swiftly closed the distance between them as if they'd been sitting still.

"We've got company," Henry informed the others in a cold voice. "Behind us. Look out the window."

Glancing out his portal, Francis gasped. "Heaven help us. The creature, it's here! My god it's big!"

"Somehow it knew we were in the cave," Justin whispered. "And was clever enough to figure we'd have to come out eventually. Where we're at the disadvantage. We can't use the launchers from inside the sub, can we?" But Henry knew Justin already knew the answer to that.

"No, we can't."

"And it's pretty much invulnerable in the water, remember?" Justin reminded him. The two men exchanged looks. That night on the lake when they'd first encountered the leviathan was still fresh in their memories.

Henry glared at the monster through the glass. It was circling the sub, examining them with hungry, diamond-black eyes. It was so damn *big*. Its eyes locked with his and a chill shivered through his body, though he was sweating. And Henry realized in that awful moment that the sub's defenses would never be a match for the behemoth. Now his hands were shaking.

He looked around and recognized the terror in the other's eyes. They all remembered what had happened to Lassen and the Deep Rover.

Henry leaned over to instruct Francis, "Get us back to the cave. We haven't got a chance out here in the water. You said this ship was fast, now prove it."

Francis didn't argue. "We'll make a run for it. Tighten your seat belts, boys. Here we go."

The pilot turned his attention to the controls and did what he did best.

Henry felt the craft wildly shift direction and accelerate. It became a bullet flying through the water, its destination the yawning mouth of the cavern they'd just exited.

"Don't look now but our voracious friend's *behind* us again," Justin moaned. "Moving up quick."

Each man looked out the nearest portals, their hands tightly holding onto any nearby solid surface, preparing for the ride.

If this sub goes any faster, Henry thought, we're going to hit warp speed.

The entrance to the cave was looming ahead.

"I think it's through fooling around," Justin's voice trembled. "It's coming in for the kill."

Henry had to hand it to his team, not one of them cried out as the monster rammed them. Greer cursed under his breath and Justin muttered something feverishly. Sounded like he was praying

The Big Rover bucked in the water and rocketed to the right, the shock of the hit sending it radically off course. Francis was jerked in his seat, but maneuvered the craft back on course. Sweat trickled down his face, leaving dirty tracks through the grime. He tried to outrun the nightmare stalking them.

The beast would not be shaken, nor left behind.

Every time they got close to the cavern's mouth, the creature slapped the Big Rover away, as if it were a toy, and kept it from entering.

"I'm turning on the electrical juice." Francis's fingers flipped a few toggles. "Full force."

But when the creature hit them again, it reacted as if it hadn't felt a thing.

"I'm firing the missiles. That'll get it." But the beast dodged the weapons and the rockets were lost in the lake's murkiness. Francis swore out loud.

Justin and Henry looked at each other.

"Oops, that didn't work." Justin's face was a shade of white Henry had never seen before.

Heaven knew where the missiles would end up or what they'd blow up. If they were lucky, it'd be some underwater rock formations or a foundation along one of the islands and not a line of boats anchored at Cleetwood Dock.

"Sorry, the missiles weren't meant to chase

down crafty, agile water dinosaurs," Francis apologized. "That's it. The extent of our defensive weaponry.

"I'd like to believe we're going to get out of this alive," he then said gently, shaking his head. "But I'm not sure."

The men didn't have time to dwell on their plight. The creature, now quite agitated, was relentlessly crowding against the hull of the sub.

"Damn," Francis snarled. "How can it do that? I've got the voltage as high as it'll go."

"Because the electricity's not affecting it, that's why," Henry replied. Suddenly he was very tired. Their situation wasn't looking very good and, on top of it all, he had a splitting headache.

"Nope, electricity doesn't seem to faze it," Justin deadpanned. "Its skin must be too tough or too thick. And it's not scared of us. We can't hurt it. We're as vulnerable as Lassen was in the Deep Rover."

"Shit," Greer breathed.

"Yeah, oh, shit," Henry echoed. "Switch the juice off, Francis, it's only making the SOB angrier."

Francis shut off the probes.

Henry had to give the pilot credit because he'd nearly gotten them to the cave.

The next shove was so forceful that the men's bodies were fiercely jostled inside the cockpit. For a second, Henry thought his neck had snapped. The beast had hit them with all it had. A few more of those friendly slaps and something would jar loose inside his head for sure or the sub would burst open like a watermelon dropped on concrete from ten stories up.

The sub spun in a crazy circle and with a loud screeching sound slammed up against a ledge of underwater rock. A huge tail wrapped tightly around the craft and squeezed. Henry could almost hear the metal crunching. Teeth scratched against the hull and claws raked the metal creating horrendous grating noises. A monster eye was plastered outside the portal's glass near him. It reflected a malevolent intelligence as it blinked. The creature knew they'd been trying to kill it. It *knew.*

Henry's mind reran a similar scene from an old movie. *Twenty-Thousand Leagues Under The Sea.* That was the film. But that had been a movie. Fiction. This was the real thing; exactly what had happened to Lassen, except this time it wasn't happening to someone else, but to them.

"Lord, I don't want to die like Lassen did," Francis exclaimed, furiously working the submersible's levers, trying to get the sub out of the monster's grasp.

The Big Rover's engines were grinding in protest as the creature grabbed a hold and violently shook it back and forth. Its occupants slammed around in its belly, jelly beans in a jar, bouncing against the hard surfaces.

A seatbelt snapped and Henry howled in pain on impact.

The mutant pushed their sanctuary downwards, then, unbelievably, released them. But the submersible's engines had stalled and it was sinking to the bottom.

"Is everyone okay?" Henry asked as soon as his senses returned. In a small metal tomb with the weight of over nineteen hundred feet of water lying on top of them, and a monster lurking outside waiting to have them for supper, Henry was disoriented. Everything had a dreamlike quality to it, even the terror.

Francis had hit his head against the hull and had put his hand up to cover the wound as blood burst from between his fingers. "Oh, I've been hurt!" was all he said, face going blank, and then he fainted in his seat, held in by his harness.

Greer had to catch him from behind and pull him out of the restraints or his head would have thudded down on the controls.

Henry reacted as only someone with emergency training would–throwing himself behind the controls, knowing Greer would take care of Francis. He frantically fought to recall what Francis had taught him days before about working the sub. He hesitated, unsure, the control panel blurring before him.

"Drive it, Henry!" Greer shouted. "Get us out of here!"

The monster was closing in. But the Big Rover was dead in the water. Even the lights inside had dimmed to a frightening twilight. If it went pitch dark, Henry thought, he'd scream for sure. The stench of fear and unwashed bodies were cloying in the compacted space.

"I'm trying!" he hissed, and what he so desperately needed to recall came flooding back. He restarted the engines; they sputtered and kicked in.

Thank God. For a heartbeat he'd been alarmed they wouldn't. He didn't want to die as Lassen had, either. He didn't want anyone to die.

They sputtered away from the monster, sparks crackling in the water around them. The beast was mesmerized by the fireworks and held back to play with the pretty lights, a delay that probably saved all their lives.

As they left their attacker behind, the submersible motored, crippled but still plugging along, through the cloudy waters.

The men were silent as their eyes observed the creature frolicking through the glass openings.

Henry fervently wished he could escape the sub, breath gulps of real fresh air. Swim away. Wished he could get out because the walls were suddenly closing in.

Justin's eyes were dilated in fear. "My head's whirling. My heart feels as if it's ready to explode." Groaning in his chair, his eyes were glued to the water world and the creature diminishing in the glass windows. "Why in the world did I agree to come along? I must have been insane," he grumbled. But Henry knew he was just letting off steam. Relieving his fear.

"Francis has been hurt," Greer announced. "He's unconscious. I don't know how bad, breathing shallowly, but alive. His pulse is strong. I stopped the bleeding." He'd laid the pilot on the floor between them. "But we're going to have to drive this thing ourselves from here on in."

Greer settled into the seat Henry had vacated as the Big Rover wobbled towards the cave and, with

Greer's co-piloting, entered the main cavern before the creature noticed they were gone. Henry brought the submersible to the surface, but was unable to get it completely flush with the rocky shore as Francis had done. He wasn't that good of a pilot yet.

"Sorry," he told the others. "We'll have to swim for it. Looks to be about ten feet."

"Then let's do it," Greer rasped. "Before the bastard sees we're gone and decides to come after us. We need to get in position to fight it."

"You mean we can't just slip into a side tunnel, squeeze into a place the beast can't get to us?" Justin inquired half-heartedly, as the three hurriedly gathered their stuff, and the weapons, and prepared to depart.

"No, sorry," Henry told him. "We need to face it now. Destroy it once and for all. No more running. I'm sick of running."

Greer's face confirmed the decision. "He's right. We have to take care of it. Now. We have the weapons and the opportunity. It'll never let us out of the cave anyway."

"You're right about that." Justin gave in.

"Justin, when we get away from the sub you watch over Francis. Greer and I will take care of the creature."

What Justin said then made Henry proud. "I'll get him to a safe place first, but then I'm going to help you two fight that thing. There's grenades in your arsenal, aren't there?"

"Yes?"

"I played baseball when I was a kid." Justin grinned in the dim light of the submersible's interior, pack strapped to his back, ready to leave. The others were ready, too, heading for the exit. "I was a great pitcher. Got a mean arm. I can hit anything at almost any distance. Don't leave me out of this. I want to help. Three fighting that monster is better than two. It's also my survival. Besides, if something happens to you two, and Francis doesn't come to, I'm stuck in this cave. I can't operate the Big Rover at all."

"You got some valid points. All right, you can help us fight. If you get Francis to a safe place first."

"Deal."

The three of them escaped from the Big Rover, bringing along an unconscious Francis. Greer and Henry also assisted Justin, who wasn't a swimmer, get to the cave's floor. When Francis and Justin were safe on dry land, Greer swam back to retrieve the grenade launchers. He stood on the top of the Big Rover and tossed them, one at a time, to Henry.

Henry had the second RPG-7 in his arms when behind him Justin howled, "Earthquake!" The word reverberated and bounced eerily around the rock cavern, repeating itself over and over.

"Shit," Henry railed, crouching down to keep from tumbling over with the heavy weapon. "And it's a bad one!" Of all times!

The initial rattling of the earth, as the water surged, knocked Greer off the sub into the water. He swam through the choppy waves to the others as rocks, some the size of a man's skull, thundered down around his comrades from the roof of the cavern.

Smaller stones pelted Justin and Henry as they huddled, waiting for Greer, cutting the flesh on their faces, slashing their clothes. They tried to protect themselves. Justin, grunting as the falling rocks hit his back, hunched over and covering Francis's body.

Now there was no way they'd be able to hide deeper in the cave, even if they'd wanted to. It was collapsing, the walls crumbling.

"If we're going to kill that thing, we'd better do it," Justin yelped at Henry, as the ground rumbled and the water around the submersible boiled and changed colors as active lava tinted it. "This cave is no place to be right now."

"Soon as it shows itself. We'll take care of it." Henry's words were barely heard over the rumbling of the earth and the screaming of the dying cavern. His hands fumbled with unpacking the weapons, but his eyes were on the water as a great churning arose near the submersible.

The monster hadn't yet made an appearance. That was about to change.

Greer burst from the water. He only had time to warn, "*It's* behind me. Give me a grenade launcher!" when the monster exploded out of the water like a monstrous jack-in-the-box.

The creature's first lunge almost gave it Greer. It didn't seem to care it was raining rocks and the cave was shaking itself to pieces.

It wanted the men.

Greer moved faster than one of those painted wooden men on a toy stick with the string that Henry used to play with as a child and narrowly got away. It was remarkable how fast a man could swim when there was a monster chasing him. He pulled himself up onto the rocks and stumbled towards Henry.

Justin was preoccupied with getting Francis to a safer spot as Henry shoved a launcher, ready to fire, at Greer, and claimed the other for himself.

The ranger fell to his knees, but Greer remained standing, as they raised their weapons. Their faces were shiny with sweat and the flickering of the fires that'd broken out all around them in the cave. The lava was seeping through the earth's crust, creating burning rivers and turning it into an inferno.

Greer yelled something, but Henry couldn't make out the words because of the ruckus the earth was making. It didn't matter.

For the monster was hulking above them, filling the cave with its giant presence and its angry voice. Rocks were slamming against it; a large boulder hit its head, near one eye, and distracted it for a few precious seconds. It shook its bloody head, dazed, then its gaze cleared and malignant eyes zeroed in on the humans.

Nothing would deter it from its desire to get its meal. The world was crumbling around it and yet it wouldn't give up the hunt.

Was its vendetta personal? Henry wondered. The creature was intuitively cunning. It remembered, and planned. They'd declared war on it, came after it and tried to hurt it. Shocked it with electricity. Shot missiles at it. Did it know they'd destroyed the other eggs, its unborn sisters and brothers, deep in the cave? Did it know it'd be alone now forever?

Henry wouldn't put that knowledge beyond the beast's awareness.

And did it sense they were its sworn enemies and if it could vanquish them as it had all the others it would be the supreme victor? The king of the hill? The boss? The one with the most strength, best defenses and ferocity would win. As in prehistoric times, it was survival of the fittest.

The victor would be king of the park.

The monster spooked Henry. It wasn't some dumb killing machine. It seemed cognizant of what was going on and what it was doing.

Greer was sighting it in with the RPG-7, using the lava's fire to see by, as the earth rocked beneath his booted feet. He fought to remain standing, the metal barrel of the weapon kissed by dancing beams of crimson reflected from the burning lava.

We. Have. To. Get. Out. Of. Here!" Justin had crawled over to the two men, leaving Francis behind a large boulder. He'd been hesitant to drag the unconscious man into the tunnels because of the quake. "The cave's unstable."

"We haven't anywhere to go. It's blocking us from the sub," Henry shouted.

Greer lifted the launcher to his shoulder. "We take a stand and kill it or we don't leave. Grenades are in my pack, Dr. Maltin."

The creature emerged from the water.

"Oh, Jesus. We're all going to die," Justin muttered, rummaging in the backpack on the ground. He didn't run. He could have. With the monster coming towards them he had to be as panic-stricken as that night on the lake or on the rim when they'd last crossed paths with it. Instead, trembling, Justin yanked out a couple of hand grenades. Greer had shown him how to use them when they'd first entered the cave.

The monster was practically on top of them.

"Fall back, Ranger!" Greer shrieked. "If I don't get it, you'll have your shot."

Neither one of them had to be reminded one shot each was about all they might have. The beast was too big, too swift, for them to have more.

Justin prepared and threw the first of the grenades. His arm was shaking so badly, though, it went off course and exploded in the water, missing its target completely. He pulled the tab on another one and aimed it for the monster's looming and now open jaws. At the last moment, the jaws swung to the side, and a claw swiped the tiny bomb away like it was hitting a baseball. The grenade struck the side of the cave. The detonation showered stone and debris over the men.

Justin gave his comrades a sheepish grin but continued tossing grenades.

Greer, in the meantime, had shot off the first of his specially-made phosphorus rockets. The monster hunkered down and the rocket narrowly missed its head, disappearing into the water behind it. Greer wasted no time and reloaded.

As frightened as Henry had been in the submarine, he was dead calm as he loaded in a rocket. His hands didn't shake. Unlike the shooting incident years ago, he felt in control. He had no other choice but to stand and fight. He was going to end the situation once and for all. Here. Now. Or die trying. No more running. No more fear. Knowing that was a relief.

That creature not only killed his friends, it'd changed his world. He wanted that world, that life back. All of it. The park the way it had been. The happy visitors swarming all over. The peace. Purpose. He wanted the tranquility and contentment back. The sweet life he and Ann had had since they'd arrived in the park.

And he wanted revenge for George, Lassen and all the others.

Henry aimed and shot the RPG-7 and time seemed to stand still as the rocket hit monster flesh somewhere in the abdomen and burst into flame. The moments afterwards seemed to last an eternity; every motion made, even the crashing rocks around them and the cracking earth, existed in another time and place. Henry had to keep shaking his head to avoid spinning off into space. It was such a strange sensation. Here he was firing rockets at a prehistoric monstrosity straight out of a science fiction nightmare. How unreal.

The creature howled and the sound boomed about the walls of the cavern and spiraled through the connecting tunnels, an out-of-control siren. The creature's screams made the men's minds numb. Froze them like store mannequins.

What took place then happened so quickly, that later Henry wouldn't be able to recall it without dizzying confusion and gut-sickening horror.

Greer thawed and sent off another shot, an arc of dazzling light that sped towards the creature as it hunkered down at the men's level with barred teeth and jaws stretched open to devour. Inches from Greer's head.

Somehow the rocket found dead center of the beast's head.

The monster let loose a screech that would have made a banshee envious, worse than before, nearly breaking their ear drums, as it rose up in surprised pain. It went berserk, swinging its arms in the air, stomping the shuddering earth in fury, tail whipping so the men could feel the wind from it. It gnashed its teeth and, throwing up its head, roared.

Dry-mouthed, Henry wanted to drop the RPG-7, cover his ears and run away.

Then it struck. It was burning from the inside but reached down and plucked Greer up as if he'd been a helpless doll. The weapon clattered to the earth.

"Greer!" Henry wailed in despair. "I'll save you!"

Henry heard the other man shrieking over the chaos; crying for Henry to fire, not to worry what happened to him. *Kill it,* Greer screamed.

But it had him! Henry couldn't fire another rocket while it had Greer in its clutches. The ranger stood there, indecisive, horrified at the awful turn of events.

"I'm a dead man, so kill it…kill–" Greer's agonized plea dissolved into a gurgling death rattle.

"Do as he says, Henry. Shoot! Kill it now!" Henry heard Justin begging from behind him. "The cave floor is ripping open. We have to get to the Big Rover or we're all dead."

Justin stumbled across the quivering ground to collect Francis as Henry glanced at the crack in the cave's floor. It was a chasm full of bubbling lava and fire yawning deeper and wider, rippling into thousands of smaller fissures, spreading and widening towards them. Tearing the cavern floor apart. Soon there'd be no cave, just molten lava and boiling water.

Henry experienced a terrible loss, as he accepted Greer's death and perhaps his own. No way were they going to get out of this mess alive. Any of them. But he could kill the beast and rid the world forever of its threat. He could do that.

Henry turned and fired straight into the creature's mouth.

That'd surely kill it. But he didn't have time to cheer. Greer was dying.

In the illumination of the collapsing chamber Henry had a last look at his captured friend. Held high and impaled on the monster's claws, Greer was something bloody and mangled that barely resembled a human being any longer. But the man was beyond pain, his body limp in the monster's embrace.

Phosphorus from the rockets had lodged deep in the monster's flesh and glowed in circles of glittering fire. Still it stood, unwilling to die. Unwilling to go away.

Grabbing for him now.

He was out of rockets and fated, too, for the monster's jaws, as Greer before him. There was nowhere to run. A ravine was gaping open behind him. The monster in front.

He shut his eyes, prepared to die, his last thoughts on Ann and the love he had for her. On his daughter and granddaughter. He opened his eyes when nothing happened.

Before him the monster bellowed in outrage and defeat as the spreading crevasse behind Henry zipped around him, leaving him safe on a small island of earth, and opened up beneath the creature instead. Its bulk toppled into the precipice and into flaming oblivion.

Henry stood there, smoking launcher in hand, staring in shock at the abyss around him, feet away, and at where his enemy had just been and was no more.

"I'll be damned," he swore. Nature, in its own way, had taken care of its mutant creation. As if the earth had realized it'd spawned an unnatural creature out of its time and had simply, finally, stepped in to rectify the problem.

"I'll be damned," Henry exclaimed again.

Justin was beside him. He'd seen what had happened and was grinning like a happy kid.

"Let's get the hell out of here," he shouted. Francis was in Justin's arms. He was strong for such a thin person, Henry thought, as he nodded, speech beyond him, and helped carry the wounded man into the water.

Together, Henry and Justin, with a still unconscious Francis between them, made their slow swim to the sub, which was rocking wildly in the water. Justin didn't sink once. He was swimming. Amazing how necessity forced people to do things they never thought they could or things they were terrified of doing. Justin's courage rose to the occasion.

They'd left the packs and the grenade launcher behind.

As they crawled into the sub, Henry stole a last look at the cavern they were leaving behind. But it was already gone, as was most of the cave probably. Nothing remained but a quivering pile of smoldering rock sinking into the water and vanishing before his eyes as he shut the hatch. The Big Rover shifted in the water. It was so hot he could barely breathe. Time to go.

Justin maintained later they'd fled the place in the nick of time. Active lava erupting from the disintegrating cave would have fried them alive, or the catapulting rocks would have smashed them, if they wouldn't have left when they did. Seconds away from death.

Henry was unsteady operating the submersible alone and he was worried about Francis, who'd not yet regained consciousness. He felt awful about Greer, his emotions unable to grasp the circumstances of the man's death or the knowledge that he could have, should have saved him; not let him die that way. While his mind told him nothing could have saved Greer. He'd done all he could have done, and that gave him some relief. Still he grieved for the man and the new friendship he'd lost, on the heels of losing his best friend, George, so recently as well.

But, at least, he'd returned with three alive and the creature was dead. Gone forever.

The lake was seething and roiling from the

earthquake, but Henry got the sub going in the right direction and somehow coaxed the crippled machine into the main part of the lake.

Once within range of the shore, working the radio, he called for backup and aid. So there were people at the dock by the time they arrived to talk him in and to take care of Francis, who was rushed to the hospital. Henry was thankful he was going to live. The pilot had a concussion, but would recover.

The first question Superintendent Sorrelson asked as Henry and Justin pulled Francis's limp body from the Big Rover was, "There were four of you? Where's Greer?" Sorrelson was angry no one had cleared the mission through him, but there were too many reporters around snapping pictures and writing down everything said, that he had to put on a happy face no matter how upset he was. As a rising politician, bad publicity was something he had to avoid.

"He didn't make it." Then Henry's grimy face glanced towards a frantic Dr. Harris, who'd been grilling Justin about the safety of his beloved dinosaur and who'd just heard it, too, was no more. "Your precious monster ate him alive, before the earthquake ate it."

Harris's expression was horrified…for the dinosaur's demise.

Henry turned away from the senior paleontologist in disgust as soon as the man began railing about how unacceptable it was that such a wondrous, unique creature had been allowed to expire. Not a word of sympathy for Greer's death, or spoken relief that the other three men had made it back alive. All Harris cared about was now there was no longer a prehistoric animal to capture and make him famous.

None of Harris's bitching mattered because the monster was dead. In Henry's heart, he knew it had to be. And he was ecstatic it'd never harm or kill another human being.

Everyone else, Patterson included, said it had been a miracle they'd come through the terrible earthquake, which had been an eight pointer easy and had centered under the caldera itself, must less escaped the monster. There'd been massive damage done to areas in the park as well as to the nearby towns, Henry's rangers reported. There was a lot of clean-up to do.

Patterson was the only other one who knew the truth about their mission. He was the only one Henry informed that they'd fired rockets into the beast before the fissure swallowed it. That they'd dealt with the monster before the earthquake had finished it off. Patterson had congratulated Henry, but he grieved for his friend's death.

Henry told everyone else, Dr. Harris, Sorrelson and the reporters, the earthquake had destroyed the creature, and left it at that. A half-truth. Why get in any more trouble than he already was? He wasn't a fool. He liked his job too much to put it at risk, if he didn't have to.

The creature was gone, that was all that mattered.

"Too bad, that the beastie had to die that way, huh? Such a rare animal. Truly a shame," Patterson had commented to Henry and Justin, with a sarcastic grin, playing along in front of a raving Harris. It'd killed his friend, too. So good riddance to it. It'd gotten what it deserved.

"Yeah, too bad," Henry had expressed mockingly.

Justin was heard to say, "Dr. Harris, all is not lost. There's still the buried fossils at the dig. You can't forget how great a discovery they are."

But Harris wouldn't be consoled. "I'm demanding a full investigation of this. You're hiding something," he'd blustered, jumping about like a mad scientist on acid.

Justin threw up his hands. As Henry, he was exhausted to the bone and hungry. He only desired to get away from the clamoring people and the questions and find some peace with those he loved.

Henry said as little as he could about where they'd been and what they'd been doing in the Big Rover to the reporters, all greedy for information and photos. He'd decided to save the real story for Ann and the Klamath Falls Journal. That story and the video should do it.

"You want a ride into town?" Henry asked Justin, as they walked away from the crowd, after promising Sorrelson he'd have a written account of every move they'd made the last week, doctored of course, in the man's hands as soon as possible. As bleary-headed and used up as Henry felt, more than anything he wanted to see his wife and his family. It seemed a century since Henry had last seen Ann's smile and had had her in his arms. He assumed Justin wanted to see Laura and Phoebe in the same desperate way.

"Sure."

The two men got Patterson to drive them to the lodge, which had become a temporary ranger headquarters until a new one could be built, and Henry called his wife. She was really happy to hear from him. Ecstatic, in fact.

Then, with dragging steps, they found their way to Greer's old car, climbed in, and fighting the whole way to stay awake, Henry somehow got them to Zeke's house where two women were very glad to see them.

CHAPTER 17

Epilogue

Justin and Laura were married at the end of the summer, soon after Laura, with her father's help, located Chad and received a no fault divorce, and earned her high school diploma. Justin's mother, father, and a sister he'd never met, attended the wedding in Ann and Henry's cabin, content to have found their son and eager to resume a relationship with him and his new family. Justin and his parents made peace with each other. In fact, they turned out to be nice people and Henry and Ann ended up liking them much more than they'd thought. Apparently, time had wrought some changes in all of them, not only Justin.

Henry had observed his new son-in-law with his parents. Justin's father had beamed with pride over what Justin had become and over his heroism at Crater Lake. And Justin, happier than he'd ever seen him, ate it up. Ann said the shadow she'd seen lurking over the boy was gone.

After the wedding, Justin and Laura remained in the park because Justin was working at the dig and busy writing a scientific paper on it and the fantastic discoveries they were uncovering. Later, if Justin had to travel for his job, Laura and Phoebe would go with him. But for now, they were happy where they were and Justin expected them to stay in their cozy new little cabin in the woods for a long time. The dig was turning out to be even more important than anyone had expected. There was lots of work to do.

Laura had liked school so much she'd decided to keep going at a community college.

Justin encouraged her and both of them seemed happy.

Laura considered her father and Justin heroes. They'd rid the park and the world of a terrible monster and had come out alive. And all the surrounding towns thought they were heroes, too, since Ann's prize-winning series of stories on the *"Summer of the Monster"*, had run, though some crucial parts of the story had been left out. Ann had hinted between the lines enough for most people to glean what really happened in the cave, without incriminating her husband and jeopardizing his job. Everyone was a winner.

And the infamous video had become a phenomenon. The monster, in vivid living color lived and breathed on it for the world to see and exclaim in horror over. The five minute tape had been run on every station for weeks. It was everywhere. Photographic stills had been captured and had been printed in every newspaper in the world. All over the web. Even *The National Inquirer*. The residuals had been huge. Ann had taken the money and stashed it in the bank, for Laura's college and for their retirement someday. The amount was still growing.

The video, the stories and the fossil site made Crater Lake Park even more famous world-wide. The tourists flocked to see where the adventure had taken place, to see where the only known living dinosaur had lived and died. Someone was even dedicating a museum to the dead prehistoric beast in the park. Next spring the park would boast a life-size replica of the dinosaur in its own building complex along with movies and a written history recreating the legend. Crater Lake Park had become Dinosaur Park. Crater Lake, Dinosaur Lake. Everyone wanted Henry to give daily oral recounts of his fateful trip into the fiery bowels of the underwater cavern as they'd tracked down the fiendish predator. They'd offered him a lot of money.

Ha, Henry had put his foot down, *leave me out of all that*. That memorial was one place he wouldn't be wandering in too soon. Who needed to see a fake? He'd seen too much of the real thing when it'd been alive.

Now that the voracious beast was dead, they were making a damn money-making legend out of it. People!

At least Ann's articles had taken the heat off Henry and his men when the army had rolled in the day after Dr. Harris had pressured his politician friend to deploy them, unwilling to accept that the creature was truly dead. The soldiers had swarmed over the lake area and park for days searching for the monster. Of course they never found it. Eventually, that and the printed stories convinced the army the creature had expired in the great earthquake and they moved out, after they'd helped clean up and rebuild the destruction from the earthquake. In fact, the army helped a great deal, even Henry had to admit, and he'd been grateful, as had been the nearby towns.

Dr. Harris had wanted Henry fired, suspecting he'd been the cause of the creature's death all along, but Sorrelson and the park authorities had refused to prosecute a national media hero and Henry kept his job.

No one else except Justin, a recovered Francis, and Henry, would ever know about the destroyed dinosaur eggs or that other amazing wall of frozen dinosaurs inside the caves. Justin joked that Dr. Harris would have a heart attack if he knew about either of them. So no one would ever tell him.

The weeks went by and the horror of that fateful expedition faded a little in Henry's mind. The nightmares stopped after a while. But he often thought of the four of them in their awkward cave gear bravely stumbling through those hot caves and fighting the good fight. Slowly, he even grew to cherish some of the memories. Justin had been right. It'd been an adventure of a lifetime. Nothing, Henry was sure, would ever top it. Not that he wanted anything to, he was ready for the quiet life with Ann in his beloved park, for as long as he had left.

The summer had been a nightmare and he was grateful to have it behind him.

He and Ann were happy. She never forgot she'd almost lost him forever. Or that she herself was lucky to be alive. It'd made their lives more precious.

He was getting ready to go on duty; had been heading out the door one fall morning when the phone rang. In uniform and grinning, he felt like the old Henry. Ann said he was the old Henry and she was glad to see him back, too.

"The kids are coming over for supper tonight," Ann said.

"Again?" Henry teased. "Isn't that the third time this week?"

"Well, yes. But Justin loves my cooking."

"Don't I know it."

"Laura wants to talk about her new college classes. Justin says he has some more pages of the book he's thinking of writing on the dinosaur to show you. You don't mind do you, honey?"

Henry stood by the table, his hand on the back of his recently vacated chair. He leaned over and gave his wife a soft kiss on the lips. "No, you know I don't mind. I love having them over. You know that. Anytime." He was also thinking about challenging Justin to another chess game. That kid was always beating him and Henry was sure this time he'd figured out the strategy that would give him the match for once.

"Good. They'll be here at seven. Don't be late, sweetheart."

"What are we having?"

"Fried chicken. Justin loves my chicken."

Henry laughed. He loved Ann's chicken, too, and gave his wife a goodbye hug and a lingering kiss. "I'd better get going. I have an early meeting with Sorrelson. He's letting me hire four new rangers. Isn't that great? The increase in tourists are running us ragged. We need the extra help. He says we've got the funds, no sweat. We're getting the new bigger ranger headquarters and anything else we want, as well. He'll approve any budget I put in front of him."

"That's great, honey. The summer wasn't for nothing, then, was it?" Ann's voice was gentle, though.

"No," Henry answered, but couldn't keep the touch of melancholy out of his voice. Every time his thoughts touched on the summer, he remembered George, Lassen, Greer, and the other deaths. It'd always made him sad.

"See you tonight, honey," he said. "Have a good day at the paper."

And he knew she would.

***

Ann walked him to the door and stepped out on the porch to watch him get in his new jeep and drive away.

She didn't go back in the house immediately, but settled down on the swing to enjoy the sweetness of the autumn woods around the house. Summer was over. There was snow expected tonight, a lot of snow, though it was only late September. She hoped she'd be home snug in front of a fire long before the white stuff started. Her husband warm by her side. She smiled wistfully. Everything was back to normal. Almost.

She went back into the house and got ready to go to work. All the publicity from the monster, the exclusive video, had saved the Klamath Falls Journal. The circulation had gone through the roof as they'd hoped. In the beginning, people heard about the monster on the evening news and wanted to know more. For a while the only place to read more about the doomed dinosaur was in the

Klamath Falls Journal.

Then after Ann was sure the paper was back on its feet, she'd sold the story and the video to larger newspapers across the country. She'd received amazing employment offers from three of those newspapers and turned them down. Zeke needed her. And she liked her life the way it was. Comfortable as an old shoe. In the park with her husband and her family. That's where she wanted to spend the rest of her days. No more excitement.

She thought about George Redcrow often. She hadn't known Greer as well, so George was the one she missed. He was the one, after all, who'd saved her life and had been her friend. He'd been in her stories, a remembered hero, like Lassen and Greer.

She'd had guilt over George to work through. At first she'd blamed herself.

If she wouldn't have gone out there that day to get a story and pictures, he'd still be alive. If she would have moved quicker. Yelled, grabbed at him, or something. Done something other than what she'd done.

Eventually Henry and Justin had convinced her he might have died anyway, whether she'd been there or not. Many men had died that day. George had been on duty; he'd been a ranger. It wasn't her fault. But, in the end, it'd been what Henry had confided in her late one night when he'd caught her weeping behind the bathroom door that had finally healed her blue heart. He'd said if George would have had a choice of a way to die, he would have picked that way, doing his job, being a hero, while saving a friend. George had admired Ann. Liked her. Known how much Henry had loved her. He hadn't died a useless death. He'd saved another's life and in doing that other's lives as well. That would have made him happy.

And George had confessed to Henry he'd dreaded getting old and ending up a human vegetable in a lonely nursing home. With no relatives, wife, or children that was what he'd feared it would come to some day. Maybe she'd saved him from that indignity.

After she'd gotten enough of the wood's beauty, Ann went to work, smiling, her thoughts on her husband. She knew she'd almost lost him and these days their marriage had a special poignancy. They were newlyweds all over again.

***

At the same moment, Henry, sitting on a rock overlooking Crater Lake from the rim and killing time until his meeting with Sorrelson, wasn't thinking about his wife. Not at that moment, anyway.

He was staring out at the water as he'd done every day since the monster had been swallowed by the earth below the lake.

Half of him still expected the creature to suddenly emerge from the water and resume its rampage. The other half was sure it was dead, stuffed and rotting in the earth's reclosed fissure deep under the lake.

The earthquake, which had been officially a 8.2 on the Richter scale, hadn't noticeably damaged the caldera or the land around it. Though it had transformed the underwater terrain, geologists believed, collapsing many of the lava tunnels and caves beneath the lake. Maybe all the underwater caves were now gone or closed off. Henry prayed they were, because when he thought about that underwater cave they'd been in he saw again the piles of human bones and the eggs waiting to hatch. If the caves had collapsed, there'd never be any more eggs. Never be another creature.

But he often wondered…were there more of those eggs somewhere under the lake in a cave even now, incubating, waiting to hatch? Ready to birth more potential monsters that would terrorize humanity?

It was something he didn't want to dwell on too long. It gave him the willies.

Things were finally back to the way they'd been, and he'd be the first one to admit, he'd never been so glad to see those nosy, noisy park visitors as he was when the park had reopened. Routine was comforting.

If only they wouldn't all pester him about telling the tales of the dinosaur. He hated reliving it so much. Oh, well, nothing was perfect, was it?

Laughter played on the air off to his right, gulls called to each other over the lake as a chill breeze ruffled his hair. He appreciated the beautiful fall day. It was sweet to be alive.

Henry sighed as he watched the tour boats putter across the water far below. The old boys were back, as were the locals and the workers in the restaurants and shops. It was good to have the park full of people again.

The homeless had returned to their original

camp. Now it was Henry and Ann who took them supplies and helped them when they could. With the newspaper's help, Ann had found some of them jobs. It was the least she could do for George. She'd written heart-tugging stories about them, as well, and people sent in money, clothes and food. There'd been enough money so some of the families had been moved to modest houses in town. Ann had become dedicated to the cause and it made her happy to help.

George would have been proud of her.

It was downright cold today, Henry thought. The metallic odors of winter were already in the air, crisp and tangy. He'd had to wear a jacket, and he pulled the collar up tighter around his bare skin. Never should have gotten that haircut. He missed the warmth on his neck. He'd need gloves by the time he went off duty if the temperature kept falling. The skies above were filled with puffy, fat grayish clouds he recognized well enough. Snow was coming. The water mirrored the sky's grayness. The water wasn't crystal blue today, the way George had liked it.

He missed George. Nobody to gobble down donuts and coffee with at the ranger station in the mornings anymore or to gossip with over the newspaper at the lodge. No more strange Indian stories. No more venison left at his back door. He thought of George as his eyes traveled the land around the rim. George had loved to come up here, too, to stare at the sparkling water below, to weave stories and recount memories.

Sometimes on the brink of twilight, Henry

would trek up here and look down at Wizard Island or the Phantom Ship and he'd swear he could see the Deep Rover glimmering just under the water line as it glided past the islands. He liked to believe Lassen was down there exploring the lake's floor and the caves…forever.

He focused his eyes on the woods behind him. And if he tried real hard he fancied he could almost see his Indian friend, along with Greer, standing in the trees' shadows, waving and smiling at him. Laughing. They weren't resentful they were dead and he wasn't. They were happy he'd made it through alive. That he was with Ann and his family.

For Henry, they'd always be there now, in the park, along with the others who'd died. And with him, their friend.

They were leaving now, fading back into the trees. *Goodbye George. Farewell Dylan*

The Deep Rover slipped beneath the water again. *See you later, Lassen.*

Glancing down at his watch, Henry knew he should be going, too. It was time for his budget meeting. Time to start planning the new ranger headquarters. Then check on the scientists at the dig. Life went on.

He stood up, brushing the dirt and grass from his uniform pants and repositioning his hat, and with one last longing look at the serene water and a final smile for the ghosts, he turned and walked down the path towards the lodge. It was time to return to the world.

It was time to go back to work.

** If you liked this book you can continue to read further adventures of Ranger Henry Shore, Crater Lake and more...dinosaurs...in its sequels: Dinosaur Lake II: Dinosaurs Arising and Dinosaur Lake III: Infestation.*

Please leave a review of this book on Amazon...I'd sure appreciate it.

Twenty of my novels are now also available as audio books at Audible Audio Books.

About **Kathryn Meyer Griffith**...

Since childhood I've been an artist and worked as a graphic designer in the corporate world and for newspapers for twenty-three years before I quit to write full time. But I'd already begun writing novels at 21, over forty-four years ago now, and have had twenty-two (ten romantic horror, two horror novels, two romantic SF horror, one romantic suspense, one romantic time travel, one historical romance, two thrillers, and three murder mysteries) previous novels, two novellas and twelve short stories published from Zebra Books, Leisure Books, Avalon Books, The Wild Rose Press, Damnation Books/Eternal Press; and I've self-published my last six novels with Amazon Kindle Direct and my Dinosaur Lake novels and Spookie Town Mysteries (Scraps of Paper, All Things Slip Away and Ghosts Beneath Us) are my best-sellers.

I've been married to Russell for thirty-six years; have a son and two grandchildren and I live in a small quaint town in Illinois, which is right across the JB Bridge from St. Louis, Mo. We have a quirky cat, Sasha, and the three of us live happily in an old house in the heart of town. Though I've been an artist, and a folk singer in my youth with my brother Jim, writing has always been my greatest passion, my butterfly stage, and I'll probably write stories until the day I die…or until my memory goes.

2012 EPIC EBOOK AWARDS *FINALIST* for my horror novel **The Last Vampire**-*Revised Author's Edition* ~ 2014 EPIC EBOOK AWARDS *FINALIST* for her thriller novel **Dinosaur Lake**.

***All Kathryn Meyer Griffith's books can be found here:**

http://tinyurl.com/oqctw7k

***All her Audible.com audio books here:**

http://tinyurl.com/oz7c4or

Novels and short stories from Kathryn Meyer Griffith:

*Evil Stalks the Night, The Heart of the Rose, Blood Forge, Vampire Blood, The Last Vampire(***2012 EPIC EBOOK AWARDS*FINALIST* in their Horror category)**, *Witches, The Nameless One short story, The Calling, Scraps of Paper (The First Spookie Town Murder Mystery), All Things Slip Away (The Second Spookie Town Murder Mystery), Ghosts Beneath Us (The Third Spookie Town Murder Mystery), Egyptian Heart, Winter's Journey, The Ice Bridge, Don't Look Back, Agnes, Before the End: A Time of Demons, The Woman in Crimson, Human No Longer, Four Spooky Short Stories Collection, Forever and Always Romantic Short, Night carnival Short Story, Dinosaur Lake (Dinosaur Lake was a 2014 EPIC EBOOK AWARDS*FINALIST* in their Thriller/Adventure category), Dinosaur Lake II: Dinosaurs Arising and Dinosaur Lake III: Infestation*

My Websites:

https://www.facebook.com/pages/Kathryn-Meyer-Griffith/579206748758534

http://www.authorsden.com/kathrynmeyergriffith

http://www.goodreads.com/author/show/889499.Kathryn_Meyer_Griffith***

https://kathrynmeyergriffith.wordpress.com/

https://www.amazon.com/author/kgriffith

****E-mail me at rdgriff@htc.net I love to hear from my readers. ****

Made in the USA
Lexington, KY
27 February 2017